'It's ...
feel-good stories'
Sunday Express

'Heartwarming and positive . . . **will leave you
with a lovely cosy glow**'
My Weekly

'Books by Cathy Bramley are brilliantly **life affirming**'
Good Housekeeping

'This is **delightful**!'
Katie Fforde

'As **comforting** as hot tea and toast made on the Aga!'
Veronica Henry

'Thoroughly **enjoyable**'
U Magazine

'This book **ticks all the boxes**'
Heat

'Reading a Cathy Bramley book for me is like coming home from
a day out, closing the curtains, putting on your PJs and settling
down with a huge sigh of relief! Her books are **full of warmth,
love and compassion** and they are completely adorable'
Kim the Bookworm

'Full of **joy and fun**'
Milly Johnson

'Perfect **feel-good** loveliness'
Miranda Dickinson

'I **love** Cathy's writing and her characters –
her books are **delicious**'
Rachael Lucas

'The **perfect** tale to **warm** your heart and make you smile'
Ali McNamara

www.penguin.co.uk

'Between the irresistible characters and the desirable
setting, *Wickham Hall* is **impossible to resist**'
Daily Express

'Delightfully **warm**'
Trisha Ashley

'A **fabulously heart-warming** and fun read that will make you just
want to snuggle up on the sofa and turn off from the outside world'
By the Letter

'Another absolute corker from Cathy Bramley. **She just
gets better and better** – creating beautiful locations,
gripping and lovely storylines and fantastic characters
that stick with you a long time after reading'
Little Northern Soul

'A **delightful** cast of characters in a setting
where I felt right at home instantly'
Rachel's Random Reads

'**Truly delectable**'
Sparkly Word

'**Warm, funny and believable** . . . grab a copy of the book
and a mug of tea then curl up on the sofa and enjoy!'
Eliza J. Scott

Cathy would love to hear from you! Find her on:

Facebook.com/CathyBramleyAuthor

@CathyBramley

www.CathyBramley.co.uk

HETTY'S FARMHOUSE BAKERY

Cathy Bramley

CORGI BOOKS

TRANSWORLD PUBLISHERS
61–63 Uxbridge Road, London W5 5SA
www.penguin.co.uk

Transworld is part of the Penguin Random House group of companies
whose addresses can be found at global.penguinrandomhouse.com

Penguin
Random House
UK

First published in Great Britain in 2018 by Corgi Books
an imprint of Transworld Publishers

Copyright © Cathy Bramley 2018

Cathy Bramley has asserted her right under the Copyright,
Designs and Patents Act 1988 to be identified as the author of this work.

This book is a work of fiction and, except in the case of historical fact,
any resemblance to actual persons, living or dead, is purely coincidental.

Every effort has been made to obtain the necessary permissions with reference to
copyright material, both illustrative and quoted. We apologize for any omissions in this
respect and will be pleased to make the appropriate acknowledgements in any future edition.

A CIP catalogue record for this book
is available from the British Library.

ISBN
9780552173940

Typeset in 11.5/13pt Garamond MT by Jouve (UK), Milton Keynes.
Printed and bound in Great Britain by Clays Ltd, Bungay, Suffolk.

Penguin Random House is committed to a sustainable future
for our business, our readers and our planet. This book is made from
Forest Stewardship Council® certified paper.

1 3 5 7 9 10 8 6 4 2

This book is dedicated to everyone who dreams of starting
their own small business from home.
I hope Hetty inspires you!

EDINBURGH LIBRARIES	
C0048582530	
Bertrams	21/03/2018
	£7.99
NT	DO NOT USE

Chapter 1

The journey from Sunnybank Farm to my daughter Poppy's school could take anywhere between twenty-five and fifty minutes depending on tractors, tourist traffic and time allocated. Obviously, the less time I had, the longer it would take.

I gripped the steering wheel tightly and willed the tractor in front of me to turn off. The driver had twice beckoned me to go around him, but on these narrow country lanes and in my ancient Renault Clio, I didn't dare attempt it. I didn't want to be late for parents' evening, but I didn't want to end up under an oncoming lorry either. Today had already earned itself the label of being 'one of those days'. I didn't need any more stress.

Deep breaths, Hetty. Okay. I wasn't late *yet*; I could still make it on time. My fourteen-year-old Border collie Rusty might be very poorly, but he was in safe hands with the vet, and even though this tractor was slowing me down, it gave me a chance to appreciate the wild flowers growing in amongst the long-grass verge. And as I rounded the bend and began a steep descent, the glorious vista of the Eskdale valley came into view.

My heart lifted and along with it, my spirits. The beauty of Cumbria never ceased to move me.

Despite the distances necessary to complete a simple task – like getting to school or popping out for milk – living here had many, many plus points and I wouldn't swap my little village for the world. The beguiling landscape with its craggy peaks puncturing the clouds and its valleys threaded with lakes and tarns; the simple joy of emerging from dark green woods to discover a waterfall tumbling over mossy rocks, or an ancient stone bridge forming a perfect arch over a crystal stream; it never grew old. I loved the timelessness and the feeling of belonging somewhere special. And even though Cumbria was a Mecca for other explorers, if you picked your route with care you could walk for miles and not bump into a soul, with just a happy dog for company. Unless your dog was at this minute undergoing multiple tests and quite possibly might never walk again . . .

I squeezed my eyes shut for a millisecond to block out the image of poor Rusty, and turned on the radio to distract myself.

At last the tractor turned off and I could finally put my foot down. I glanced at the time on my car's dashboard: with a bit of luck and a following wind, I just might make it.

I got the last free space in the school car park. I quickly ran a comb through my dark copper hair and applied an ancient stump of lipstick.

At college, I'd once been described by one particularly toxic girl as a poor man's Kate Winslet, at which point Dan Greengrass, the boy I'd had a crush on since for ever, leaned over and looked at me so intensely that my stomach flipped. He whispered that if that was the case he hoped he'd be poor for the rest of his life and would I go out with him. My heart virtually exploded all over the common room and my acceptance came out as a squeak and a nod. Today my cheekbones were less prominent than Kate's, my hips a little more padded and my locks had sprouted their first grey. By contrast, Dan still looked pretty much as he had back then, but with even more muscle. We were also still poor.

I got out and was brushing the red dog hairs – don't think about him – from my cardigan when I spotted my best friend Anna by her car. She worked here and was loading a cardboard box into her boot.

'Hey! Hetty Spaghetti,' she yelled across the car park, her customary wide smile lighting up her pretty face.

'Anna Bananna!' I laughed and waved.

My school nickname had been coined due to my long thin legs; now it was more likely to refer to my messy hair. Her nickname didn't mean anything, but it was fun, which meant that it suited her.

I kissed her cheek. 'Good. We can walk in together now and I won't be last to arrive.'

'I'd rather be last.' Anna arched an eyebrow playfully. 'I like to make an entrance.'

I always felt like a giant next to Anna. She was tiny and birdlike with short blonde hair and eyes the colour of sapphires, which danced permanently with mischief. She slammed the boot and opened her handbag.

'No Dan?' She peered over my shoulder before applying a posh lipstick which still had its pointy end, unlike my old thing.

I shook my head. 'A section of electric fence has come down; he had to stay and mend it. They're escape artists, those sheep. I'm sure they patrol the edges of each field looking for weak spots.'

She laughed at that.

'And it would help if parents' evening was actually in the evening instead of three thirty in the afternoon,' I added.

'I suppose it's hard for him to take time off in the daylight. He's a grafter, your husband.'

'So am I!' I retorted.

'I know you are; you are Super Woman!' She whipped out her mascara and flicked it over her pale lashes. 'I've seen you racing across fields on a quad bike in winter to rescue a new-born lamb, your red hair flying. I'm in awe. You even look sexy in a woolly hat and wellies. Whereas I look like a garden gnome.'

She could never look like a garden gnome. I smiled,

watching as she took her time to do her face, even though we were already late. In many ways we were chalk and cheese, but she was as close as family; the sister I never had.

We met when we were sixteen. My parents had just emigrated to Cape Cod, leaving me home alone. They'd planned on waiting until I went to uni, but Dad received an offer to buy his business unexpectedly and so after reassurance from me that I'd be fine, they'd decided to go early. I'd thought living on my own would be fun, but I'd been lonely and, although I hadn't liked to admit it, a bit scared too. Mum called constantly to check I was okay. I'd said I was fine, but secretly I wanted them to come back.

Then Anna came along. She'd been living with her glass-half-empty grandmother since her mum had died and the two of us gravitated to each other like magnets. Before long she'd unofficially moved in and we'd been close ever since.

Dan sometimes grumbled about Anna and me living in each other's pockets, but I thought it was par for the course when you lived in a small village like we did. Besides, he was probably a bit envious of our friendship. His own best friend, Joe, left home after college and never came back. I'd been sad about it, but my husband was a man of few words and shrugged it off as 'one of those things'.

'You're right; Dan does work longer hours than me,' I admitted. 'But it frustrates me sometimes. Introduce yourself as a farmer and everyone puffs out their cheeks, sympathizing with what a hard life you have. But say you're a farmer's wife and people go all misty-eyed imagining a contented, apple-cheeked woman in an apron, sliding pies into the oven before settling down to bottle-feed an orphan lamb . . .' My voice petered out. Anna tried to suppress a snort. Okay, so that was me to a T.

'Oh, shut up. Anyway, Poppy's last report was less than glowing and I would have liked some moral support this time.'

'Wouldn't we all?' she replied with a sigh.

I grinned at her. 'Really?'

Anna was a single parent; her son Bart was in the year above Poppy. He was my godson and I loved him almost as much as I loved Poppy. Anna had attended every appointment and meeting since the day he was born and was rightly proud of how well she coped on her own. But she was exceptionally protective of Bart and a bit of a control freak.

She pulled a face. 'Okay, probably not, but sometimes I think it would be nice to share the burden.'

To be fair, I did most of the domestic and childcare duties by myself too; it was part of my job description as a farmer's wife. Besides, being a farmer wasn't exactly a nine-to-five job; if it was light, Dan was at work and if it was dark . . . well, he'd probably still have things to do.

'The *burden* being your gorgeous, caring, well-mannered son?' I nudged her arm playfully. 'Poor you.'

'Good point well made.' She inclined her dainty head. 'Come on, stop fannying about or we really will be late.'

She locked the car and set the pace at a swift march across the car park towards the school entrance, where our children would be waiting in the hall. She pulled a bottle of perfume from her bag without breaking her step and spritzed it liberally in a cloud around us both.

'Sorry, but I honk,' she said, laughing as I began to cough. 'I've had unprotected sex, two asthma attacks, a vomiting incident in the PE toilets and an unexplained two-inch gash to a forehead and I need to get rid of the smell of disinfectant.'

'What an image.' I winced. 'I've made ten pies for the old people's monthly luncheon and some little gift bags for my mother-in-law for this week's Women's Institute raffle. I thought that was enough.'

I'd also sat up half the night in front of the Aga with Rusty as he'd been struggling for breath and too weak to make it up to his usual spot on the landing outside my bedroom door, but I kept that to myself. Anna and I shared everything usually but it would only take the slightest kindness to make me cry; she knew how much I loved that dog.

'Honestly,' she went on, 'being a school nurse in a secondary school is worse than working the Saturday-night shift at A&E. Hold on, nearly forgot.'

We'd reached the bottom of the steps which led to the revolving doors. She stopped to roll up the waistband of her skirt, then pulled a pair of stilettos out of her bag, swapping them for her sensible shoes.

I had to smile; she was thirty-three, but sometimes she acted like the teenager she'd been when I met her. 'You'll embarrass Bart doing that.'

'Pfff. He's only a baby; he doesn't notice that sort of thing.'

Somehow I managed to hold my tongue; she was kidding herself there. Poppy said he was very popular with the girls. 'What are you doing it for, anyway?'

'*Who*, you mean. Look out for Bart's form tutor, Mr Purkiss. I mean, what a name, it's got purr and kiss in it.' She winked. 'Plus, he's hot to trot.'

That was the other thing about Anna that hadn't changed: she was always on the lookout for the perfect man.

Inside, the hall was packed with gangs of teenagers, all doing their best to stay with their friends and away from their parents for as long as possible.

Anna scanned the room for her son, while I looked for Poppy. Bart wasn't difficult to spot; he was tall for his age and had the same white-blond hair as his mother. He stuck his hand up self-consciously, Anna went straight over and I smiled at him, feeling a sudden wave of sadness that his father would never know what an amazing human being he'd helped to create. Bart was the result of a one-night stand early on in Anna's gap year and she had no way of tracing the father. She'd arrived back in Carsdale with a baby boy. But other than knowing he'd been named after his father, Bart knew nothing about him and I sometimes wondered how he felt not having a man to call Dad.

'Mum? How's Rusty?' Poppy sidled up, her face, under a heavy fringe of auburn hair, was etched with concern. She had a crumpled appointment card in her hand, her shirt was untucked, there were two large holes in her tights and pen drawings all over the back of her left hand. She reminded me of me at her age and my heart filled with love for my only child.

'Doing okay.' I resisted the urge to stroke her face, but gestured to her appointment card instead, avoiding her eye. 'He's at the vet's now. Sally's giving him a full check-over; we'll find out later. Card please.'

Her fingers brushed against mine as I took the card from her and she gave my hand a quick squeeze. Hugging your mother at school was social suicide, but I could see she was dying to fold herself into my arms.

'He'll get through it,' she said. 'He gets through everything.'

'I hope so.' I looked at my girl, wondering when she'd started sounding so grown-up, and wished I could believe her. She was almost as tall as me now, her blazer was looking a bit tight across the chest and short at the sleeves too; she must be having another growth spurt. Another expense we could do without.

She leaned in towards me. 'We could just skip this and go and find out?'

'Nice try. Sally will call us as soon as she knows anything.' I looked down at the list of teachers' names. 'Come on. Who's first?'

Together we walked into the cafeteria where all the teachers were sitting behind small tables in rows and clusters of eager parents were hanging around trying to jostle for earlier appointment slots.

'Maths.' Poppy's shoulders fell. 'Ugh. I mean, seriously, who even cares?'

7

'I love maths!' I retorted.

'I know. Mum, please don't say that so loud,' she muttered. 'It makes you sound weird.'

I mimed zipping my mouth. 'What's your teacher's name?'

'Mr Purkiss,' she groaned. 'He hates me.'

'I've heard he's hot.'

Poppy gasped in horror just as Mr Purkiss looked up and beckoned us to his table. He half stood to shake my hand. His hands were warm but dry, thank goodness. It was amazing how many teachers got clammy hands during parents' evening. I could see what Anna meant about him, though: he was quite attractive. In a boyish way. He had floppy dark blond hair and a slim-fitting navy suit, which made the colour of his blue eyes pop. His face was clean shaven and he smelled of something harsh but manly, as if he'd just had a good spritz of deodorant in the staff room.

'Mrs . . . Greengrass?' he said, looking at Poppy for confirmation. She nodded reluctantly, her pretty face slightly pinker than usual.

'That's right,' I said with a smile. 'Pleased to meet you, Mr Purkiss. Goodness, you're young.'

Poppy's jaw dropped. The poor teacher gave a bark of embarrassed laughter. I'd meant that he was young for Anna. And I hadn't meant to say it out loud.

'Sorry, ignore me,' I continued, willing myself not to blush. 'It just popped out!'

'No need to apologize.' He cleared his throat and pulled Poppy's report from the pile.

I sat down, placing my handbag at my feet to avoid his eye.

'Not that you're *too* young. I'm sure you're old enough for . . . well, anything really,' I blathered on. Poppy looked on the verge of committing matricide. 'Anything at all,' I went on with a shrug.

Mr Purkiss looked scared. He scratched his head.

'Um. You're young too,' he said gallantly. 'You don't look old enough to be Poppy's mother.'

'I was a child bride,' I said, brushing off the compliment with a wave of my hand.

'Oh?' He looked a bit taken aback.

I wondered how to get this conversation back on topic. Once one embarrassing comment slipped out, it was as if the floodgates had opened and there was no end to my ability to humiliate myself and my child.

'No you weren't.' Poppy frowned. 'You were twenty-five.'

'I did marry at twenty-five.' I smiled at Mr Purkiss, who was looking left and right as if he might be contemplating his escape, or possibly looking for a security guard. 'But I'd already had Poppy by then, at a very young age. A legal age, I hasten to add, I wasn't fifteen or anything.' I laughed, to show him that nothing untoward had happened. No crime had taken place. 'And I did marry her *father*. I don't want you to think I was off willy-nilly having affairs during my teenage years.'

Mr Purkiss clasped his hands in front of him and swallowed. 'I wasn't thinking that.'

'No. Why would you?' I laughed a bit too loudly, aware that my face felt hot. 'How old are you, incidentally? Asking for a friend.'

'Oh my God,' Poppy muttered, sinking low in her chair.

'Twenty-six.' He cleared his throat and made a show of finding Poppy's name on the list in front of him.

I nodded thoughtfully. 'Not *too* young.'

That would make it a seven-year age gap. Probably the biggest Anna had had but I don't suppose she'd say no. I looked across at Poppy who was staring at me as if I'd gone mad. I bet she was wishing I'd stuck to talking about my love of maths after all.

'So.' She launched herself forward and leaned on the table that separated us from her maths teacher. 'Shall we discuss my last test results?'

'Yes,' said Mr Purkiss with evident relief.

Five long minutes later I was shaking his now very clammy hand.

'For the record,' Poppy said through clenched teeth, 'Dad can come next time. Not you.'

Forty minutes later, we'd nearly finished. Most of the teachers agreed that Poppy was a bright and competent girl but needed to work harder in school. I could see their point, she could drive the tractor now that her feet reached the pedals, stay up all night to help with the lambing and had her own business selling eggs to the teachers at school, but ask her to analyse a William Wordsworth poem or list the properties of sound waves and she stared at you blankly. She and I both. There was just one teacher left on the list – Poppy's least favourite. She groaned as Miss Compton beckoned us to her table . . .

'It's simple: you need to engage more.' Miss Compton was not only Poppy's form tutor but her English teacher too. She turned to address me. 'The class was studying *A Christmas Carol* last lesson and I asked Poppy to pick out an example of use of imagery. She couldn't answer because she didn't even know which *book* we were reading.'

'Oh dear,' I replied. It occurred to me to ask why on earth the teacher thought that reading a Christmas story in May would ever interest a class of twelve- and thirteen-year-olds, but I managed to restrain myself.

'But, Miss, there was a pair of robins outside the window, and each time they landed on the fence, their little beaks were stuffed with insects to take back to the nest; I couldn't stop watching.' Poppy turned to me for support. 'Robins make such good parents.'

My heart leapt for my girl; she loved being outdoors, would spend all day on the farm if she was allowed. A Victorian novel would never hold any appeal for her.

'I'm sure they do,' I said, 'but you can see Miss Compton's point of view, Popsicle.'

I realized my error straight away: never use her nickname in public.

Poppy sunk down in her chair, muttering 'so embarrassing' under her breath.

'Do you even know the main character's name, Poppy?' asked Miss Compton.

Poppy tilted her chin. 'Do you know how many trips per day a robin makes to the nest to feeds its babies?'

'No, but I don't need to.'

'Yeah, well, I feel the same about Dickens.'

The teacher and Poppy glared at each other for a moment and then Miss Compton looked at me for help.

'Your education is important, especially English; you must concentrate,' I said firmly, earning myself a nod of approval.

'What's the point of reading stuff like that? When am I going to use it?' Poppy asked, quite reasonably.

'Well, because . . .' I faltered, and smoothed down the front of my shirt while I ferreted about for a suitable reply. 'You'll use it when . . .'

I wasn't much of a reader either, unless cookery books counted. A few options occurred to me, such as the information might come in handy in a pub quiz, or because it will keep the teachers happy, but before I could formulate something more motivational the teacher leaned forward and cocked her head to one side.

'Who inspires you, Poppy?' she asked.

'What do you mean?' Poppy's eyes narrowed.

'She's only twelve, she . . .' I hesitated, I was about to add that she was only a child but that would have earned me more black marks.

'Almost thirteen,' Poppy put in.

'So?' Miss Compton continued. 'Who's your role model? You'll leave home one day, perhaps go to university, travel the world; whose footsteps do you want to follow?'

The teacher and I both looked at Poppy and I held my

breath. I didn't for one second expect it to be me; I liked to think I was a good person, kind, happy-go-lucky, but I'd done nothing remarkable with my life, nothing that would seem brave or inspirational to a twelve-year-old. Nonetheless at that moment I'd never wanted anything more.

Poppy's eyes met mine and she smiled, and my heart began to beat a merry tattoo. 'Auntie Naomi's quite cool, isn't she?'

I swallowed and somehow managed to return her smile. 'She is.'

Dan's sister, Naomi, had converted a little row of farm buildings her dad had left her in his will into an award-winning farm shop. She had a head for business, she was good to her staff, gave fantastic customer service and on top of that was the best sister-in-law I could have wished for. And right now I felt inordinately jealous of her.

'Naomi Willcox, from the farm shop?' Miss Compton gave a bemused smile. 'I was thinking of someone a little further afield.'

'Why?' Poppy frowned. 'I don't get all this "go out and see the world" stuff. What if I like it in Carsdale?'

Poppy and I were alike in looks, but complete opposites in other ways; I'd been dying to leave when I was her age. For once, the teacher hadn't got a ready response but pulled a face as if she was chewing a wasp. I cleared my throat and picked up my bag from the floor; this discussion wasn't going anywhere.

'I take all your points on board, Miss Compton, and my husband and I will see to it that Poppy starts showing more interest in her studies.'

'Good.' The teacher started to shuffle her papers. 'Because her schoolwork has to take precedence over her love of nature.'

Poppy pushed her chair back and stood up. 'Do you want your usual half-dozen eggs tomorrow, Miss?'

Miss Compton's cheeks turned pink. 'Er, yes please, Poppy.'

Poppy nodded. 'Okay, but you still owe me a pound from last week.'

The teacher fluttered her hand up to her neck and smiled sheepishly at me. 'I didn't have any change.'

'Scrooge,' said Poppy, hefting her school bag over her arm.

'I beg your pardon?' Miss Compton's head reared up.

'The main character in that old book,' she replied innocently. 'And the answer to *my* question is up to one hundred times a day.'

'Oh right, yes.' The teacher's blush deepened. 'Well done.'

One nil to Poppy, I thought, with a rush of pride as we walked out of the school hall.

Chapter 2

'Home?' Poppy asked, pulling off her school tie and flinging it on to the back seat a few minutes later when we'd made it back to the car.

I grimaced as I did up my seat belt. 'Sorry, love, shopping first.'

We set off to the sound of Poppy complaining that for once she'd just like to get home at the same time as normal people. She usually travelled on the school bus, which due to its circuitous route took over an hour to reach Sunnybank Farm. I reminded her that at least she'd only got one more day before school finished for a week and promised her a treat if she pushed the trolley for me.

I was keen to get home too but couldn't pass up the opportunity to visit a proper supermarket while we were in town. Carsdale only stretched to a couple of little grocery stores, both of which were very pricey, and although I bought local as much as I could to support them, it was nice to do a big shop every now and again.

With Poppy steering the trolley and me tossing item after item into it, we soon managed to accumulate a mountain of food and after half an hour we headed to the tills. The shop was busy and by the time we'd loaded all our shopping on the conveyor belt, quite a queue had built up. Poppy wasn't keen on packing, so while she retreated to sit on the bench with her pot of pomegranate seeds, chosen as her treat, and check for vitally important messages on her phone, I began loading the bags.

And then an image popped into my head: my little blue purse sitting on the kitchen table.

'Oh no,' I said suddenly, with a bolt of panic.

I'd taken my purse out of my bag to pay a bill over the phone this morning. I reached for my bag now, already knowing it wouldn't be there.

'What's wrong?' asked the cashier, a pale-faced girl who, judging by the long and consonant-heavy name on her badge, may have been Polish.

The other people in the queue stopped to stare as I rummaged in my bag. My phone, car keys, bottle of water and tub of dog treats: all present and correct. No purse.

'I haven't brought my money,' I said, feeling the heat rise to my face. And my armpits. 'I'm so sorry; I can't pay for my shopping.'

A collective groan went up from the queue, two of whom had already started unloading their shopping on to the belt. The two behind them pulled away from the queue and dashed to the other open till.

'No cards at all?' The girl blinked at me with large worried eyes.

'Poppy?' I called, grasping at the ultimate straw; I didn't even know why I was asking. 'You haven't got any money on you, have you?'

Bless her, she reached into her blazer pocket. 'How much do you need?,' she said, holding out a handful of coins.

'Ninety-five pounds,' said the pale-faced assistant, chewing her lip. 'You might have enough to pay for the pomegranate.'

Yep. Definitely one of those days.

Poppy strode out ahead with the car keys, leaving me to return the trolley. I stowed the empty shopping bags back in the boot and we headed for home.

Before long we'd left the supermarket and relative

15

metropolis of Holmthwaite behind but my darling daughter was still laughing.

'Only you could do that, Mum,' she snorted after she'd finished messaging all of her friends about my disaster. 'You should have seen your face. You're hilarious.'

'You might not think that when you see what's for dinner,' I said stoutly, turning on the radio. 'Check my phone in case the vet has called, will you?'

The smile dropped from her face and she scooped my phone out of my bag, but there had been no word from Sally yet.

'That probably means he's absolutely fine,' Poppy said lightly as we passed what counted as the high street in Carsdale and took the steep lane up towards the farm.

I glanced across at her and my heart squeezed with love for both her and Rusty. She had never known life without him. He'd guarded her proudly when she was a baby sleeping outside in the big old Silver Cross pram which had been Dan's and Naomi's before that; and when she'd learned to walk, it had been Rusty who'd stood patiently, letting her grip his fur as she'd planted one wobbly foot in front of the other. Being brought up on a farm had exposed her to the sharp end of both life and death, but Rusty was more than just an animal, he was a big part of our family.

'I hope so, Poppy, I really do.'

We turned in through the farm gates, rattled over the cattle grid and followed the track between a long sweep of hawthorn hedge. Finally, we rounded a bend and there, amongst the soft hills that led down to the River Esk at the bottom of the valley, and up to the distant peaks that were often snow-covered long after spring had sprung elsewhere, was Sunnybank Farm.

Home.

The farmhouse might not win any prizes for design but as far as I was concerned it was the most beautiful house in the world. The main part of it was a sturdy white rendered building with sash window frames painted soft blue, a central porch sheltering a front door that we rarely used, and a slate roof. Scattered around the edge of the yard were a random assortment of stone outbuildings, wooden lambing sheds and tumbledown barns. To the left of the house stood a huge log store which held a winter's worth of seasoned wood at a time and in front of that my haphazard vegetable patch and a pond beloved of the hens. To the right was the track leading to the orchard and the meadow currently home to Dan's new project, the rare-breed Soay sheep, and beyond were our fields of black-faced Swaledale sheep, which, according to my mother-in-law, had been grazing here for at least four generations of Greengrass farmers. And if you followed the track right across the farm to the far edge of our land, you'd end up at the Sunnybank Farm shop, owned and run by Naomi.

I parked the car between the farm-shop van – which meant that Naomi was here – and the Land Rover and Poppy jumped straight out and ran indoors. At this time of day, as it glowed in the early-evening sunshine, Sunnybank Farm suited its name perfectly. And on grey days when it rained or when the clouds came down so low that we could barely see the roof, it cheered me up with its twin plumes of smoke from the chimneys at either end of the house, the slate planters on the front step full of fragrant thyme, little tête-à-tête daffodils in spring and hardy fuchsias in summer.

Normally I'd be greeted by Rusty, not as boisterously as he'd done as a young dog, but nonetheless with waggy-tailed love and adoration in his eyes. Today I walked across the yard unaccompanied and as I approached the kitchen door I could hear Poppy already regaling Dan and her favourite and inspirational Auntie Naomi with the supermarket saga. They were standing side by side next to the sink as I came in, clasping giant mugs of tea and grinning.

Dan was tall and broad, with gentle eyes, hair the colour of autumn acorns and a complexion that could only come from a lifetime spent out on the Cumbrian hills. Naomi was the elder by seven years and had just celebrated her fortieth birthday. She had similar colouring to her brother and was almost as tall. And although her work mostly kept her indoors, she was a keen fell runner and spent much of her time on the hills. Consequently, she was as thin as a lath and the contents of her wardrobe comprised ninety per cent fleece and ten per cent Lycra.

'I hear you forgot something?' Dan nodded to the centre of the table where my purse sat in pride of place.

'Yeah, we only had enough to pay for one thing!' Poppy said with glee, shrugging off her blazer and dumping it on top of her school bag in the middle of the floor. 'Luckily it was *my* thing. But I'm still starving.'

She helped herself to the last banana in the fruit bowl and sat at the kitchen table to eat it.

'I was mortified,' I said with a shudder as I put my purse back in my bag where it belonged. 'Wheeling an empty trolley out of a supermarket is worse than doing the walk of shame in last night's clothes.'

Dan's eyes flashed with amusement. 'And when did you ever do that?'

I held his gaze, a smile playing at my lips. 'Oh, you know, hypothetically speaking.'

My husband grinned back: a confident smile that implied he knew me inside out. And he did. Mostly.

Apart from what I'd done during the weeks I'd spent in Cornwall, the summer after our A levels. Dan had broken up with me and I'd fled, broken-hearted, to Padstow to distract myself while I waited for my exam results.

Gil, the son of the owner of the Cornish pasty shop where I'd had a summer job, had been my therapy. We'd had fun, he'd taught me to smile again and, yes, I had done the walk of shame, tiptoeing barefoot in the early hours of the morning through the narrow streets, heels in my hand. But then Dan and I had got back together and I'd put my Cornish adventure behind me. Since then there'd only been Dan, my first and only real love.

'I did the walk of shame once after a Young Farmers' ball in a full-length puffy taffeta dress. Mother went barmy.' Naomi sighed dreamily into her mug. 'Worth it, though.'

Poppy made a choking noise. 'Nooo! Stop, Auntie Naomi, please, it makes me feel ill.'

'I know,' Naomi winced, 'me in taffeta: I looked like a giraffe in a frock. Awful.'

We laughed as she leaned forward and ruffled Poppy's auburn hair and I crossed to the sink to kiss Dan's cheek. He smelled of fresh air and damp grass and he was wearing his farmer's uniform: rough wool checked shirt, rolled at the sleeves, over a faded T-shirt and old jeans. I felt a familiar pull of love for him, a love that had changed over the years from the frantic fireworks of our first few months, to the gentler glow of a log fire. But the spark was definitely still alight.

I'd fallen for him instantly: Dan had looked a bit like Harrison Finch, a TV presenter who I'd always had a soft spot for, he had his own car, and even at seventeen, he'd looked like a man, unlike his best friend Joe who had a baby face and coveted Dan's stubble and muscles. But more importantly than that, I'd never met a kinder boy. My mum once said that kindness is a reflection of a person's true beauty. I'd never forgotten that. He was still a kind man, and I still loved him for it.

'That tricky ewe's finally gone into labour,' he said, turning to put his empty mug in the sink.

'The one who lost her lamb last year?'

Dan nodded.

'How's she doing?'

The rest of our flock of Swaledales had already lambed. There was rarely any need for intervention but Dan kept an eye on them even so. And sometimes, like with this one,

19

he'd bring them into a pen if they'd had issues in previous seasons.

'Restless but okay, touch wood.' He rapped his knuckles against the solid wood worktop that ran the long run of cream painted units. 'But one of last night's triplets died. I wasn't surprised; he'd been weak and struggled to suckle right from the start.'

'Poor thing,' I said with a sigh.

Poppy and I exchanged glances; no matter how much we accepted that the survival rate was never going to be a hundred per cent, we always got upset when one of our little ones died.

'Sounds like you've all had a tough day with one thing and another,' said Naomi. She'd helped me lift Rusty into the back of my car this afternoon after Sally had advised me to bring him into the surgery. I nodded, swallowing back the lump that rose as soon as I thought about him.

'And being told my child isn't paying enough attention in school didn't help either,' I said.

'Poppy, school is important,' Dan said with a growl.

'Not again, please! Mum's already gone on at me,' Poppy groaned. 'I'll do my homework straight after dinner. Promise.'

'You need to make the most of every opportunity to—' he began again.

I held up my refereeing hand. 'Dad's right, it is important.' Although not important enough for Dan to make it to parents' evening, I thought to myself. 'But we trust you to do the right thing. Don't we?'

Dan and Poppy folded their arms at exactly the same moment and I couldn't hide my smile; she was her father's daughter all right.

Naomi regarded me for a moment then shook the teapot to see if there was anything left in it. There wasn't. 'Let me make you some fresh tea.'

'Oh, thank you, I'd love one.'

I'd got used to her treating my kitchen like her own a long time ago. Because, of course, this had been hers; this had been the family home until she'd married Tim and moved out to a cottage a couple of miles away. They still lived there, and up until last September when they left for university, their twin boys, Oscar and Otis, had lived there too.

When I'd first moved in, Dan's mum Viv had still been here and this had been her space. Over the last ten years, since she'd moved out, it had begun to feel more like mine. We had kept the rather utilitarian wooden table which seated sixteen and the huge Ordnance Survey map of the area on the wall above it. But with the addition of curtains to soften the big windows, cushions to soften the hard benches and chairs and my collection of pottery vases for stuffing with wild flowers, these days it reflected my tastes. I'd set two cosy armchairs by the log fire and although the room was cavernous, on a winter's night with the fire lit there was no cosier spot on the planet.

'Fill this up as well, while you're at it,' said Dan, pulling an ancient Thermos flask out from under the sink. 'I'm going to sit with that ewe; I don't like the thought of her struggling on her own.'

Poppy and I pulled 'ahhh' faces.

'And I'd better sort out dinner,' I said. 'Though goodness knows what it'll be now I haven't done the shopping.'

'Didn't I see you making a load of pies?' Dan scanned the kitchen as if they might be hiding somewhere. He headed for the cake tin while I surveyed the fridge for the makings of a meal. It was slim pickings indeed: a punnet of cherry tomatoes past their best, half a jar of olives and a mottled chunk of mature cheddar.

'Yes, five sausage and leek and five beef and celeriac. But they were for the old people's luncheon club,' I said with a smile, remembering the look of delight on the vicar's face when I'd delivered them, still warm, to the village hall earlier. He'd only paid me for the ingredients, as agreed, and not my

21

time but the thought of Carsdale's elderly enjoying my food was reward enough.

'You are good at pies, Mum,' said Poppy kindly, looking up from her phone. 'I'll give you that.'

'I'm not just good at pies,' I replied, seizing my chance to be as inspirational as Naomi. 'I'm good at . . .' I racked my brains to think of something that might impress her. 'MATHS! Yes, I'm very good at maths.'

'As long as it's pie charts,' Dan said, winking at Poppy.

'And last time you helped me with my maths homework I got it wrong.'

'Technically, I was right,' I said defensively.

But I'd used a more advanced formula to calculate the nth term and the teacher had marked her down because he'd assumed she'd copied it off the internet.

'Technically, it was me who got in trouble,' Poppy put in.

Everyone laughed, including me. The joke might have been at my expense but we were all together and happy and, really, what else mattered? So what if I didn't exactly cut an inspiring figure for Poppy? I was a farmer's wife and a mum, with a passion for pastry. I'd just have to find other ways to be a role model for her, by being a good person, warm-hearted and kind. I'd have more hope of achieving that than by wowing her with my achievements outside of the home.

Naomi poured some tea into a mug and handed it to me. I carried it over to the old stone larder which was where Dan's ancestors would have kept food cold and now housed my collection of jams, pickles and tinned foods.

I'd never got as far as having career aspirations; I'd simply planned to do a degree in maths and then see what turned up. But instead, when Dan had arrived in Cornwall to beg me to come back to him, he also had terrible news: his father, lovely Mike Greengrass, had suffered a massive heart attack and died, aged just fifty-five. Dan had been planning to study to be a vet but instead had been named in Mike's will as the heir to the farm business, while Naomi received the land and buildings on the other side of the farm, which she converted into the farm shop. Dan's life on the farm became mine and all thoughts of going to university were forgotten. For both of us.

My hunt through the shelves had yielded two tins of baked beans, and they were only there because I'd bought the no-taste, healthy ones by accident and none of us liked them. But we always had fresh eggs and I could probably grate the floury layer off that cheese.

'So egg, cheese and beans on toast it is, then,' I said, placing the tins on the table.

'No bread,' said Dan, swallowing the last mouthful of cake. 'I finished the last bit up with some of your jam. Sorry.'

Naomi scooped up the keys to the van. 'I had a load of sausages to sample from a new supplier today. You could cook them and give me your verdict, if you wouldn't mind. Plus, I've got a tub of potato salad about to go out of date, so eat that and you'll be doing me a favour. If Poppy comes back with me, we can nip in and get it.'

'Cool.' Poppy jumped to her feet and dropped the banana skin in the compost bucket at the door. 'See, Mum, that's why she's my hero.'

She began to recount the earlier conversation between her and Miss Compton, and Naomi's jaw dropped open in surprise.

'Thanks, Pops,' she said, sounding a bit choked. 'For that I might even find you a tub of ice cream.'

'And I thought she might say *I* was her role model,' I said, only half joking.

'Oh, Mum,' said Poppy indulgently, patting my arm. 'You are funny.'

I watched them leave and let out a deep sigh.

Dan caught my eye. 'Don't take it personally, you know what they say: you're never a hero in your own land.'

'I'm not even a hero in my own kitchen.' I smiled wanly at him, appreciating his sentiment, even if he did mean 'prophet'.

Dan held up the teapot, offering me a refill; his way of showing me that he cared.

He wasn't the demonstrative type. Neither was the rest of his family. It had been one of the biggest differences I'd noticed between my parents and his when we first met. My dad had never even popped out for a newspaper without giving Mum a peck on the cheek. I'd loved that about their relationship and they were equally loving towards me as well. When Dad died after a complication with heart surgery, Mum's own heart was broken too. But as she'd said when I flew over to America for the funeral, at least they had had five years of living their dream, and Dad had met Poppy, and had loved his little granddaughter fiercely.

Mum was still living in Cape Cod and had a new companion, a divorcee called Al who treated her like a queen, but she said he didn't give hugs like Dad did. We Skyped weekly and she visited occasionally, but it wasn't the same as having her arms around me whenever I needed it, so I'd brought Poppy up on a diet of cuddles and kisses instead. I dreaded the day when she said she was too old for all that fuss.

'You've made a good life for her here, Hetty; she'll see that when she's older,' Dan said, picking up his Thermos flask.

'But is that enough?' I said quietly, as much to myself as to him. 'I want her to shoot for the stars, not put any limits on her aspirations. I sometimes worry that I should have aimed higher myself.'

Dan looked at me sharply. 'Isn't the farm enough for you? We both agreed to make sacrifices; it's a bit late to be having regrets now.'

He was right, all those years ago when we were both eighteen, taking on the farm together had been a massive commitment, we'd both given up our plans for the future, but I'd loved Dan with all my heart, I still did, and whilst I did sacrifice a university education, I'd never regretted it. Besides, it was never too late to try something new if I really, really wanted to, was it?

Dan's eyes were still searching mine, waiting for an answer, and I wrapped my arms around his waist and hugged him. 'Of course not, I'm being silly. No regrets at all. Shall I come with you to check on the ewe?'

His face relaxed. 'You can do; you always help soothe them when they get anxious.'

Another skill to add to my pastry prowess, I thought wryly as I pulled on a pair of mud-caked boots and trudged with Dan across the yard: sheep whisperer . . .

Chapter 3

'I saw Bart at school earlier,' I said, waiting in turn to wash my hands at the sink inside the barn. We'd stopped off to feed Dan's two dogs and needed to make sure we were germ free before handling the labouring ewe. I handed a towel to Dan as he turned, shaking the drips off. 'He's so tall now and turning into a man so fast, not that Anna can see it, I think she's trying to prolong his childhood as long as possible.'

'She mollycoddles him.' He dried his hands roughly while I washed mine. 'She panics if the lad goes out on his bike without his helmet.'

'Only natural, I suppose, he's the centre of her world,' I said in her defence. 'Anyway, seeing him looking so grown-up made me think how few male role models he's had in his life.'

'Apart from the various "uncles" over the years,' said Dan wryly. 'You're right, he hasn't had anyone steady, but that's about to change.'

'Oh?'

Hands clean, we walked over to the sheep pens while Dan told me that Bart had cycled over after school and had watched while the last family of lambs had been tagged and checked. 'He seemed keen to help,' said Dan. 'He asked if Poppy worked on the farm and when I told him she did, he looked really envious.'

26

I twinkled my eyes at him, already guessing what was coming. 'When does he start?'

Dan rubbed a hand through his hair sheepishly. 'Saturday. I told him it's a four-week trial and I can only offer minimum wage. I know we can't really afford it but . . .' He shrugged.

'You big softie.' I nudged Dan's arm with mine. 'That was good of you; I bet he was thrilled.'

He grimaced. 'He was; I thought he was going to kiss me. Right, let's see what's going on in here.'

The sheep pens were housed in an open-sided low barn. Each ewe had her own wooden pen with a thick layer of straw. Only two of them were occupied: the ewe now in labour and the one who'd given birth last night to triplets and had lost one.

'These beauties can wait until the morning before I turn them back out into the meadow,' said Dan, entering the pen and picking up each lamb in turn to check it over. Finally, he stooped to examine the ewe's teats. 'She's doing well. Another night's rest and she'll be fine.'

He went to wash his hands again while I collected one of the foldout camping stools we kept out here and opened the gate to the pen where the pregnant ewe was lying on her side. I'd hardly had a chance to sit down in the corner when she made a long straining noise and the water sack slid out of her rear end. The lamb was on its way.

'Dan,' I called, 'quick, the head's out.'

He dashed into the pen and dropped to his knees. The water sack popped and the lamb's little nose appeared.

'Damn,' he muttered, pulling away the mucousy layer from the lamb's nostrils. He swept his fingers around the ewe's vulva.

'Problem?'

'Only one foot has presented. Can you get me the thin rope and the lubricant?'

'Sure.' My heart sank as I leapt to my feet; the poor thing

27

had lost her lamb last year, we didn't want a repeat performance. A lamb should be born front feet, then nose first – literally diving into the world. If one or two feet were caught behind, its mother would struggle to push the lamb through the birth canal.

'Are you going to call Sally?'

Dan shook his head. 'I can manage.'

'Of course you can.' My heart swelled with pride as I let myself out of the pen. Dan had such a calm and confident aura about him; there was no doubt in my mind he could do it.

He never said as much but I think he quite relished the challenge of a difficult birth and prided himself on attempting what many farmers would quail at. I headed for the table where he kept various bits of kit. I found what he needed, cutting off several lengths of rope and bringing everything over to him, along with some clean rags.

He poured some lubricant into his hands and massaged it in up to his wrists. I knelt at the ewe's head to steady her, making soothing noises. The poor thing; if she thought life couldn't get any more uncomfortable, she was in for a shock.

She bucked a bit and I pushed myself closer, gripping her wool while Dan looped a piece of rope gently around the lamb's neck. The first time I'd seen this, I'd been worried to death that it would choke, but Dan knew what he was doing.

'That's it, in you go.'

Gently, he tucked in the lamb's ears to streamline the head as much as possible and pushed the lamb back up the birth canal and into the abdominal cavity with all his might. The ewe was strong, her every instinct was to push, and beads of sweat were popping up along Dan's forehead.

I'd been helping out at lambing for years, and I was a lot less squeamish these days. Even so, I swallowed nervously as Dan struggled against the ewe, feeling around inside her for a foot. 'Got it,' he panted.

Slowly he brought out one of the front feet, secured it with rope and went back in for the second.

The ewe was starting to get distressed and heaving to push the lamb out, and it was taking all my strength to hold her steady.

'Shit.' Dan knelt back to catch his breath. 'If she could only understand we need her to work with us.'

My heart was beginning to pound. That lamb would suffocate from lack of oxygen if we didn't get it out of there soon. And it was too late to call the vet now.

'What can I do?' I asked, licking my dry lips.

Dan flicked me a glance. 'We're going to have to flip her on to her back, let gravity help us. Can you do that?'

I nodded and rolled the struggling ewe over. Dan managed to keep the lamb from emerging from the birth canal and deftly secured a rope around the other foot. Seconds later the lamb, limp and lifeless, slid out on to the straw.

'Oh, thank goodness,' I said, tears of relief springing to my eyes. 'Is it okay?'

'We'll soon know.' He lifted the lamb away from its mother, letting the umbilical cord break away, and began rubbing clean straw over its body to help massage its lungs. The lamb's front feet kicked and Dan smiled at me. 'It's breathing. *She*, I should say. It's a gimmer.'

I exhaled happily. A female lamb.

He placed it at the ewe's nose to encourage her to lick her lamb clean and the little thing made a tiny mewing noise.

'Well done, Mum!' I said, rubbing the ewe's neck. 'You can have a rest now.'

Dan sat back on his heels and wiped an arm across his forehead. 'Not for long she can't; she's carrying twins, according to her scan.'

'Oh, look at them,' I whispered, getting up to perch on the stool to give them some space.

For a moment the two of us fell silent, watching as the mother and her new-born bonded, doing exactly as they were supposed to do, naturally. It took me right back to an April night seven years ago when I'd sat in one of the pens with Dan witnessing a much smoother birth than the one we'd just assisted with. Poppy had only been little and she was inside, tucked up in bed. It had been a cold night right at the start of the lambing season and I'd been sitting on the camping stool wrapped up in layers, marvelling at the way the ewe had calmly and quietly delivered her two lambs and wondering why I couldn't do the same. It had been only eight weeks since my miscarriage. Physically, I was fine; mentally I was finding the loss of my baby difficult to deal with. My eyes had filled up with tears at the injustice of Mother Nature.

Dan had turned to me suddenly and the look in his eyes told me that he was thinking exactly the same thing.

'Remind me why we aren't married?' he'd said in a low voice.

'Because I haven't asked you,' I'd joked through my tears.

The truth was that we'd always intended to get married but to begin with we'd felt too young, living as teenagers under Viv's roof. Then we were too busy running the farm and starting a family, not to mention being strapped for cash.

'Well, I can't wait any longer.' He'd knelt in front of me, taken hold of my hands and said, 'So I'm asking you. Hetty, will you marry me?'

And I knew that what he was really saying was that together we were strong, a team, a family, and that his love for me didn't depend on anyone or anything else. And whether we had more children or remained parents solely to Poppy it didn't matter, we had all we needed to be happy.

So I'd said yes.

'Seven years since you proposed,' I murmured now, marvelling at how fast time had flown by, how much had happened, and yet despite that how I still felt like the same person inside. Just with a more pillowy bottom.

I dragged myself out of my reverie to find Dan looking at me oddly. 'Not fed up of me yet, are you?'

'Of course not,' I said, shocked. 'Why would you think that?'

'Just, you know . . .' He paused and shrugged. Getting my husband to express himself could be torturous, so I waited patiently. 'What you said earlier: you should have aimed higher.'

'I didn't mean it like that,' I said, lowering myself down to the straw and wrapping my arms around his neck. 'All I want is to be at Sunnybank Farm with you and Poppy.'

He grinned. 'Glad to hear it. I won't hug you back because—'

'Yeah, I know,' I laughed, 'because you've had your hands up a sheep's bum, you old romantic.'

'You go back inside,' he said, as I eased myself up from the straw, 'I'll shout if I need you.'

I gave the ewe and her lamb one last look before letting myself out of the pen.

'Hetty . . .' Dan turned quickly. 'I was talking to Ian this morning.'

'Oh yes?' Ian Kirk was a friend and fellow farmer. He owned Woodside Farm on the other side of the valley and kept sheep and cattle. His flock shared the same common areas on the fells as ours.

'He thinks his dog Nancy is pregnant.'

'Ah, that's nice.'

He chewed his lip. 'I was just thinking, if Rusty—'

'Don't say it,' I blurted quickly, shaking my head. 'I'm not ready to think about that.'

Dan gave me a sympathetic look. The sound of rapid footsteps closed the discussion down as Poppy came into view, holding my mobile phone in front of her like a relay baton.

'Mum!' she yelled. 'It's the vet!'

Thirty minutes later, I stood in the vet's consulting room, resting against the examination table, reeling from Sally's

31

words. Rusty was lying in front of me, in a sphinx position; his bony head pressed against my stomach, still woozy from his biopsy. The fingers of my right hand were threaded through his fur, my left hand swiped at my tears. My brain felt as if it was throbbing with the new knowledge. I suppose I'd known deep down that Rusty was very ill. But I'd been shutting it out, hoping that I was wrong. His prognosis was even worse than I'd imagined.

'It's the kindest thing, Hetty.' Sally managed a smile, her chin wobbling with the effort of remaining professional. She'd been looking after all the animals from Sunnybank Farm for years and I knew she had a soft spot for my dog.

I nodded. My throat was so tight with emotion that it hurt. I knew she was right: Rusty was old, the tumour in his throat was huge and getting bigger. There were no guarantees that surgery would be successful at his age, or save his life. And even if he survived that, the biopsy on the lumps on his flank had proven them to be malignant too. In short, Rusty was riddled with tumours, his life would be painful and difficult. But even so . . .

I looked at my beloved Border collie lying passively on the examination table and he returned my gaze, his wise old eyes filmy now and cautious, but as trusting ever. This was one of the hardest days of my life.

A sob welled up and out before I could stop it. Sally pressed a gentle hand to my arm and tactfully turned away to tap into her computer. I knew what she'd be typing and I couldn't bear it.

I leaned over him and hugged him tightly. His thick red and white fur made him seem such a big dog, but his muscles had been wasting away since Christmas and I could feel every rib along his precious body, every nobble of his spine. His breathing was wheezy and laboured and every in-breath was an effort for him. I lowered my head to his, hoping he could feel the strength of my love, my sorrow, anything but my guilt at being the one to make the decision.

'Goodbye, Rusty, old boy,' I whispered. 'We've been through a lot together you and me. What am I going to do without you?'

I stroked his one white front paw with my thumb, remembering so clearly the day when Dan bought him into the kitchen fourteen years ago. His little ears pricked, his pale blue eyes taking everything in, his plump body wriggling to be set free. I'd only just moved in with Dan and his mum and the transition from living in a normal semi-detached house to a sprawling, smelly farm on the side of a steep hill was proving harder than I'd anticipated. I was blissfully in love, excited for the future and full of ideas for my new role, but even so, I was only eighteen and for a girl who'd planned on doing a three-year maths degree, with nothing and no one to think about but herself, this sudden change of direction had taken some getting used to.

'To welcome you to the farm,' he'd said, placing the bundle of fur in my arms. 'Your very own sheepdog. A redhead, just like you.'

The farm had black-and-white Border collies, who slept outside in kennels, but they weren't pets, they were workers and responded to Dan's every word and gesture. This puppy was just for me.

It had been love at first sight and Rusty and I had been inseparable ever since. Incidentally, his aptitude for sheep herding was a perfect match to my talents as a shepherdess – poor. But with Rusty by my side I'd explored every nook and cranny of the farm: where the best blackberries grew, where the skylarks nested in spring and even, to Dan and his mum's delight, a gully where a ewe and her twin new-borns had fallen and couldn't get back up to freedom. Finding a role for myself alongside Viv had been tricky to begin with, so I'd taken a job in the village post office and gradually, as she eased herself into life without her husband, I'd taken on new responsibilities: the vegetable garden, the orchard of damson and apple trees, helping out with lambing and, later, looking after Poppy. And Rusty was always beside me, my lovable, dancing shadow.

'But what fun and adventures we've had, boy, eh? You have been the best dog. The best.'

Sally cleared her throat softly. 'Shall we get this over with?'

I took a deep breath and met her gaze with a nod. This was possibly the bravest and worst thing I'd ever had to do.

After I'd stopped crying long enough to string a sentence together, Sally showed me out via the staff exit so that I wouldn't have to walk back through reception with a tear-stained face and no pet. Rusty would come back home to be buried on the farm, but there was no way I could be the one to drive him.

Back outside I walked to the car, head bowed. It seemed impossible that less than an hour had gone by since I'd arrived; dusk had begun to fall, a cool May breeze was tickling the cherry blossom from the trees and a football match was taking place on the field behind the village primary school. I sat in the car for a few minutes to pull myself together and I was doing really well until I spotted Rusty's tartan blanket on the back seat. I pulled it towards me and folded it up small, stuffing it back behind my seat out of sight. There were reminders of him everywhere at the farm-house; I'd text Dan, I decided, he could prepare the way for me when I came home without him . . .

A wave of anxiety rose up inside me. Poppy would be devastated – she had never known life without Rusty.

Losing animals was part of farm life. In its simplest terms it was our business. A stillborn lamb, a poorly ewe, a fatal injury – it happened and we mourned every loss; but a dog was different, even Dan had welled up when I'd called him to let him know the results of the biopsy. Rusty was as much a part of the farm as the house itself. I took a tissue from a packet in the glove box and wiped my eyes.

On the other hand, although Poppy was an animal lover, she was pragmatic; she might even deal with it better than me. Either way, I'd show her that expressing your emotions was perfectly okay, whatever they were.

I flipped down the vanity mirror, checked my face, wished I hadn't and then turned the keys in the ignition. It was the end of an era; Sunnybank Farm without Rusty was going to feel very different indeed and for once I was in no rush to get home.

Chapter 4

The next day dawned just as any other: the birds began their twittering symphony as soon as the light eased its way in stripes through the curtains; the cockerel made his harsh presence felt at about six and below us in the valley bottom, the lowing of Ian's cows provided a baritone bassline to the sounds of the morning. I made Dan some breakfast while he showered and once he'd gone out to check on last night's new lambs Poppy staggered down, school shirt untucked and tie askew, at seven fifteen. She was too late for breakfast but just in time to catch the school bus as it passed the end of the lane. I stuffed a packet of breakfast biscuits in her bag and pressed a hurried kiss to her cheek as she stomped out of the door, only to run back and collect the egg boxes for her teachers.

And then it was just me.

I propped the kitchen door open and clasping a mug of tea, gazed from the fields intersected with their zigzag of drystone walls up to the fells which rose to the east at the back of the house, green then brown then a smoky blue at the summit. This precious time, this breathing in the sharp morning air, had been my ritual as long as I could remember. Rusty and I, dog and mistress, sizing up the day ahead together. All of a sudden Rusty's absence hit me like an avalanche, and I felt heavy under its weight and the tears appeared soundlessly on my face. I whisked myself back in and shut the door. There was no use sobbing again, at least not all day anyway.

Last night had been bad enough. Poppy and Dan had eaten by the time I'd got back. Dan had watched over the delivery of the second lamb while Poppy had cooked the sausages. She'd left some for me in the bottom of the Aga, but I couldn't eat. Instead, she and I curled up together on the sofa for a good cry and Dan took himself outside on the pretence of checking the sheep before bed and came back blaming a touch of hay fever for his red eyes. He hadn't fooled me for a moment; he was a big softie underneath that tough, nothing-gets-to-me Cumbrian exterior.

But back to today; my eyes roamed the kitchen looking for a job I wanted to do. I'd keep busy, do something I loved doing rather than the usual Friday chores, I decided. I flung the kitchen door open again and set off for my potting shed.

The vegetable garden had once been Dan's mum's domain. It was Viv who'd introduced me to the joy of planting peas and courgettes, come-again salad leaves and tiny outdoor tomatoes, and I'd found great pleasure in watching my seeds sprout and the seedlings grow into edible crops. There wasn't really a place for flowers on the farm and Viv wasn't a flowery person. But I loved them and always managed to squeeze a few annuals into pots and borders, like the sweet peas which clambered up the runner-bean plants, and the marigolds in between the rows of broad beans.

The potting shed had been my thirtieth birthday present from Dan. It was my second favourite place after the kitchen and was by far and away the newest building on the entire farm. It was wooden with windows that opened up to let out the summer heat and crammed with shelves made from old pallets, plus one deep shelf at the back where I headed now. On the shelf I found the last of the autumn crop of Bramley apples. Taking the box back to the kitchen, I put on an apron and began unwrapping each large green apple from its layer of newspaper until I had enough for my favourite pie recipe: apple and dark chocolate. The perfect antidote to my melancholy.

I'd peeled the apples and set them to soften in the Aga with sugar and a cinnamon stick and was taking out the ingredients for pastry when the door opened and Naomi came in. She was wearing her fleece embroidered with the Sunnybank Farm Shop logo and smelled vaguely of cheese.

'Poppy dropped this in my car last night.' She held up a small key which I recognized as my daughter's school locker key.

'Thank you, she's forever losing that. Coffee?' I held up the kettle, pleased to have company, although I doubted she'd have time to stay for a drink.

'Er . . .' Her eyes flicked automatically to the square of rug under the kitchen table where Rusty used to sit whenever I was cooking. And then our eyes met.

'Dan called me. I'm so sorry. How are you coping?'

'I'm taking my mind off him,' I said in a wobbly voice. 'I feel . . .'

I looked at her kind, caring face; my unflappable, intrepid sister-in-law who inspired my daughter.

She might be an amazing businesswoman, but she was also a dog person and had been in bits when she lost her Lakeland terrier, Bracken, a couple of years ago. She'd understand exactly how I felt – at least about losing my dog, anyway. I didn't think she'd understand how I felt a failure in the 'role model' department, how I always felt a bit of a lightweight next to her. I think she'd have been quite shocked if she knew that I was wondering if it might not be time to start challenging myself, forcing myself out of my comfort zone. She wouldn't comprehend that because she'd been challenging herself business-wise for years.

So all I said was, 'I feel empty and lost. I don't know what to do with myself.'

And that was enough to bring the tears close to the surface again.

'Oh, love.' Naomi strode over, removed the kettle from my hand, filled it from the tap and flicked it on.

'You're baking,' she said briskly, rubbing my arm, which was her idea of a maximum demonstration of affection. 'Good sign. Very therapeutic.' She pushed her short hair behind her ears and cleared her throat. 'Did you manage to sleep last night?'

'Eventually.' I blinked away the tears, took out a mixing bowl and tipped 250 grams of flour and a pinch of salt into it. I didn't weigh the flour; I could make pastry in my sleep I'd made it so often.

We'd gone to bed at eleven as usual but by midnight, my juddering sobs had begun to get on Dan's nerves. I'd murmured my apologies and edged towards him, hoping for a cuddle, but he'd turned away and thumped his pillow, muttering that he had to be up at dawn and at this rate he might as well not bother trying to sleep at all.

Not quite the sympathetic reception I'd hoped for, but fair enough; the poor man needed his sleep. I'd crept out, aiming for the spare room, but had tripped over Rusty's bed at the top of the stairs which had resulted in a fresh wave of sorrow. I was on the verge of sinking down on to his doggy mattress when Poppy called me into her room. She had been too upset to sleep too. And eventually, after cradling her in my arms, I drifted off, soothed by the thud of my daughter's heartbeat and the rhythm of her breathing.

'Good, good,' Naomi nodded, seemingly mesmerized by the way I was lifting the flour and letting it fall through my fingers as I rubbed in the fat. 'Listen, you're probably too busy but I'm going to ask anyway: I need your help.'

'Of course.' I looked at her properly; she looked agitated.

She finished making the coffee and set two mugs on the table. 'I've cocked up big time.'

I abandoned my shortcrust pastry crumbs. 'What is it?'

She flopped into a chair and sighed. 'The farm shop open day is tomorrow.'

I nodded. It was celebrating its fifteenth birthday this year and Naomi and her small team of staff had decided to hold an event on Saturday as it was a bank holiday weekend. They'd arranged various activities, taster sessions and demonstrations. She'd taken out advertising in the *Westmorland Gazette*, and there was even talk about the local TV news programme featuring it if their scheduling permitted it. 'Poppy and I can come and help out if you need us?'

'No. Well, yes, possibly,' said Naomi, chewing her lip. 'But it's not shop staff we need. The problem is the bakery.'

I frowned. Sunnybank Farm Shop had a deli, an organic fruit and vegetable department, a cheese counter and a bread and cakes section. It didn't have its own bakery. At least not yet; the rate Naomi was going, she'd be rivalling the supermarket in Holmthwaite before too long.

'Do you mean one of your suppliers?' I asked.

She looked at the big map on the wall, her eyes roaming from left to right as she sipped her coffee.

'Yes, the Crinkle Crags Bakery: a husband-and-wife team. They sent me an email weeks ago to inform me that they are having a month off because they've just adopted a baby. And it completely slipped my mind. Totally my fault. I phoned in my order this morning and it wasn't until I heard the voicemail announcing the arrival of six-month-old baby Maggie that I remembered.'

I hated letting anyone down but I shook my head. 'I can't make bread. I really can't. Mine comes out doughy and full of air holes.'

I stood then, remembering the apples I was cooking for my pie. I opened the Aga and the smell of caramelized apple and cinnamon filled the air.

'That's okay. I don't buy my bread from them.'

'No?' It must be cakes then. I raised an eyebrow, mentally working out whether I could realistically produce a Victoria sponge to shop standard. I slid the dish of softened fruit on to a pot stand.

'I buy pies.' She looked at my mixing bowl of sifted flour and then peered at me hopefully. 'Shortcrust-pastry pies.'

'Oh, then your worries are over,' I beamed. 'Pies are no problem.'

'Phew.' Naomi smiled. 'I was hoping you'd say that. But you're going to need a bigger bowl.'

The following morning, I was up at six. The shortcrust pastry for Naomi's pies was made and had been resting in the fridge overnight. I normally only rested my dough for an hour at most, but needs must and if I was going to deliver twenty-four pies, all perfectly baked, by eleven o'clock, I needed a head start.

But first tea and toast. I opened the back door tentatively, determined not to let Rusty's absence reduce me to tears again. And there, sitting on the step as if awaiting my appearance, was Birdie, the boss lady of our herd of farm cats, whose skills included terrorizing mice, chickens and even on occasion the dogs. Jake and Fern, Dan's working dogs, were terrified of her. None of the cats were interested in human affection, no matter how hard Poppy and I tried. However, maybe it was intuition on her part, or maybe today she just wanted to share my patch of early-morning sun, but either way, I was extremely glad of her company. And as I lowered myself down on the step next to her, she inched closer, sniffing my slice of buttered granary toast, her sleek black fur glinting in the light, and I felt, if not the undisguised love of Rusty, a companionable silence in which to absorb the rhythm of the farmyard.

'Thank you, Birdie,' I murmured when I'd finished my tea. I offered her my last crust but she simply stared at me as if I'd gone bonkers. I risked stroking her head, half-expecting her to lash out with one of her razor-sharp claws, but to my surprise she butted her head against me and began to purr as deeply as one of Dan's tractors.

'Same time tomorrow?' I said, getting to my feet. She

dived into the warm spot I'd vacated and curled into a ball. I was taking that as a yes.

Dan was already out doing the rounds on the quad bike with his dogs. There was a heavy dew on the meadow but it was starting to steam in the morning sunlight. It was going to be a lovely day and Naomi's farm shop would be heaving with visitors.

She had really tested my flavour combinations to the max with her pie requests. After admitting that she'd invited members of a regional business network to which she belonged to her open day, to show off her shop and taste her wares, she further confessed that she'd promised to provide a pie lunch for all the suppliers who were taking part too. She'd asked me to deliver some piping hot and some at room temperature and I was going to do my best to comply. My heart went out to Naomi; she had invested so much time and money into making the open day a success, it was hardly surprising that she'd forgotten that her usual bakery was closed. But I was happy to help and although I didn't mention this at the time, being set a giant task which would take up most of my day and keep my brain busy was the perfect way to cushion me from the loss of Rusty.

I glanced at the clock and a twinge of adrenalin shot through me: it was time to get baking.

I took the pastry out of the fridge and tied on my apron, mentally running through the order in which I should tackle the job. I decided to make four at a time; that was the most I could fit in the Aga in one go and I could make the next four while the first lot was baking. Yesterday I'd made five fillings: two sweet, three savoury, as per Naomi's instructions, almost solely made with ingredients from her shop.

My pies were special, if I said so myself. Poppy wasn't exaggerating on Thursday when she said that I was good at making them. My pastry was light and soft; it melted in the mouth without being too fatty or too crumbly. I used a mix of butter and vegetable shortening – a bit old fashioned, but it worked – and I always added egg yolk to give richness and a lovely golden colour. My favourite shape was a free-form pie, roughly circular, baked straight on to a baking sheet with a domed centre promising a generous filling and – my speciality – a twisted crimp hinting at the skills I'd picked up working in the Cornish pasty shop.

But all of these factors faded into the background compared to my fillings. This was where I let my imagination run wild. A pie made with sweet pears might be delicious, but with the addition of honey and a few crumbs of blue cheese it became sublime. To tender chunks of lamb, I added mint, fresh peas and asparagus tips for a pie that tasted like a Cumbrian spring morning, while slivers of strong local Cheddar inserted into slices of our home-grown Bramley apples sent everyone's taste buds into overdrive. For me baking was alchemy, a blending of flavours and textures wrapped up in a crispy pastry crust – the more unusual, yet complementary, the better. And I was yet to bake one that didn't get hoovered up; everybody loved them.

Poppy emerged an hour later just as I pulled four golden-crusted apple, walnut and Cheddar pies from the Aga. She was dressed only in the vest and shorts that she wore as pyjamas because they were too small to be decent these days.

'Is there any custard?' She perched her chin on my shoulder as I eased a palette knife underneath the bottom of one of the pies to free it from the baking sheet. 'I can have some of that for breakfast.'

'Oh no you can't. This is for the farm shop,' I said, kissing my daughter's cheek and inhaling her toasty just-woken-up smell.

I directed her to the tray of bacon in the top oven instead and she made herself a bacon sandwich while I popped four pear and honey pies in to bake.

'I'll make pastry decorations for the next batch,' she said, after she'd polished off her sandwich and a mug of milky tea.

I fetched her an apron and sent her to wash her hands and

43

then poured myself a coffee while I watched her cut letters out of my pastry remnants.

'There,' she said, standing back, head to one side as she examined her handiwork. 'The next pie can have our name on it.'

'Very apt,' I agreed, taking a heavy earthenware dish out of the fridge. 'Because this pie sums up the very best of Sunnybank Farm: spring lamb, pearl barley and thyme. Except I'm making four of them, so can I have more letters please?'

'Ooh.' Poppy looked impressed. 'Very fancy.'

She chatted away, telling me about a boy at school who was a brilliant footballer. He only had one hand but he never let it stop him doing anything and Poppy, judging by how many times she called him 'awesome', obviously had a bit of a soft spot for him. While she talked, I rolled out four more circles of pastry for the lamb pies, waiting for her to get bored of pastry cutting. It wouldn't be long; she'd be cleaning out the chickens and then joining her dad for a bit of shepherding before I knew it. But for now, she was in my world, my cosy farmhouse kitchen, and I was content just to enjoy her company and drink her in.

Chapter 5

'Cooee!'

A familiar voice cut through our conversation and Anna let herself into the kitchen. She skipped over to Poppy who was nearest to the door, and gave her a hug. Poppy was already taller than Anna; she'd be catching me up soon too, no doubt. 'Hello, gorgeous girl. Any coffee going, Hetty?'

Anna had her blonde hair scooped up into a ponytail and looked fresh and youthful in jeans, a blue-and-white striped T-shirt and lipstick which matched her pillar-box red Converse. Whereas I, I noticed, catching sight of my reflection in the small mirror next to the umbrella stand, had a red face, dried-on egg wash up my arms and probably floury handprints on the seat of my jeans.

'This is a lovely surprise!' I beamed, pleased to see her. 'Coffee coming up.'

'Ahh, look at you two baking together.' Anna sighed. 'Like something out of a nineteen fifties TV ad for lard.'

'Lard?' I snorted.

'Well, I don't know about baking, do I?' She waved a hand at the floury table. Anna was one of Naomi's best customers: buying readymade dishes which simply needed heating up. She'd got good at cooking lamb, though, because I supplied her with meat from Sunnybank Farm on a regular basis. 'What *are* you wearing under that apron, Poppy?'

'Not much,' I said, answering for her, and regarding my

daughter properly for the first time. I made a mental note to take her to be re-measured for a new bra. Soon. 'Perhaps you should get dressed, Pops.'

'Mum!' Poppy sighed heavily. 'I'm fine; no one's going to see me.'

Anna and I shared a grin; we'd been exasperated by our own families at just the same age.

'I think she looks great,' said a voice that managed to span two octaves in one short sentence. It was Bart, poking his head into the kitchen. He coughed to clear his throat.

His voice was breaking, bless him, and there was the faint hint of a blond moustache above his mouth. I would have scooped him up and hugged him if it wouldn't have horrified him.

'You see, Hetty.' Anna winked at me, poured herself a small cup of black coffee and added sugar. 'My boy knows. You're just out of touch with fashion.'

'Bart!' Poppy gave a yelp and scampered out of the room towards the stairs. 'I'm just going to . . . I'll be down in a minute.'

Bart stared after Poppy for a long moment and then gave himself a shake. 'I'm starting work at the farm today.'

'Of course!' I said. With all the events of the last day and a half, it had slipped my mind. 'Would you like a drink or did you want to go and find Dan?'

There was a rumble outside as the man himself came speeding into the yard on the quad bike.

Bart looked over his shoulder and then smiled shyly. 'I'd better pass on the drink; tell Poppy I'll catch her later.'

I pressed a hand to my chest and sighed.

'Those two are so cute,' I whispered to Anna. 'Imagine if they ended up together.'

My best friend looked appalled. 'No, don't say that!'

'Why not? We'd be related; I think it would be fab!' I said, surprised at her response. Wasn't my daughter good enough for her precious son?

'Ignore me,' she said with a soft laugh. 'I'm just not ready to relinquish my position as the top female in his life.'

I pulled her into a hug. 'I'm sure you'll be his *numero uno* for a long time yet. And anyway, Poppy has just been very sweetly telling me all about another boy, so I don't think she sees Bart in that way.'

Anna's face relaxed. 'Phew.' She rolled her eyes at her own over-the-top reaction. 'Listen to me; Poppy is adorable and you know I think the world of her, but think of the problems it would cause if it didn't work out for them. I'd hate it if anything came between you and me.'

My heart tweaked for her; she was so invested in Bart, so involved with every aspect of his life, determined that he wouldn't miss out simply because his father wasn't around. I sometimes worried about how she would cope when he finally flew the nest.

I realized Anna was now talking about exactly that: how life would change when Bart left home and I gave myself a shake.

'Listen, I know you like to keep your relationships light and casual,' I said diplomatically, 'but isn't it time you looked for something a bit more long lasting? That way, when Bart does leave home, you won't feel quite so lonely.'

She wrinkled her nose. 'I think it would be difficult for Bart to accept a man in the house. He and I have a great time together; I don't want to ruin that.'

'You're a good mum, you know,' I said, smiling warmly at my friend, 'but I'm sure he wouldn't want you to make such sacrifices for his sake.'

Anna pulled an unconvinced face and then we both turned to look out of the kitchen window as the dogs began to bark like crazy. Bart had climbed on to the quad bike and Dan was showing him the controls while Jake and Fern were doing their utmost to get run over by dancing round the bike's tyres.

Anna sucked in air. 'He will be okay on that contraption, won't he?'

'Don't worry, he's in safe hands,' I said with complete confidence, watching my husband give the teenager the thumbs-up to drive the vehicle forward.

My heart fluttered then, wishing as I did from time to time that we'd had the big family I'd hoped to raise in this beautiful place. Dan would have loved a son of his own to carry on the Greengrass name. Never mind, I thought, stoically, he'd be in his element showing Bart the ropes today and he had a daughter whose heart would for ever be at Sunnybank Farm, whatever she ended up doing with her life . . .

'Hetty?' Anna shook my arm and sniffed the air. 'You're miles away. Can I smell burning?'

'Yikes, my pear and honey pies!' I leapt to my feet, brandishing my oven gloves.

Right on schedule, all the pies were ready, the kitchen had been cleaned up and so had the cook. I gave my reflection a final once-over in the mirror by the door to check for stray crumbs-on-cheek and was pleasantly surprised: the recent spell of warm weather had brought colour to my cheeks and the rare swish of eyeliner coupled with the blue of my denim shirtdress did wonders for my green eyes. Dan always liked me in blue, which was lucky seeing as I spent most of my time in jeans.

I collected the last crate of pies and let myself out of the kitchen, taking care not to bash any corners on the way out.

Anna had already taken most of the pies up for me, so I only needed to make one trip now and after flattening the rear seats in my little car, I'd just about got enough room. I slid the crate in and did a quick count-up: five lamb pies, complete with Sunnybank Farm pastry letters; five chicken, chestnut and sherry, and four sheep's cheese, chard and poppy seed. The first two were proven winners, but the last combo was a brand-new invention and I hoped Naomi would approve; she'd had all the ingredients in her shop yesterday and coming from a sheep farm, it was an apt choice, and

48

brimming with the local provenance people seemed to go wild for.

The aroma of the still-warm pies was wonderful and the windows had started to steam up by the time I'd fastened my seat belt. My stomach rumbled, reminding me that it was a long time since breakfast; I hoped there'd be plenty of food to try at the shop. Preferably not pie; I was all pied-out for today. I set off, driving with infinite care along the track to the farm shop, creeping at a snail's pace over the cattle grids to avoid arriving with nothing but crates full of crumbs.

When I got there, there were no free parking spots; even the last disabled space had just been filled, so I reversed up to the front door between two big old water troughs which were now home to bright displays of foxgloves, pansies and nasturtiums. There was a trestle table full of little plants for sale too, next to a display of organic vegetables in a lovely old wooden market barrow.

Naomi and her assistant Tess appeared to help me unload before I was even out of the car.

'Hooray for Hetty's pies!' Naomi pressed a hand to her chest in relief. 'Thanks so much, you're a lifesaver.'

'Pleasure's all mine,' I said, feeling the by now customary lump form in my throat. 'I've been too busy to cry over Rusty this morning.'

Naomi pulled a sympathetic face and Tess wrapped an arm around my shoulders.

'Lovely plant display, Tess,' I said, nodding to the troughs.

'Thank you. Next year I shall take orders for hanging baskets, but I wanted to start small to begin with.' Tess smiled proudly and then made a show of looking me up and down. 'A dress? Not used to seeing your legs. If I had such shapely pins, I'd be flashing them in miniskirts. As it is I've got two tree trunks and folks will be happier if I keep them under wraps.'

I flapped a hand, secretly pleased. I wouldn't normally get

myself dolled up to go to the farm shop but Naomi had asked me if I'd stay at the open day a while and I'd felt obliged to get changed.

'Oh, I don't know,' said Naomi with a smile. 'Some men appreciate a sturdy pair of thighs. You could be known as Tree-trunk Tess.'

Tess shot her a look of mock indignation. 'Thanks. I'll put it on my Tinder profile.'

She was a single mum in her early forties with grown-up children who'd both flown the nest over the past year. Since then she'd been dividing her time between eating her body-weight in crisps and keeping tabs on how long it had been since she'd had sex, until Naomi had suggested she take up a hobby to fill up her new-found free time. So after giving it some thought she'd started up a small plants business on the side. She was now supplying plants to the farm shop *and* had lost a stone in weight. Unfortunately, she still hadn't bagged herself a man, but now she claimed she was too busy anyway.

'I was under strict instructions to make an effort,' I said, nodding to Naomi, who also looked extra smart in black trousers, crisp white shirt and ballerina pumps. 'I didn't want to let the side down.'

Tess hooted with laughter. 'No, she's got me to do that. She's already had to wrestle the sloe gin samples out of my hand.'

'Only when you and Tim started your Kiki Dee and Elton John duet,' Naomi muttered.

I grinned. That meant my long-suffering brother-in-law Tim had been roped in to help too.

'Ah,' Tess nudged her boss, 'don't go breaking my heart.'

'I couldn't if I tried.'

The two of them burst out laughing, and I thought how lovely it would be to work with someone day in day out and still get on so well. Which Dan and I did in a way, I suppose, but female camaraderie, well, it was something different, wasn't it?

'Ooh, get a whiff of them!' Tess inhaled deeply as I opened up the boot.

'These look amazing, Hetty. We can start serving them straight away.' Naomi dived into the back of the car so eagerly that she nearly ended up on top of the pies.

'Steady on,' Tess chuckled, grabbing the back of Naomi's shirt. 'She's all at sixes and sevens since she found out the TV is coming to interview her for the news.'

'They're definitely coming, then?' I winked at Tess. 'Now I see why she's ditched the fleece for a change.'

'For your information, ladies, I will be wearing my fleece for the interview because it's got our logo on. But all this running around has made me hot.' Naomi bent over the pies and pulled out two crates, handing one to Tess and the other to me. 'And I didn't tell you to make an effort; all I said was take your pinny off and check your face for flour smears.'

A sudden thought occurred to me. 'We aren't all going to be on TV, are we?'

Naomi shook her head, turning back to the car. 'No, no, no. I just wanted you to meet the Sunrise Breakfast Club members.'

I smiled. 'Oh, how sweet! Are the children here now?'

'Ha, it might sound like a kids' group,' Tess's body shook with mirth before heading towards the shop, 'but it's grown men and women who meet up for a chat and a bowl of corn-flakes of a morning before work.'

I grinned at my sister-in-law. 'Sounds fun.'

'Hardly,' said Naomi primly. 'It's a very serious business group. We discuss real issues and do valuable networking while most other people are still slobbing around in their pyjamas.'

'I see.' I nodded solemnly. It sounded like a dreadful way to start the day to me.

'Gosh, those are adorable,' she said, spotting the pastry letters on the lamb pies. 'In our last meeting we were discussing making the most of Carsdale skills and products, and your pies are part of that, so thanks for coming.'

I shrugged. 'A pleasure. It was either that or going out into the meadow to check lambs' bottoms to see if they needed worming . . . so hardly a choice at all.'

Naomi tucked a crate under each arm, determined to carry more than everyone else. 'That's the problem with the warm weather; brings the flies out in hordes.'

An elderly couple making slow progress arm-in-arm up the ramp leading to the shop entrance shot us a worried look.

'Flies?' said the woman in a loud whisper. 'I hope they're going to cover those pies.'

'Don't worry,' Naomi called, bestowing a calming smile on her customers as she strode by. 'There are no flies on us, plus we'll be giving away free samples while they're still warm. And make sure you come and try our local cheeses too.'

'I'll get the last crate, then you can move the car,' said Tess, bustling back out as I stepped inside.

I paused just for a second to breathe in the atmosphere of the shop, feeling the familiar wave of joy I always got in here. It was such a bright and happy place, full of charm and character and bulging with deliciousness.

The interior décor was testament to Naomi's talents, even though it had been done on a shoestring; a local joiner had been commissioned to knock up some shelving to break up the vast space. Lighting suspended on wire tracks gave the illusion of a lowered ceiling, even though the eye could see right up to the vaulted beams above. Straw bales covered with white cloths gave a quirky rural feel to display areas and each department – fruit and veg, preserves, deli and cheeses, drinks and the baked goods section – had its own particular feel. Today, Naomi's proud artisan producers had been shoehorned into every spare nook and cranny, giving demonstrations and tasters of their wares.

'Wow, the shop looks amazing!' I said, following her into

the back office and depositing the pies in the space she waved me towards. 'Where do you get your ideas from?'

She laughed. 'Having the ideas is the easy part; it's making them happen that takes effort. Luckily I've got you and your pies to help with that.'

I basked in the glow of her praise for a moment before nipping out to move the car. She made it sound so simple, but in the early days, it had been anything but that . . .

Chapter 6

When I'd first come to Sunnybank Farm, this traditional Cumbrian stone barn had been derelict, along with the low single-storey buildings adjacent to it. It wasn't until Naomi had the bright idea of converting it into a shop that it had had a new lease of life. Dan's father Mike hadn't agreed, or at least that was what she had thought at the time. However, after he died, Viv admitted that Mike had had a change of heart and had applied for planning permission for Naomi's plans. Naomi had been stunned by his actions, but it was a bitter-sweet victory as her beloved father would never see her complete her dream.

A lesser woman would have faltered, given herself time to grieve. But not Naomi, she set to work straight away; while building work was going on inside, she set up a stall in the yard selling fruit and vegetables, fresh farm eggs and plants, and did a roaring trade in Christmas trees that first winter. Her boys were still little, only just old enough for school, and Tim had taken a job working away in Scotland, three weeks on, three weeks off. And yet, even with all that going on around her, she'd pulled it off beautifully.

Someone was just pulling out of a narrow space so I quickly nosed my car forward and into it and ran back into the shop. Naomi was deep in conversation with a woman with a mass of red curls. She caught my eye, gave me an apologetic smile and held up her hand signalling that she'd only be five minutes so I went to find Tim instead.

There were so many customers milling about, wielding the traditional wicker baskets that Naomi had sourced locally, that it took me some time to spot my brother-in-law: he was perched on an oak barrel behind a tray of tiny plastic cups of juice.

'Ah, Hetty!' He stood, pushing his newspaper aside, and put a moustachioed kiss on my cheek. 'Can I interest you in a drop of rhubarb juice? You can either use it to strip paint or add it to vodka, which I'm told will result in a rather lively cocktail.'

He pushed one of the sample cups towards me. It reminded me of the little paper cups of pink liquid you get at the dentist.

'I'll pass,' I said, pulling a face.

'Go on,' he whispered. '*Mein Führer* says as soon as this lot has gone, I can go home and put my feet up. I've already downed ten.'

'Shush,' I said with a giggle, checking that no one could hear him. 'The supplier might be here.'

Not that Tim would be remotely bothered. He always reminded me of Winnie the Pooh and had the figure and temperament to match. He was older than Naomi, shorter than Naomi and considerably stouter than her too. But the two of them were such a perfect couple in every other way that their physical differences were simply brushed aside. He worked in the oil industry, living away from home much of the time, in a little flat in Inverness, but when he was here, he followed her round like the cade lambs – the orphans – followed me. Where she was full of ideas and plans, he was happy to take life as it came, when she went out running, he'd take a stroll down to the river and mess about on his little boat for an hour. They were yin and yang and for them that seemed to be the key to a happy marriage.

'I wish that were so,' said Tim, tugging the collar of his

shirt, which, now I looked properly at it, looked . . . different. 'Because then he or she could flog their own acid, I mean nectar.'

'Tim, your shirt.' I tipped my head to one side to study it. 'It's rather . . .'

'Avant-garde, I think, is the phrase you're looking for.' He smoothed down the front of it and then took the points of the collar in his fingertips. One side had a tiny almost non-existent point like a cat's ear and the other side had a huge flap like a Spaniel's. 'From a young British designer going by the name of Otis Willcox.'

'Ah. All is now clear. It's fantastic; Paul Smith, eat your heart out.'

Good old Tim for wearing his son's creation. He straightened his arms to demonstrate the sleeves. The fabric was a sheeny brown colour apart from its extra-deep yellow cuffs, which seemed to flare from his elbows.

Tim chuckled, hoisting himself back up on to his barrel. 'Twin boys, identical at birth, who've received exactly the same parenting and yet Otis and Oscar couldn't be more polar opposite if they'd planned it. How can that be?'

I shrugged. 'It's a mystery. I love those two boys dearly but they are a mystery to me. I'm an only child, so is Poppy. The only experience I have of sibling relationships is of Dan and Naomi—'

'Who are incredibly alike,' he put in.

'Uncannily so,' I agreed.

'Nature versus nurture, eh?' said Tim ponderously, running a hand over his sparse dark hair.

We stared into space for a second, lost in our thoughts. Otis was studying fashion in Leeds. He had a unique sense of style, a severe asymmetric haircut and thought nothing of waxing his eyebrows before a night out. Oscar never noticed what he was wearing; clothes, shoes, personal grooming . . . none of that featured highly, if at all, on his agenda. His university degree was in ecology and conservation, and he was never as animated as when he was discussing the properties of soil with anyone who'd listen.

'Gosh, that looks like it might be super-healthy!'

The voice jolted me out of my thoughts. It was the red-haired woman I'd seen chatting to Naomi. She had a stack of leaflets in her hand and strapped to her front was a tiny sleeping infant with soft fluffy orange hair. She was leaning over the tray of samples peering at the pink liquid.

'Which is usually a cause for concern in my book,' I said, bending to get a closer look at the baby.

'True,' she said with a laugh, her eyes sparkling. She picked up the rhubarb juice bottle and turned it round to read the small print. 'Oh good! Locally made too!'

'Hello, little one,' I whispered, resisting the urge to stroke the baby's downy cheek. There had been a time when other people's babies made me tearful with longing for another child of my own. I still had the odd pang of regret, but now that Poppy was almost thirteen, the thought of a sibling for her felt wrong somehow.

'Try some,' said Tim eagerly.

'I'll swap you for a leaflet,' she said, holding one out. She gave me one too. 'I'm Freya Graythwaite, by the way, and this is Baby Tilly.'

'*Cumbria's Finest*,' I read aloud. '*Your regional food group, showcasing the very best food and drink from the area to customers both home and away.*'

'I've taken over the role of recruiting new members for the group.' Freya's eyes widened as she knocked back the juice Tim had given her. 'I heard about the open day and thought I'd pop over while my husband is with our eldest at ballet.'

'Ah, a ballerina in the family,' said Tim. 'How old is she?'

'He. Artie, and he's three. Named after his great-uncle, not that *he's* a dancer,' she giggled, 'he's a retired farmer.'

'So they do retire then?' I said with amusement. 'I'm married to a farmer and I can't imagine him ever leaving Sunnybank.'

Freya's eyes lit up. 'Ditto! We run two farms, which is a bit full-on. Although my main role is the tea rooms at Appleby Farm; oh, and the wedding business and the vintage holidays. But I know what you mean: I can't imagine Harry leaving the farm; it's bad enough trying to get him to take a holiday.'

'A holiday,' I joked, 'what's that?'

Another Wonder Woman. I was smiling but inside my stomach was in knots. On top of running those businesses she looked after two children and had just taken on a recruitment role for Cumbria's Finest. All I did was bake a few pies and help Dan out on the farm and I wasn't even very good at that: I was useless when a sheep got flystrike, I wasn't strong enough to shear and I still shed a tear when a lamb died. Pathetic.

'Retirement,' said Tim wistfully, 'can't wait. Although when you're married to a Greengrass like Hetty and I are, you're pretty much married to Sunnybank Farm too.'

'Oh, you're Hetty Greengrass!' she exclaimed. 'Silly me; I just realized. You made those fantastic pies. I am in *awe* of you. Your pastry is to die for.'

I loved her. I totally loved her.

'Thank you. I am Hetty, yes,' I said proudly.

Just then her angelic child awoke and let out a squawk to rival our cockerel.

'Oh crumbs, and I thought I'd get round the whole shop before she needed feeding.' She pressed her lips tenderly to Tilly's head. 'Yes, yes, lunch will be served immediately, darling. I'd better go, but lovely to meet you.'

'You too,' Tim and I said in unison.

She gave me a warm smile. 'And good luck!'

I raised my eyebrows. She dashed off, red curls flying, before I could ask what she meant and the next moment, someone stumbled into me.

'Crikey! Sorry, darlin'.' It was a man with a tanned face, sunglasses clamped on top of his bedraggled hair, huge shoulders and a scruffy goatee beard. His appearance, added to his Australian accent, told me he was probably a shearing contractor. It was the start of the British shearing season and the time when Antipodean farmers were having their winter and consequently work in that part of the world dried up. There was one particular caravan park ten miles from the farm which was almost solely inhabited by burly men with amazing biceps for the whole of June. All my girl-friends had tried to get jobs there when we were younger.

'It's fine,' I reassured him with a smile.

'Is this alcoholic?' he asked, picking up a taster cup.

'Only rhubarb juice,' Tim answered apologetically. 'But it's extremely good for,' he lowered his eyes to his lap for a millisecond, 'vitality, if you get my meaning.'

The man smirked and nodded. 'Oh yeah?' And then pro-ceeded to knock them back like vodka shots, grimacing after each one went down.

Tim and I stared at him. After about his eighth, the man suddenly choked, realizing how it looked. 'Christ. Not that I need any help, you know . . .'

'Down under?' Tim finished for him, tongue in cheek.

'Exactly, mate.' The Aussie rubbed his nose, dropped his sunglasses down and swaggered off.

Tim rubbed his hands together with glee. 'Okay, four left. That's two each and then I can slip away unobtrusively.'

'Unobtrusively? In that shirt?' I said. 'You'll be lucky.'

Nonetheless, we both picked up a plastic taster cup and knocked them together.

'Down the hatch,' said Tim.

'Excellent!' boomed a deep voice at my shoulder. 'The famous rhubarb juice.'

I turned to see six or seven smartly dressed people with earnest faces and all wearing bright yellow name badges.

'This is what Naomi was suggesting we served at the next meeting,' said a lady with silver hair pinned up in a bun. Her badge proclaimed her to be Janet. She looked disappoint-edly at the tray. 'Oh, have you run out?'

59

Tim sighed, reached under the counter and pulled out a new bottle and some more plastic cups. 'Not at all,' he said in a jolly voice, winking at me. 'Plenty more where that came from.'

He began pouring out samples and Janet handed them round.

'So, you're the Sunrise Breakfast Club, then?' I said to the nearest man, remembering that Naomi had expressly said she wanted me to meet them. 'I've heard about you from Naomi. I'm Hetty, her sister-in-law, and this is her husband, Tim.'

We shook hands and he introduced himself as Matthew. He'd clearly already sampled some pie; he had crumbs in his beard and a telltale splodge of sheep's cheese and spinach on his suit lapel.

'We're the leading business group for local entrepreneurs,' Matthew exclaimed smugly.

'I'd love to hear more,' I said, arranging my features into my most interested gaze.

He rocked back on his heels as if preparing to give a lecture and my heart sank.

'We're a networking group, we meet, share business leads, motivate each other and help hone each other's personal mission statements.'

'Gosh, sounds . . .' *absolutely hideous*, I wanted to say. I caught Tim's eye and he waggled an eyebrow, clearly thinking along the same lines. 'Riveting.'

'I like the fact that I can grow my business before the office even opens, and of course we also have breakfast,' added Janet.

'I'm with you on the eating,' said Tim. 'But I struggle to motivate myself out of my pyjamas in the morning, let alone motivate someone else to greatness.'

Just then Tess walked up with a tray of biscuits spread with some sort of pâté.

'Local smoked duck and port terrine on oat crackers,' she

said, plunging the tray into the middle of the group. Hands dived in to help themselves. 'Available on our deli counter.'

'What's your mission statement, Paul?' I said, turning to a grey-faced man with one bushy eyebrow higher than the other, which lent him an expression of extreme suspicion. He wolfed down two crackers and then did a phlegmy cough into a napkin.

'Glad you asked,' he said, spraying a mouthful of crumbs in my direction. 'It's to use my charisma and talents to breathe life into my new business.'

'Bravo,' murmured a lady called Heidi, who seemed to have matched her jacket to her yellow badge.

'And what *is* your business?' Tim enquired, topping everybody up and draining the bottle. He took Tess's last cracker and popped it in his mouth.

'An abattoir,' said Paul without a hint of irony.

Tim began to choke on his cracker and my cheeks were aching with the effort of not laughing when Tess drew me aside.

'Can you go and see Naomi in the back office?' she whispered. 'She wants to check something with you.'

I left Janet banging Tim on the back and Heidi trying to tip rhubarb juice down his throat and made my way to Naomi.

The office still smelled of my warm pies and three of them, I noticed, were still untouched. Naomi had rolled up her sleeves and was standing at her desk behind a pile of cardboard. She looked up shiftily as I entered.

'Hi,' she said, slipping a sheet of paper underneath the cardboard. 'Having fun?'

'Oh yes. Your Sunrise Breakfast crowd are an entertaining bunch,' I said diplomatically, trying to see what it was she'd swiftly shoved to one side.

'Quirky lot, aren't they?' She gave me a wry smile. 'Networking is a necessary evil these days and the shop does get a lot out of it. Besides, it fills an hour after my morning run before the shop opens.'

'Phew.' I sat on her revolving office chair and span round. 'I'd hate to think of you at a loose end at seven thirty in the morning.'

'Ha ha. You can mock.' She poked her tongue out in concentration as she tucked flaps into slots. She appeared to be assembling a box from a flat piece of cardboard. 'But since the boys left home, conversation in the mornings has been pretty thin on the ground and I like company at breakfast. Especially when Tim's working away.'

'Mmm,' I said vaguely. Me too; until Thursday I'd shared my breakfast with Rusty: a mouthful for me, a titbit for him. On the step if the weather allowed, or huddled in front of the fire in the armchair if it didn't. Although in his last week his appetite had vanished and not even the fatty bits of my bacon could tempt him. 'Tess said you wanted to check something with me?'

'Yes.' Naomi met my eye. 'Look, I know this is a bit of a cheek, but what do you think of these?' She pulled out the thing she'd hidden and passed it across to me; it was a sheet of self-adhesive labels. Each circular sticker was around five centimetres in diameter. In the centre was a tiny illustration of the farmhouse and behind it a simple line drawing of a hill with two little cartoon sheep on it. The words 'Sunnybank Farm' arced above the hill like a rainbow.

'Nice,' I said, trying to work out why she'd used an illustration of our farmhouse, rather than the shop's logo.

'I thought so,' she said, going a bit pink. 'Otis ran out of money last month so I agreed to top up his loan if he designed a new logo.'

'A logo for . . . ?' I looked at her, confused.

She slid one of my pies into the box she'd assembled, closed the lid and stuck a sticker on it. 'For Sunnybank Farm Pies.'

She passed me the box. 'I've been toying with the idea of an own brand for the shop; Crinkle Crags Bakery were supposed to be trialling them for me but . . .'

'But their baby arrived,' I supplied, nodding my head. I

couldn't drag my eyes away from the box. My pie, packaged up and labelled like a proper product, like something you'd see in a shop. Just the sight of it made me feel all tingly. 'You know, I've never heard of Crinkle Crags Bakery, where are they?'

Naomi rubbed her nose. 'You wouldn't have, they're specialist, very niche.'

'Shortcrust-pastry-pies – niche?' I said dubiously.

'I mean trade only,' she said hurriedly. 'They don't sell direct to the public.'

'Wow.' I picked up the pie box reverently and stroked my finger over its little cellophane window. The box was slightly too big for the pie; it had too much room to slide about, but even so, I thought it was marvellous. 'A Sunnybank Farm pie.'

'You don't mind, then?' Naomi heaved a sigh of relief. 'I'm so glad. It's just with the TV cameras coming I didn't want to pass up the chance to talk about my plans.'

There was a flurry of activity outside the office in the front area of the shop and the other member of staff, Edwin, appeared. He coughed politely to announce himself.

'The TV crew are here,' he said, fingering his bow tie nervously. 'They're asking where they need to set up.'

Naomi did an audible gulp. 'Thank you, Edwin, will I do?'

He stepped forward, tugged her sleeves down and brushed a speck of fluff from her shoulders.

'You'll do magnificently.'

He gave a little bow and turned on his heel. Edwin used to be a butler for a posh house in London but he had left after being criticized by his Lordship once too often for his whistling nostrils and fled to Cumbria. He'd since had his sinuses drilled, which had alleviated the problem, but he said he'd never go back to a life in service.

'Break a leg,' I said, holding up the pie in a box.

She inhaled deeply to calm herself, stepped forward and took it from me but stumbled over the wheels of the swivel chair I was on.

'Ouch,' she yelled, dropping the box in my lap.

'I didn't mean literally,' I said. 'Are you all right?'

She dropped to the ground, kicked off her flimsy ballerina shoe and clutched her foot. 'Stupid shoes. I think, ow, ow, ow, I think I might have broken a toe.'

'Ice,' I said, jumping to my feet, taking care not to let the chair roll over her feet again. 'Where's the freezer?'

She grabbed my arm as I made for the door. 'Get Edwin or Tess to fetch the ice.' There were tears in her eyes and she squeezed my hand. 'You'll have to show the TV company the Sunnybank Farm pie. Please, you're the best person to talk about it.'

'No, this is your moment,' I insisted. 'You'll be fine in a second.'

Even as I said it I could see that she wouldn't be. Her face had gone grey and clammy and when I looked down at her foot it already looked red and swollen.

'All right, I'll do it.' My stomach wobbled with nerves as she smiled her gratitude through gritted teeth. 'And I'll try not to let you down, although I can't promise anything.'

Tess came to the door, looking frazzled. 'Hurry up, I sent Edwin in to get you. Blimey, Naomi!' she gasped, catching sight of her boss on the floor. 'Now what are we going to do? The news reporter is getting restless out here.'

'Hetty's taking my place. Help me up,' Naomi said, wincing as she reached a hand out to Tess. 'And don't fret, Hetty, it's not live and they'll only want a quick soundbite. You go.'

And pie in hand, I did as I was told.

Back out in the shop a crowd of beaming customers were jostling for position behind Kirsty, our bubbly and enthusiastic local reporter, who today was all teeth and tweed as befitted a country girl. She held her microphone as if she was about to burst into song and the atmosphere in the shop was buzzing with the prospect of being on the TV. In front of her stood an androgynous sort of person with long hair, a willowy body and a chunky camera. A red light appeared on the top of the camera and Kirsty cleared her throat.

'Today we're here in Carsdale on the banks of the glorious River . . .' Her eyes slid sideways and Edwin whispered 'Esk' lightly just out of shot.

'I can't believe she doesn't know the river's name,' muttered the old lady who'd been concerned about flies on pies to her husband.

'Esk,' Kirsty continued smoothly, 'visiting the wonderful Sunnybank Farm Shop run by Naomi Willcox.' She lowered her eyes this time to some scribbled notes on a card in her hand. 'Her family, the Greengrasses, have been farming here for generations, but it was Naomi's dream to bring this traditional Cumbrian stone building to life again.' She paused, noticing me holding my boxed pie at this point, and gestured for me to join her. 'Naomi has curated all the best produce from the area under one lovely slate roof and today the shop is celebrating its fifteenth birthday, isn't that correct, Naomi?'

She shoved the microphone so close to my lips that it vibrated against my skin and I flinched.

Kirsty was giving me a rictus smile; she was clearly waiting for me to speak but I had completely forgotten the question.

'Hetty Greengrass,' I said hesitantly, leaning over the microphone.

Kirsty shot an anxious look at her camera person and then at the pie box. 'And is this one of your products?'

I flicked open the box and lifted it up to the camera. 'Yes, this is one of my favourites: spring lamb, pearl barley and thyme picked fresh from the farm garden this morning.'

'It smells lovely,' Kirsty said, smiling into the lens. 'And you don't make it in a tray, I see?'

'Free-form pies are my speciality,' I said, relaxing now I was on familiar ground. 'You can't beat cutting that first slice out of a pie and seeing layer upon layer of filling.'

Kirsty nodded intently as if she'd never heard anything so interesting in her life.

'And what's the secret to a good piecrust?' She turned to smile at the customer behind her. 'If it's not a trade secret, that is!'

Everyone laughed obediently, even though it wasn't really funny.

'Well, strictly between us,' I said, getting into the swing of it, 'you have to keep the filling dry; there's no soggy bottom on my watch!'

The laughter increased and I even managed a smile myself.

'And Sunnybank Farm is a sheep farm, isn't it?' Kirsty asked.

'Yes, mainly Swaledales and our rare-breed flock of Soays.'

'So is that one of your lambs in there?' She wrinkled her nose and pointed at the pie.

Oh crumbs.

And it was all going so well. I felt my mouth dry up and floundered for something to say. I had a dirty secret where Sunnybank Farm lamb was concerned. No one knew; well, no one except Anna and I'd sworn her to secrecy.

'Well, is it your lamb?' Kirsty gave a sharp laugh. 'Or not?'

'It's Cumbrian lamb,' called Naomi, limping towards us. Kirsty pivoted towards her and the crowd parted to let her through. At last, I was out of shot, thank heavens. 'We don't have a butcher's counter at the Sunnybank Farm Shop yet, although we do have plans for expansion . . .'

I felt someone tug my sleeve and turned to see Tim's friendly face smiling at me. 'Shall we?' he whispered, nodding towards the door.

I put my pie down gratefully and fled.

Chapter 7

At six o'clock, the three of us were all back in the kitchen ready to catch up on each other's day over dinner. I ladled out dishes of lamb and spinach curry while Dan chopped up a fresh red chilli to sprinkle over his. Poppy filled a jug of water and set glasses on the table.

Naomi had phoned earlier to thank me for the pies. In spite of her injured toe she had had a brilliant day: the shop takings had been through the roof and she was thrilled with the media coverage and the turnout and all the feedback she'd had from the Sunrise Breakfast Club. The news piece was apparently going to be aired this evening at six thirty and she and Tim planned to celebrate with a glass of champagne, although, she confided, he had a bit of a dodgy tummy from too much rhubarb juice. I'd laughed at that; if he was suffering, imagine what the Aussie sheep shearer was going through. Her toe was too swollen to drive, but Tim had driven her round to Anna's, who declared it 'a right mess' and strapped it up for her. As far as Anna could tell, there were no broken bones so she should be fit for her twenty-two-mile fell race in two weeks' time. I'd needed a sit-down just listening to that.

'My pies went down well,' I said, scraping the extra rice into a bowl for Rusty before I remembered. I gave myself a shake and put it in the fridge instead. 'But I came away feeling like I was the biggest underachiever in the family. Even the other farmer's wife I met was running multiple businesses, bringing up multiple kids and holding down a day job.'

'Don't feel bad, Mum,' said Poppy. 'Not everyone is destined to be a high-flier.'

I sighed, sliding plates in front of Dan and Poppy before fetching my own. I knew she meant well and I didn't especially need to be a high-flier, but getting off the ground would be nice.

'And don't underestimate how much I need you on the farm, Hetty,' Dan said kindly. 'Without you we'd have to pay a full-time farmhand to help with shepherding and that would eat up most of our profit.'

'I know,' I said with a sinking heart. Dan meant well too, but all his comment succeeded in doing was to make me feel guilty for wanting more out of life.

We had a lad, Cameron, from agricultural college helping out three days a week; he was starting up his own flock at his parents' beef farm and wanted the experience. And it had been the same way for the last fifteen years: relying on students to get us through the busiest times of the year – birthing, shearing and getting the lambs ready for market. How did Freya Graythwaite manage, I wondered, juggling both farms and holding down a job?

'You've got me as well now, Dad,' Poppy piped up. She shovelled in her curry as quickly as she could, probably due to the 'no screens at mealtimes' rule. 'It's half-term this week, I can help.'

Dan nodded absentmindedly. 'And Bart seems keen; the dogs responded well to him. It'll be good to get him trained up.'

'I'm keen,' Poppy reminded him hotly. 'And I can already work with the dogs.'

'I know, love,' said Dan patiently. 'But you're only twelve—'

'Nearly thirteen.'

'Okay, nearly thirteen. I know you want to help now, but when you're older you might want to get a job in the village.'

'At a shop or a café?' Poppy said in disgust.

Dan looked at me for assistance. Sometimes I felt more like a referee than a wife and mother.

'Anywhere,' I said. 'You can go anywhere, do anything. Maybe a shop or maybe helping out Sally at the vet's.'

'But why?' Poppy sat back, her green eyes flashing with frustration. 'Dad, I see what you're doing, just because he's a boy, you're giving Bart all the attention. Well, girls can be farmers. I'm not letting what happened to Auntie Naomi happen to me. It is so not fair!'

When Mike died and Dan inherited the farm, he had been devastated. Partly because his hero had died so suddenly, but also because he knew his plans to train to be a vet would have to be placed on permanent hold, even though it had always been Naomi who'd taken the greater interest in farming. But Viv was adamant that Mike's wishes were to be carried out and besides, Tim hadn't wanted to live on the farm. And so Naomi threw herself into setting up the farm shop and Dan had taken over the reins. There'd been no way the farm could have supported two families; it simply wasn't profitable enough. And as it was, we'd taken out a mortgage to buy Viv her own home when she decided to start a new life away from the farm.

It would be different for us: there was only Poppy to inherit. Right now, staying on Sunnybank Farm was Poppy's dream life. And while I knew Dan was secretly proud of that, he was also determined that she'd get a chance to explore the world beyond Sunnybank Farm.

He smiled at his daughter. 'You're right, he did get more attention today, but that's because he's new and if I don't watch him he could have an accident. Whereas you're a pro.'

He shifted in his chair and shot me a sideways glance, evidently proud of that reply.

Poppy wasn't so impressed. 'You even let him go on the tractor today. On his first day!'

'Bart's feet reach the pedals, love,' Dan laughed. 'On your first day on the farm you were shorter than most of our ewes.'

'Exactly,' she said darkly, 'because farming's in my blood.'

Dan held up his hands to curtail further argument. 'He's taller than you and stronger than you. You can't fight facts.'

The phone rang, breaking the tension, and I got up to answer it. It was mounted on the wall by the back door, handily positioned so that you could come in from the farmyard, lean in and make a call without having to take off your boots.

'Sunnybank Farm, Hetty speaking.'

'You'll be having your dinner.' It was my mother-in-law. Six o'clock was and always had been dinner time; it just seemed to fit in with the chores on the farm. 'I shan't keep you.'

She always said that and usually contradicted herself by talking for England. Not that I minded, I loved Viv, and loved having her so close by. She'd been a substitute mother for me, especially when my parents had first left the UK and I'd missed having them to talk to.

'I don't mind either way, Viv,' I said. 'It's only curry.'

What I meant was, it was only *lamb* curry and I'd got a thing about lamb. Unfortunately, it was Dan's favourite meat; he would eat it every day if he could. I couldn't.

'I was on the bus coming back from the hospital and when we came down the hill towards Carsdale I saw some of your tups in Harry Sadler's barley field.'

'Thanks, Viv, I'll let Dan know.'

The tups – or rams – were in a field of their own at the moment, separated from the ewes for the summer until the mating season, or tupping, began again in autumn. If Viv said the tups were ours, they would be. Each farmer had a distinct mark and every ewe, lamb and tup was marked so we could identify whose is whose. Ours had a red line across their back. Plus, our tups were Swaledales, and the only other farmer near enough, Ian Kirk, kept Herdwicks and no retired farmer's wife would mix those two up.

'Don't tell me.' Dan sighed, scraping up the last of his curry. 'Bloody sheep have got out.'

'Yep,' I said, coming back to the table and filling him in on their whereabouts.

'As my dad used to say, sheep have two aims in life: to escape and—'

'To die,' Poppy finished for him.

'Exactly.' Dan grinned at her. 'You know.'

'As I said,' said Poppy archly, 'farming is in my blood.'

Dan sighed in defeat and I bit my lip to stop my face breaking into a smile as she stood up, stacked her plate in the dishwasher and walked into the living room.

'I'll get the telly on ready. I'm putting it on Snapchat.'

Dan caught my eye and grinned. 'And I'll text Harry. Let him know I'll be over as soon as my wife's had her first TV appearance.'

Five minutes later, Dan and I were sitting on the sofa and Poppy was kneeling on the floor in front of the TV with her phone held up ready to capture my big moment. My stomach was churning.

'I'm more nervous now than I was at the time,' I said, glad Dan was here so I could bury my face in his chest if it was awful.

'You'll be great.' He lifted his arm to make room for me as I snuggled up to him. 'And you've got a lovely smile; you'll be good on TV.'

I breathed in his familiar scent and felt my heart rate calming. 'Aw, thank you. Naomi warned me I'd probably only be in view for a few seconds. A soundbite she called it.'

'Shush, shush, this is it!' Poppy yelped and started to record it on her phone.

The camera panned across the front of the shop and paused on the flower troughs outside while a voiceover introduced the piece. And then there was Kirsty, all toothy smiles and flicky hair, standing in the shop and talking to the camera with that big microphone in her face and forgetting the name of the River Esk. I smiled at Edwin's voice softly prompting her from the wings.

'I'm there, just to the left of her,' I hissed to Dan, pointing at the screen.

'Shush,' he chuckled, 'and can you loosen your grip?'

I looked down to where I'd balled his shirt up in my fist. 'Sorry.'

'Her family, the Greengrasses, have been farming here for generations, but it was Naomi's dream to bring this traditional Cumbrian stone building to life again,' said Kirsty.

'Like me,' said Poppy pointedly, giving Dan a haughty look. 'I'm the next generation of Greengrasses.'

'This is me now,' I squeaked. 'Oh . . . ?'

They'd done some cutting and pasting with the film and instead of Kirsty beckoning me to join her, it jumped to some interior shots of the shop, showing customers tasting food, ending on a close-up of my pie in a box in my hands.

'Naomi has curated all the best produce from the area under one lovely slate roof and today the shop is celebrating its fifteenth birthday, isn't that correct, Naomi?' Kirsty continued.

And then there was Naomi, still looking a bit uncomfortable after her accident and talking about how proud she was of her shop and her expansion plans for the future. I pushed myself up from Dan and leaned forward.

'This is supposed to be me talking about the farm and my pies,' I muttered.

'And finally, we spoke to farmer's wife Hetty Greengrass who told us her secret to a perfect Sunnybank Farm pie,' said the voiceover while I yacked soundlessly away in the background to Kirsty. Until suddenly there *was* sound:

'You have to keep the filling dry,' said the telly version of me, grinning like a lunatic at the camera. 'There's no soggy bottom on my watch!'

72

'And there you have it, ladies and gentlemen.' Kirsty finished her report standing outside the farm shop. 'There are no soggy bottoms on Sunnybank Farm.'

'So that was my soundbite,' I groaned, dropping my head into my hands. 'About soggy bottoms. What a buffoon.'

'Never mind, Mum,' said Poppy, hooting with laughter. 'I still love you even if you are a buffoon.'

'Me too,' said Dan, fighting to contain his mirth. 'And for what it's worth, you've got a lovely bottom.'

'Ugh, Dad, I don't want to think about you thinking about Mum's bum, thank you very much.' Poppy shot him a withering look. 'Auntie Naomi was good, though, wasn't she? I hope I'm as confident as her when I'm older. Mum? Mum, are you crying?'

My eyes burned where I'd pressed my palms against them and I fumbled in my cardigan pocket for a tissue.

'Come on, Hetty, it doesn't matter what you said.' Dan patted my leg. 'You helped Naomi promote the shop and you've been on TV. Not many people can say that.'

Poppy squeezed herself in beside me and added her love to the hug. 'The pie looked amazing, and they showed the one with my letters on. Told you it was a good idea. There's no need to cry, Mum, you did a good job.'

'Dad didn't wash his hands after chopping chillies,' I said, half laughing. 'And then he rubbed the chilli juice on to mine. That's why I'm crying.'

Sort of.

The truth was I was fed up of not being taken seriously by anyone. I'd had enough of just helping other people; I wanted to do something for myself. Something had to change. The question was: what?

Chapter 8

'Hup, hup, hup!'

Dan walked behind the last few ewes, waving his arms to get them to move from the meadow into the paddock and whistling to the dogs. Fern and Jake rounded up the stragglers, alert to Dan's every command. Finally, the ewes and their lambs were all in safely and I lifted the metal gate and swung it towards the post in the wall.

The ewes called frantically for their lambs and once everybody was paired up again, they got stuck into feeding on the new green grass.

'Look at them munching away,' I called over to Dan, securing the gate firmly. 'The grass has doubled in height in here since the last time I looked.'

It was the end of May and halfway through the half-term holiday and everything seemed to be growing at a rate of knots: the grass, the young plants in my vegetable garden and, of course, the lambs. They'd stay with their mothers, getting fat on milk until they went to auction. We'd keep a few back as usual to replenish the flock and once the majority of the lambs had gone, the rest would be weaned and the ewes would be free to get themselves in tip-top condition, ready for tupping again in November.

Dan bent down to give Fern a scratch on her head. 'A bit of rain followed by a bit of sun and everything grows like the clappers. If this warm weather holds for June, we might need to clip them early or they'll be keeling over in the heat.'

The weather had been fine for the last week, which meant being outside was more pleasant to work in. But only a couple of weeks ago, the weather had been really wet, which unfortunately was the perfect breeding conditions for maggots. Awful for the sheep, and not pleasant for the shepherd either.

We wandered through the flock, checking for any illness or injury. Dan spotted a lamb that appeared to be limping and grabbed hold of it to look at its front feet; he examined the gap between its hooves and sprayed it with a can of antiseptic he kept in his pocket.

'Scald?' I asked, joining him. Scald was nasty, an infection between the two hooves. If you didn't catch it in time it could lead to foot rot, which was even worse.

He nodded. 'We've had a few in this lot. I'll have to tell Cameron to check the ones in Top Valley too.'

'You'll do,' he said, releasing the lamb, who sprang back to its mum with evident relief.

There was always plenty of shepherding to do at this time of year: vaccinations, flea and worm treatments, rescuing daft animals from slippery rocks in the middle of the beck or those stuck head-first down trenches, not to mention rounding up some of our regular escape artists from roads and rivers. But there was a calm and happy busyness to it, quite different to April's 'up and out all hours of the day and night' activity. Some of our earliest lambs had almost reached sale weight and would be heading off to market before long. The ewes – in most cases – were good mothers and although we'd had an unusually high proportion of triplets this year, we'd managed to get almost all of our single-lamb ewes to foster a spare and the few cade lambs we'd ended up with were doing well too.

'That old girl will be leaving us this year; she's barely got any teeth left.' Dan pointed at a mule with a dappled brown face and a round belly who, much to Jake's frustration, was resisting his attempts to get her to join the rest of the flock. She stopped to tear up some grass and ignored him.

'Mind you, we've had six crops of lambs out of her so I can't complain. And with mutton getting fashionable again, she should fetch a tidy sum.'

Giving birth six times would make her seven years old. Not a bad life, I supposed, glancing round the paddock, over the drystone wall to the fields and fells beyond. She'd been free to roam over our hills with her family all that time, to do as she pleased, just coming back down for a bath and a haircut now and again.

She finished chewing and with a spurt of energy rejoined the flock. One of her lambs sought her out and buffeted against her, almost knocking her off her feet in its haste to get to her milk. She bleated so loudly in protest that Dan and I laughed.

'She's a feisty mum,' I said, 'with a pretty face.'

He gave me a sideways look. 'My favourite sort.'

'I don't know what you mean.' I smiled back. I didn't class myself as pretty and as far as I knew I didn't think I'd ever been particularly feisty either. Unlike the person just pulling into the yard.

'Anna's here,' I said, nudging Dan.

'Again? Tell her I've given Bart a chainsaw and told him to fell some mighty oaks by himself.'

I chuckled. Each time Bart came to work on the farm, Anna called by on some pretext or other, checking up on his safety; I'd never seen so much of her. 'I wonder what today's excuse for dropping in will be.'

'Tell her she can help with worming,' said Dan. 'That should put her off.'

'I don't think she's dressed to work on a farm,' I said, watching as she got out of the car and began picking her way over the clods of mud in her high-heeled boots. She wore a tiny black leather jacket and had a leopard-print bag over her shoulder. 'I'll go and see what she wants and make lunch for us all while I'm at it. Will you go and shout to the kids?'

Anna was leaning on the drystone wall scanning the fields when I reached her.

'Cameron has taken Poppy and Bart over to Beck Field, if that's who you were looking for,' I said, 'with the mobile scales. Dan reckons some of the early lambs are ready for the off.'

Anna's brow furrowed. 'He won't be using any dangerous machinery, will he?'

I gave her a pointed look. 'No. Dan would never allow it. Anyway, look at you, all gorgeous!' I kissed her cheek, keeping my hands well away from her jacket. 'Don't tell me: date with Mr Purkiss from school?'

She flapped a hand as we walked towards the farmhouse. 'No. Too young and too easily intimidated. I've found a real man. And why are you holding your hands away from me like that?'

'Lanolin. Very sticky,' I replied. 'And not a good mix with leather and leopard print.'

We went inside and she took mugs from the cupboard while I washed my hands and filled the kettle.

'Bart says there's a dog called Nancy in the village having puppies in eight weeks, he's already asked if we can have one,' said Anna, spooning coffee into mugs.

I opened my mouth to say that an exuberant Border collie at home all day while she was at work wasn't a good idea but she shook her head. 'Don't worry, I've already said no. The last thing I want is a woof-machine. But have you thought about maybe . . . ?'

Her eyes flicked to the spot in front of the Aga which until recently had always been occupied by Rusty.

'No,' I said quietly. 'I can't explain it, but Rusty and I grew up together and now he's gone it feels like the end of an era.'

'Enough said. Hugs.' Anna wrapped her arms around me. 'You'll know when the time is right.'

77

I gave a small sigh; I hoped so. I couldn't quite put my finger on it, but change was in the air and I felt uneasy and out of sorts. A new puppy was not on my radar at the moment.

'And instead of it being the end of an era,' she continued, 'how about thinking of it as a new beginning, and focus on something positive in your future?'

I squeezed my friend and managed a smile. 'Thanks, lovely chum. And talking of the future, you were saying something about a real man?'

'Wilf,' she said with a wicked gleam in her eye. 'And he is snog-on-a-stick delicious.'

I opened the fridge to get the milk and she told me about the gorgeous Aussie she'd met in the village on Sunday. He was here for a few days sorting out contracts and accommodation for his team ready to start shearing next month.

'I might have met him at the farm shop, ask him if he drinks rhubarb juice.'

'Okay, if there's time between all the kissing.'

I grinned, shaking my head. 'But you do know he'll only be here for a few weeks and then he'll be gone? I thought you were ready for a serious relationship?'

'I know, but I couldn't help myself. He hypnotized me with his testosterone, I was powerless to resist,' she said with a giggle. She twirled a lock of her hair around her finger. 'He said he was at a loose end tonight and I said so was I since my best friend stole my son.'

'Although Bart will be finished at four,' I reminded her.

The kettle came to the boil and she made us both a drink while I got sandwich materials out of the fridge.

'Exactly, he's coming round for a drink first. So would you mind keeping Bart for dinner?' she asked.

'Not at all. He and Poppy are getting on a lot better now she's realized she can boss him about.' I chuckled until I noticed Anna pursing her lips.

'It's fair enough,' I said, defending my daughter. 'She's

been helping on the farm all her life and Bart seems happy to follow her lead.'

Too happy, according to Poppy, who thought he was trailing after her a little too much and had tried to fob him off on to Cameron.

'Good for Poppy, I suppose. I'm all for girl power. Bart's loving it here; I thought he might,' said Anna wistfully.

'And Dan loves having him,' I laughed gently, 'much to Poppy's disgust.'

She set a coffee mug down on the worktop next to where I was slicing a fresh granary loaf. She sipped her coffee and stood next to me, gazing out of the window.

'It's good for him, learning some practical skills. Could come in handy later in life. On another level, it's nice for him to feel part of a family for a while.'

I put my arm around her shoulders. 'We *are* family. Or as good as. What is it you used to say at college?'

'Sisters from another mister.' She smiled, leaning her head on my shoulder.

'Better than sisters,' I put in. 'We never had any of the bickering or sibling rivalry to contend with.'

'You're so lucky, you know,' she sighed, 'having all this, belonging to the farm, having Dan. Sometimes I envy you.'

I glanced sharply at her. Where was all this coming from? Normally she was full of feminism, telling me how fulfilling it was to make her own way in life, unfettered by male egos and opinions.

'I've always envied you too,' I admitted.

She looked at me in surprise and snorted. 'Me?'

I nodded. She'd had a tough time training to be a nurse while single-handedly bringing up Bart but she'd never let her circumstances hold her back. I'd love to be more like her.

'You're brave and independent, and not afraid to take risks.' I met her eye. 'You know what you want and you go for it.'

'Ah, thanks.' Anna gave an embarrassed laugh. 'But that's not always a good thing.'

'It's more than I've ever had the guts to do.'

'Not true,' she argued. 'You were brave to give up your university education to move in here with Dan after his dad died. That was a risk.'

I wrinkled my nose at that, unsure whether I agreed. At the time it had seemed the only thing to do, I couldn't have contemplated any other course of action.

She pressed a swift kiss to my cheek and put her empty mug in the sink. 'And on that note, I'm off to take another risk: with a sheep shearer called Wilf. Bye!'

'Don't do anything I wouldn't do,' I called after her.

She stopped at the door and arched an eyebrow. 'Anything?'

We both laughed.

'Good point,' I conceded. 'Forget I said that, just enjoy yourself.'

Poppy suggested having lunch outdoors in the sun at the picnic bench. It was sheltered from the breeze by my potting shed and once everyone had washed their hands, Bart and Cameron helped me carry the food out while Poppy went to check on the cade lambs and Dan checked his voicemail messages. Cameron was a self-contained young man of few words who wore T-shirts featuring bands I'd never heard of and shaved his own head with clippers. He ate his lunch sitting in the tractor cab listening to grime (very apt given the state of his jeans). But Bart was happy to chat to Dan and Poppy about the jobs for the afternoon. I served them mugs of soup and thick cheese sandwiches and then went back inside to fetch some cake. The phone was ringing when I got to the kitchen and I picked it up, guessing it would be the supplier of our sheep pellets who had been expected this morning and hadn't turned up. Either them or someone reporting more runaway sheep . . .

'Sunnybank Farm, Hetty speaking.'

'Hello, this is the Duck and Feathers pub in Holmthwaite.'

It was a woman shouting at the top of her voice to make herself heard over the background noise of chinking glasses, men's laughter and music. 'I've got a pie here and I want to put it on today's dessert menu. How do I heat it? Can I microwave it slice by slice?'

'Reheat the whole pie in the oven and cut when it's hot. Never microwave shortcrust pastry,' I replied. 'Never. Or it will go—' I stopped myself from saying 'soggy'; I'd had quite enough of soggy bottom jokes. 'The pastry won't be crisp.'

'Right,' said the woman doubtfully. 'Won't it burn?'

I told her to cover the top with a piece of foil and to keep the whole pie warm after she'd taken it out of the oven and rang off, wondering whether the Duck and Feathers had in fact got one of my pies, or if I was simply the first person who came to mind for asking this sort of information.

In the past five days since I'd been on TV, I'd had quite a few pie-related enquiries. Most of them had started with, 'Is that the pie lady from the farmhouse?' I appeared to have become a shortcrust pastry guru in a short space of time. Which reminded me: this morning I'd had a message on the answerphone from Freya, the farmer's wife I'd met at the open day, who'd apparently got one of my pies too. I made a mental note to call her later this afternoon, but right now I had a hungry team of shepherds and trainee shepherds to feed so I flicked on the kettle and began cutting a chocolate and cherry loaf into thick slices.

Lunch was never a long drawn-out affair; it was simply a chance to refuel. As soon as Dan swallowed his last mouthful of cake he stood up and the others followed his lead. Dan went back into the paddock and Cameron took the dogs and the youngsters off to finish weighing the early lambs. And for the next couple of hours I sat in the kitchen ploughing through a stack of farm-related paperwork and replying to emails.

'How these government departments have time to create

all these ridiculous forms is a mystery,' I muttered to myself crossly. I looked longingly at the remains of the cake and wondered if my efforts should be rewarded with a second slice. *Most definitely*, came back a little voice immediately. I got up to make tea for myself and Dan, and nearly leapt out of my skin when the door flew open and Naomi appeared, breathing heavily.

She braced herself against the door, her tall frame filling the space and winced as she circled the foot with the injured toe.

'Sorry to interrupt but we need to talk.'

Chapter 9

My stomach swooped.

'Come in. Everything okay?'

She shut the door behind her and gave a nervous laugh. 'Yes, fine, fine. Do you remember meeting Freya Graythwaite on Saturday?'

'Of course. Actually, she left a message for me to call her earlier, but I haven't had a chance yet.'

'Good,' she said, exhaling. 'That's good.'

She began pacing the length of the room, twisting her hands in front of her. The suspense was killing me and even though my sister-in-law wasn't one for physical contact I caught hold of her busy hands and forced her to look at me.

'Please spit it out, my heart's hammering here. What's happened?'

She straightened up.

'Okay, here's the thing. And you've got to remember that I've done what I've done because I thought – *think* – it's the right thing and once you've had time to let it sink in so will you. Although if you really don't I suppose we can pull out. Nothing's irreversible.'

'That might make perfect sense to you, but I'm completely lost,' I said firmly. I pulled out a chair at the table and guided her to it. 'Why not start at the beginning.'

Naomi sighed and did as she was told and I fiddled with

the teapot so as not to look directly at her while she attempted to get her words out.

'Hetty, your baking is amazing. The way you can turn out pie after delicious pie, multiply your quantities for bulk orders and make it look so simple; that takes skill, real skill, and the flavours you put together, I mean that sheep's cheese one . . .'

'With the chard? Did you like it?' I said, beaming as I dropped two teabags in the pot.

'Everyone did. It was inspired. It was like something off a TV baking competition. Which is why . . .'

She paused to clear her throat and I was suddenly flooded with terror.

'You haven't volunteered me to be on that *Bake Off* show, I hope?' I stared at her, pausing from pouring water into the teapot.

She wrinkled her nose. 'Of course not. But I did give one of your pies to Freya Graythwaite.'

'Thank goodness! Is that all?' I said, clamping a hand to my chest. 'You had me going then, I thought—'

Naomi grimaced.

'That wasn't all, was it?' I said. I stirred the tea, popped the lid on the pot and poured it out.

She shook her head. 'Not quite. Freya came into the shop a couple of weeks ago and signed us up as a member of the regional food group. She's also been set the task of encouraging local artisan producers to enter the Cumbria's Finest competition. Apparently Cumbria stopped running this competition a few years ago and now some new executive has been brought in to beef up the profile of food from the Lakes.'

'But you're not a producer.' I frowned and handed her a mug.

'No, but you are.' She took a slurp of tea, eyebrows raised in hope.

'I am not.' I extended an arm to take in the kitchen. 'I'm just plain old Hetty with a farmhouse kitchen.'

Although . . .

If I was going to start a business, not that I was . . . because, I mean, how? When? Not to mention why? Okay, I knew why, but if I was to do it, producing pies would be the perfect thing.

She tutted as if that was a minor detail. 'You *could* be a producer. Look, I've wanted to start doing some own-brand products for ages. I've looked into preserves but everyone else is doing them. I thought about flavoured gin, or maybe soup. But pies, filled with local ingredients?' She eyed me shrewdly. 'What could be more exciting than that?'

My heart filled with longing. 'Almost nothing.'

'So I thought I might as well get the ball rolling and enter you into the competition. Whether we win or not doesn't matter, the point is, the farm shop gets publicity for its new range of pies, baked and supplied by you. And it gives us a platform, do you see? So what do you think? Your choice, obviously.'

I folded my arms. 'Is it? It seems to me that I've had little choice in any of it so far.'

By rights I should have been really annoyed, but my stomach was bubbling with possibilities and my brain had started whispering, *What if* . . . ?

'Just think, Hetty,' she continued, ignoring my comment, 'your own food business. I know you help Dan out on the farm, but this would be *your* venture.'

I nodded thoughtfully, my eyes drifting to the Ordnance Survey map on the wall. This could be the change I was looking for. Making pies was something I loved; I was good at it and I could do it in my sleep. Bringing in a bit of extra cash would be handy too. I'd never have thought of it on my own. And all because the other bakery had adopted a baby, what a happy coincidence.

I squinted as a grease blob on the map drew my eye and there, next to it, were the words 'Crinkle Crags'. I gave an involuntary gasp and tapped the mountain on the map. She followed my gaze and grinned sheepishly.

'Whoops.'

'There is no Crinkle Crags Bakery, is there?' I narrowed my eyes.

She shook her head.

And I shook mine. 'I wondered why I'd never heard of it.'

She chuckled into her mug. 'I think I did quite well to come up with that name on the spur of the moment; "crinkle" made me think of the crimping around a piecrust.'

I gazed at her incredulously.

'You've been plotting this for ages, haven't you? Those pie boxes you just happened to have in your office, the labels designed by Otis . . .' I sat down beside her, my head spinning.

'And asking you for cool pies so that it would be easier for me to box a couple straight away and load them into Freya's car.' Naomi's face was a mixture of contrition and glee. 'It all went so smoothly; I could hardly believe it.'

'I feel silly for just falling in with your plans.'

'With respect, Hetty,' she stood up, in control once again, and found Dan's favourite mug in the cupboard, 'you've been falling in with other people's plans since you arrived at Sunnybank Farm. I love you dearly, but I've watched you tinker about, making yourself useful on the farm, fitting in, doing anything and everything you can to help other people. You're a wonderful mum to Poppy and there isn't a community group that you don't help. And yes I admit,' she turned and fixed me with those determined eyes, 'that I've steamrollered you into this but now I hope you take the opportunity to make your own plans.'

My own plans. The fizz of excitement in my stomach was bubbling over like hot sugar syrup in a little copper pan.

Naomi poured milk into Dan's tea and chinked the spoon on the edge before dropping it in the sink. 'Come on then, lass, we'd better break the news to that husband of yours.'

The fizz stopped fizzing and the bubbles burst; I had a sneaky feeling that Dan wasn't going to like this one bit.

We found him in the small field with his Soay flock. I loved the Soays; they were dainty little things compared to our boisterous Swaledales. They'd been on the farm less than a year and so this was their first crop of lambs. Hardly any meat on them and their chocolate-brown wool wasn't worth a bean, but helping to increase numbers of a rare breed had been on Dan's wish list for a few years and he'd said it made a nice change to do something purely for the love of it without trying to make it pay.

He was rebuilding a section of drystone wall which had crumbled near the gatepost where Bart had reversed into it with the tractor this morning. He took his tea and leaned his elbow on the wall while Naomi and I filled him in on the Cumbria's Finest competition.

'So you tricked Hetty into it?' He scowled at his sister.

'"Tricked" is perhaps a bit harsh,' I said diplomatically.

'I meant to tell you on Saturday,' Naomi confessed. 'But the shop was so busy, and then I hurt my foot. It slipped my mind until I had an email from Freya saying that all entrants would be contacted by phone if more information was required.'

'And you've passed Hetty's pies off as your farm shop's produce?' He set the mug down and folded his arms.

My heart sank. '*Sunnybank Farm* produce,' I corrected. 'Ours.'

'The rules are that the product must be made in the area and the ingredients sourced locally wherever possible.' Naomi shrugged. 'So we comply.'

Dan was shaking his head. 'This is you all over, Naomi. You go off like a rocket without considering others.'

'Rubbish.' She shook her head impatiently. 'Think of the benefits for the farm: a branded product from Sunnybank Farm, out there promoting your lamb.'

Technically, it wasn't our lamb, I thought to myself, it was simply 'Cumbrian lamb'.

'What if Hetty doesn't want to enter a competition?' Dan demanded. 'What if she doesn't want to be judged?'

87

'Actually, I don't mind,' I said, realizing that it was time to assert myself in this debate. 'But I agree with Dan, in future please consult me before doing anything like this.'

'I apologize wholeheartedly,' Naomi said. 'It was impetuous of me, Dan's right. But I saw an opportunity to shine a light on your baking and I took it. I figured if I told you about it up front, you wouldn't have submitted an entry.'

'Good point,' I conceded. 'I probably wouldn't have.'

Dan tipped the dregs of his tea away and I took his mug from him.

'Of course she wouldn't have entered because she doesn't run a bakery,' Dan said, still frowning at her. 'Are Hetty's pies even eligible? She's a home baker, there are no health and safety policies, no hygiene regulations followed. No record of the ingredients. Where do we stand if she poisons someone?'

'Thanks for the vote of confidence,' I said huffily.

His face softened. 'I didn't mean it that way, love. But I'm guessing there was no label on the box, no allergy information, no instructions on how to store, how to reheat?'

Naomi and I exchanged worried looks. The box had been a plain cardboard carton with one of Otis's labels stuck on it. Perhaps that was what Freya wanted to tell me: that I was breaking goodness knows how many laws. Dan leaned back against the wall and stared at us grimly.

'Um, well,' Naomi began, clearly unwilling to let her younger brother get the upper hand, 'that was what prompted me to call in. Freya needs a list of ingredients.'

'I can write one,' I said hurriedly, 'retrospectively. Most of the pie fillings were made from farm shop stock so it won't be hard to trace everything. And I'm sure the safety stuff will be straightforward, I'll look into it.'

'I'll just tend to eight hundred sheep on my own, then,' Dan grumbled.

His moaning was slightly diluted by the appearance of Cameron on the quad bike with Jake and Fern riding

88

shotgun in the trailer behind him and Poppy and Bart laughing and running alongside them. Cameron carried on to the farmyard to put the dogs in their kennels and the two youngsters joined us in the field.

'Phew, here comes the cavalry,' said Naomi with a smirk.

'But no one's as good at spotting any injuries as Hetty,' Dan said sulkily.

'For goodness' sake,' Naomi muttered under her breath.

'It's fine, I can do the list later,' I said breezily. This pie competition had planted a seed and if it was going to sprout into life, I'd need Dan on side.

'I'm as good as Mum,' said Poppy, out of breath, her red hair tangled and windswept around her pretty face. 'Better even, because I'm a faster runner so I can catch them easier. And if I find any abscesses, I love popping them.' She mimed the pressing action around a lump and blew a raspberry.

I winced and I could see poor Bart was doing his best not to look disgusted.

Dan looked at me, his face softening into a slow smile, and I held his gaze, understanding without the need for words that he was apologizing for being childish. I smiled back.

'Go and do the paperwork, Hetty,' he said softly, rubbing a hand through his hair. 'Looks like I've got plenty of expert help.'

I nodded, smiling back, and Poppy punched the air.

'Catch.' Dan threw his daughter a can of antiseptic spray. 'Show Bart how to check for scald on the Soays. We don't want any more with foot rot.' He turned to Cameron, who'd come back from the kennels. 'You're in here with me, lad, we can finish this wall that Bart demolished and then take a ride over to the valley bottom.'

Cameron immediately picked up a rock and wedged it in place on the wall.

'It's green slimy stuff between their toes,' Poppy began explaining to Bart, striding up to the nearest ewe and her lamb.

Naomi bumped her arm against mine as we walked back to the farmyard where she'd parked her van. 'So if Freya calls, you'll say that Sunnybank Farm is definitely entering the competition?'

'Definitely,' I confirmed.

She heaved a sigh of relief and opened her van door. 'You won't regret it,' she said with a grin.

'Oh,' I called just before she slammed the door shut. 'One thing I meant to say, I'll be telling Freya that the pies aren't from the Sunnybank Farm range.'

My sister-in-law's mouth opened to protest but I jumped in quickly.

'I'm taking over the project,' I said firmly. 'So I'll choose the name.'

'You're the boss,' said Naomi with a grin.

That night, after Poppy had texted me goodnight from her sleepover at a friend's house and Dan had gone to bed, I gave the dying fire a poke to spread out the ashes, made myself a hot chocolate and took a seat at the kitchen table with the laptop. The clock ticked, the fire made occasional hissing sounds and upstairs I could hear Dan turning on taps and padding across the creaky floorboards and into bed.

It was peaceful here: just me in my kitchen, the heart of Sunnybank Farm. It was a cosy, homely space and the aroma of the rhubarb and apple pie we'd had for dinner filled the air with sugary sweetness. The ancient Kilner jar full of utensils on the window-sill, the lovely long table pitted and scarred from countless family mealtimes, the embroidered cushion in the small of my back, a memento from when this had been Viv's domain, and the pen marks on the door frame recording Poppy's growth over the years ... These details were what made this room special and I felt more at home here than in any other place on earth.

I'd said to Naomi earlier that I was just plain old Hetty

with a farmhouse kitchen. But you know what? That was fine. A smile settled over my face as I set up and named a new folder on the laptop: Hetty's Farmhouse Bakery.

And as I began to type a list of ingredients for the pie Naomi had entered into the Cumbria's Finest competition, a vision of my own cottage industry began to form in my mind. I would make pies for the farm shop right here, at my kitchen table, using the very best of local produce to create unusual flavours that would delight Naomi's customers and have them returning for more. It would be a small business, baking as many as she could sell in a day, so that they'd be perfectly fresh every morning. I could bake at night, in the quiet hours when the farm chores were done . . .

The clock struck eleven; the last hour had whizzed by and I was normally in bed by now. I finished the list, glad that Naomi had insisted on me concocting recipes from what the farm shop had on offer, thus making the job a whole lot easier, and emailed it off to Freya. I turned off my laptop and went up to bed.

''Bout time,' Dan muttered with a yawn. He flipped his pillow over to the cool side, something he did constantly through the night. 'Busy day tomorrow. Tagging and tailing. You'll help, won't you?'

I pulled a face in the dark. Lambs didn't mind having their ears tagged; docking their tails was a different matter.

'Of course.' I slipped under the duvet and felt for his hand. He wrapped his fingers around mine and I kissed him goodnight. I listened as his breathing slowed and grew deeper and gradually the pressure of his hand in mine lessened as he fell asleep.

My mind was still racing too much for sleep. There was so much to do, and learn, but the thrill of it, the mere thought of creating something for me, of my own, sent pinpricks of excitement down my spine. I'd tell Dan all about it just as soon as I'd got some firm plans. He loved me therefore he'd be happy for me, wouldn't he? I let out a quiet sigh. In my heart of hearts, I knew I was kidding myself; he'd grown so used to me being on hand to help him out. What I needed, I realized, as my eyelids began to grow heavy, was an ally, someone he couldn't say no to . . .

Chapter 10

'A pot of tea, apple pie and cream, a Belgian bun and a spare plate?' The young waitress set the tray down with a smile, admired Viv's chiffon scarf and sauntered off.

'So it makes good business sense really,' I said, resuming my Get the Mother-in-law Onside campaign as I cut the pie in two. Tactically, I put the largest half on the spare plate for her. 'Naomi wants to sell home-made pies filled with Cumbrian produce and I get to earn some pin money.'

'Hmm.' Viv smoothed down her apricot-coloured bob, pulled her chair in closer to the table and tucked a paper napkin into the neck of her jumper. Her face gave nothing away.

She looked lovely today, I mused. When I'd first met her she'd been perpetually hidden under a big striped apron. Over the years, she'd rebranded herself: styling her hair, adding little accessories, wearing make-up. She was slimmer too, which she put down to not having to cook big farmer's meals which she'd invariably eaten. Mike would hardly recognize her these days, although her facial expressions had remained the same and she was as difficult as ever to impress.

'She won't be happy until she's as big as Sainsbury's, that one.' Viv shook her head, her lips pursed. She wasn't fooling me: she might try to hide it but she couldn't be prouder of Naomi. Or any of her family.

93

'The farm shop is just what the village needs, though, and the open day last week was fantastic. Hats off to her, I say.' I held up my cup for Viv to pour the tea.

'I had my doubts about that shop, you know,' she said with a sigh. 'When I think of what her life could have been like.'

I stared at her. 'What do you mean?'

Viv flushed. 'Oh nothing, I just mean, well, you know, if she and Tim had gone up to Scotland to be nearer his job.'

She was hiding something but I knew better than to push.

'Well, selfishly I'm glad they didn't go. Naomi's always been like a big sister to me, and I don't know what I'd have done without you all when Mum and Dad first went away.'

'You wouldn't have ended up baking pies for a living, that's for sure.'

'True,' I laughed. 'I've got a lot to thank you all for, you especially.'

My meals with Anna had been heavily pasta-and-pesto-based until I started coming to the farmhouse regularly. At first, Anna had been a bit grumpy about me spending so much time with Dan, but when I started bringing home portions of shepherd's pie, dishes of hotpot and slices of home-made pie, she soon changed her tune. But it wasn't until I moved into Sunnybank Farm that Viv started to give me cookery lessons. She'd only just lost her husband, Dan was finding his voice with the two old farmhands that had used to work for Mike and I, at eighteen, had still felt like a child staying in someone else's home. It had been around the kitchen table, mixing pastry, that Viv and I had found a way to really get to know each other while my new puppy lay asleep in his basket near the fire. I'd already learned how to make a pasty in Cornwall, but making the shortcrust pastry itself was a skill I'd learned at Sunnybank Farm.

'How is your mum?'

I smiled at the memory of our recent late-night conversation. I'd been up late again tinkering with my cherry and almond pie recipe when my phone had started to buzz with a Skype call.

'She's making the best of her life,' I replied fondly. 'Just like you.'

Both women had been widowed far too early, both of them had had their lives turned upside down as a consequence. Viv had chosen a busy existence at the heart of the community she'd always lived in. And Mum . . .

'She was on her way out to watch the sunset when she called.'

'America,' said Viv disparagingly. 'When you could live here.'

She nodded through the glass windows of the café I'd driven us to at a National Trust property. The scenery was lush and green and the rolling fields and long silver ribbon of the lake below us were breathtaking. But there was no way we could sit outside today; the temperature had plummeted and the rain had barely stopped all day.

'Yeah, sun, sea and sand,' I rolled my eyes mischievously, 'I don't know how she stands it.'

Viv sniffed.

'I thought Poppy might come with us today?' she said.

'I did invite her but Dan was taking Bart to his first auction with twenty lambs,' I said, handing her the milk jug. 'She wanted to be the one to show him the ropes.'

Viv chuckled. 'Chip off the old block.'

'There's no doubting she's a Greengrass.'

'How's Anna's lad doing on the farm, enjoying it?'

I paused before answering. 'He's strong, which goes down well with Dan, and he's keen.'

Privately I thought that he was more keen on Poppy than on shepherding, but as I'd got my head bitten off by Anna when I'd mentioned that, I kept it to myself.

'I'll never forget the first time Dan brought you home and made you help him fix a puncture on his car in the yard.' She helped herself to jam and piled it on to her scone.

'Neither will I,' I said indignantly. 'I got oil on my new jeans.'

'Mike watched you pick up that heavy tyre and dunk it in a tin bath of water to check for leaks and he looked at me and said, "She'll do."'

I blinked at her, my heart twisting. 'He approved of me?'

She patted my hand. 'We both did. We knew you'd make a great farmer's wife. Eventually,' she added in a lower voice.

I wasn't sure whether she was referring to Dan and me not getting married straight away or whether I took a long time to fill her shoes; either way, Viv didn't hand out compliments very often, so I'd take it.

'Thanks. I don't think Dan really wants me to take on something that will take me away from the farm. I think he thinks baking pies is frivolous.'

'Raising those daft Soays is frivolous,' she said huffily. 'And anyway, what he means is that he likes having you as free labour. I never did, you know.'

'You never worked on the farm?'

I cast my mind back to life on the farm when Viv and Mike had been running it together. Memories of Mike pootling about on his little tractor, sometimes with little Oscar and Otis squished beside him, but always with his favourite dog, Bess, running alongside. We still had that tractor in the shed, it was a vintage machine now and Dan always said that one day he'd do it up and take it to shows. Mike had loved being on the farm, never wanted to leave it, not even for a holiday, and Viv was never far away either: shelling peas on the picnic table outside, or red-faced and perspiring as she decanted hot sticky blackcurrant jam into jars, or, come autumn, wrapping apples in paper to keep them for winter.

'Not shepherding, no. It was part of the deal. I helped out with lambing, of course. Then it was all hands to the pump. But not the rest of the time. When the kiddies were small, I worked as a dinner lady. I was an Avon lady for a while. That was like flogging a dead horse round here; all the women I knew only wore make-up on their birthdays and at Christmas. But I had this sudden yearning for a dose of glamour. It was fun while it lasted. Then Naomi's twins came along and I helped with them. And then, of course, you turned up, scared of sheep and needing training.'

'You make me sound like one of the dogs!'

'Kids, dogs, husbands, they all need taking in hand at one time or another.'

'So I should go ahead with my pie idea, you reckon, and try to win Dan over?'

'My son has had his own way for long enough; it'll be no bad thing for him to realize you've got aspirations too.'

My heart swelled with anticipation. Naomi was right, it didn't matter whether I won the Cumbria's Finest competition or not, just taking part had inspired me to give baking a go. I'd come to Sunnybank Farm and been absorbed into Dan's life. Somewhere along the way I'd lost my own identity. Hetty's Farmhouse Bakery would redress the balance. And for the first time in ages I felt excited for the future.

'So what do you think of this pastry?' I asked, looking at Viv's scraped bowl.

'What do *you* think?' she replied with a chuckle, knowing exactly what I was going to say.

I leaned forward to whisper discreetly. 'Soggy bottom.'

'Yours is far nicer. Even than mine,' said my mother-in-law, patting my hand. 'You get my vote, love.'

And with Viv behind me, I thought as I floated home, how could I fail?

The following Tuesday Dan and I spent the afternoon moving the ewes and the twin lambs up on to the lower slopes after all the rain over the weekend. Cameron wasn't working because he was sitting an exam at college and Poppy was due back from school any moment. The meadow, where they'd been, was too boggy now and hundreds of little feet had churned the ground to sludgy mud. Despite their thick fleeces, the sheep didn't like the rain and had spent much of the last two days huddled in close to the wall and under the clump of hawthorn trees in the top corner. Now, though, the stiff wind was drying the grass out nicely and the swirling air made the lambs spring and kick and run around in gangs with excitement.

Their antics made Dan smile, I was glad to see. He was quiet today. It would have been his dad's birthday and although he didn't like talking about it, I knew he'd been up to the grave early this morning to pay his respects.

I was quiet too; my stomach was as churned up as the meadow. The results of the Cumbria's Finest competition had been collated yesterday and Naomi and I had read through the details over a glass of wine in her cottage last night. There were fifteen entrants in my category. The winners would be contacted first and standard letters would be sent to the rest. My spring lamb, barley and thyme pie had been entered into the category of savoury Cumbrian pie and the farm shop was competing with nine others for best Cumbrian farm shop. We'd told ourselves we didn't mind not winning, we were just happy to be involved in anything that helped promote food from the region, and then burst out laughing at our blatant lies.

There was another thing keeping me awake: the money I'd need to spend on the kitchen if I was going to make pies professionally. I'd done a bit of research and reckoned on a thousand pounds. The thought made me feel a bit sick; it was an awful lot of money to fritter away on what was little more than a whim. It was roughly how much we'd get at auction for a hundred lambs. And that was before we took our costs out of it.

'One or two lame ones,' shouted Dan, pointing at a cluster of energetic youngsters who were zigzagging across the long grass, enjoying themselves.

That was the thing with lambs: a poorly leg didn't stop then joining in the fun, thus compounding the problem.

Dan whistled and Jake herded them in our direction. Dan caught hold of one of the limping lambs and checked its feet while I grabbed a gimmer and rolled her over, running my hands over her legs and feeling for injuries. She was smaller than some of the others and there was a sore on her back and two nasty-looking scabs on her knees.

'I'll give her a shot of antibiotics, if you've got one?'

Dan handed me a syringe from a leather pouch in his pocket, then jogged away to catch another lamb.

Suddenly Jake bolted off, sprang up on to the wall and began barking and wagging his tail. And there in the distance was Poppy, her school bag bumping on her hip as she ran. Close behind her was Naomi. Not wasting time using the gate, Poppy hopped over the wall and came careering towards me and the lamb.

'Hello, darling!' I looked up briefly. The lamb sensed I was distracted and bucked against me. 'Whoa, whoa, calm down.'

'Hey, Mum,' she panted, her entire body bristling with energy. 'Auntie Naomi drove me up the lane. Hurry up!' she yelled at Naomi, who had taken the more civilized route through the gate.

'Hetty, you've done it!' cried Naomi, crashing the gate shut in her haste. She was waving something in her hand.

The noise of metal against metal made the flock turn and stare before scampering as far away as they could.

My heart pounded.

'Right. I'll be with you in two shakes of this lamb's tail.'

Poppy huffed and started fidgeting in front of me.

I had thirty kilos of wriggly lamb between my knees and a loaded syringe. I took a deep breath to stop my heart racing as I plunged the needle into her thigh, trying to concentrate. I released the lamb, replaced the cap on the syringe and finally straightened up.

'Hetty?' Naomi's breath was coming in short spurts, her face wreathed in smiles. 'Did you hear me? You've won!'

She thrust the piece of paper at me. It had been battered by the wind but the Cumbria's Finest logo in shades of green and brown was at the top and unmistakeably, in big bold letters, were the words:

GOLD-STAR WINNER OF CUMBRIA'S FINEST
Hetty's Farmhouse Bakery Cumbrian Spring Lamb Pie

'I've won.' My voice emerged as a strangled croak, barely audible over the whoosh of my pulse in my ears. 'My pie won.'

My head and my heart were a blur of emotions. I had achieved something. I'd done something well. I was a winner!

'Yay for Mum!' Poppy dropped her school bag and launched herself at me, squeezing me tight. 'Is there a cash prize?'

I looked at Naomi who shook her head.

'But you can use the winner's logo on your packaging,' she said.

'Like a badge of honour,' I said, returning Poppy's hug.

'What's going on?' Dan came to join us. I handed him the sheet of paper, my eyes bright with tears.

'Congratulations, Hetty,' said Naomi warmly. 'I knew you could do it. The farm shop didn't come anywhere so I'm glad there's at least one winner in the family.'

I opened my mouth to commiserate but she flapped a hand.

'This is your moment,' she said and lowered her voice. 'Also there's a second page to the email with all the details on, you can read that yourself later.'

'Good stuff, love,' said Dan, passing back the email. 'I'm chuffed for you. What does that mean now?'

'Told you you're good at pies. I'm so proud of you, Mum,' Poppy squealed.

Mission accomplished.

'It means . . .' I looked from my daughter to my husband and swallowed. 'It means everything.'

Chapter 11

Later that evening when we ate dinner, I picked up the email and read it through properly.

'Listen to this!' I exclaimed. *'Regional category winners from around the UK are invited to submit an entry to the Britain's Best Bites final to be held in London at the Hyde Gate Hotel in Bloomsbury.'* I lowered the page and stared at my family. 'I had no idea about this!'

I hadn't been to London for years. I felt a whoosh of elation and a tremor of nerves at the same time. 'I can't believe it; I'm going to London.'

Poppy leaned across me to read it too.

'I'd love to go to London!' she said, wide-eyed. 'Can I come?'

I scanned the page for the date. 'It's the day after your birthday, the twenty-ninth of June, returning the next day. No, sorry, you'll be at school, love.'

'So unfair.' Poppy's shoulders slumped. Dan scraped his chair back from the table and went to consult the calendar on the wall.

'You can't go either, Hetty. The twenty-ninth is a Friday; we'll be getting lambs ready for market. I might even take the ewes that day too. I can't manage without you, I'm afraid.' He shot me an apologetic look.

'I'm sure you could,' I teased. 'It's not like I'm *that* good with the lambs.'

'Sorry, love.' He picked up his plate and stacked it in the dishwasher. 'Anyway, better to finish this pie lark on a high; you're the best in Cumbria. Be content with that.'

Pie lark – I bristled a bit at that, wishing he'd take my endeavours more seriously.

'Finish?' I said indignantly. 'I've only just started.'

'I could stay off school and help, Dad?' Poppy piped up, ever the chancer. 'So that Mum can go.'

I scanned the rest of the email: Britain's Best Bites awards to be handed out by a celebrity TV presenter . . . 'And Harrison Finch is going to be there!' I gasped. 'He could potentially eat one of my pies and if I won, I'd get to meet him!'

'Oh Dad,' Poppy laughed, 'you've got to let her go now. She's always had the hots for him.'

'I wonder if they'll film the awards for an episode of *Countryside Matters*,' I said dreamily.

'It doesn't matter if they do.' Dan, tight-lipped, began to head back outside. 'As I said, I need you here so you can't go.'

The kitchen door slammed, leaving Poppy and me speechless.

Things were a bit frosty between me and Dan for the rest of the evening until about nine o'clock when he called to me from upstairs.

'Hetty, can you come up please? I need you.'

He was standing at the bathroom door when I got there, looking very contrite.

'Is everything okay?' I scoured his face and hands for wounds, which was the normal reason he needed my assistance.

'I hope so,' he said, taking my hands in his. 'I'm not very good at this sort of stuff,' he said. 'I don't tell you enough how much I love you and what a wonderful woman you are. And how sorry I am that I'm such a grumpy old git. But all of that's true. So enjoy . . .'

He opened the bathroom door and a cloud of fragrant steam billowed out.

'Oh Dan, this looks gorgeous!' I gasped.

The bath was brimming with bubbles. There was a tiny bottle of champagne and a single glass perched in between the taps. The edge of the bath was dotted with scented candles and on top of a pile of towels sat this month's *Foodie* magazine. On top of that there was a little handwritten note.

Congratulations on winning the Cumbria's Finest competition, and for the record, you've always been a winner in my eyes.
   Love always, Dan xxx

I turned back to the door to tell him that I loved him too, but he'd already gone and closed the door behind him. It was only when I lowered myself into the bubbles that I realized that he might have apologized, but he still hadn't changed his mind.

By Friday I'd forgiven Dan for his less-than-enthusiastic reaction to my invitation to London, but we hadn't talked about it again since. My plan was to get all my ducks in a row first and then wow him with my ideas.

Over the previous couple of days, I'd done a lot of reading – not my usual recipes or food blogs, but stories about entrepreneurs. Success stories, tales of derring-do and risk-taking, about people with such a strong passion for their businesses that they stuck at them through thick and thin to get them off the ground. Foodies who'd tasted something so wonderful that they felt duty-bound to share it with the world, organic crusaders who believed in a better, healthier way of feeding people and, most exciting of all, farmers and farmers' wives who'd set up field-to-plate enterprises to boost their farm takings. From sausages to soups, juices to jams, vinegars to vodkas, preserves, puddings and pies . . .

Britain was full of amazing small producers and the more I looked, the more awestruck I was at the sheer ingenuity and doggedness of others. And the more determined I became to join them.

Dan had given Cameron a list of jobs to do this morning and then set off with Jake to meet a farmer looking for a mate for his red-and-white-coated Border collie bitch. I had felt a huge pang of loss for Rusty when Dan showed me a picture of her: she looked just like his mum had done. This wasn't the first time Jake had been drafted in for stud duty. He was a very special dog: his herding instincts were spot on and he'd shown promise from the day he'd arrived on the farm at only a few weeks of age, bravely barking at two old tups and not flinching when they lowered their curly horns to him. Up until Jake, Dan had trained all our dogs himself, but Jake had got VIP treatment with a top sheepdog handler. Pricey but worth it because now Jake's stud fee made a handsome contribution to the farm's coffers.

And with Dan gone, I had a few hours to myself and I decided to call the council to ask if they could help me with complying with hygiene laws. To my surprise, the man I spoke to was incredibly helpful and offered to visit the farm and give me some free advice.

'You can come a week today?' I sat bolt upright in surprise at the kitchen table and regretted it instantly. I'd been out with Anna last night; I obviously couldn't handle my drink these days. I cradled my poorly head in my hand. 'That's great, Mr Lucas!'

'I'll be there at two.'

'And do I need to do anything special?' I asked.

'No, Mrs Greengrass.' There was a pause followed by a laugh. 'Although a cup of tea always goes down well.'

I assured him that that would be no problem and ended the call, striking a line through the first thing on my to-do list. Just then, the sound of a piano rang out from my mobile phone. It was the bluesy riff which I'd chosen for text messages from my VIP contacts: Dan, Poppy, Naomi, Viv and Anna. I picked up my phone to read it; it was from Anna.

Who runs the world?

Girls!

I smiled as I typed my reply, quoting lyrics from the Beyoncé track we'd sung last night, walking down the middle of Carsdale high street at nearly midnight. The last time we'd sung that song it had been my hen night. Some things never grow old.

Anna typed straight back:

You're damn right we do. Especially the world of pies. Mind you, I've got a terrible hangover. Must be getting old.

We are. Never again xx

Ha! Till next time. Anyway, just wanted to repeat how pleased and proud I am: your baking ROCKS xx

My hangover was terrible too. I'd called Anna to tell her about my win and she'd insisted we go out to celebrate. I reminded her that we only lived in a village and of the three pubs, only one of them wasn't usually chock-a-block with farmers, but I got dressed up and met her in Carsdale where we proceeded to toast my success and commiserate over the fact that Wilf had gone to do a shearing contract in the Midlands and wouldn't return for a month. It had been a great, fun evening and had taken me right back to our younger days, when I'd tried to stay sensible but had quickly given in and let Anna lead me astray. The only difference was that these days my hangovers took twice as long to wear off.

Still, now I'd got an appointment with the council and in a week's time I'd know whether or not the idea of running

Hetty's Farmhouse Bakery from my farmhouse kitchen was feasible or not. I was proud of myself for getting this far, but a part of me was still nervous about what Dan would say. The more ammunition I could get to convince him that I was serious about this, the better.

A week later I was in the kitchen waiting for Mr Lucas from the council. Ten days had gone by since I'd become a winning pie baker and it felt as if every spare moment had been taken up with making, selling or thinking about pastry.

And I'd reached a decision.

Going to London to represent Cumbria in the Britain's Best Bites competition would be incredible. Truly unbelievable. In fact, sometimes I *couldn't* believe it and had to keep looking at the email from Cumbria's Finest to check that I hadn't misread anything.

But it was just a day and a half in my life. And if Dan really didn't want me to go then I wouldn't; our marriage was more important. But my idea for Hetty's Farmhouse Bakery, suppliers of perfect pastry pies, was another matter. I *did* want to do that. And somehow I needed to make it happen.

My first challenge was to sort out the kitchen. Right on time, at two o'clock, the doorbell rang.

'Come in, Mr Lucas,' I said, answering the front door. This door was rarely used and our feet echoed on the tiles as I led the way to the back of the house. 'The kitchen is through here.'

I stood back to let the baby-faced man from the local council in ahead of me, pleased with the state of the kitchen.

I'd scrubbed and cleaned and polished and even piled up nice-looking logs in the grate to make the fireplace look welcoming. There was a bunch of wild flowers picked from the meadow in a vase on the window-sill and a warm pie resting on a cooling rack next to the Aga.

It was like an advert from one of those country magazines.

'Thank you,' said Mr Lucas. 'It's a lovely old place,' he said, clutching a slim wallet of papers to his chest. 'Very traditional.'

I put the kettle on and worried whether being traditional was a bad thing when it came to matters of health and safety.

'Do look around,' I said, trying to sound normal and not like someone who was worried that Birdie might have managed to sneak a dead animal in here in my thirty-second absence. 'I use the Aga for cooking and the table for preparing and the sink . . . for washing up.'

Even to my own ears I sounded moronic. I mean, where else would I do the washing-up?

Mr Lucas shuffled his feet and made a sort of cough-laugh noise. 'Mrs Greengrass . . .'

'Hetty, please,' I insisted. 'Mrs Greengrass makes me sound like my mother-in-law.'

'Call me George.' He blushed. 'And yes, George Lucas is a daft name. Before you ask, my parents are *Star Wars* fans. They also had a catering business in Kendal called May the Fork Be with You. So I know what I'm talking about.'

While he described the absolute essential things I needed to do to comply with the law, I caught sight of my reflection in the mirror. My cheeks were pink and my eyes were huge, but I looked like a woman with a purpose. Which was true; I'd spent the last week being very purposeful, and happier than I'd felt for a long time too.

'So the sink,' said George, peering into it.

I peered into it too. 'Yes.'

'You use it for both washing-up and food preparation?' His brow was furrowed and I could tell this was a bad thing. 'Because you really should get a double one.'

'Right,' I said despondently, wondering how much extra that would cost. 'But there is a sink in the downstairs loo for handwashing.'

'Good.' George nodded and scribbled something in his notes.

Just then there was a thump on the door and when I opened it Dan blundered in, hands held aloft.

I made the introductions as Dan headed for the sink.

'Hello,' said Dan, nodding at George.

George held his hand out to shake. But Dan sidestepped him and jerked his head to the tap. 'Turn it on for me, Hetty.'

'Lanolin,' I explained to George. 'Off the sheep's fleece. It gets quite runny on a warm day like today.'

'Not this time.' Dan soaped his hands, the water and bubbles spraying all over the draining board and I noticed George's eyes sliding from side to side anxiously. 'One of the ewes has had a prolapse. Lucky I was there to pop it back in. But I'm going to nip her over to the vet's to be on the safe side.'

He grabbed a towel and dried his hands and then extended his right one to George.

George shook it politely and cleared his throat.

'Right-o, I've seen all I need for now,' he said. 'I'll leave these with you.'

He handed me some more leaflets to add to my groaning pile and headed for the door, resisting my attempts to offer him a cup of tea.

'You'll need to get all sorts of policies written up for things like fire hazards and provenance before you can start trading,' he said, standing back while I opened the door for him.

On the front step, predictably, Birdie was hunched over a dead mouse, batting it with her paw.

'I will,' I said, surreptitiously kicking the rodent out of his eye-line.

'And I'd get that double sink as soon as I could, if I were you,' he added.

'Thank you so much for coming.' I shut the door behind him and breathed a sigh of relief.

Dan was still in the kitchen; he was drinking the tea I'd poured for George.

'Why was that man here?'

My stomach swooped with nerves and I took a deep breath. Now was my chance to tell him the truth. But before I could formulate a sentence the phone rang. I leapt at it, grateful for the reprieve.

'Sunnybank Farm, Hetty speaking.'

'Hello, Hetty. This is Joe.' There was a pause. 'Chief executive of Cumbria's Finest.'

I felt my insides wobble. Freya's new boss. She'd told me about him over the phone. He'd been headhunted to revive the food group and had set them all ambitious targets to make Cumbrian produce part of the narrative about British food. Whatever that meant. His accent was local so he couldn't have been headhunted from far away.

'Hello,' I said.

'I just thought I'd congratulate you on your fantastic . . .' There was a sound of rustling papers. 'Spring lamb pie. How apt, coming from a sheep farm.'

How thorough of him to have researched our farm. But I supposed it was his job to know about such things. There was something familiar about his voice, although I was sure I'd remember if I'd met an executive.

'Thank you, I'm delighted to have won,' I said, avoiding Dan's eye. 'I normally only bake for fun – you know, for the family – I don't do it professionally.'

'Oh, really?'

'Is that a problem?' I bit my lip, wondering if I'd succeeded in disqualifying myself.

'No, no, no. Nothing that can't be . . .' He coughed. 'Anyway, I wanted to call and stress how much I, we – Cumbria's Finest – really want you to be part of the delegation heading down south to the Britain's Best Bites competition. It would be lovely to see you. Meet you. Lovely to meet you.'

'I don't think I can come to London.' I shot another glance at Dan, who was now staring openly. 'I've got other commitments.'

Joe continued as if I hadn't spoken. 'And of course we'll put you up in a five-star hotel, there's a gala dinner celebrating regional winners, that's you,' he laughed, 'and there's an opportunity to meet the best producers, like yourself, from around the country. Anyway, give it some thought. I'll need your answer by Monday.'

Joe. It was the laugh that did it. I was pretty sure I knew this man, *we* knew this man. My spine tingled.

'I'm sorry,' I said, licking my lips. My mouth had gone totally dry. 'I didn't catch your last name, but your voice reminds me of someone.'

He laughed again. 'I was wondering if it might. It's me, Joe Appleton. A blast from the past, eh? Oh damn. My other line is ringing, I need to get this. I'll call you next week, Hetty.'

'Joe Appleton?' I gasped. 'I knew it!'

'Bloody hell.' Dan grabbed the phone from my hand. 'Joe? Joe? Is that you?'

But the line was dead.

Dan and I stared at each other. His best friend had vanished from our lives fifteen years ago.

And now he was back.

Chapter 12

Joe Appleton from Carsdale, last seen on A level results day, at least by us, his closest friends, had resurfaced as the chief executive of Cumbria's Finest and wanted me to go to London with him. It was too bizarre for words.

'I don't believe it.' Dan replaced the phone on the cradle.

'Me neither.'

I sat down at the table, stunned. I couldn't wait to tell Anna; she'd be amazed.

'And what's he got to do with this . . . ?' Dan flapped his hand. 'This pie business?'

'He's taken over the running of the food group recently,' I said with a shrug, secretly annoyed with the hand flap. 'That's all I know. Freya said that she had a new boss who'd been tasked with raising Cumbrian produce to new heights. I had no idea it was Joe.'

He looked at me as if to say 'Who's Freya?' and I supressed a sigh. Sometimes I wondered whether he listened to a word I said.

'Joe clearly knew who I was. He let the conversation run right until the end before telling me his name,' I said thoughtfully. Why would he do that? Why not come straight out with it? I had so many questions. 'Shall I try to ring him back?'

Dan shook his head. 'Get it up on the laptop. Let's do a bit of digging first.'

I searched for the Cumbria's Finest website. The home page was filled with news of the competition winners, done in a grid, with a photograph and a description of the winning entry for each category, me included.

'I'm famous, look!' I was pleased with that picture of me; Poppy had taken it. I was standing behind my kitchen table, with my apron on, smiling at the camera while I sifted flour through my fingertips.

'Hmm,' said Dan, scooting closer to me to read the screen. 'Click up there.'

There was something about that *hmm* that made me wonder if he had a problem with me being in the limelight but I didn't want to get into that now, I was too intrigued to know more about Joe.

He pointed to the 'About Us' tab and sure enough the first picture on the page was of Joe and underneath it was a summary of his career. I zoomed in to enlarge it and we both fell silent while we read.

Joe had always planned on joining his family bakery, Appleton's in Holmthwaite, but after he disappeared without a word, Dan went to visit Joe's mum and discovered that he'd taken a management trainee job in Lancashire at one of Britain's biggest bakeries instead. Dan left his mum a message to give him but Joe never got in touch and after a year of trying to contact him Dan had given up. I'd never been able to understand that; I was sure that Anna and I would never lose touch. In our small community, friendships were intense; the bonds people made as children usually remained strong for the rest of their lives. But whenever I broached the subject with Dan he dismissed my concerns, saying that it was different for blokes and if Joe wanted to move on without us, he could.

And it seemed he had. According to his bio, he'd risen swiftly through the ranks and had a series of high-flying jobs ever since. I wondered what or who had drawn him back to Cumbria.

I looked at his photograph again and a warm feeling trickled through me. He'd aged, of course, hadn't we all? But he still had the unruly sandy hair, gentle brown eyes and cheeky smile. He was wearing an open-necked shirt and jacket in this shot; I think, with the exception of the leavers' ball, I'd only ever seen him in jeans and sweatshirts.

'So he's always worked in the food industry,' Dan marvelled, shaking his head. 'Just like he said he would. I wonder whether he ever married.'

'Probably,' I said fondly. 'He's ringing back on Monday for my decision on going, so we'll find out more then. I've always wondered what happened to him that summer.'

Dan frowned. 'Let bygones be bygones, Hetty. Don't go raking all that up again. Be polite, obviously, let him down gently about London and—'

There was a knock at the kitchen door. Dan and I looked at each other and he groaned.

'Damn.' He shoved his chair back roughly, scraping it across the tiles, and rushed to the door. 'That'll be Cameron, I told him to get that ewe in the trailer ten minutes ago to take her to the vet's. I'd forgotten about it. I'd better go.'

After he'd gone, I glanced at the clock; there was an hour before Poppy was due back from school. I sent Anna a quick text to tell her about Joe, although she wouldn't be able to reply until the end of school. I knew she'd be on the phone as soon as she could. Until then, I had just enough time to rummage in the loft for my old sixth-form yearbook. I was in the mood for a cup of tea and a slice of nostalgia . . .

I found it in a box along with my old maths books, a stripy teddy bear with 'Good Luck!' embroidered on its tummy, which Mum had sent me before my exams, and a faded copy of the estate agent's house details which arrived on the day of my last exam when the family home had gone up for sale.

I carried the yearbook downstairs, made some tea and settled in the armchair, tucking my feet underneath me.

I flicked past the introduction by the principal and turned to the first page of students whose surnames began with A. I laughed when I saw Joe's picture halfway down the page: his pose for the camera was identical to the one on the Cumbria's Finest website. His hair had been almost strawberry blond but he preferred to call it 'sandy'. He'd been like a big gentle bear, the butt of Dan's jokes a lot of the time, but so easy-going that he never rose to the bait. He'd been desperate to grow a moustache in that last term, but could only manage a covering of soft blond hair. Dan, on the other hand, had been having a full shave since the age of sixteen and by the time we left sixth-form, he had a hairy chest too. Joe had been really jealous of that.

I turned the pages to get to kids whose name started with 'C', Anna Croft was the last of them. Her big blue eyes leapt out from the page, she was slightly side-on to the camera and she was staring at the lens with a knowing look. She'd had dark hair extensions put in underneath her natural blonde (I'd been super jealous of them at the time), and she was in her velvet tracksuit top. I smiled as a memory came back to me of the two of us lusting over Juicy Couture tracksuits in *Cosmopolitan*. They were wildly out of our budget, but we'd found some cheap and nasty knock-offs at the market and wore them till they dropped to bits.

Next came Dan. My heart flipped at the sight of his face; I'd forgotten how handsome he'd been as a teenager. He was the oldest in our year, born on the first of September, and I was the youngest, born 364 days later. I peered more closely at the checked shirt he was wearing and laughed to myself; that shirt was still hanging upstairs in his wardrobe; he never threw anything away if it still had life left in it. Last, right at the back of the book, was me: Hetty Wigglesworth as I was then, a name which I'd thought made me sound about eighty. I smiled at my photograph. Why had I always thought I was plain? I'd been lovely: fresh-faced and freckly, bright-eyed and full of the-world-is-my-oyster optimism.

We'd been so young: eighteen – well, almost, in my case – and on the brink of our adult lives. I was head over heels in love with Dan and still remembered how deliriously happy I'd been when he'd said 'I love you' for the first time. Joe was single at the time and Anna didn't have anyone serious, but they got on well as friends and at the start of that summer the four of us had been inseparable.

Which had made it all the more inexplicable that Joe had suddenly decided he didn't want us in his life any more. I'd found his desertion hard, even more than Dan had seemed to. But then he'd been grieving his father and adjusting to his new life as a farmer, so perhaps there simply hadn't been any room in his head to process the loss of Joe too.

I took a sip of my tea and closed the book on my lap, feeling my eyelids grow heavy in the warmth of the sunlit kitchen.

And as the sun's rays shifted their way effortlessly from one window to the next, and my tea stopped steaming and eventually cooled to the point of being revolting, and my legs grew stiff underneath me, I let my mind drift back to that summer. When everything, and it seemed everyone, changed for ever.

Throughout May and June, we'd worked really hard, revising for our exams. Joe was probably the most studious, even though he'd been adamant that he didn't want to go to university like the rest of us. He reckoned he didn't need three years of studying and getting into debt just to end up at Appleton's Bakery where he was guaranteed a job. Academically, Anna was the brightest. She'd been predicted straight As and was confident she'd get a place at medical school. Dan hadn't waivered in his dream of becoming a vet and despite their disappointment that he didn't want to join the farm, Viv and Mike had been proud that their son had set his sights so high, the first one in the family to go to university. Naomi, although just as smart as Dan, had never wanted to go; she'd been a buyer for a supermarket until the twins had come along and, like Joe, didn't see the point.

The weeks flew by, exams came and went, and we soon settled into the serious business of enjoying our long summer of fun before the results were published. There were days spent doing nothing but sunbathing, all-night parties, club nights at the one dodgy club in Holmthwaite interspersed, for Anna and me at least, with our part-time jobs, hers at the local pub and mine at the post office. Dan and Joe both worked long hours at their family enterprises: Dan on the farm and Joe doing the early-morning shift at the bakery. We talked loosely about all going on holiday together, but we never got as far as booking anything. My parents had offered to pay for flights to the States to visit them but the thought of unclamping my face from Dan's had been too awful to contemplate.

August came around and while I was starting to get nervous about my results and wondering what I'd do if I'd failed them all, Joe, Dan, Anna and a group of others packed rucksacks with camping equipment and headed off to north Wales to complete their final expedition for their Duke of Edinburgh award.

I was sad not to be going with them, but the survival training sessions back in spring had clashed with an extra maths course I'd committed to and I hadn't been allowed to join the expedition without being properly trained. I was irritable and bored stiff without my friends and missing Dan terribly but I consoled myself with the knowledge that at least I had a shower, clean clothes and a comfy bed at night, unlike them on a blustery Welsh mountain, and I threw myself into buying what I'd need for my room in university accommodation instead.

The D of E group was due back at college on the evening before results day. It had started to drizzle and I was damp and perspiring inside my waterproof jacket by the time I'd cycled down to meet them. My stomach fizzed as the mini-bus pulled into the car park; this had been the longest Dan and I had been apart since we'd been a couple and I couldn't wait to see him. The parents who'd arrived to collect their offspring moved in like a swarm of honey bees. I spotted Viv and went to stand beside her. First off the bus was Tasha, or rather, Tasha's crutches. Then, aided by the teacher in charge and Joe, was Tasha with her ankle in plaster. Poor girl. She looked ashen. My heart fluttered, hoping that no one else was injured.

Next came Dan. I jumped up and down, waving and call-ing his name, hoping he'd run over and swing me round in his arms in front of everyone, saying how much he'd missed me.

I didn't get the reaction I'd been hoping for.

Dan, Joe and Anna were so tired they could barely stand. There was no laughter, none of the usual banter; in fact, it was almost as if they weren't even on speaking terms. The mood was tense and when I asked Anna if she was okay, she'd been close to tears and said she'd had the worst time of her life.

I hugged Dan and tried to find out what had happened but after returning the briefest of kisses he brushed me away, telling me that he stank. Viv shot me a look of sym-pathy and asked if I wanted to come back to the farm with them. Dan interrupted her, bundling his rucksack into the back of the Land Rover and saying that he just wanted to go home to sleep. After he'd squeezed my arm, promising to talk to me tomorrow, he clambered into the car and closed his eyes. Joe disappeared with his mum and even Anna said she was going back to her gran's for the night. Within a few minutes the car park was empty again and I was alone. I was bitterly disappointed that none of my friends had seemed pleased to see me, but I put it down to tiredness and perhaps the stress of the trip and Tasha's accident. I got back on my bike and made my way home.

The next morning, I went to college to collect my results and met Anna and Dan in the foyer. There still seemed to be an atmosphere between them but I assumed it was nerves. Anna went into the hall, leaving us alone, and Dan told me that Joe had already left, after collecting his results – three straight As. I was thrilled for him, but uptight about my own results. I laced my fingers through Dan's as we walked into the hall. For once he didn't pull away as he usually did when we were in public. But his usual healthy glow was gone: he looked pale and queasy. I teased him, telling him I'd still love him even if he'd flunked them all. Results envelopes were being given out alphabetically and we each headed towards our allotted section.

Five minutes later, Dan and I were outside on one of the benches.

'Two Bs and a C!' I said, heaving a sigh of relief. 'Not enough for a place on *University Challenge*, but it will get me to Lancaster. How about you?'

He ran a hand through his hair. 'Yeah, good. All As like Joe. So vet school in Bristol here I come.'

'That's brilliant!' I kissed him and tried not to think about the fact that in only a few short weeks we'd be living in different cities, hundreds of miles apart.

'And I'm so chuffed for Joe, the sly fox,' I laughed. I hadn't realized until this moment how heavily the exams had been weighing me down. Now I felt free and exhila-rated. 'We should go out tonight for cocktails and celebrate. I'll find Anna and tell her. You ring Joe.'

I looked round for Anna but couldn't spot her in the crowds of teenagers in various states of nervous excitement.

Dan stood up and held his hand out to me. 'Let's go for a walk away from everyone.'

'Sure.' I got up, pleased that at last he wanted to spend some time alone with me.

Hand in hand we walked around the side of the college, towards the football field, leaving the noise of the other students behind us. Suddenly he stopped still and turned to face me. He exhaled and when he spoke his voice was wobbly and unfamiliar.

'Listen, Hetty, there's no easy way to say this . . .'

But he said it anyway. I blinked at him, confused by the change in tempo of the moment, hardly able to take in his words. How he'd felt we were getting too serious and that a few days in the wilds of Wales without me at his side made him realize how dependent we'd become on each other. We were too young, he urged, he wanted me to go off to university and not be tied to him. He said we should be having fun, being reckless, enjoying our freedom . . .

I stared at him through my tears and said that I was having fun and I'd been supposedly enjoying my freedom for almost two years since Mum and Dad left for Cape Cod and actually it wasn't all it was cracked up to be. But he'd apologized, saying that he hadn't meant to hurt me. He kissed my cheek, like I'd seen him kiss his mum, held me one more time and then left. I sank to the ground and sobbed for ages. Then I called Anna, hoping she'd come outside and comfort me, but she didn't pick up.

I managed to dodge the rest of our friends at the front of the college and made my way miserably back home.

When I got there, a note had been pushed through the letterbox. It was from Anna to say she hoped I'd done well but things hadn't gone well for her; she didn't have the grades she needed and would have to resit and she was too miserable to talk at the moment. Poor Anna, her note made me cry harder. No sooner had I stemmed the flow of tears than Mum phoned to see how I'd got on and also to break the news that the house had been sold and how quickly did I think I could move out?

It was the final straw; I couldn't hide my sadness from Mum and burst into tears again. She tried her best to cheer me up, telling me what fun I was going to have at uni and how everything seemed overwhelming now but I was on the cusp of a new adventure, I'd meet new friends, explore a new city and before I knew it my heartache would fade.

She might have been right, but later that night when I went to bed in an empty house I'd never felt more alone in my life. And the idea of waking up knowing me and Dan were over filled me with dread. Suddenly I had to get away, I didn't want to spend the next few weeks avoiding him until I left for university. So I got back out of bed, packed a suitcase, phoned for a taxi and spent the night in the bus station waiting for the first coach to Cornwall the next morning. I wasn't sure what was in store for me, but taking back control felt like a positive move. I wanted a change, to do something drastic, meet new people, or at least avoid old ones.

Dan and I splitting up was the end of an era; our little gang had disbanded, the four of us had not been together again since.

The summer of fun was officially over.

Chapter 13

The following day, I was in my vegetable garden tethering pea plants to their stakes when the Land Rover and trailer rumbled into the yard. The hens scattered in all directions and the dogs in the kennel barked at the return of their master. Cameron jumped out, nodded at me in greeting and went around the back of the vehicle to unhook the trailer. It was empty. Good sign. That meant the lambs had fetched at least their reserve price at auction. Dan got out more slowly and stretched his neck and shoulders.

'How did you get on?' I shouted, keeping my fingers crossed for a good result.

We were sending lambs to market every Saturday now and this was the time of year we made our profit. All the money we put into the flock over the year: the feed, medication, treatments against disease, vet's bills ... It was an expensive business, not to mention risky, as so many things could go wrong.

He stuck up a thumb. 'Bloody brilliant! We got an average of a hundred pounds per lamb!'

'Gosh, well done!'

I felt a rush of adrenalin from my toes to my head. I'd been waiting for the right time to talk to Dan about my business ideas. A moment when he was in a good mood. This might be it.

'Yep. The buyers were on fire today,' he continued,

fetching a ten-pound note out of his wallet and handing it to Cameron, then slapping him on the shoulder. 'Well done, lad. The supermarkets will have lovely Cumbrian lamb on the shelves this time next week. From our farm. Makes it all worthwhile when it goes well.'

It did. It had been a good week financially, with that and the stud fee Dan got for Jake last Friday. The bank balance would be well in the black for a change.

'We'll celebrate tonight.' I grinned at him. 'I'll nip to the butcher's for some steak and we can open a bottle of wine.'

'Champion,' he replied.

It was good to see him happy. Farming was an incredible way of life in so many ways, but it was tough too. Moments of triumph like these were definitely ones to treasure and they kept us going in the midst of winter when the water pipes were frozen or sheep had been attacked or the monthly vet bill arrived.

'I'll go and make lunch,' I said. I secured the last pea shoot with twine and tucked my secateurs into my tool belt.

'Great, I'm starving.' Dan lifted a hand in response and disappeared across the yard towards the shed where he kept an assortment of farm machinery.

Ten minutes later I'd made a stack of cheese and pickle sandwiches and a pot of tea but neither Cameron nor Dan had arrived. I stuck my head out of the doorway and found Cameron loitering outside, hands in pockets, kicking his toe against a lump of dried muck in the yard.

'Lunch is ready, help yourself,' I told him, knowing he would never come inside without a direct invitation. 'I'll fetch Dan.'

I smoothed a hand over my hair nervously and took a deep breath. This was it. This was the moment to tell him about the funds I needed to get Hetty's Farmhouse Bakery off the ground.

My initial estimate had been right: I needed a thousand pounds to put in a double sink, an extra oven and some new worktops. I ran over my key points as I walked to the sheds: short-term outlay, long-term benefits, a few big regular orders (slightly massaging the truth here) and I'd easily cover my costs. And the farm generated most of its income during the summer months; my pies would help bridge the gap over winter. It wasn't that Dan was tight; it was more that we had, through necessity, to be cautious with money. We didn't have much in the way of savings and what we did have we called our emergency fund and we used it for things like building repairs and new machinery and, very occasionally, new vehicles. Spending money on a perfectly serviceable kitchen was not an emergency.

We had several sheds, in varying states of disrepair. The biggest was fairly watertight and we used it to house straw bales and the milk powder we bought in for our orphan lambs. And it was in there that I found Dan, in the corner, sitting on his dad's vintage tractor and staring into space. The tractor hadn't moved for over a decade and was allegedly going to be one of Dan's projects when he had time. The tyres had started to disintegrate, the engine had seized and there were thick cobwebs covering the peeling red paintwork.

'Hi there.' I coughed lightly so as not to make him jump. 'Is this a good time to talk?'

He looked up, surprised to see me, and gave himself a shake.

'I was miles away. This was my granddad's old tractor before he gave it to my dad.'

I nodded. This was a tale he'd told and retold over the years. I walked slowly up to him and leaned my head against his shoulder. He tucked one arm around me and ran a hand over the crude metal steering wheel, laughing softly under his breath.

'Granddad said I wasn't allowed to drive it by myself until I was ten. So five a.m. on my tenth birthday I came down and rode around the whole farm on it before anyone else woke up. I got as far as Top Valley when it ran out of fuel. I had to run back for a can of diesel before my granddad woke up and found it stranded in a field. Never run so fast in my life,' he chuckled.

'When I got it back into the yard, my dad and grandad were waiting to use it for the harvest and I thought I was in for a good hiding. But Dad said that as I was already in the hot seat, I could help them. Eight hours later, my backside was covered in bruises from bouncing on that hard seat all day and I couldn't wait to get off.

'Dad had laughed at me walking like John Wayne, but he was proud of me. "We'll make a farmer out of you yet, lad," he said. And I said . . .' Dan hesitated and scratched the stubble on his jaw. 'I said that I didn't want to be a farmer, I wanted to be a vet. I thought he was going to cry. I ruined that day for him. And for myself. He drove the tractor himself the next day. I felt awful.'

'He came round to the idea in the end, though,' I reminded him.

'I hope Dad would be pleased with the way I'm running his farm, even though I wasn't that keen at first.'

'He'd be proud as punch,' I said, 'although he'd have probably felt guilty that you didn't get to vet school after all.'

'No point dwelling on "what ifs". Besides, we're happy enough, aren't we?'

He turned to me and I nodded.

'More than enough.'

He climbed down from the tractor and together we walked towards the shed door.

'I've decided that the time has come to get the tractor going again,' he said. 'Seeing as we've done all right money-wise recently. I thought about having it towed away and getting it done up for Poppy's birthday. I can't think of a better way to spend the money, can you? Plus, it would be a nice tribute to Dad and Granddad.'

What could I possibly say to that? Her own tractor. It might not be every thirteen-year-old girl's dream gift but I knew Poppy would be over the moon. And I loved Dan for even thinking of it.

'No,' I said, swallowing the lump in my throat. 'No I can't.'

So that was that. No money left in the pot for me.

For the rest of the weekend I vowed not to think or say or do anything more pie related. It had begun to take over my every waking thought and I needed some space from it. Luckily, living on a farm there are always plenty of distractions. The weather had remained warm and perfect for bringing in the hay to make the haylage, which would feed the sheep over winter, and so Dan and I hit the phones to call for back-up.

Sunnybank Farm didn't have a large enough crop to warrant investing in huge automatic machinery to do it all for us, so we brought in the hay the old-fashioned way with a tractor, an ancient baler and plenty of pairs of hands. I begged Anna to come with Bart. Tim was working away but Oscar and Otis were back from university for the summer so Naomi roped them in to help. Poppy was in her element having both Bart and her big cousins to boss about; Naomi and Dan tried to outdo each other in terms of who was working the hardest and the dogs tired themselves out running in circles through the cut hay. Anna and I alternated between reminiscing about Joe and wondering what it would be like to see him again and playing a childish game of sneaking up and stuffing hay down each other's backs all day and Dan had to occasionally intervene sternly when our bouts of giggling interfered with the job. Viv was there too and temporarily reclaimed my kitchen to throw together a picnic which we ate in the fields. It was hard work but great fun and it turned into one of those glorious English summer days which sustained us through the cold and windy winters.

By nine o'clock on Sunday night we were sun-kissed and sleepy. Poppy disappeared in a panic to do a last-minute piece of homework and Dan had already been asleep in the armchair for an hour when the phone rang. I snatched it up quickly so as not to wake him and slipped out into the sultry evening air to talk.

'Hello?' I said softly as soon as I'd pulled the door behind me.

The dogs in their big kennel looked up at the disturbance and, not wanting them to start barking, I took the path around to the vegetable garden.

'Well.'

I smiled. How my mum could squeeze quite so much indignation into one word was incredible.

'Hi, Mum.'

'Twelve days I've waited for you to tell me about your success in that Cumbria competition. Twelve!'

'Sorry, I should have called,' I admitted. 'How are you?'

'Leathery.' There was a slurping noise while she took a drink. 'And loving it.'

'Ha. Same here.'

I could picture her sipping iced-tea, looking at the ocean from under the little covered porch that ran the length of her white clapboard bungalow, sheltering from the afternoon sun. Meanwhile, I sat on the old split-pine bench beside the potting shed and rested my feet on an upturned plant pot, gazing up at the shadowy hills. We were approaching the solstice and up here in the north of England it didn't get properly dark; the sky turned purple rather than black but the stars still managed to put on a magical display and the gentle noises of the night were comforting and familiar.

The hills rose to my left and right and I could just make out the blobs of white, some big, some small, as the sheep nibbled their way round the fields before snuggling up with their lambs for the night. Birdie materialized from nowhere and bumped her head against my shins until I scratched behind her ears.

'So my daughter bakes the best pies in Cumbria *and* gets invited to London to meet Harrison Finch, whom I know she adores, and doesn't tell me about it. My maternal radar is going wild, here, Hetty.'

'Sorry. Busy time on the farm, you know, with sheep sales, and haymaking . . .' My voice petered out. It was a poor excuse and we both knew it. 'Anyway, who told you?'

'Poppy, of course! She Skyped me as soon as you got the news. She was almost bursting with excitement; I could hardly make out what she was saying!'

My heart swelled. 'If nothing else comes out of this, I'll be forever happy that I've made her proud.'

'It must be nice,' Mum said evenly, 'for your daughter to be proud of your accomplishments.'

'I'm proud of *you*!'

'Humpf.'

'I probably don't tell you enough, that's all,' I admitted. 'After Dad died I thought you'd come back to the UK. I thought you might not be brave enough to live in America by yourself. But you've moved house, made new friends, taken up hobbies, you've created a life that suits you. I'm proud of you for that, Mum. I'm even . . .' I hesitated. 'I'm even proud that you've found love again with Al.'

'Really? That is good to hear.' Mum sounded so grateful, my heart pinged with love for her. 'He'll never replace your father, but he treats me well.'

We were both silent for a moment. I was thinking about Dad. About how much I missed him. He'd been the first man to buy me flowers on Valentine's Day and I'd made a pact with myself right then to find a man who would treat me the same way. Last Valentine's Day, Dan had traipsed right to the other side of the moors to pick me a posy of wild heather which he'd tied with baler twine; I'd been over the moon with it.

'You weren't quite so proud when we moved to America, were you?' she continued.

It was a rhetorical question; I'd been verbal about my disapproval, at the time and since. In front of me Birdie lifted her leg elegantly behind her ear, like some sort of advanced yoga pose, and began to give herself a wash.

'I was sixteen and selfish. I couldn't see it as your adventure. I processed every event according to the way it affected me. And I missed you both terribly.'

'And we missed you. It was a huge wrench leaving you, you know that. We nearly gave up and came home several times.'

'Yeah, I know, but you did the right thing. It was important that Dad enjoyed the life he had left.'

'And he did enjoy it.' Mum sighed softly. 'Owning his own boat, fishing in the ocean and sitting for hours on the veranda watching the water, or the sunset, or even the lightning storms; his last few years were his most content. I have no regrets. Our only sacrifice was you.'

I stifled a yawn; the day's labours were beginning to catch up with me. Above me Poppy's bedroom light went out, just as ours was switched on. Dan had gone up to bed; I wouldn't be far behind him, hopefully. 'It worked out in the end. It's getting late, Mum—'

'I notice you've managed to move the subject away from pies?'

'Not deliberately but it's complicated . . .'

But I resigned myself to telling her anyway. About my pipe dream to run my own business from home and about the costs involved that we just couldn't justify and how leaving Dan to run the farm while I swanned off to London wasn't fair. And about how Joe Appleton had resurfaced after all these years as the head of Cumbria's Finest.

'Oh goodness me,' she said irritably, 'Dan's a big boy; he'll cope without you for a day or two. You can't always please everyone, Hetty. No one knows that more than me.'

'What do you mean?' I asked.

'I mean, leaving you behind when we came to the States. I was caught between you and your father. But he persuaded me that you might relish the freedom; being a teenager and being able to set your own rules. We thought giving you your independence would help you when you went away to university.' She sniffed. 'Anyway, you gave up a lot for Dan; it's time you did something for yourself.'

I smiled softly into the dusky night. This was one of Mum's soapboxes: how I gave up my place at university for life on a farm.

'I have no regrets, Mum,' I said, echoing her words.

'Fibber. That's why you haven't told me about winning the competition. Because you knew I'd tell you to go for it. I can lend you the money to get the kitchen done, so that needn't be an issue.'

'Thank you, but no,' I said swiftly. 'I don't want to borrow money. You brought me up to be independent, remember?'

Mum tutted. 'Clever clogs. Okay, I'll *give* you the money. I ought to, anyway, because at the rate I'm burning through it, you won't be getting an inheritance.'

We both laughed and my eyes filled with tears of love; it was at times like these I missed her most.

'Thanks, but no thanks, Mum, I'd rather you carry on spending it yourself. Besides, it was just a pipe dream, some things aren't meant to be.'

'You could call it Pie in the Sky,' she said, ignoring my last comment.

'No, I've already got a name: Hetty's Farmhouse Bakery.'

'I thought you're not going ahead with it?'

'Um . . . I'm not.' I paused. 'I don't think.'

'Darling, don't be afraid to do something for yourself. And if not for yourself, for Poppy.'

'That is a good reason,' I admitted.

'And as far as *my daughter* representing Cumbria in a *national competition* is concerned, that would give me something to crow about at the tennis club next week,' she added innocently.

'And that's another good reason. I'm glad you phoned. Thank you for your advice.'

'Darling, that's what I'm here for, to make you see sense. Anyway, you must go to London, how else will you find out why Joe lost contact?'

Three incontrovertibly good reasons. I wondered if Dan would agree . . .

Chapter 14

The next morning, the clear skies of yesterday were a distant memory and the clouds were heavy and grey.

'I'll be in the tup field with Cameron this morning, tarting them up,' said Dan, swallowing the last mouthful of a bacon sandwich. 'There's a few with horns that need cutting down and we're going to make a decision on which tups to show and sell.'

The Carsdale Show was a big date in the farming calendar. Every year, we took some of our best Swaledale tups to compete. A winning ram could fetch a colossal sum; Dan's friend Ian from Woodside Farm got ten thousand pounds for one of his last year. Dan could barely speak to him for a week he was that envious.

'Hang on, I'll fetch you some tweezers,' I said, handing him a big box of sandwiches and two flasks to keep them going.

A part of tarting up the tups was removing the stray white hairs from their black faces. They also had the tips of their horns filed down if they were growing too close to their cheeks, peat rubbed into their wool to give the fleece a lovely grey colour and nearer to the auction, they'd have their white legs washed too. Sometimes I thought the male members of our flock had a better beauty regime than me.

As if reading my mind, Dan smiled his thanks and then did a double take. 'You look nice today.'

'Do I? I'm only in my jeans,' I said. 'I've brushed my hair, that's all.'

'And you've got make-up on.' He narrowed his eyes teasingly. 'Have I forgotten something? A birthday? Anniversary?'

'The only thing you've forgotten is how nice your wife *always* looks.'

He shook his head confidently. 'I'd never forget that.'

'Flattery will get you everywhere.' I turned to the door so he didn't see my blushing face. Joe Appleton was due to call today and I was feeling on edge about it. Yes, I knew it was only a phone call, but somehow making an effort with my appearance gave me an extra bit of confidence, whether Joe could see it or not.

I quickly found the tweezers, handed them over and as soon as I'd run through the list of jobs I'd got planned for the morning, Dan left.

The first few chores took longer than planned because I kept coming back into the kitchen to check the phone for messages. But at eleven o'clock I stopped for a cup of tea. Despite staring at the phone and willing it to ring, I still jumped when it did. Speaking to Mum last night had helped me sift through my conflicting thoughts; if this was Joe, I knew what I was going to say.

I caught sight of my reflection in the kitchen mirror as I reached for the phone. Eyes bright, cheeks flushed; I looked like what I was: a woman about to go behind her husband's back . . .

'Sunnybank Farm, Hetty speaking.'

'Hetty, it's Joe.'

'Hi.' My heart hammered and I took a seat at the kitchen table. 'I can't believe it's really you.'

'Look, first of all I owe you an apology. I should have come clean and said who I was straight away last time we spoke.' His words came out all in a rush as if he'd been rehearsing them.

'Yes, you should,' I said. I paused, waiting for him to

133

explain himself, but no reply came so I decided to launch straight into a speech of my own. 'The Britain's Best Bites competition would be a great opportunity to—'

'It is!' he urged, interrupting me. 'I'm so glad you agree!'

'To see *you* again,' I finished. 'To fill in the missing years. Joe, what happened to make you cut off all ties so completely?'

'Oh gosh, that was a long time ago,' he said. 'I don't really think about those days now. We just finished sixth-form and went our separate ways. I'm sure there are other people from the college days you don't keep in touch with.'

'True.' My brow furrowed. He was right: Anna, Dan and I had lost contact with most of the other students who'd moved away. But Joe wasn't 'other people', he'd been part of our gang, Dan's best friend. Even after all these years it was still bugging me.

'Now, Hetty, I really want to persuade you to come to the Britain's Best Bites awards. Do you have time to meet up?'

'When?'

'Today, preferably.'

I looked around the kitchen; there was nothing that a quick spruce-up wouldn't sort out. 'Of course, and I'm sure Dan would like to see you.'

'No, no,' Joe said swiftly. 'Somewhere neutral; I mean, halfway. I'm at the office in Kendal.'

'Okay.' I glanced up at the map on the wall and then at the clock. Appleby Farm in Lovedale was roughly halfway, plus Freya had asked to try a fruit pie: I could kill two birds with one stone. 'Appleby Farm in an hour?'

We ended the call and I ran upstairs to get changed. The rest of the chores could wait.

I turned off Lovedale Lane through an open gate that stood between a rustic honesty box selling eggs, pots of herbs and bunches of fat radishes on one side, and a wooden sign for Appleby Farm Tea Rooms on the other. I drove up the bumpy track and parked in a small field marked 'Visitor Parking'. There were several cars already there and I wondered if Joe's was one of them.

I was nervous. I hadn't attended many formal meetings in my life. Most business dealings in farming were conducted at great decibels in the auction ring or, depending on the time of day, companionably and quietly over a pint or a cuppa. And to be honest, I wasn't quite sure what I was even doing here.

But this was just Joe, I reminded myself, smoothing down the skirt of my one decent tea dress and lifting a caramel apple pie from the back seat. Just sweet-faced Joe, adored by all the girls for his quiet and thoughtful gentlemanly ways, even at eighteen.

'Hetty!' Freya descended on me, arms outstretched. She wore a baggy denim pinafore dress over a polka-dot T-shirt and had a matching scarf tied in her mass of curls. 'Congratulations again!'

'Thank you! It's still sinking in.' I gave her a one-armed hug and then handed over the pie. 'Serve warm with thick cream. I still haven't quite worked out how I'm going to bulk bake legally, but . . .' I ended with a shrug.

She wrinkled her nose. 'Ach, all that health and hygiene stuff is easy enough to navigate once you get the hang of it.'

I thought about the expression on the council inspector's face when Dan had come in to wash his hands in the kitchen sink after a close encounter with a ewe's undercarriage and said nothing.

She hung her nose over the pie. 'This smells amazing. Is it the recipe you'll be taking to London?'

'Well, I . . .' I started to tell her that nothing was official yet, but she set off across the farmyard and carried on talking.

'Actually, I think I've already put you down for that lamb one.' She pulled a face. 'I wish I was going with you, but Tilly is still too small to leave overnight. But I expect you to bring me all the gossip. Especially about Joe. He's a lovely boss, but talk about closed book; I normally wheedle stuff out of everyone, but so far nothing from him.'

'I know lots about him when he was a teenager. He was my husband's best friend through school.'

Freya stopped in mid-flow. 'Never!'

Her eyes widened when I told her we hadn't seen each other for fifteen years.

'Really?'

'He wasn't one of the judges, was he?' I said, suddenly realizing I might have shot myself in the foot. 'Because I don't want to be accused of cheating.'

She shook her head. 'They were a panel of experts from outside of the county, to avoid favouritism. None of the team was involved with the voting. Wow, though, childhood friends.'

She was still staring at me with interest.

'Talking of children, where are yours?' I said to cover up my awkwardness.

'My mum's taken them up to Clover Field where the shepherd's huts are. We've got guests checking in later. Come on, I'll give you a quick tour before Joe arrives.'

Fifteen minutes later, we'd done a whistle-stop tour of Appleby Farm, which had ended at the tea room. Freya told me how she'd converted it a few years ago from a disused barn, furnished it on a shoestring and decorated it with bunting, adding her mum's collection of vintage tea sets to complete the look. It was light and bright and very pretty, and I was completely bowled over by her talents. She introduced me to her right-hand woman, Lizzie, and installed me at a table to wait for Joe. No sooner had I scanned through the menu and drooled over the delicious-sounding cakes when soft footsteps approached my table. My spine prickled with anticipation. I looked up.

'Hello.'

And there was Joe, instantly recognizable even after all these years. No longer a big gangly teenager, slightly unsure of himself, but a tall, cuddly bear of a man, with a neatly shaped beard, a broad chest, a slight curve to his tummy and signs of a hectic life ingrained into the lines on his forehead. But the warm dark eyes, gentle smile and tufty sandy hair were unmistakeable.

In a flash I was out of my chair and flinging my arms around him. 'Joe!'

'Whoa,' he said, taken aback, placing a leather document wallet on the table. 'It's good to see you too.'

'You look great,' I cried, taking in his linen jacket and the smart polo shirt and jeans. 'I love the beard, makes you look rugged.'

He grinned boyishly. 'You too, Hetty Wigglesworth. You look great, I mean, not rugged.'

I laughed. 'I haven't been called Wigglesworth for a while; Dan and I have been married for seven years now.'

'And no sign of the seven-year itch?' He cocked an eyebrow and took the seat opposite mine.

'No!' I said, pretending to be aghast at the suggestion. 'We're as happy as ever.'

Joe held his hands up. 'Sorry. Bad joke.'

'Hey, no worries.' I handed him a menu. 'Shall we order? I'm dying for a drink.'

'And how is Dan?' He opened the menu and for a moment I lost sight of him behind it. 'I bet he was surprised to hear you're meeting me today.'

I opened my mouth, wondering whether to admit that Dan didn't know anything about it but luckily Freya arrived to take our order and the moment passed.

She returned to our table almost immediately, delivering tea for two, a plate of her home-made scones, a jar of her Auntie Sue's bramble jelly and a bowl of thick cream courtesy of Kim, their Jersey cow.

'I'll leave you two old chums to catch up,' Freya said, beaming from Joe to me, 'and I'll join you for the businessy-bit in a while.'

'This is . . . well, this is lovely,' said Joe simply, when she'd gone. He laughed under his breath, shaking his head. 'Strange after all these years, but lovely.'

I couldn't take my eyes off him. So many memories kept popping to the front of my mind, like when he used to call in to my house after his shift at the bakery, bringing Anna and me left-over sausage rolls and sponge cakes. Coming with me to the dentist when I was nervous and Dan was too busy on the farm to come. Roaming the streets with us for hours, helping us look for next-door's missing cat after I'd volunteered to feed it while they were away. Joe had always been there for us with a helping hand, a thoughtful deed and a friendly smile.

'It is, very lovely. I can't quite believe it.'

I reached for his hand across the table. He left it there for a second and then withdrew it, saying, 'Shall I be mother?'

'Talking of which, I am now a mother too . . .'

And while he poured the tea and plonked enormous scones on plates I showed him photos of Poppy and Dan and even a picture of Rusty, which brought a tear to my eye, and in a few sentences I managed to sum up the last fifteen years of my life.

'And you, Joe?' I asked, finally, cutting my scone in half and dolloping on some jam. 'Has life treated you well?'

'Oh yes.' He shifted in his seat and added more cream to his already mountainous scone. 'I've done all right for myself, been promoted once or twice, moved around to keep things fresh. Then this job with Cumbria's Finest came along and I decided that the time was right to come home. It's a three-year contract, and after that . . .' He shrugged casually. 'Well, who knows?'

Blimey, he'd managed to cram his life story into even fewer words than me.

'Is there a Mrs Appleton?' I probed. 'Any little Appletons?'

'Nope.' Joe looked down at the front of his jacket, where one lone crumb had stuck to his lapel. He flicked it away.

'There was briefly a wife, but not long enough to produce kids. My CV looks a bit thin on that score.' He gave me a resigned smile. 'Still. More tea?'

He reached for the pot, making it clear that he was uncomfortable talking about his personal life, but I had to know more.

'And your family bakery in Holmthwaite?' I continued. 'Your mum sold up, I heard?'

He set the teapot down carefully, nodding. 'She had an offer she couldn't refuse a year or two back and sold the business. Now she lives in Windermere in a complex for the over fifty-fives with a view of the lake, and bistros, galleries and boutiques on her doorstep.'

'I quite fancy that myself.'

Tension hung in the air between us.

The elephant in this room was so big we were in danger of being crushed beneath it. I studied Joe as he added a drop of milk to his tea and then stirred. Despite what he'd said on the phone earlier about not thinking of his college days any more, we couldn't ignore his mysterious disappearance from our lives. My insides were completely twisted up with the effort of not demanding answers. I had to say something.

'Joe, why did you leave without saying goodbye?' I held his gaze. His expression gave nothing away but a tiny flicker in the muscle under his eye told me how much he didn't want this conversation. 'We were so confused.'

He glanced up sharply. 'Not everyone was confused. What did Dan say about it?'

His words stole my breath; so there was something. Did Dan know more than he was letting on after all? If so, that would explain why he'd pushed Joe's disappearance under the carpet and scarcely referred to it over the years. But Dan and I didn't have any secrets. My stomach flip-flopped at the thought and I pushed my cream tea away.

'He told me nothing.' I leaned forward, forcing him to

look at me. 'Tell me, please. You cut off all contact from me, Dan and Anna, your friends? Why?'

'I grew up. We all did.' He busied himself taking papers from the leather wallet on the table. 'As I said on the phone, there's nothing else to say. My A-level grades were better than college had predicted and I was headhunted by Fairbrother's to their trainee programme.'

'I get that!' I said crossly. 'But your new life needn't have stopped you keeping in touch with the old.'

'It was easier that way.' Joe clamped his mouth shut, his jaw set.

'Not for us it wasn't,' I retorted. 'Dan could have used a friend after losing his father.'

He rubbed a hand over his beard.

'Can we stick to business?' he asked quietly. 'I'm sure you're busy and we need to talk about your entry to Britain's Best Bites. Freya said you'd brought a pie, I'd love to try it.' He looked over his shoulder, as if trying to attract Freya's attention.

'For goodness' sake, Joe,' I said sharply. 'This was a mistake; I'm going. I can't sit here discussing shortcrust pastry while you pretend that turning your back on your friends and then picking up fifteen years later without an explanation is perfectly normal behaviour.'

My chair screeched across the wooden floor as I pushed it back and stood, preparing to leave.

Joe flung his pen down. 'All right,' he barked.

The babble of conversation in the tea rooms stopped. The other customers turned to get a good look at who was arguing and Lizzie and Freya were looking worried too.

He ran a hand through his hair, leaving it standing in tufts.

'All right,' he repeated more calmly. 'But if I tell you, can we then drop it and move on?'

'Deal.' I sat back down. My heart was pounding hard and I felt ridiculously close to tears. The onlookers, sensing that the drama was over, returned to their own conversations and gradually the atmosphere lifted again.

Joe leaned his elbows on the table and dug the spoon in the sugar, stirring it round and round.

'I left because I was in love. Properly in love. It was more than a teenage crush; it was all-consuming. In fact, it overshadowed and ultimately drove a wedge through my marriage.'

I swallowed. 'Who were you in love with?'

He lifted his gaze to me and shook his head. 'Doesn't matter now. She never knew. I thought . . . I thought that if I waited long enough, showed her that I cared, eventually I might stand a chance, that she might notice how I felt. And then one day that summer, I realized that I was wasting my time; she'd never love me because she loved someone else.'

I reached a hand out to cover his and realized that mine was trembling. 'Oh Joe, I wish you'd confided in me, or even Dan.'

He quirked an eyebrow. 'It wasn't that simple.'

'Okay, maybe not Dan,' I conceded. 'He's not great at talking about his feelings, unless it's about Poppy, he adores her, or if one of the dogs gets injured. Or conversely, if one of his prize tups does a Houdini act, he's quite verbal with his emotions then.'

'And does he adore *you*, Hetty?' he asked.

He was looking at me so intensely, trying to read my body language, and it suddenly felt very important that he thought well of Dan and me and the life we'd built together. I thought of the champagne bubble bath Dan had run for me recently and the toast cut into heart shapes he'd left by the side of my bed on Saturday morning, before leaving for the sheep sales, and a thousand other little things he did to show he cared.

'He does,' I said, my eyes softening. 'In his own way.'

'Good.' Joe gave me a tight smile. 'Now can we please talk pies?'

We both breathed a sigh of relief when Freya came to join us with baby Tilly, who disappeared straight under Freya's T-shirt for her lunch. And after Lizzie had cleared the remains of our scones, she brought us fresh tea and left us to talk shop.

'We've got sausages, preserves, cider, gingerbread, chocolates, breakfast cereal, oils . . . loads of stuff, all from Cumbria, as well as your pies,' said Freya, beaming proudly. 'Our stand at the London show is going to be amazing!'

'Hetty hasn't confirmed yet that she's definitely coming,' Joe corrected her. 'But I agree, the quality of food from our small businesses has astounded me.'

'Ah,' I said, 'about the "business" bit . . .'

I explained that Hetty's Farmhouse Bakery was still, technically, only at the ideas stage and that a lack of funds to make improvements to the kitchen had temporarily halted proceedings.

'Hmm, I see.' Joe was trying desperately to be blasé about the top of his sales manager's boob being visible during a meeting. He scanned through the small print on the Britain's Best Bites website to check eligibility. 'Have you registered your company name? Do you have orders? A bank account?'

I nodded and crossed my fingers under the table; I had Naomi's firm order, if that counted, and a bank account wouldn't take five minutes.

'Then you're in. Simple.' He shrugged a shoulder. 'All we need is to find a way round the health and safety issue when you bake your competition entry.'

And find a way around the 'Dan' issue to comply with my marriage, I thought with a flicker of worry.

'You don't look convinced?' said Joe, furrowing his brow.

'Um, it's just . . .' I couldn't say my husband had forbidden me to go to London, it made him sound like a Dickens character and made me look like a spineless wimp. And neither was true. But I could see that it might look that way. And I was sure once Dan understood how important it was to me to go, he'd be fine.

'We'll organize transport and cover all costs. All you have to do is bring yourself and your Hetty's Farmhouse Bakery pie.'

Joe's words sent a volley of shivers down my spine. My pie, in London, competing with proper food companies from around the country. I wasn't completely sure how I'd got here, but now that I had I liked it. A lot. And I didn't want the adventure to end yet.

From her seat at the table, Freya was communicating to Lizzie via a series of mimes to keep the tea rooms running smoothly, whilst still keeping an ear on our conversation *and* feeding Tilly. If she could multi-task so effectively, so could I.

'You've convinced me,' I said determinedly. 'I'm in.'

'Great.' Joe clapped his hands together and grinned. 'And you never know, if you come first in Britain's Best Bites, you could be walking away with the five-thousand-pound prize.'

My eyes stood out on stalks. 'There's a prize?'

Freya winced. 'Didn't I mention that in my email?'

'Probably,' I said, not wanting to get her into trouble. My brain was whirring; imagine what we could do with that sort of money . . . I probably wouldn't win, but I had to give it my best shot. Even Dan would see that, wouldn't he?

Chapter 15

Dan stared at me, hands on hips, his forehead creased in disbelief.

'You've been to see Joe? Behind my—' He stopped himself just in time. 'Without me?'

I carried on mashing potato but Viv and Poppy, sitting at the table with their hands in the biscuit tin, stopped their conversation to listen.

'You're making it sound underhand and it wasn't,' I said, trying not to sound defensive. I hadn't deliberately gone behind his back, but I hadn't exactly made an effort to tell him either.

'Humpf.' He moved to the kitchen sink, washed his hands and poured himself a glass of water.

'I would have called you, but there's no signal on the moors, is there?' I said reasonably. 'And I didn't think I needed your permission to pop out?'

'Of course not.' Dan tutted irritably, leaning back against the sink. 'But this was meeting Joe. That's way more than just "popping out". And you're in a dress. You were in jeans this morning.'

'Yeah, you look hot, Mum.' Poppy pinched her thumb and first finger together in approval. 'You should get your legs out more often.'

Dan raised an eyebrow. Poppy wasn't exactly helping.

'Thanks, love.' I shot my daughter a smile for her support.

I wished I'd got changed when I'd come home. Silly mistake. At least then I could have told Dan about meeting Joe in private. But I'd been away from Sunnybank Farm longer than planned; Joe and Freya had made me fill in all the forms there and then, plus they'd wanted to go through the travel arrangements and show me the artist's impressions of the Cumbria's Finest exhibition stand. I'd come back and thrown myself into the rest of the day's farmyard chores, which had involved changing the straw in the orphan lambs' pen (not ideal in a dress), checking up on a couple of poorly ewes and their lambs in the paddock, a quick half an hour in the vegetable garden pinching shoots and picking produce, and making two rhubarb pies which Viv had requested to take to the hospital café where she was a volunteer.

'It was a spur-of-the-moment thing. He wanted to meet to discuss . . . my winning pie.' I'd been about to say 'London' but stopped myself just in time, I'd lead up gently to that. 'So we met in Lovedale at the vintage tea rooms at Appleby Farm.'

'I love that place,' Viv piped up.

'So what did he say?' Dan asked, ignoring his mum.

'About what?' I replied, swallowing hard.

He lifted his arms up. 'Come on, Hetty. About the radio silence for the last fifteen years?'

I held his gaze. 'He seemed to imply you might know.'

'What? Of course I didn't know.'

There was an edge to his voice now and Viv cleared her throat pointedly.

'Shame you two lost contact.' She shook her head. 'And odd in this day and age of the internet when everyone feels the need to share every aspect of their lives from videos of their sleeping dogs to pictures of their dinner.'

'I don't,' Dan grunted.

'That's because you don't have a life, Dad.' Poppy grinned. 'Who's this Joe you're getting all salty about, anyway?'

'A friend of Dad's from a long time ago,' I explained,

wiping a hand across my brow. 'Can you pass the cheese from the fridge please?'

She hopped up obediently and went to fetch it.

'Did he ask about me?' Dan wanted to know.

I spooned the mash on top of the chicken and mushroom pie filling. 'Of course.'

Sort of. *Does he adore you, Hetty?*

The thought of Joe's question made me flush. He'd looked at me so intensely, as if he was looking deep into my soul. Right now I felt more like I was on the business end of the Spanish Inquisition than cherished.

'But we spoke mostly about business.'

'Yeah, London, baby!' Poppy chimed with a fist-punch to the air. I groaned inwardly as Dan's ears pricked up.

Great. Now I had no chance of introducing the subject gently. I fetched the cheese grater from the cupboard.

Before Dan had arrived back from the moors, the three of us women had been having a lovely time debating dating etiquette. Poppy thought it was ridiculous that most girls waited to be asked out by a boy and had told us of her vow to do the asking when the time came. She also spent about ten minutes listing all the attributes of a boy called Niall. Not the first time she'd done that; he was the boy in her year with one hand, the brilliantly funny football player. Viv had then stunned her by saying that she'd asked Poppy's grand-dad out for their first date and the two of them had been married eight months later, which Poppy thought was awesome. I'd let the feminist side down by admitting that Dan had asked me on a date but secretly I was glad it had happened that way round. It had given me a huge ego boost that the gorgeous Dan Greengrass had chosen me when all the other boys fancied Anna.

Then Dan had come in and noticed my dress and the mood had descended from there.

'London?' Dan said confused. 'But I thought we'd agreed you weren't going.'

'Dad?' Poppy flung herself back against her chair aghast. 'Course she is!'

I glanced up from grating cheddar over the potato topping at my daughter's indignant face. I couldn't let her down now.

'We agreed nothing of the sort,' I replied calmly. 'I said I'd like to go and you said I couldn't. Big difference.'

'Daniel!' Viv gasped. 'I never had you down as a bully.'

'It's okay,' I said swiftly. I could not have my mother-in-law intervening on my behalf; this matter had to be sorted out once and for all, and I had to be the one to do it.

I took a deep breath.

'Dan, this is important to me. I know we're busy and I know I'm letting you down when you need help but it's only for a short time and I need to do this. I've agreed to represent Cumbria in London and I'd like to think you'll support me and be proud.'

'Hetty?' Viv whispered, nodding at the pie dish. 'Easy on the cheese, love.'

I looked down to see a mountain of grated cheese on top of the pie. I patted it down absentmindedly.

Poppy crossed the kitchen and wound her arms round my waist. 'I'm proud, Mum, definitely. Even if Dad's not.' She eyeballed her dad viciously.

'London.' Viv rootled in her bag for a tissue and dabbed her eyes. 'You'll be representing Sunnybank Farm too. Mike would have been over the moon.'

I stared at dan. He stared at the floor.

Viv got her diary out. 'When is it, love?'

I told her the dates and she scribbled something down.

'That's that sorted.' She sniffed at Dan. 'I'll come over and stay the night, and feed the cade lambs in the morning. Are you at the sheep sales the next day, son?'

Dan nodded warily.

'Then I'll help you with the sorting.' She intercepted Dan's objections with a stern look. 'Once a shepherdess, always a shepherdess. Unless you think I'm past it?'

I suppressed a giggle as Dan scratched his head. 'Course not,' he muttered.

'Right then.' She stuffed her diary back in her bag and winked at me. 'Come on, Popsicle, show me how this egg business of yours is doing.'

The two of them set off outside, leaving Dan and me in silence, staring at each other across the kitchen table. There seemed to be a gulf opening up between us all of a sudden and my stomach twisted uneasily.

'Please be happy for me,' I said softly. I put the pie in the Aga and walked to him. 'I really want this. It feels like the right time to push myself. Take on a challenge.'

He ran his hands down my arms gently. 'It feels like the farm's not enough for you any more.'

'That's not the case at all,' I argued. 'Loads of farmer's wives have other jobs. I love being here with you on the farm, and building my own food brand is something I can do without even leaving home, it's a perfect fit around my other work.'

He lifted his eyes to mine. '*Your* own brand. Not Sunnybank Farm's. *Hetty's*. Clue's in the name.'

My heart sank.

'Don't be like that. The pies will be made here on the farm and I like the name Hetty's Farmhouse Bakery; I think it sounds more friendly, more home-made.'

'True.' He puffed his cheeks out. 'Sorry.'

He pulled me to him and I threaded my arms around his neck and leaned against him. Outside I could hear Viv telling Poppy diplomatically that she wasn't ready to go in yet and please would she show her the Soay lambs. Dan pressed a kiss on the top of my head and I felt my body sigh with relief; friends again. 'And I'm ready for an adventure of my own, I suppose.'

He stiffened and lifted his head away. 'That's what I'm most bothered about.'

I frowned. 'What do you mean?'

He exhaled wearily. 'If I'm honest, I'm jealous.'

My eyes widened; I was amazed. 'Because of Joe? There's no need. There's only you for me. There's only ever been you.'

I had a flashback then to Gil in Cornwall, with his sun-lightened blond hair, freckly face and wide smile, the boy who'd made it his mission to piece me back together after Dan had finished with me that summer. And after three weeks he'd succeeded. But that time in Cornwall felt like a dream now. This was my reality and I never wanted that to change.

Dan laughed softly and stroked my cheek. 'No, not because of Joe. Because you're doing something different, I suppose.'

'But so are you! Look at your Soay flock doing so well with the new lambs.'

His mouth twisted. 'It's still sheep. It's still at Sunnybank Farm.'

'Are you saying that the farm is no longer enough for *you*?' My eyes scanned his face; I couldn't imagine us anywhere but here. But if Dan needed an adventure too then I wouldn't be the one to stop him.

He pulled a face and shrugged, as if struggling to find the right words. 'The farm has swallowed me up. I didn't get the chance to be the man I wanted to be.'

My heart melted for my lovely man.

'Darling, don't say that. You're kind and hardworking, a wonderful dad . . . Not to mention being a tiny bit gorgeous. I think that's quite enough achievement for one man.'

'When you put it like that,' he said gruffly, his lips twitching.

'Do you still sometimes have regrets that you didn't become a vet?'

He gave me a wan smile. 'From time to time, yes. But it's not just that. The landscape here is wide open, I have all the space I need, all the fresh air I can breathe, but some-times . . .' he paused, rubbing a hand over the stubble on his jaw. 'Sometimes this life seems a bit small. There's a whole world out there and I worry that I'm never going to get the chance to see any of it.'

I nodded fondly. After more than fifteen years together I could guess what he was thinking. Last year, he'd been glued to a TV series about the conservation of the Great Barrier Reef in Australia. He'd said if he ever won the lottery, he'd treat himself to a month over there as a volunteer. I'd never been bothered about having money, but seeing the wistful look on Dan's face made me wish I could afford to book him on the first plane out there.

'Anyway.' He gave himself a shake. 'I suppose I'm going to have to let you go to London, aren't I?'

'You don't have to,' I said, cupping his handsome face and kissing his lips. 'Because I'm not asking for permission. But I'd prefer it if you were on my side. We're a team. The best team. And you, me and Poppy – that's all I want.'

He nodded, shamefaced. 'Me too. I love you, Hetty.'

'Ditto.'

His kiss took my breath away, just as it always had.

'But please tell me if you're going to see Joe again. No more secrets?'

I smiled at him, my heart full of joy; watch out, Britain's Best Bites, Hetty Greengrass is coming to get you.

'No more secrets.'

While I ran a bath later and sat on the side watching it fill up, it occurred to me that Dan and I were open books to each other. We'd never had secrets. And living and working side by side, I guess we were used to sharing everything. That said, there were two things he didn't know about me. One was that I couldn't bear to cook our own Sunnybank Farm lamb and the other was the full story about my time in Cornwall.

He knew that I'd found a cheap attic room to rent at the top of a tall thin cottage overlooking the harbour in Padstow. He knew that I'd got a holiday job in a shop serving traditional Cornish pasties to tourists. But he didn't know that after hours Gil taught me how to make the pasties that his family bakery was famous for, and how to crimp the pastry edges so that the filling didn't ooze out. Dan most definitely didn't know that we sat up long into the night, just talking and sipping beer, and that one night – on my eighteenth birthday – we'd slipped out into the moonlight, when everyone else was sleeping, run along the path to St George's Cove, dropped our clothes on the soft damp sand and run giggling into the dark freezing water and then later made love on the beach. I'd walked home at dawn, humming happily to myself, and as I walked through Padstow's narrow streets, I caught sight of my reflection in a shop window. I was smiling and happy and even though my heart wasn't truly mended, I knew it could be and I'd be forever grateful to Gil for that.

And why hadn't I told Dan? Because later that morning, when I turned up for work, Gil couldn't meet my eye.

'You've got a visitor,' he'd said.

'Who?' Outside of work, I knew no one in Cornwall except my landlady.

But he simply jerked his head to the little staff room at the back of the shop and my stomach twisted with a sense of foreboding. I hurried through to the back and found Dan, slumped in a chair, his head forward on the table, his clothes creased and his hair dishevelled.

'Dan?' I'd gasped from the doorway.

He sprang up and wrapped his arms around me, burying his head in my neck as his body shook with shuddering sobs.

'I'm sorry, Hetty, I made a mistake. A bad one. Please come back,' he said when he could finally get his words out. 'Please come home. I can't manage without you.'

His dad Mike, he told me, had died two days before of a heart attack out on the moors. Viv was in a state of shock and Naomi, already a mum by then, was distraught too. The poor boy had driven through the night from Cumbria to find me, while I'd been frolicking on the beach with Gil without a care in the world.

'We might be young,' he'd said, holding my face close to his, 'but I know without any doubt that you're the girl I love, will always love, and if you'll give me a chance, I never want us to be apart again. Please say you'll have me back.'

'Yes,' I'd said, kissing his lips again and again. 'Yes. Let's go home.'

I'd never stopped loving him, not truly, and it didn't occur to me to make him suffer for the heartache he'd caused me. From that moment on, Dan was my home and I'd never regretted it for a single day.

I made my apologies to my boss, said a hurried and rather awkward goodbye to Gil in front of Dan, and then I packed up my attic room and drove us both back to Carsdale, the longest drive I'd ever done since passing my driving test, with Dan in an exhausted sleep beside me.

Back in Cumbria it was all change. Anna, after not getting into uni, had decided to take a gap year and go travelling and Joe too had slipped off the radar. At Viv's insistence, I'd moved into Sunnybank Farm the day before Mike's funeral. And from then on I was part of the family. Those days were so emotionally draining that it took us a couple of weeks to realize that Joe hadn't been in touch. And when Dan took a drive up to Holmthwaite to Appleton's Bakery, Joe's mum proudly told him that he was a management trainee at a big company in Lancashire now and was too busy to come back home. I was desperately disappointed on Dan's behalf; my man was grieving for his dad and could have done with a friend. Dan was more philosophical about it and moved on, but until today I'd never understood it.

When Viv and Mike's solicitor called Dan in for a meeting, things became even more complicated. The estate had been split between the siblings, with Dan now owning the farm and Naomi having the buildings she had wanted for the farm shop.

Dan had only just turned nineteen, yet he was faced with a difficult choice: become a farmer and continue the Greengrass tradition, or follow his own dreams of training to be a vet. If I hadn't been there to prop Dan up during that gut-wrenching time, he might have crumbled, but we talked and talked, night after night, until together we came to a decision. Both of us would put our plans for university on hold for five years and throw ourselves into farming. The rest, as they say, is history.

The bath had filled while I'd been reminiscing and the bathroom was misty with steam. I stripped off, lowered myself into the water and then, doing the thing I always told Poppy off for, I picked up my phone and sent Anna a text.

Can you talk?

A reply came back straight away.

YAY! Yum face! Just who I need to entertain me. Am in a dry-as-a-bone school governors' meeting. Some guy from the council is wittering on about illegal parking. But no one can see my hands, so I can text. What's up?

I met Joe Appleton today

WTF? Bear with. Will escape to loo

I lay back on my little inflatable pillow with my hair in a bun and prayed I wouldn't drop my phone in the water. Anna called me less than two minutes later.

'Bloody hell! Joe Appleton? Tell me everything,' she squealed.

'He's handsome, Anna, and lovely. He's Joe.' I shrugged casually, even though she couldn't see me. 'The same as ever.'

'But where has he been? And why the disappearing act?' she demanded. 'I wish I'd known; I'd have come too!'

'It was a spur-of-the-moment thing,' I began and then proceeded to tell her all that I knew.

I'd just got to the bit about his mum retiring to Windermere when there was the sound of a toilet flushing and then a tap running and Anna talking to someone.

'Hetty, I'm going to have to go,' she hissed. 'But do you know what made him disappear?'

'Yes. That's the strange thing,' I said, feeling my throat tighten. I thought about Joe withdrawing his hand from mine and the way his eyes had searched my face. *Does he adore you, Hetty?* 'It was unrequited love. He was so in love with a girl he couldn't bear to be around her.'

Anna gasped. 'Oh, the sweet, sweet boy. Did he say who the girl was?'

I swallowed. 'Not exactly. And this might sound daft, but I think it was me.'

'Blimey.'

'I know.'

The only girls he spent a lot of time with were Anna and me and he'd specifically said that the girl he loved, loved someone else. It had to be me because Anna had been single at the time.

'But that's not daft,' she said and I could hear the warmth in her voice. 'You're an absolute goddess, I'd fancy you myself if I wasn't so pro-testosterone. Bloody hell, gotta go, I think they've sussed me out. Let's talk soon; we need to discuss outfits for London. Love you.'

'Love you too.'

I was laughing as we ended the call and I dropped my phone on to the floor.

Absolute goddess, that's me, I thought as I slipped beneath the caress of the bubbles.

Chapter 16

In the farm shop, the sound of a heavy wooden table being dragged across the floor made me lean my head out of the work area at the back of the shop to see what was happening.

'Here you go. Now you can put your afternoon tea hamper display at the back by the jams,' Edwin insisted. 'You've got more space to spread out.'

'No thank you,' Tess replied hotly. 'You do your emergency camping provisions idea *at the back*. Mine needs to go at the front where people will see it.'

'Naomi did say my idea was fantastic,' Edwin put in.

'Fantast*ical* more like,' Tess huffed. 'I've already sold one hamper and that was before I'd even had a display. I'm a born saleswoman, me.'

'You don't need to be at the front, then.' Edwin folded his arms with a smug smile.

I went back to rolling my pastry on the stainless-steel worktop, leaving them to their bickering.

I listened with amusement as the power struggle continued. Tess reminded Edwin that she'd been here the longest, while Edwin pointed out that while that might be so, he had trained at the British Butler Institute and was impeccably well versed in the art of anticipating clients' every whim.

'Ahem. Customers,' Edwin warned suddenly as the sound of voices approached.

155

The debate was suspended as both members of staff switched into customer-service mode.

It was Friday and Naomi had left them jointly in charge while she went to Inverness to spend a long weekend with Tim for their wedding anniversary. It was a bit of a busman's holiday for her as she was doing a tour of delis and farm shops while he was at work, but they would spend quality time together in the evenings. Edwin and Tess had promised her faithfully that things would run like clockwork in her absence.

I was glad she was having a break, she was usually as reluctant as Dan to leave Sunnybank Farm and I knew Tim would be happy to have his wife to himself for a change. But she hadn't gone until she had helped me solve the dilemma of how Hetty's Farmhouse Bakery could possibly satisfy the Britain's Best Bites rules so that my entry was valid.

Freya had confirmed via email that I had to make the pies in an inspected and approved facility and be able to demonstrate that I had a viable business. Part one of that was quickly sorted: Naomi had offered me space here using the pristine facilities at the shop. The downside was that there was no oven on site, so once the pies were made, I had to nip home to bake them. Which was probably entirely against the rules, but it was the best we could do at short notice. Part two was to secure some orders. No matter how small, I needed customers. Sunnybank Farm Shop would be placing a regular order, as would Appleby Farm Tea Rooms, but as one was family and the other was connected with Cumbria's Finest, I needed someone else. So today's mission, once I'd finished these pies, was to parcel up the pies I'd baked yesterday and take them on a tour of local shops.

I gave an involuntary shudder; one week today, I'd be on my way to London. I hoped I'd managed to get a promise of some orders by then. I cut a large pastry circle, arranged apple slices over it, crumbled creamy Wensleydale cheese on top and I was fitting the lid when Edwin glided through to put the kettle on.

'Tess's just sold another afternoon tea hamper for fifty pounds,' he said, looking put out. 'So I suppose I'll have to admit defeat. This time.'

He straightened his bow tie and peered over my shoulder as I crimped the edges of the pie, pinching and turning as I went. 'Gosh, where did you learn to do that?'

'Ha. The result of a misspent youth,' I said proudly. I dipped a brush into a pot of beaten egg just as Tess came to join us.

'Misspent?' she said, raising a quizzical eyebrow. 'I spent *my* youth trying to make potato moonshine in my gran's shed and tattooing a dolphin on my own thigh.'

She hoisted up her skirt to show us. Edwin went pale and fanned his face with his hand.

'Hmm.' I looked at the blurry blue shape wistfully. 'When you put it like that, it wasn't really misspent, was it?'

'Perhaps you're just a late bloomer.' Tess patted my arm. 'Edwin, you'd better get out there, there's a big group of folk on the way in wearing shorts and hiking boots, with huge rucksacks on their backs. The emergency camping provisions might be about to hit the big time. If they spend more than fifty quid, the front display spot is yours.'

Edwin clapped his hands, air-kissed Tess's cheek and scurried back to the shop floor, leaving Tess to make the tea and me to ponder over her words. Was I a late bloomer? Was that why I felt so driven to start up my own business now? When I'd agreed to join Dan and Viv at Sunnybank Farm, I'd simply put aside my own plans and set about supporting Dan in the mammoth task of filling his father's shoes.

If you were to ask Dan who was the boss at Sunnybank Farm, he'd say we were partners. But that wasn't strictly true. Dan was far more knowledgeable, more capable than me. I might always know what needed doing, but he decided which animals to take to market, when we should clip, when to move the sheep up to the moors and down again. And it was to him that our suppliers deferred. None of which I had a problem with. But my pie business was different. This was mine and as each day passed I could feel my confidence growing and my desire to make a success of it growing with it.

And the best thing about it was that nothing needed to change, I could fit Hetty's Farmhouse Bakery around being a mum, wife and shepherdess, at least until I started making money from it. There was no risk, no expensive premises to fund. Even if I didn't win Britain's Best Bites (and I didn't think I could, although I got a tiny frisson of hope every time the thought crossed my mind), at least I'd tried. I could say that I, Hetty Greengrass, had represented Cumbria at the highest level. My status had changed around here from Dan Greengrass's missus, to Hetty with the pies. And on top of that – the ultimate accolade – Poppy thought I was cool.

I packaged up yesterday's pies in cardboard boxes and a smile spread on my face as I carefully laid two of them in my new wide wicker basket. Anna had bought it for me as a present and had painstakingly embroidered Hetty's Farmhouse Bakery into the corner of the gingham lining. She'd given me hundreds of thoughtful gifts over the years, but this was probably the loveliest.

I had a good feeling about my new venture; only good could come from this. We'd have more money, I'd have a little independence and Dan would have a happy and fulfilled wife. I honestly couldn't see a downside.

A few minutes later I passed through the shop on the way to the Land Rover with my basket over my arm. Edwin was at the front putting the finishing touches to his camping display and Tess was helping a man decide between three types of expensive olive oil by dipping cubes of ciabatta in little tester dishes.

'Do people buy quails' eggs when they're camping?' I

asked, looking over the impressive wheel of little jars that Edwin had built. It all seemed very high-end: as well as the tiny eggs, there were anchovies, stuffed olives, artichokes, sundried tomatoes and even minuscule jars of caviar.

'I'm pitching it aspirationally,' Edwin confided, tapping his nose. 'Camping needn't be all baked beans and bacon butties. I'm aiming for the picnic at Glyndebourne sort of market.'

There was a peal of laughter from Tess as she led the customer towards the till. She had her hand on his arm; even by Naomi's high standards of customer service, this seemed unusually attentive. I caught sight of his face and suppressed a smile; he was rather lovely looking: thick dark hair with silver streaks at his temples, dark brows and lashes and gorgeous brown eyes. His outfit was casual, just jeans, open-necked shirt, rolled-up at the sleeves, and deck shoes, but I could see even from a distance that his clothes were expensive.

'Like him?' I nudged Edwin. 'He wouldn't look out of place at Ascot.'

'Mr Brookbanks? He wouldn't look out of place anywhere.' Edwin did a little swoon and sighed. 'Alas, though, he isn't a camper, he's a local man. Naomi met him at the Sunrise Breakfast Club.'

I looked at him again; I'd never seen him before. I'd definitely remember if I had. 'He didn't come to the open day.'

'He's in retail himself so he probably works most Saturdays.'

'Ciao,' said Tess, passing Mr Brookbanks his receipt and handing him his carry bag. 'Let me know how you get on with the honey and mustard dressing, bring it in for me to taste if you like,' she added, waggling her fingers in a cutesy wave.

Mr Brookbanks mumbled something vague under his breath, stuffed the receipt in his pocket and gave us a thin smile as he passed on his way to the door.

'He can dip his bread with me any time,' said Tess, fluffing up her blonde hair suggestively, 'any time at all.'

'What's the name of his shop?' I asked, hitching my heavy basket up on my arm. It had six tasty pies in it. At least I hoped they were tasty; they were the key to my foodie fortune.

'Shops, plural,' Edwin corrected.

'Surely you recognize him?' Tess said but I shook my head. 'The Brookbanks family started Country Comestibles, they've got the main shop in—'

'What?' I gasped and dashed for the door, not hanging around to let her finish her sentence.

This was a golden opportunity to promote Hetty's Farmhouse Bakery. I legged it outside to collar Mr Brookbanks before he left the car park. I didn't dare run too fast in case I ended up with a basket full of crumbs and by the time I caught up with him, he was lowering himself into a sleek indigo-blue Porsche.

'Mr Brookbanks,' I said, panting slightly.

He paused from shutting the car door and stared up at me, brow furrowed. 'Yes?'

I looked at the pies carefully before selecting one. Country Comestibles was Cumbria's most prestigious retailer and a foodie's paradise; anything worthy of a place on its shelves had to be extra special. I decided on the steak, chilli and cheese pie. The heat of the spices was an unexpected twist and the tang of the cheese combined with the tender beef fillet I'd used was heaven on a plate. 'Can I give you this?'

I levered the box out of my basket and handed it to him.

'A pie,' he said flatly, looking down at the box in his lap.

'Yes,' I said breathily. My heart was banging. *Sell it to him, Hetty.* 'A pie made with Cumbrian beef and local Eskdale cheese.'

He regarded me for a long moment, his dark lashes blinking steadily. 'Makes a change. I usually get given casseroles.'

'Well, this is a bit like a casserole with a coat on.' I laughed nervously. Mr Brookbanks' face remained set. 'I made it. Heating instructions on the bottom.'

He exhaled. 'Do I look incompetent? Desperate? In need of looking after?' he said snappily.

'No,' I said, taken aback. This was new; I was used to my pies getting a warm reception. 'You look handsome, I mean smart. I just thought . . . Sorry, it was a spur-of-the-moment thing.' I tried to get the box back from him, mortified, but he hung on to it firmly.

'Okay.' I took a deep breath. 'I'm trying to launch my new range of pies, that's all, and when I heard you were from Country Comestibles, I—'

'This is for the shop?' Mr Brookbanks ran a hand through his hair. 'Ah, right.'

I frowned at him. Why else would I run up to a stranger and thrust food at him?

'Well, that's just for you to sample, really. Or your pie buyers.' I tucked a strand of hair behind my ear with a trembling hand. I was going to have to work on my sales pitch for next time.

His lips twitched. 'My pie buyers?'

I shrugged one shoulder. 'I'm still learning.'

He set the pie box on the passenger seat and swung his feet out of the car. 'Watch out.'

I stood back to let him get out.

'Let's start again.' He stuck his hand out to shake mine. 'Gareth Brookbanks. And you must be Hetty.'

I nodded, glancing down at his smooth fingers, tanned like Dan's, although Dan's were rough and calloused and never one hundred per cent clean. 'Hetty Greengrass. From Sunnybank Farm. And I'm starting a pie company.'

'Pleased to meet you.' His eyes flicked up to the moors where several hundred sheep were grazing amongst the heather. 'So it's a field-to-plate business.'

'Exactly.' I smiled. 'My strapline is: From my farmhouse to your fork, with love from Hetty, kiss kiss.'

161

I'd paid Otis to redesign the logo for me. It now featured a pie with beams of sunshine radiating from it and the words 'Hetty's Farmhouse Bakery' written below it. The strapline would be printed separately on the boxes. I loved it. So did Poppy. So much so, in fact, that she was thinking of getting her own logo for some branded egg boxes for her egg business.

He nodded appreciatively. 'I like it; it fits with our ethos. Maybe lose the "kiss kiss". Do you shop at Country Comestibles?'

'Um.' The Greengrass budget didn't stretch to the likes of Gareth's fine establishment. 'I window shop there. All the time. Maybe one day, if I make my fortune selling pies . . . ?' I gave him a hopeful smile and he laughed softly.

'I can't promise anything, but I do have a soft spot for authentic farm produce. I tell you what, I'll serve it up to a very discerning customer tonight and let you know.'

'Really?' I had to stop myself from flinging my arms round his neck. Instead, I grabbed his hand and shook it again. 'So you do have a pie buyer?'

'I have a six-year-old daughter,' he grinned, 'and believe me, she's not easy to impress.'

'Thank you, so much, Gareth, thank you.'

He started to get back into his car and paused. 'And I'm sorry I was rude. I lost my wife earlier this year and I've been bombarded with divorcees and do-gooders thrusting food at me.'

'I'm terribly sorry to hear that.' My heart ached for him and his little girl. 'And I'm neither of those.'

'I can see that now.' He lifted the lid of the box and smelled the pie. 'I love the free-form style of this and it looks better than my pastry.'

'You cook?'

He nodded. 'Sara, my wife, did the gardening and the kitchen was my domain.' He rubbed his neck. 'Unconventional, maybe, but it worked for us. So now Ella and I still eat well, but the garden is a wilderness.'

'I could help?' I found myself offering. 'I'm more of a veggie grower, but—'

'You've got enough on your plate. No pun intended.'

We shared a smile and he tucked the flap back down on the Hetty's Farmhouse Bakery box.

'My wife would have loved this. You're an entrepreneur. Cumbria needs more people like you and I wish you lots of luck. Goodbye, Hetty.'

My spirits soared as I waved him off. *An entrepreneur*, wait until I told the rest of my family about that . . .

Meeting Gareth gave me a huge boost and for the next couple of hours, I floated around the nearby villages on a cloud of confidence, handing out pie samples to two cafés, a delicatessen, another farm shop and the little general store at the camping and caravanning site where the sheep shearers from Australia usually stay. And by the time I bumped up the track to the farm with an empty basket at two o'clock, I was feeling very pleased with myself. I'd had a couple of missed calls from Dan but as I was nearly home, I'd decided to carry on rather than pull over and call him back.

That was possibly a bad move, I thought, when I pulled the Land Rover to a halt next to my old Renault. Dan was pacing the farmyard, one hand in his hair, the other glued to his phone. Still, I was here now and I was sure he'd be pleased for me about my day.

'Finally,' he said gruffly, shoving his phone in his back pocket.

'Ah, it's nice to be missed,' I said, leaping out of the vehicle. 'I've had a fantastic morning.'

I walked over to him, swinging my empty basket on my arm, bursting with news.

'Terrific,' he said flatly.

I held up my cheek to be kissed and he obliged grudgingly.

'Ooh, stubbly,' I complained, rubbing my face where his lips had grazed my skin.

'I'm too busy to shave in the mornings, Hetty,' he said with a scowl. 'I'm rushed off my feet today and you going AWOL with the Land Rover hasn't helped.'

'Sorry, darling.' I pulled a face. 'But your clever wife has secured four firm orders for pies this morning. My first proper pie orders! How cool is that? Plus, I met Gareth Brookbanks who—'

'How many?' he said smoothly.

'What?' I said, taken aback.

'How many pies have been ordered exactly?' He folded his arms.

'Well, only four,' I said huffily, 'but mighty oaks, little acorns and all that.'

Dan shook his head. 'So four actual pies,' he remarked coolly. 'And how much has it cost us to secure those orders?'

'Er.' I swallowed nervously. 'Roughly?'

He nodded. 'If that's all you've got.'

I was still getting around to working out my costings. There were the obvious things like the ingredients. They were expensive, but I was making a top-quality product, I couldn't stint on them. I'd spent money on packaging, the logo, and I supposed if you were going to be pernickety about it, I'd spent money on diesel driving around with my samples. The Aga was on all day anyway so that didn't cost anything extra and once I was a proper business, I'd have to factor in a cost for my time. Dan stared at me, waiting for an answer.

'Not much,' I said weakly.

'Oh Hetty, love.' He exhaled. 'Ask yourself, do we really need this extra work now? Do we need any more commitments? It's not as if we're going to see profit any time soon.'

'Yes, we do need it,' I argued. 'At least, I do and it's not just about the profit. We've been through this, Dan.'

He sighed and looked down at his boots, kicking at a clod of dry mud.

'I think you need a reality check. *You said* it wouldn't impact on the farm. *You said* it wouldn't get in the way of anything.'

'And it won't,' I said hotly. 'I've checked the cade lambs this morning, cleaned out the hens for Poppy and I went to Top Valley first thing because someone phoned to say they thought they saw one of our ewes with her head stuck in the feeder. Which there was, so I sorted that out and checked over the triplet lambs while I was there. *And* I made your lunch. All before making pies.'

He rubbed a hand over his face. 'When you put it like that . . . Now I feel like a slave driver.'

'You are sometimes.' I stepped closer, running a hand up his back. 'Why can't you ever just be pleased for me?'

'Because you took the Land Rover and I needed it.'

I'd taken it because although neither of our vehicles were really suitable for visiting potential customers, at least that one aligned to my farmhouse bakery brand. Sort of. But I hadn't thought to tell Dan I was borrowing it.

'I'm so sorry. I didn't think.'

'No you didn't.' He swiped the keys from my hand. 'Because all you think about is your bloody pies.'

'That's not true,' I gasped. 'Besides, I thought you were going to be in this morning and wouldn't need it?'

'I was but I had a call from a guy in Penrith with a Soay flock like ours, he invited me to go and see a couple of his males for a potential swap. That way we can get a new bloodline going free of charge. I had an hour or two free and I thought I'd go. Now I'll have to fit it in another time.'

'Free of charge?' I cocked an eyebrow. It was one rule for him and another for me; that wasn't fair. 'The Soay flock takes up loads of your time. They also take up space. We have to pay to feed them in winter and keep them healthy. We've invested hundreds of pounds in them and you'll probably never see a return. You did it because you wanted to. For a little project on the side. We could have had a holiday last year, Poppy could have felt sand between her toes, but we didn't say anything because we could see how much it meant to you.'

Dan frowned. 'Hetty, this is a farm, we keep sheep. And rearing a rare breed gives us an extra string to our bow.'

I lifted my chin. 'And so does having a field-to-fork business. I haven't got good enough facilities yet, but there's a five-grand prize up for grabs at this London competition and if I win, I—'

'If you win . . . ?' Dan laughed in amazement. 'Have you even looked at who the other competitors are? You're a great cook, but you won't win.'

I stared at my husband, crushed by his comments. 'That is the cruellest thing you have ever said to me.'

Dan puffed out his cheeks. 'I didn't mean to be cruel, but face facts, Hetty.'

The low rumble of the quad bike slowly approaching up the track that led to the farm shop made us both look round. Fern was padding alongside it, her long tongue lolling, and Cameron was at the wheel. He had the small trailer attached to the back of it and in it, bleating plaintively, was one of our biggest tups.

'Oh hell, now what?' Dan groaned.

Cameron turned the engine off. 'Broken leg, by the look of it.'

We went over and the sight of the animal in pain and distressed, its back leg at an odd angle, made me queasy. 'Oh, the poor thing,' I murmured. 'It must be in agony.'

'Another bill from the vet,' Dan tutted.

He stormed off towards the Land Rover, yelling for Cameron to help him load up the injured tup, and a couple of minutes later they'd gone.

I stood in the yard with my empty basket, too chock-full of emotions to move. My ego was bruised, I was humming with indignation, aching with disappointment and, more than anything, I was scared of the splinters that had appeared on the surface of my marriage.

Right now, I had no idea what to do or say to make matters better. My phone rang and I grabbed at it gratefully, shuddering with relief to see Anna's name pop up on the screen.

'You must be psychic,' I said with a wobbly laugh. 'I'm so glad you called.'

There was a hesitation on the line. 'You might not be so glad when you find out why I've phoned.'

My heart froze. 'What's wrong? Is it Poppy? Is she okay?'

'She will be,' said Anna calmly. 'But I'm afraid you're going to have to collect her from school.'

Chapter 17

I drove like the clappers, or at least as fast as my old car would allow. I'd let Dan know and he and I had put aside our row, both of us worried about our daughter. He couldn't leave the vet, but I promised I'd send him news as soon as I could. The traffic was kind for once and I made it to school in twenty-five minutes.

'Poppy Greengrass, Form Eight B. I'm her mum.'

'Push the door.'

The school receptionist buzzed me through the first set of security doors and told me to wait on the hard little sofa while she called the nurse.

I perched on the edge of my seat, heart hammering. Poor Poppy. According to Anna, she'd hit her head on a wall outside and fainted.

'Hetty?' Anna stood in the doorway, holding open the door to the rest of the school. 'Come through.'

'How is she?' I flew over to her. She gave me a quick hug and together we marched towards her little office-cum-sickbay.

'Mostly wounded pride.' She squeezed my arm and smiled. 'She's recovering already, she'll be fine. Matilda is sitting with her.'

In the nurse's room, Poppy was sitting on the bed, shoulders slumped, pressing her hand to a bandage above her left eye. Her skin was as pale as milk and her green eyes looked huge in her little face. Her friend was holding her hand, looking grave.

'Oh, love,' I said quietly, fighting tears. 'Look at you.'

She raised her eyes to mine and gave me a wonky smile. 'I hope I get a black eye. I've always wanted one of those.'

Anna and I exchanged looks. I sat on the bed next to Poppy and gathered her to me. Matilda edged away, awkwardly. Poppy relaxed against me and I breathed in the scent of her shampoo and school disinfectant and teenage bodies.

'You gave me such a fright,' I said. 'Are you all right?'

'Apart from my head feeling like it's been hit with a hammer and feeling like a total idiot, yeah.'

'You were amazing, Poppy,' said Matilda gravely. 'You are *so* cool in this school right now.'

Poppy perked up. 'D'you think?'

Matilda nodded, wide-eyed, and Poppy snorted with laughter. I let out a breath; she was fine, panic over.

'Can I go to the loo, Miss?' she asked.

I smiled at Anna; I'd forgotten Poppy had to address her formally at school.

Anna nodded. 'Go together. Matilda, you can go back to your form afterwards and Poppy, you come straight back here please.'

The two girls left and I flopped back on the bed, exhausted.

'What a day,' I groaned.

'Two ticks and I'll be back with some tea for us both,' said Anna. She slipped my shoes off and lifted my legs on to the bed. 'And then you can tell me all about it.'

She was back two minutes later with two mugs and a glass of water for Poppy.

'She'll be ages yet.' Anna grinned. 'For some unfathomable reason, the girls' toilets hold great allure for our students; they can be gone for hours.'

I sat up to take my tea from her and sipped it.

'Heaven.' I closed my eyes and sighed with pleasure.

'You relax.' She sat at her desk and began scribbling some notes. 'I just have to file a report about Poppy's injuries.'

'I haven't stopped today, despite what my husband might think.'

'Oh dear, is everything not rosy in your marital garden?'

'Humpf. You could say that. Dan has told me that I won't win this London competition and so it's not worth going.'

'Wow.' She looked at me, bemused. 'That was a bit caveman of him. You're not pulling out, are you?'

'I don't want to.' I groaned softly. 'We had such a row.'

'Oh don't.' She stuck her fingers in her ears. 'You two are my beacon of light in a dark, dark world. You're meant to be together, it's written in the stars.'

'You daft thing,' I said, grinning.

'I mean it.' She gave me a lopsided smile. 'As you know, I've never had any joy with men. I have seriously considered denouncing the opposite sex for good and becoming a nun. And then I look at you and it gives me hope. It can be done, I think to myself, as I call time on yet another failed relationship. If Dan and Hetty can fall in love and stay that way, it is possible.'

'It doesn't feel possible at the moment, he's upset with me and I don't appear to be making him happy either.' A thought occurred to me and I gasped. 'Hey, Joe joked the other day about the seven-year itch. Perhaps this is it?'

Anna frowned. 'Ignore Joe; he hasn't seen how happy you two have been for the last decade and a half. Don't give up on love. For my sake. Or I really will have to take the veil.'

The two of us laughed and I took another sip of my tea.

'Look,' she hesitated, 'I don't mean to pry but – and let's face it I'm no expert so feel free to ignore me . . .'

'What?' I said, laughing. 'Come on; out with it.'

'Well,' she pursed her lips as if choosing her words carefully, 'are you both making an effort, you know, in the romance department? I mean, please tell me it's not all buttoned-up nighties and thermal pyjamas.'

I nearly snorted my tea out through my nose. 'You do know we don't have double glazing, don't you? Our bedroom is freezing.'

'But you have each other,' she said fiercely.

My eyes softened. 'We do.'

She was right, we'd let life get in the way, or to be more precise, *pies*. I couldn't remember the last time he and I went on a date together, at least not one that didn't involve winning rosettes for our sheep. I'd make a determined effort to put romance firmly back on the menu as soon as I was back from London. I'd just have to hope he was still talking to me by then.

'I'm not giving up on love.' I sighed. 'It just seems like I'm the one making all the sacrifices, that's all.'

'That's love, though, isn't it?' she said simply. 'The more we love someone, the bigger the sacrifice we'll make for them. Look at me and Bart; prime example.'

'What do you mean?' I hitched myself back on the bed and stretched my legs out like a patient.

'When I was younger, I had one goal and that was to study medicine. No one in my family, as far as I knew, had ever gone to university, let alone become a doctor. It was more than just a dream; it was my driving force. Nothing, no one, was more important to me than that. I never let boys come between me and my studies.'

'I remember,' I said. 'You always dumped them after a couple of dates. You still do.'

'Hmm,' she agreed. 'Sometimes I lie awake at night psychoanalysing myself. Part of me wants a man to sweep me off my feet and take care of me, the other part wants to punch any man who'd even dare to suggest such a thing in the goolies.'

I chuckled. 'I think you have control issues.'

'You think?' She twirled a blonde curl round her finger contemplatively. 'Anyway, stop changing the subject. I'm trying to tell you a tale about sacrifices.'

'Sorry.' I mimed zipping my mouth.

'Heading off travelling after sixth-form wasn't planned but when I didn't get the grades for medicine I decided to make the most of the opportunity until my re-sits. I didn't even own a passport before I left college. I'd been nowhere, I was no one. I was scrawny little Anna Croft from the rough end of Holmthwaite. I thought doing the gap year thing would give me something to talk about at med school when I eventually did get there and all the posh kids were talking about their private schools and long-haul holidays.'

'Oh Anna.' My heart ached for her. 'You were *so* not a nobody. You were the brightest star in my orbit, even then.'

'Apart from Dan,' she said, looking at me with a grin.

'True enough.' I smiled, acknowledging she was right. 'I was besotted with him. And then . . . ?'

She shrugged. 'I had a ball at first. I partied in Australia and then continued to Thailand.'

'When you realized you were pregnant?'

She swallowed and nodded. She didn't need to tell me the rest, I already knew that she'd taken up a volunteering role in Thailand at a maternity hospital being run by a humanitarian charity project. A month after she'd been there she became ill and her supervisor checked her over, thinking she may have picked up a virus. But it was just a case of good old-fashioned morning sickness. The project organizers wanted to send her back to the UK but Anna begged to be allowed to stay. The only family she had at home was her grandmother and she knew she'd be livid with her for getting pregnant; and with no other means of supporting herself, she wanted to stay put and finally they agreed. The baby came early, but he was a strong and healthy little thing and when he was three months old, she decided to come back to Cumbria.

'I still wish that you'd told me,' I said softly. 'I'd have flown out to you. You needn't have gone through it alone.'

She put her pen down and swivelled her chair round to face me.

'I was so eaten up with guilt, I was better on my own.'

'Why? What was there to feel guilty about?' I sat up to study her pretty face.

She picked up her mug and stared down into it. 'I'd made such a mess of things, let people down.'

I reached a hand out to her knee. 'No one thought that. If anything, I was in awe of how well you were coping. Nineteen and a single mum. If you hadn't turned up with Bart, Dan and I probably wouldn't have started a family so young. Thank goodness we did.'

We shared a wan smile. When I miscarried a baby when Poppy was still small, I was told it was unlikely I'd ever be able to carry another child to term. I'd been heartbroken at the time, as had Dan. Anna had been my rock. I don't know what I'd have done without her.

'Good did come out of it,' she agreed. 'Anyway, we're digressing. The point I am trying to make is that although I'd set my heart on medical school, when Bart came along, I realized I couldn't go. My gran disagreed, she said I should go to uni and put him up for adoption. Can you imagine?'

I shuddered, thinking of that lovely boy growing up as a stranger, never knowing his mum.

'Unthinkable.'

'Exactly. So I sacrificed my dream career. I threw myself into caring for Bart and trained to be a nurse instead; it was easier to study nursing part time. Medicine would have been impossible. I have no regrets on that score. None whatsoever.' She wrinkled her nose. 'Okay, sometimes when I look at my bank balance I get a little twinge. But I feel rich in other ways.'

I nodded slowly as it dawned on me what she was trying to say.

'I am rich in other ways, admittedly,' I said, thinking of Sunnybank Farm with its hills and river and animals and the wide, ever-changing sky above. 'But why should I have to give up on my business idea, for the sake of my marriage?'

173

Anna took a sip of her tea and then set down her mug with care.

'I can't answer that for you, Hetty Spaghetti, but what I will say is this.' Her blue eyes stared fiercely into mine. 'Not all of us get to marry our dream man, not all of us get our happy ending. Think carefully about what you've got to lose and how much of a risk you're prepared to take. Because there are plenty of women out there who'd swoop in on Dan before your side of the bed was even cold.'

Her warning sent a shiver down my spine and an image of Gareth Brookbanks surrounded by divorcees and do-gooders popped into my head.

'Don't worry,' I murmured, giving her a hug. 'I won't do anything rash.'

'What's this: the Middle-aged Women's Appreciation Society?' said Poppy as she came back in and squeezed on the bed beside me.

'Cheeky.' I bumped my shoulder against hers and caught Anna's eye. 'Thanks for the pep talk.'

'Any time.' She held my gaze for a moment before turning her attention to Poppy. 'Sorry your daughter looks like a pirate.' She bent down in front of her and neatened the edge of her bandage. 'But if she will behave like one, what can she expect?'

I forced Poppy to sit up. 'Explain please?'

Poppy sighed emphatically and examined her nails. 'All right, but let me finish before you jump to conclusions, okay?'

I nodded.

She jutted her chin out. 'I got into a fight.'

My jaw dropped. 'Poppy!'

'Before you go bananas, just listen,' she said calmly. 'Remember that boy, Niall, I told you about . . . ?'

Anna and I listened as requested as Poppy recounted the incident. At lunchtime the boys were playing football in the playground and she and her friends were sitting on the wall watching. After the game finished, Poppy, inspired by Viv's tale of making the first move on Mike and egged on by the other girls, went up to Niall intent on asking him out on a date.

Anna looked at my daughter in surprise. 'Good for you, Popsicle.'

She lifted a shoulder nonchalantly. 'I'm a feminist; why should men make all the decisions?'

Sometimes, I thought, bursting with pride, I could do with taking a leaf out of my own daughter's book. Then I remembered that she was sitting in the sickbay wearing a bandage . . . 'Go on, Poppy, what happened then?'

'But the boys in year nine grabbed the football and started throwing it at Niall when he wasn't looking. It was horrible. He can catch but it's harder for him with only one hand, and they were doing it deliberately when they knew he wasn't expecting it.'

Anna looked aghast. 'Year nine boys? Please tell me Bart wasn't among them?'

Poppy shook her head.

'Poor lad,' I said. 'And Anna, I'm sure Bart wouldn't do anything like that.'

Anna pursed her lips. 'Hormones have a lot to answer for, believe me. I've seen it all.'

'This wasn't hormones.' Poppy grimaced. 'This was abuse, bullying, whatever, and I couldn't stand by without saying something. So I shouted at them to leave him alone.'

'That was brave of you,' I said, flicking a worried glance at Anna. As much as I applauded her independent streak, she'd be asking for trouble if she tried this outside of school.

Poppy gave me a withering look. 'I know how to look after myself.'

Anna coughed and raised her eyebrows at her bandage.

Poppy frowned. 'Anyway, Niall was laughing it off, but I could see he didn't like it. The older lads were jeering at him, saying he was worse at catching than a girl.' Poppy's eyes flashed. 'That was it. I was so mad, I charged at Andrew Margate, who's the worst of them, and kicked his shin really hard. He squealed and fell to the floor, crying; you should have seen him. Such a drama queen,' she added scornfully.

My heart melted for my feisty and fearless daughter. Bless Poppy for standing up for Niall. But I could only imagine how embarrassing it would have been for him.

'Kicking another child is never right, darling,' I said, squeezing her hand. 'No matter how good your intentions are.'

'The boys thought it was hilarious that a girl had come to Niall's rescue.' Poppy hung her head. 'Except for Niall and Andrew. Niall gave me such an evil look and then yelled at me to butt out of his business. I was so embarrassed. I turned to go back to my friends and the next thing I knew Andrew jumped up and shoved me in the back. I fell forward and hit my head on the wall and then I went a bit dizzy.'

'One of the girls ran for a teacher and we got her into my room,' Anna added.

'Niall will never go out with me now.' Poppy began to cry and dropped her head to my shoulder. 'There's no point even asking him.'

'Oh Pops,' I said, pressing a kiss into her hair. 'I think you're incredible.'

There was a sharp knock at the door and Anna got up and opened the door just enough to see who was there. It was Bart.

'Hey, you're the talk of the entire school,' he said, impressed.

'Really?' Poppy swiped at her tears. 'Cool.'

He squatted down in front of her, steadying himself with a hand on either side of her knees, and winced at the sight of her eye. 'That'll be a right shiner.'

'D'you reckon?' She smiled mischievously at him. 'Good.'

'It's your birthday soon, isn't it?'

Poppy nodded warily. 'Next week, why?'

He glanced briefly at his mum and then at me, his cheeks

turning crimson. 'I thought to celebrate you turning into a teenager, we could, you know, go out somewhere.'

I suppressed a smile; I'd always thought he had a soft spot for her.

Anna gasped and opened her mouth but before she could interrupt Poppy shook her head firmly.

'Sorry, it's against my principles.'

'What, why?' Bart sat back on his heels, crestfallen. 'Just because I work for your dad?'

'You work for *us*,' Poppy reminded him. 'And no, not because of that, because I want to do the asking for the first date I go on. It's important to me.'

I shook my head incredulously; where had my baby girl gone . . . ?

'No, sorry, not in my sickbay please, kids,' said Anna, running a hand through her blonde curls. 'The bell is about to go so—'

'Bart, will you go out with me?' Poppy blurted out.

'Sure,' he replied, looking a bit shocked.

'No way!' Anna and I said in unison.

'Why not?' Bart and Poppy demanded together.

'Because, because . . .' Anna's mouth flapped open and closed like a goldfish. Bart was growing up and it seemed as though she was doing her utmost to ignore it. Nonetheless, I came to her rescue, as I knew she would mine.

'Because you're grounded,' I said firmly, pulling Poppy gently to her feet.

Anna's shoulders sagged with relief.

'What?' Poppy stared at me amazed.

'Sorry, but you've been caught fighting at school, did you think that would go unpunished?'

'Well, pardon me for standing up to bullies,' Poppy protested, rolling her eyes at Bart. 'Adults. I will never understand them.'

Chapter 18

I set plates in front of Poppy and Dan stacked with American-style pancakes topped with rashers of crispy bacon.

'Happy birthday, darling.'

I wrapped an arm around her slim waist and pressed a kiss into her smooth shiny hair. She was still in pyjamas but she'd already straightened her hair. She must have been up at dawn.

'Thanks, Mum,' Poppy chimed.

'I love this birthday breakfast tradition.' Dan grinned, adding swirls of maple syrup to his own stack before passing the bottle to his daughter.

'Yeah, me too,' Poppy giggled. 'Except that year when Mum asked for kippers.'

The two of them shuddered and then laughed.

I sipped at my coffee and smiled; it was lovely to see them enjoying each other's company. They'd have even more time together when I disappeared off to London tomorrow, leaving Viv in charge of my kitchen for two days. There was still so much to do; I hadn't even thought about what I was going to take with me, I had pies to bake, lists to leave for Viv and, if I got the chance, I really wanted to spend some time with my husband to convince him that Hetty's Farmhouse Bakery could be good for us in the long term. My stomach swooped with nerves. I wouldn't think about that now; it was Poppy's birthday and even though we'd got up early to factor in time for breakfast and presents, we didn't have all morning.

'Can I start?' Poppy asked through a mouthful of pancake, pulling her pile of presents towards her.

'Yes, do,' said Dan with one eye on the clock. 'I've got a woman coming over early to try and sell me some new stuff for sheep scab.'

'Open this one,' I said, passing her a soft air-mail package.

'Wow.' Poppy's mouth formed a perfect 'o' as she unfolded a bikini sent by my mum.

My angel was growing up. Her face had changed over the last year, her jaw had lost it roundness and she looked like a young woman with her defined brows and cheekbones and lovely heart-shaped face. Her body was becoming more womanly too. I could look at her all day.

'Blimey, there's not much to that, is there?' Dan looked alarmed.

Poppy rolled her eyes. 'Dad, I'm a woman now, get used to it.'

'Right.' He pulled a face.

She then ruined it by slurping from a glass of blueberry smoothie and giving herself a huge purple moustache.

Dan and I laughed.

'We have a teenager, Dan,' I said softly, catching his eye.

He held my gaze and nodded. 'Yeah, I think we're doing okay, aren't we?'

I reached across the table at the same time as he did. Our fingertips touched and the ripple of relief that washed over me almost emerged in a sob. He hadn't come near me in days.

A truce, his eyes seemed to say. At last.

We stayed that way and watched as Poppy opened a package from Otis containing a hand-printed T-shirt with poppies on it; a build-your-own solar panel from Oscar, whose gifts were always ecology themed; new jeans and a couple of best-selling books about being a shepherd from Naomi and Tim; a pair of posh wellies from Anna and a necklace from Bart with a silver poppy hanging from it.

There was just an envelope from us left on the table.

Dan pushed himself up. 'Hold on a sec before you open it, Popsicle, I think I heard a car.'

Poppy groaned as Dan let himself out of the kitchen. As he opened the door, Birdie sashayed in and sat expectantly at my feet.

'He could be ages,' said Poppy, frowning. 'If I miss the bus, it's his fault.'

I dropped a piece of bacon for the cat, smiling to myself. 'He won't be long.'

Sure enough, seconds later, a diesel engine rumbled closer and closer.

Poppy wrinkled her nose. 'That sounds like a tractor, not a car.'

'Go and look,' I said, doing my best not to give anything away.

'I'm not dressed.' But she hopped over to the door and opened it. Her hand flew to her mouth and she squealed. 'No way! Mum, look!'

I went to join her. Dan was sat astride his granddad's vintage tractor. It was sparklingly clean, its red and blue paintwork shone, and there wasn't a speck of mud on it. We had tied white ribbons and balloons on it last night and it looked, for a tractor at least, very pretty.

'Happy birthday, Poppy.' Dan turned off the engine and held up the key. 'Your first set of wheels. Every farmer should have her own tractor.'

'It's really mine?' she gasped.

Dan nodded. She squealed again and flew outside, wrapping her arms round his neck. 'Thanks, Dad, Mum. I love it, I love it so much.'

Dan climbed down so Poppy could get into the driving

180

seat. She turned the engine on and released the brake. My stomach lurched.

'Dan,' I yelled, 'is that wise?'

Dan prodded Poppy's leg. 'Footwear,' he shouted above the engine noise, pointing to her flip-flops. 'Never operate farm machinery without decent shoes on.'

'Sorry.' Poppy pulled a face, realizing her mistake. She turned the engine off immediately and got down, still beaming. Dan and I exchanged proud looks. She'd be sensible; she knew how important safety was.

She crossed to where I still stood at the kitchen door and hugged me tight. 'Thanks again.' She kissed my cheek and then kissed Dan.

'You're very welcome, darling. Time to get dressed,' I said, ushering her towards the hall.

She started to dash off but paused at the door. 'I know I said I didn't want a party, but could I have a few friends round tomorrow night? We could have a sleepover in the living room. I really want to show them my tractor.' She clapped her hands together with joy. 'I even love saying it. *My* tractor. Best present ever.'

'Well, I'm away in London.' I looked at Dan. 'But Viv will be here to help out.'

'I can cope with a group of teenagers,' he said testily.

'Course you can, love. How does takeaway pizza and ice cream sound?'

'Amazing. Thanks. Don't get big-headed or anything, but you're seriously cool parents,' she said breathily.

'Oh Poppy,' I said, filling up. Dan cleared his throat in a manly way.

Poppy turned to go and then stopped again. 'I know I'm only a day older than I was yesterday, but I feel different. I feel . . . invincible.'

Dan and I watched her go. I slipped my arm around his waist. It was the first time we'd held each other since our row almost a week ago.

'She's got you wrapped around her little finger,' I said. 'Which, I think, is as it should be.'

'Maybe, but I draw the line at *all* the women in my life running rings round me.' He reached for his phone from the kitchen table, simultaneously extricating himself from my embrace. 'It feels like my opinion doesn't matter any more.'

'That's not true,' I protested, stunned that that was how he felt.

'Isn't it?'

'Dan?'

But he shook his head and left for the farmyard, muttering that he had a farm to run.

'Thanks, love. Now I'll have to hurry you, I've still got five more collections to make before setting off down south.'

The courier, a portly man with a white comb-over and a snug uniform of polo shirt and cargo trousers, swallowed down the last of his tea and stood up, anxious to go. Naomi took his empty mug from him and put it in the sink.

'There.' I pushed my hair from my sticky forehead and stepped back to admire my handiwork. Four pies in Hetty's Farmhouse Bakery boxes, baked to perfection, though I said so myself. 'All finished, in the nick of time.'

I'd been up since five, baking the pies for my competition entry. I had to supply four, all the same, and on the advice of Naomi, I'd stuck to the lamb recipe which I'd already had success with in the Cumbria's Finest contest.

Naomi stacked the four pie boxes into the big cool box which I'd bought specially and tucked ice packs around them and put bubble wrap on top.

'If there are points for aroma,' she said, 'you're a dead cert. They smell incredible.'

She held out the heavy bag to the courier, who in return passed me an electronic device to sign.

I scribbled my signature. 'You will be careful with them,

won't you? They're free-form shortcrust and prone to splitting if they get flung about.'

Some of the other competitors from the larger producers had got their own exhibition stands at Britain's Best Bites, but others, like me, would just have a presence on the Cumbria stand. Freya had arranged a specialist food courier to transport all the smaller producers' entries safely. Now all I had to worry about was getting myself there.

'Of course.' He winked. 'Unless I get hungry and then I might make one split on purpose.'

'As long as you don't start tucking into the Lyth Valley damson gin, you'll be fine,' said Naomi, showing him to the door.

I watched anxiously as he loaded the cool box into the back of the van.

'Right. Gone.' Naomi rubbed her hands together. 'You can do no more. What's next?'

'Next I do this.' I flung my arms around my sister-in-law and squeezed her tight.

'All right, steady on!' She peeled me off her and smoothed down the front of her T-shirt.

'I've got so much to thank you for,' I said, letting go of her reluctantly. 'I'd never have contemplated doing any of this if you hadn't nudged me in the right direction.'

'Nudge? Full on fireman's lift, you mean,' she said, chuckling. 'And don't thank me. Just win, that's all I ask.'

'Is that all?' I laughed. 'There'll be entries from all over the UK. Some of them will have been in the food business for years. Just getting this far is reward enough. That and meeting Harrison Finch, of course.'

As well as handing out the prizes tomorrow, the *Countryside Matters* presenter would be the guest of honour at tonight's gala event. I promised Poppy I'd try to get a selfie with him. Not that she liked him, but she thought it was hilarious that I'd had a crush on him for years.

'If you don't get your skates on you won't be going at all.' Naomi looked at her watch. 'Are you getting changed?'

I nodded and told her to follow me upstairs to help me pack while I put on some clean clothes.

'That'll do,' I said, zipping up my overnight bag five minutes later, after changing into a clean dress and running a brush through my hair. 'Ready when you are.'

Naomi followed me back downstairs and collected her car keys. 'Is Dan not coming back to the farmhouse to say goodbye?'

I checked my bag for the train tickets for the umpteenth time, not meeting her eye. 'We said our goodbyes earlier on. He and Cameron are on the upper slopes this morning bringing the sheep down, ready for clipping next week.'

We'd had a bout of flystrike earlier in the week; a common affliction suffered by sheep but one that needed urgent treatment. Without going into too much detail, it involved maggots. In some cases, Dan opted to shear them straight away to clean them up. And this time he'd given Cameron the chance to clip them and his first efforts had been impressive. So much so that Dan had decided that we'd shear our own flock this year instead of bringing in the contractors. It would mean a lot of hard work over the next couple of weeks, but it would save us a huge amount of money.

Naomi nodded. 'I'll be helping with that.'

'As a shearer?' I said, surprised. 'You're brave, most of our ewes weigh over ninety kilos and last year, some of them took great delight in struggling against the clippers for the entire time it took to relieve them of their fleeces.'

'No, I'm not that daft. Dan's asked me to be a catcher,' she said casually, walking towards the door. 'Let's go.'

I froze. 'That's normally my job. Why has he asked you?'

'I asked the same thing.' Naomi pressed her lips into a thin line. 'We had sharp words about it. Dan said he couldn't rely on your availability any more and asked if the boys were around. But they're away so I said I'd help, but I also said that I was sure you'd be there. He hadn't been so sure.'

'He said that?' I swallowed. I'd been so selfish, not realizing the impact I'd had on Dan. I'd been too wrapped up in my own little world to notice. 'He can't rely on me any more?'

'You've got a new focus and he feels threatened. He'll come round and in the meantime, I don't mind helping out.'

'But we're a team,' I murmured sadly. 'At least we were. I haven't missed shearing for fifteen years.'

What was happening to us? For the last few weeks, all we'd done was fall out and make up again on a continuous loop. It was exhausting.

I pulled out a kitchen chair and sat down, train journey forgotten for the moment. I felt terrible that Dan had felt the need to find someone to replace me. The sheep were our livelihood. The farm was everything. Hetty's Farmhouse Bakery was just a way for me to have a little independence, to do something I loved, while at the same time bringing in a bit of extra money. I'd never set out to let Dan down. And it wasn't worth it, not if it was going to continue to come between us like this.

'The last thing I wanted was to cause trouble between you two.' Naomi squeezed my shoulder. 'And if I'm honest, I didn't realize how much would be involved in running a little pie business on the side. You were making pies for all and sundry, like the old people's luncheon club, and I wanted to see you get paid for your efforts.'

'Don't feel guilty. It's not your fault, it's mine,' I said firmly. 'Poppy looks up to you because of your success with the farm shop and I wanted her to think that way about me too. I thought I could inspire her by being an entrepreneur like you.'

Her eyes lit up at that.

'Both of you flatter me. But firstly, you already inspire her every day in more ways than you know, just by being you and with the loving family life you've created. And secondly, running your own business should be guided by a burning desire within you. This is *your* journey.'

'I do have a fire in my belly for it now. In fact,' I added with an uneasy laugh, 'it's spread like wildfire. It's out of control.'

She laughed. 'I'm glad to hear it. And talking of journeys, let's get you on that train. Poppy will be gutted if you miss it. She's so proud that her mum's going to have a swanky time in London for two days.'

'She is, you're right!'

I blinked at Naomi as realization dawned: I didn't need to run a pie business to inspire my daughter. I'd already done it. I'd shown her that by doing something you love and working hard at it, you could achieve great things, and by getting as far as Britain's Best Bites, Hetty's Farmhouse Bakery had already served its purpose. I'd come back from London tomorrow night triumphant whether I'd been crowned by Harrison Finch or not; because in Poppy's eyes I was already a winner.

And that was where it would end because I was going to halt my business plans.

I'd get my marriage back on track and I'd revert to being the Hetty who always had time to help others, the Hetty who Dan loved and relied on. It was a sacrifice, because I'd set my heart on something new, but as Anna had said, the more we love someone, the bigger the sacrifice we'll make for them. And I did love Dan with all my heart.

I jumped to my feet and grabbed the notepad and a pencil. 'Please could you take my bag out; I won't be a second.'

Naomi picked up my bag and disappeared outside.

My note was only short, but I hoped it would tell Dan everything he needed to know:

Dan,
   I've decided to put Hetty's Farmhouse Bakery on ice (not literally because that would result in soggy bottoms ☺). You and Poppy and Sunnybank Farm

mean the world to me. Let's not let anything come between us again. Looking forward to shearing time with you next week.

I love you
Hetty
xxx
PS Poppy if you're reading this, STOP
PPS Go Team Greengrass!

I was humming happily to myself as I inserted the key into the door to lock it when the phone rang. I waited, letting the answerphone pick it up.

Hello? This is Gareth Brookbanks with a message for Hetty. The official taster gave your pie the thumbs-up. I'd like to trial it in four of our biggest stores. Shall we say . . . an initial order of twenty pies? Please call to discuss pricing. My number is—

I softly closed the kitchen door, not bothering to hear the rest. There was no point. I'd made up my mind. I'd go to London, I'd have my five-star adventure with my home-made pies, I'd bask in my moment of glory and then I'd come back to Carsdale and get on with the business of running a sheep farm. With Dan. And Hetty's Farmhouse Bakery would be just a delicious memory . . .

Despite all the dramas and the worries and my not inconsiderable nerves, I found myself enjoying my journey to London. The train rocked and rolled along the track, whizzing through the green fields, skimming past Morecambe Bay, so close to the coastline that I could see ripples on the sea, and then weaving through towns and cities as it threaded through the country towards London. I was served drinks and sandwiches, and chatted away to an old lady who got off at Preston and after that I sat and gazed and pondered.

Something – or rather, some*one* – dominated my musings more than any other.

Joe Appleton.

My heart fluttered every time I thought about him. I hadn't seen him again since that meeting at Appleby Farm. I'd had one or two emails, nothing more. It had been Freya who'd sent me all the details I needed for Britain's Best Bites, she who had organized my travel and my hotel and sent me the list of other local contenders. But I'd see him tonight. He was hosting a small welcome drinks thing, just for the Cumbria's Finest contingent. I had so many questions to ask him. But would I have the courage to ask the one I really wanted the answer to: which girl had stolen his heart all those years ago? Who had broken his heart so badly that he'd literally vanished from our lives? I hoped against hope that it wasn't me, because if so the next twenty-four hours would be very awkward . . .

Chapter 19

It was five o'clock by the time I slid the key card into the slot in my hotel room. My feet were aching from all the walking I'd done between tube platforms and I couldn't wait to slip off my shoes and maybe have a nap before meeting everyone in the bar downstairs. The hotel oozed old-world charm and opulence and my room was lovely: the windows had the original leaded panes of glass, the ceiling was low and had dark beams running across it. There was a double bed, a delightful French dressing table and the nightstands on either side of the bed were covered in broderie anglaise cloths. I kicked off my shoes and smiled as the floorboards creaked under foot. There'd be no chance of creeping along the corridors at night undetected in this place. Not that I would. I laughed aloud at the idea and threw myself on to my bed. The mattress was deep and luxurious, the pillows soft, and I sighed with pleasure and just as I closed my eyes I remembered a missed call from Anna. I sat up, retrieved my mobile and played the message:

Have a fab time in London, my lovely chum, enjoy every minute and make sure you get all the gossip from Joe, I want all the details. And don't even think about getting an early night and missing out on that party – I know you. Love you loads but also slightly jealous right now. Kiss kiss!

I laughed to myself, glad she couldn't see that I was already making myself comfortable on the bed, and reached

189

across to the far nightstand to put my phone down. I hadn't noticed it at first, but there was a bottle of champagne nestling in an ice bucket.

Nice touch, I thought, wondering whether this was Freya's doing. Propped up against it was a stiff envelope addressed to me. Intrigued, I reached for it, slid a finger under the flap and pulled out the card. My heart squeezed with joy: on the front was a photograph of myself as a child, kneeling on a chair in the kitchen in our old house in Holmthwaite. Propped beside me was my very first cookery book by Delia Smith. I was gripping a mixing bowl with one hand and had the electric whisk in the other. My face, my clothes, the table and the book were covered in white blobs from where I'd sprayed the cake mix by accident. But my smile was huge and my happiness was clear for all to see.

There was a lump in my throat when I opened the card and read the message from Mum.

Dear Hetty,

Look at you. I think you were five years old, do you remember? You couldn't even read the recipe by yourself. Regardless of that, and of losing most of your cake mix to the walls and every surface in the kitchen, you gave it your best shot, determined not to be beaten by any obstacle thrown in your path. You've been the same at every stage of your life. You have followed your own path, done things your own way. It has been my privilege to watch you grow and become the incredible woman you are today. And now there you are in London, competing with the best of them, because you ARE the best of them. My little Hetty, I wish I could be there to show you how much I love you. Instead, I've sent you some champagne so you can toast your achievements.

Sending you all the luck in the world, not that you need it because you are invincible.
Love
Mum xxx

I pressed the card to my chest and brushed tears from my face. Mum's choice of words couldn't have been more perfect if she'd tried. I didn't agree with them. Not one bit. It was Poppy who was invincible, not me. I gave up far too easily; I'd been taking the easy way out all my life.

'But thank you for believing in me. I love you too, Mum,' I whispered and fumbled in the side pocket of my bag for a tissue.

Instead of a tissue my fingers closed around a slip of paper. I pulled it out and my heart skipped a beat: it was a page torn from the tiny notebook Dan kept in the sheep pens to record any medication given.

My tears were now so bad I was beginning to make ugly gulping noises. I'd have to get a grip before too long or my eyes would swell. I took a deep breath and unfolded the note.

If my heart was a pie chart, the biggest slice would belong to you.
Love always, Dan xx

And then I laughed, and cried some more, and poured myself a glass of champagne because my family loved me and because I was in London being a winner.

'You know what, Dan?' I said, raising my glass to my absent husband. 'With you on my side, I think I just might be invincible after all.'

At ten past seven I was standing to attention, crammed against strangers in slinky dresses and smart suits, in a tiny but opulent private bar in the hotel. Outside this room was the main cocktail bar, equally packed with the regional food groups from the rest of the country. And at the far end of that was the ballroom where tonight's dinner would be held.

Opulent it might be, but the air conditioning was nothing to write home about and the ceiling fans were no match for the London heat, which must have been a good ten degrees higher than Carsdale's cool green hills. I flapped at the front of my rose-pink satin dress to let some air in, not wanting to be a sweaty Hetty. Poppy and Anna had helped me choose the dress. I loved it but it would be a devil for showing underarm perspiration and if I was being honest, it was a bit of a snug fit; pie-tasting had definitely taken its toll on my tummy recently. I glanced down at my legs quickly, hoping my super-fast fake tan didn't look too streaky, but decided it was fine from a distance.

I flapped at my face with a napkin and tried to catch a waitress's eye while pushing through the crowd, chin lifted as if I was looking for someone.

The two glasses of swiftly consumed champagne in my room hadn't been such a good idea, although I'd followed them up with a power nap and then a quick shower to mitigate the effects of the alcohol. And then, because I faffed about tanning my legs, I'd been short of time, so I'd made the fatal mistake of tipping my head upside down to dry my hair quickly and now whenever I caught sight of my reflection in the many, many polished surfaces in this hotel, I would get a glimpse of someone who resembled John Travolta in *Hairspray*. I had possibly never looked so much like a country bumpkin in my life.

Bouffant hair and red face aside, I was buzzing. Just being here, so far from the farm, in a glitzy dress surrounded by chandeliers and champagne, had put a massive smile on my face.

'Drink, Madam?' A waiter smiled and offered me a choice of sparkling wine, juice or water. I opted for water this time and gulped half of it straight down.

I'd been hoping to bump into Joe but by the time I'd got here the room was so packed that it was impossible to do much mingling. Despite that, so far I'd had a good chat with a lady who'd persuaded me to try adding fig jam to my apple and Wensleydale pie and I'd had an offer of a joint promotion from a couple who'd launched a range of organic gravies. It was only when I'd agreed to send a selection of pies to a farm shop in Ambleside that I remembered that after tomorrow there would be no more Hetty's Farmhouse Bakery.

The thought made my stomach quiver but I pushed it aside for now. Tonight was about being part of Cumbria's Finest, tonight I was the region's top pie maker and I was determined to enjoy it while it lasted.

I could see Joe now, he was at the far end of the room on a small stage and someone was handing him a microphone. He looked like he was about to make a speech.

I elbowed through the crowd to get a bit closer. A rush of warmth filled me just looking at my old friend, so authoritative and confident as he thanked a member of staff and took a sip from his glass. He looked ultra-handsome this evening in a caramel-coloured jacket and cream shirt, which complemented his fair colouring and thick sandy hair perfectly.

Lovely Joe. Once again I felt a pang of sadness that he'd been so unlucky in love. He deserved someone wonderful. I made a pact with myself to dig a little deeper into his personal life while I was here, to see if I could find out more about the man he had grown into, and more importantly, who he'd been running from when he left Carsdale.

He tapped the microphone to check it and a muffled sound reverberated around the room. The throng fell silent and turned towards him.

'Good evening, Ladies and Gentlemen,' Joe began.

Just then a well-known bluesy piano riff rang out. Everyone laughed.

'And welcome to the Hyde Gate Hotel.'

It rang out again. The timing was perfect. I giggled into my glass.

'I feel like I should break into song,' he said as the plinky-plonk music rang out a third time.

This time people looked round to see where the noise was coming from. A lot of them seemed to be looking my way.

'I guess now's a good time to ask you to switch your mobiles to silent,' Joe added good-naturedly.

The fourth time the ivories tinkled, someone prodded my arm.

'I think it's your phone?' murmured a lady with wiry grey hair, plump arms and rosy cheeks.

'Oh crumbs! Sorry!' I muttered.

I fumbled to mute it, not easy with a glass in my hand. It was a text alert from one of my VIP contacts. I'd had to set the volume to maximum so that I didn't sleep through my alarm earlier. I glanced at it surreptitiously. It was from Viv. Oh Lordy, please let everything be all right. The lady was now giving me stern looks so I had no choice but to put my phone back in my bag without opening the message. I eyed up the door, wondering whether to escape now before Joe began his speech properly.

'Hetty!' Joe's eyes flashed with humour as he addressed me from the platform. 'I knew you'd be trouble.'

'Me?' I stuttered, my eyes wide.

'Ladies and Gentleman, a good moment to introduce Hetty Greengrass from Sunnybank Farm in Carsdale. I think she has the honour of being our newest food brand. Hetty's Farmhouse Bakery has only been in existence for a matter of weeks, and already she can call herself an award-winning pie company. Well done, Hetty. You're a star.'

I didn't know about being a star but my face now felt like the red planet. Was that Mars? Which reminded me of the Mars bar pie I'd dreamed up earlier. I should write that down before I forgot: Mars bars and pecan nuts and possibly a dash of Bourbon too . . . I reached into my bag again

194

but the lady next to me started tutting and shaking her head crossly. I mouthed my apology and slid my hand away.

Joe lifted his glass to toast me. The rest of the room clapped and muttered their congratulations. I nodded my thanks, my cheeks aching from smiling so hard. Joe cleared his throat.

'I was brought up in Cumbria. Some of you may remember Appleton's Bakery in Holmthwaite, my family's business? I even worked there myself. I was the weedy teenager who was desperate for a broad chest and stubbly chin like my best friend Dan.'

I smiled, remembering them together. The two of them were always messing about, arm wrestling or challenging each other to eating contests. How sad that their friendship had been cut short.

'My career took me away from the area but the place, the food and, of course, the people have always retained a special place in my heart.'

I felt my cheeks redden as his gaze held mine. If he wouldn't mind getting back to his original speech soon, and away from the subject of our shared history, that would be great. A waitress stopped in front of me with a tray of drinks and raised an eyebrow.

'No thank you,' I whispered, showing her my glass of water.

'Hetty wasn't much of a cook when she was a teenager . . .'

I groaned inwardly. As if I wasn't already the centre of attention.

'In fact, I distinctly remember her serving me frozen pizza one evening.' He shook his head, laughing. 'And when I say frozen, I mean frozen. The pineapple chunks nearly broke our teeth.'

'Actually, I've changed my mind,' I said to the waitress, tapping her arm as titters rang around the room. I took a glass of champagne and knocked half of it back. If this was going to be a trip down Hetty's memory lane, I was going to need more lubrication.

Nonetheless, I couldn't help smiling at the memory his story had conjured up of Anna, him and me sprawled out on the sofas at my house watching horror movies after the pub. Dan had already gone back to Carsdale and we'd taken great delight in scaring ourselves half to death in the name of entertainment and had all ended up under one blanket, terrified. We had had great times together.

Still, I thought, sending him an admonishing look across the room, I'd rather we kept our teenage years to ourselves.

'Anyway, we've both changed since then: Hetty is now an award-winning baker and I eventually managed to grow a beard.'

The audience laughed as he scratched the end of his chin.

'Now.' His face took on a more serious expression. 'This year represents a mammoth step forward for Cumbria's Finest. We've secured significant investment via tourism channels, we have relaunched our own awards and for the first time in years, we are here in London. Not only to compete but to show the rest of the country, in fact the world, just what makes food from the Lakes unique.'

'Hear, hear,' a deep booming voice called.

'I am privileged to be in a room full of so much talent and creativity.' Joe's eyes roamed his audience all the time, but just then they rested on me. He smiled and I felt a warm fluttering sensation in my stomach. 'It is my task to curate the best our region has to offer, and I believe I've done that here tonight.'

He paused to let everyone clap. Appleton for Prime Minister, I thought, swallowing a lump in my throat. He was brilliant. I wished Dan was here to see him, he'd be so proud of his old friend.

'Cumbria not only has the best produce in the country, but also the greatest flavour innovators, recipe developers, chefs, bakers, butchers, retailers . . . You name it, if it's edible, we can make it. And I thank you. From the bottom of my heart.' Joe pressed a hand to his chest. 'Thank you for making me so proud of Cumbria. London, we're coming to get you.'

He raised his glass one last time and then, handing the microphone back to a member of the hotel staff, he stepped down from the platform.

The applause and the cheering this time was so loud, I couldn't hear myself think. For a second or two I just stood there soaking it in. Being here in this room with all these winners, I felt part of something special. I'd always loved being part of the Greengrass family, passing on the hill-farming tradition from generation to generation. But this felt different, bigger somehow. I'd done this all by myself. And it felt great.

The smile on my face was huge as I looked around, trying to catch someone's eye to strike up conversation. But everyone seemed to know everyone else and it felt rude to simply muscle in on someone else's little group. I wasn't a shy person but I was out of my comfort zone here. Posh dinners and London exhibitions were probably every day occurrences for all these professional food companies. Whereas to me it was a massive deal: bigger even than the Carsdale Sheep Fair, the village maypole festival and the pub Christmas party all rolled into one.

I decided to push my way through the crowd in Joe's direction to find him. I skirted a group of men in matching navy polo shirts and smiled my way past the lady I'd spoken to earlier about fig jam when I felt a sudden wet sensation on my back.

I turned to see a young man with straw-coloured hair blushing profusely, a champagne flute in his hand.

'Oops, sorry.' He pulled a handkerchief from his pocket and handed it to me. 'Luckily it's only champagne, not my usual tipple.'

'Oh, what's that?' I thanked him for the handkerchief and tried mopping my own back without much success.

'Rhubarb juice.' He smiled proudly. 'I've won an award for it too, actually. Here, allow me.'

I gave the hanky back and turned around so he could dab the wet patch.

'I think I may have tasted it. Did you supply bottles of it for the Sunnybank Farm Shop open day?' I said over my shoulder.

'Yes I did!' he exclaimed. 'I couldn't go myself because I was at Scout camp. I'm a leader. Not an actual Scout,' he added swiftly. 'There, that's as good as I can get it, I'm afraid.'

I turned back around and sipped my drink to hide my smile. 'Hence the hanky.'

He looked at me blankly, still blushing.

'Be prepared?' I said.

'Ah yes!' He chuckled. 'What did you think of the juice?'

I smiled, remembering the puckered face of Wilf the sheep shearer after several shots of it. 'It's . . . invigorating.'

'You're Hetty, aren't you?' His face lit up a bit more. 'I'm Rupert. I saw you on TV talking about your pies. I recorded it in case my brand was mentioned. You were very funny.'

'Not intentionally,' I said archly.

'There's no soggy bottoms on my watch, ha ha ha.'

He followed his joke up by reaching round to pat my bum. I was shocked but dealing with great hulking sheep for fifteen years had given me fantastic reflexes. Before my brain had even registered what he was doing, I stamped on his toe.

'Oof.' He doubled up, tipping the rest of his champagne over me. Down my arm this time.

'Weren't prepared then, were you?' I said, pulling the damp handkerchief back out of his breast pocket and drying myself. 'No bottoms at all on my watch.'

'I'm so sorry, I don't know what came over me,' he spluttered. 'Please accept my apologies, I'm a little overawed this evening.'

To be fair he did look shocked.

'Apology accepted,' I said, handing him back his wet handkerchief.

'Hetty!' Joe dived between us. He grabbed hold of my shoulders and kissed me on both cheeks. 'So sorry to have left you on your own all this time.'

'Actually, I wasn't alone I was talking to . . .' I looked round to see where Rupert had gone, but he'd melted into the crowd. 'Rhubarb boy.'

Outside in the corridor a gong sounded.

'That's our cue.' Joe tossed back the rest of his drink. 'I've put you next to me at dinner, is that okay?'

I was about to say that I'd like nothing more when I suddenly remembered Viv's text.

'Oh no!' I said with a gasp.

Joe looked crestfallen. 'Well, I could—'

'Sorry, no, no, it's fine.' I thrust my glass at Joe and wriggled my phone out of my bag. 'But that piano music earlier was a message from home, I'd forgotten all about it. Hold on.'

The phone had a second message alert on the screen too, this time from Poppy. I groaned as I unlocked the screen.

'Problem?' Joe asked.

'Don't know yet.'

I opened Viv's message first.

All well here. Girls are eating pizza and Dan's building them a bonfire for later to toast marshmallows. So nothing to worry about. Relax and enjoy yourself xxx

'Phew!' My shoulders sagged with relief. Poppy's message was equally lovely: no words, just a picture of her with her friends having fun.

'Everything okay?' Joe's dark eyes were full of concern.

'Yes.' I felt my heart lift. I had champagne, a five-star hotel and Joe to myself for the evening. 'Everything is perfect.'

He offered me his arm. 'Then shall we go through?'

The huge crowd in the main cocktail bar was funnelling slowly through the double doors into the ballroom at the end. Joe and I chatted easily as we ambled along, stopping to collect fresh glasses of champagne from a long table covered in a white cloth. He described the new house he was thinking of buying in Kendal and I told him about Poppy's birthday and the tractor we had given her.

'And Anna, do you hear much from her?' he asked.

'Absolutely. She's the school nurse at Poppy's school and we're still the best of friends; she makes me laugh, keeps me sane, gets me drunk . . . So you could say she hasn't changed a bit.'

'Really?' He glanced sideways at me. But he wasn't really focusing on me; he had a faraway look in his eye.

'Of course!' I laughed. 'You know what it's like where we live, friends for life . . .' My voice petered out. With the exception of him that was.

'And is she . . .' He paused to clear his throat. 'Single?'

'Yes. And I worry about that, before long her son, Bart, will want a life of his own and she's going to be lost without him.'

'Right. I'd heard she didn't train to be a doctor in the end because she had a baby.'

'Bart isn't a baby any more,' I laughed. 'He's as tall as Dan! He works for us at weekends. Lovely lad.'

'And he's into farming?' Joe said, intrigued. 'Not medicine, like Anna. How old is he?'

'Fourteen. Between you and me,' I confided, 'I think Bart is more interested in my daughter than the farm, but don't tell Dan, you'll hurt his feelings and Anna freaks out at the thought of her son going on a date.'

Joe had stopped walking and was hanging on my every word. It was the perfect opportunity to suggest he came over to the farm one day to see Dan but before I could form the words, Joe launched ahead again, steering me diagonally across the room.

'Let's check the seating plan,' he said.

There was a noticeboard propped on a stand at the entrance and Joe released my arm to study it. Three other people, two men and a woman, were doing the same thing and I stood to the side to give them space.

'There are people from John o'Groats to Land's End here tonight,' said Joe. 'Let's see if we're all mixed up or arranged in geographical order, north to south.'

One of the men laughed. 'I can't make any of it out without my glasses, the print is too small.'

His dialect was pure Cornish and my mouth lifted into a smile. With just a few words, the man had taken me right back to the time I'd spent in Padstow. How Gil and I had teased each other about our accents.

'There, look,' said the woman, tapping the board with the tip of her fingernail. 'Taste of Cornwall.'

'And we're here, Hetty, table five,' said Joe.

'Well done. Come on, Gil,' said the man, clapping his friend on the back. 'We've found our place. Table nineteen.'

Gil? I looked up at the group from Cornwall, just as one of them whirled round to look at me.

'Hetty?'

My hand flew to my mouth as I found myself looking at a man who was instantly recognizable as the boy who had mended my heart only to lose me again to Dan.

He pushed past his friends to get to me, his expression a mixture of dazed and happy. 'It *is* you, isn't it?'

'Gil Pemberton,' I murmured. 'I don't believe it.'

Chapter 20

This was mad; I had never expected to see Gil again in my life. Yet there he was, hands on hips, right in front of me, a big grin plastered on his face.

'It's good to see you!' He inched closer and I braced myself for a hug but he seemed to think better of it and patted my bare arm instead. His touch sent a shiver through my body. I felt like a teenager again.

'You too.' I scanned his face, drinking him in. 'My legs are shaking. And my hands.'

I held them out in front of me, one of them still clutching a glass.

He showed me his. 'Ditto.'

We both laughed and a ripple of joy bubbled through me.

'So what are you doing here?' He glanced at Joe briefly, who I'd completely forgotten about. Joe was staring at us, jingling his coins in his pocket.

'The food thing,' I said, flapping my hand, unable to string a sentence together. 'For Cumbria.'

'Oh, the *food thing*,' Gil teased, 'yeah, me too.'

He ran a hand through his hair. Still the colour of the Cornish sand. I was tempted to touch it to see if it was stiff with sea salt as I remembered it from early mornings spent riding foam-topped waves. He'd been slim and athletic; his muscles taut from hauling himself on to his surfboard. He'd bulked out a bit, but there was no mistaking that he was Gil Pemberton.

'Let me guess?' I raised an eyebrow. 'You're still at Pemberton Pasties?'

'Yep. Man and boy.' He puffed out his chest. 'Dad's retired now, so I'm in charge.'

I smiled, remembering his boast that he was going to surf his way around the world from championship to championship before settling down. Had he ever done it, I wondered? Or had he, like me, set his dreams aside and slipped seamlessly into adulthood?

'So Hetty Wigglesworth from Holmthwaite,' he marvelled, shaking his head. 'I'd recognize that cheeky smile anywhere.'

'You haven't changed a bit either. Except for those.' I pointed to his smart black trousers. 'I've only ever seen you in shorts.'

'I still have a "shorts unless it snows" rule.' He shrugged. 'Not that we get much snow in Cornwall.'

'I get your share,' I said. 'Usually on the days most of our ewes decide to lamb. And in Cumbria we probably only get two shorts-worthy days a year.'

'So.' He nodded slowly. 'You're a farmer's wife?'

'And pie entrepreneur,' I said airily.

Gil was still gazing at me in disbelief. 'Still got that wild red hair.'

'Copper, I call it.'

'Whatever, I loved it. Not so freckly these days, I notice?' He pretended to peer at my cheeks.

'No, but my daughter inherited my hair and my freckles.'

'You have a daughter? I have one of each.'

'Really?' I laughed. 'I thought you said that family commitments wouldn't fit in with your free-spirited lifestyle.'

'I said that?' He pulled a crazy face. 'Jeez, no, my kids are everything to me.'

'Married?' I asked.

'Yes. I found someone to replace you. Eventually.'

His brow wrinkled slightly as if he was catching hold of a

memory. I wondered if it was the same as the image my mind had, a loop of us entwined in a moonlit sea.

A hand touched my shoulder.

'You two clearly know each other well,' Joe said with an awkward laugh.

'Old friends,' Gil said easily, holding a hand out to him. 'I'm Gil from Pemberton Pasties.'

Joe raised his eyebrows, clearly impressed. 'Joe Appleton, in charge of Cumbria's Finest.'

'And isn't she just,' said Gil, winking at me.

Joe laughed. 'I'd have to agree with you there.'

I blushed; this was surreal.

Just as Gil was introducing his two friends, a couple with their own fresh seafood company in Truro, a line of black-and-white-clad waiting staff appeared from a door beside the bar.

'Take your seats now, please,' cried a stern-faced woman.

Two members of staff went to hold the double doors, and the others glided into the ballroom.

Joe placed a hand in the small of my back. 'We'd better go. Good to meet you, Gil.'

Gil and I smiled at each other. I didn't want to say good-bye, there was so much more to catch up on, so much I wanted to ask, but Joe propelled me forward.

The sight of the ballroom made my breath hitch: it was decorated with bunting, balloons and huge displays of sum-mer flowers, the perfume from which filled the air. The room was enormous and packed with table after table of happy people, dressed in their party clothes, laughing, chat-ting and chinking glasses.

Joe pointed out our table and forged in front, ploughing a path through the crowds, and suddenly Gil caught hold of my elbow.

'Can I see you tomorrow at the exhibition? Perhaps we could grab a coffee?'

I felt a frisson of guilty pleasure and nodded.

'Great, it's a date.' His lips touched my cheek and then he was gone.

I pressed my fingertips to my cheek where he'd kissed me. What was I doing? Meeting up with men wasn't me at all. 'Grabbing a coffee' wasn't me either. A loud gong sounded. I hurried after Joe and decided not to worry; I was probably reading too much into it. After all, I was in London, not Carsdale. People probably grabbed coffees with each other all the time.

'Ladies and Gentlemen,' a booming voice relayed through the speaker system, 'I give you your host for this evening, Mr Harrison Finch!'

Thunderous applause accompanied by cheering and whistling ensued. I reached my seat beside Joe just as everyone got to their feet to welcome our celebrity speaker into the room. I was busy for the next few minutes introducing myself to the others on the table, sneaking my phone out to take pictures of Harrison, who was, if it were possible, even more gorgeous in the flesh than I'd imagined. Finally, everyone settled down as plates of the most delicious lobster terrine began to appear in front of us.

I tucked into mine immediately, conscious that my food-to-alcohol ratio since arriving in London was horrendously off balance.

Joe poured us both a glass of wine. 'So how did you meet Gil from Pemberton's Pasties?'

I swallowed a mouthful of lobster and told him how I'd fled to Cornwall after splitting up with Dan and worked in his bakery.

'Free pasties and lessons in crimping,' I said cheerily, 'turned out to be the ideal therapy to mend a broken heart.'

Joe pleated the edge of his napkin. 'I was furious with Dan for what he did and the way he treated you, even if he did regret it the next day. He came to see me when he found out where you'd gone, wanting my advice.'

I blinked at him. 'And what did you tell him?'

'I told him he was a bloody idiot; I told him he'd had it all and thrown it away and that if he really cared for you, he'd leave you alone because you deserved better.' He shrugged. 'And as you know, I haven't seen him since.'

I stared at Joe. I couldn't believe he hadn't been more sympathetic to his friend, and that he could tell me about it now so casually.

'Well, I'm glad he ignored your advice,' I said evenly, 'or I'd probably still be down in Cornwall.'

He stroked a finger along his jawline. 'Would that have been such a bad thing? Gil seemed pleased to see you.'

'I resent that,' I said crossly. 'Dan and I are very happy. Besides, if I'd stayed in Cornwall I wouldn't have had Poppy and I can't imagine life without her.'

'Of course, I apologize.' He held up his hands. 'It's all ancient history now, although I wouldn't get too friendly with Gil.' He leaned forward and added in a whisper, 'He's your competition.'

I hadn't thought of that. His pasties would be in the same category as my savoury pie.

'Has he entered before?'

'Oh yes.' Joe nodded gravely. 'Pemberton's Pasties have won bronze, silver or gold for the last five years.'

'Have they really?' I said, sipping my glass of wine and making a promise to myself to make it my last. 'Then tomorrow should be very interesting indeed.'

Chapter 21

The next morning there were a few bleary eyes on the Cumbria's Finest stand at London's Olympia exhibition hall. Not mine: I'd switched to water after that first glass of wine with dinner. Joe, especially, was like a bear with a sore head, or maybe a blue-arsed fly might be a more accurate description, I thought, watching him pace the length of the corridor giving phone instructions to a lost delivery driver.

Although in his case, it was probably nerves rather than the after-effects of alcohol which had plunged him into such a dark mood. All the Cumbria's Finest finalists last night had agreed what a great job Joe had done in his first few months as chief executive, and today the pressure was on to see if all that hard work would pay off. Personally, I'd packed my low expectations along with my summer dress for my pie's performance in the Britain's Best Bites final, but I'd met such talented people last night, and tasted their wonderful food this morning, that I had every confidence that as a group we'd be returning to the Lake District weighed down with medals.

Cumbria's Finest's exhibition stand was much bigger than I'd expected and more professional too. It was on the upper floor on the balcony overlooking the main theatre kitchen where Harrison Finch would be announcing the winners later on. We had a great position next to a wide staircase, which gave us a bird's-eye view of everyone as they came up the stairs.

In fact, everything was bigger than I'd expected. Olympia was filled on both levels with every food and drink imaginable and already buyers from all over the world were strolling along the aisles tasting samples, collecting brochures and in many cases placing orders.

It hadn't dawned on me until now just what a huge event this was. I'd never been to a trade show before unless you counted the annual livestock supplies fair in Carlisle. This was far more aromatic.

'Is it me, or is it hot in here?' said Pam the Jam from behind large sunglasses. I'd got chatting to the lady with the fig jam and she'd told me to call her by her nickname – everyone did, apparently. She fanned her face with a map of the exhibition.

'It's the glass ceiling,' I agreed, raising my eyes to the curved roof above us. 'It's like being in my potting shed, but on a massive scale.'

'Everything in London is on such a large scale, you could fit my whole village high street in here.' She looked up too and then stumbled, grabbing hold of my arm. 'Oh crumbs, my head's still spinning. The bed in my room was so uncomfortable, I didn't get a wink of sleep.'

Privately, I thought the rum and cokes she'd been downing when I left to go to my room at eleven o'clock might have had something to do with it, but I kept that observation to myself. I left her spooning jam into a cut-glass dish and arranging broken crackers on a plate for tasting. Three of my pies were already set out beautifully on vintage plates that Anna and I had found in a charity shop. The fourth was right now being judged in the grand theatre kitchen.

Joe had finished his phone call and was now doing a final inspection of our stand.

'Okay, listen up,' he called, beckoning us all into the middle of our area. He cracked his knuckles nervously.

'The judges have had everything from us that they need,' he said. 'We've done all we can. There'll be an announcement in an hour or so and you'll be called to the theatre for the results. I shall stay here to man the stand but I'll be rooting for you all. Any questions?'

We all shook our heads.

'In that case, enjoy your day and network like bosses. Oh, one final thing, there's a rumour that Harrison Finch is on his way round – could be a good photo opportunity for your businesses, so make the most of it.'

My stomach fluttered; I was definitely up for that. I'd taken a few blurry ones of him last night, but I'd been so far away that he could have been anyone. In fact, from a distance, he really did look like my husband.

I'd thought about Dan a lot last night. Being with Joe, who was so attentive, and then bumping into Gil, who couldn't wipe the huge smile off his face, had really given my ego a boost. I felt feminine and desirable for the first time in ages. But that didn't mean I was about to run off and have an affair, far from it. I loved Dan and I wanted him to know exactly how much.

I was going to follow Anna's advice, I decided, and have a huge overhaul of my nightwear. I mean, no one likes to go to bed with someone in more layers than an Arctic explorer, do they? And a regular date night. That was something else we had to work on. Now that Poppy was thirteen, we could perhaps start leaving her on her own for an hour or two. We could pop out for a walk, or go to the pub. Whatever we did, we needed to spend time away from the farm, just the two of us. I'd fallen asleep dreaming up all sorts of plans for a relaunch of our love life . . .

I took my phone out of my pocket and perched on one of the display tables. Dan had texted me earlier to see how I was. He'd been up and out with Cameron taking fifteen lambs to market this morning. He'd left Viv in charge of the slumbering teenagers and had written a list of easy jobs for Bart to get stuck into before he got back around lunchtime.

I took a few quick snaps of the stand and sent the best

one to Dan. He sent me back a thumbs-up emoji and then a couple of seconds later a picture of a red Border collie puppy came through, looking the spitting image of Rusty.

'Oh, adorable,' I murmured to myself. I swallowed hard. I swiped the picture away and closed my eyes. I wasn't ready to replace Rusty with another dog, not when the thought of him could still reduce me to tears.

'It's him! It's Harrison coming up the stairs,' Pam the Jam squealed.

'Just relax,' said Joe, making a calming gesture with his hands. 'Just act naturally.'

'Food from the Lakes,' Harrison Finch said, beaming and opening his arms wide as he approached us. 'Could there be a fairer sight?'

Yes, I thought, fanning my face, I'm looking at it.

The butterflies were on the rampage in my stomach; he was so much better looking in real life than I'd imagined. I had to take some pictures; Anna was going to be so jealous.

'Oh my God, he is such a hotty!' said Pam in a choked voice. 'Look at that bum!'

She elbowed me so viciously that my phone flew out of my hands and straight into Rupert's jug of rhubarb juice. She gasped. 'Ooh, sorry pet!'

'My juice!' Rupert cried.

'My bloody phone!' I yelped, plunging my hand into the bottom of the jug.

'Keep it together, guys,' Joe hissed under his breath, stepping around the drama to meet and greet Harrison, who was looking a bit nonplussed at the lack of welcome from the Cumbrian contingent.

'That'll have to be thrown away now,' said Rhubarb Rupert, pouting. 'It's not cheap, you know.'

'Neither was my phone,' I muttered darkly. 'Besides, you owe me one after your behaviour last night.'

Rupert paled and glanced quickly at Joe to check he wasn't

within earshot. But Joe was handing Harrison pieces of Cumberland sausage dipped in delicious onion marmalade from Coniston.

I shook the phone vigorously to remove as much liquid as possible while Rupert grabbed the jug, scowling, and went to dispose of the juice. Pam repeated her apology and handed me a tissue.

'Over here,' said Malcolm from Grasmere Grains, offering me a bag of couscous. 'Turn it off and stick it in this to let it dry off.'

By the time I'd found a spare bowl and buried my phone in the couscous, Harrison had moved on to the Taste of the West Midlands stand further along and I'd missed my chance for a photograph.

'Did he even taste my pie?' I asked Pam dejectedly.

She chewed her bottom lip. 'No, love, sorry; he said he's gluten free.' She perked up. 'But he took a jar of my jam.'

Half an hour later word got round that the judges had finished their tastings in the theatre kitchen and were back in the green room making their final deliberations. I'd recovered from the phone incident, although the phone itself hadn't. I could switch it on, but nothing came up on the screen. Malcolm agreed to look after it for me and promised to tell me as soon as it showed signs of life.

The atmosphere had fallen a bit flat after the Harrison debacle and no one was in the mood to 'network like a boss' as Joe was hoping, so I was really glad when a familiar figure tapped me on the shoulder.

'Do you fancy coffee?' said Gil.

'Perfect timing,' I replied.

There was a refreshments kiosk selling drinks further along the top floor and we headed over there. The heat was stifling. I was used to being outside with no shortage of fresh air. Being in this huge greenhouse of a building was making me feel claustrophobic. I undid another button on my shirt and flapped the collar.

'Shall we go and stand near that oven?' Gil said, waggling an eyebrow. He pointed to the Essex Pizza Company stand, where a man was sliding bubbling pizzas from a clay oven on to a huge slate board. 'Just in case you feel like undoing anything else.'

I gave him a stern look. 'It's all right for you in your shorts.'

We stopped and ordered two iced coffees. I looked at his tanned legs while the barista made our drinks.

'I've been here before,' he said, handing over money and refusing my offer of cash. 'I know all the tricks.'

Just then a fire exit door opened and a man holding cigarettes and matches came through it.

'Like this one, hurry up,' Gil continued. 'Hold the door please, mate!'

The man managed to catch the door before it closed and we took our drinks over. Gil went out ahead of me.

'It's not a great view, and not sure how fresh it is, but it is air,' he said, holding the door open for me.

I laughed when I saw the view. We were surrounded by rooftops, not an inch of greenery in sight. Immediately outside the door was the small platform at the top of a fire escape, with metal stairs that wound their way down to ground level. The view below was of rows and rows of industrial-sized dustbins and recycling skips. Hunched between some of them were homeless people in sleeping bags. There was a dustbin lorry trying to reverse into the small area and two refuse collectors were attempting to move the homeless people out of the path of the lorry.

'Gosh, this makes me appreciate home,' I murmured.

Gil grabbed a plastic crate and used it to wedge open the fire door. 'There, now we'll hear if they make any announcements.'

We leaned over the railings and sipped our drinks.

'So,' we both said at the same time and then laughed.

'You go first,' said Gil.

'Um.' I picked at a bit of loose paint on the railings. There was so much I wanted to know. Like was he okay after I left, who did he marry, did he ever think of me . . . ? But I couldn't ask those things; I had no right. He'd been so good to me and I'd simply upped and left the very next day after the first and only time we'd made love. It felt wrong asking about his personal life.

'I still think about you,' he said. 'You were the first girl to break my heart.'

'I'm sorry. If it's any consolation I did feel bad about it and I still think of you from time to time.'

'Hey, listen.' He shuffled closer and bumped my shoulder gently with his. 'It was a long time ago. Tell me about you. I bet your husband's proud of his award-winning wife?'

'Hmm.' I wrinkled my nose. 'He is. But I'm needed on the farm, and he sees Hetty's Farmhouse Bakery as an unnecessary distraction. So I've decided that after today I'm mothballing the business until I have the time to devote myself properly to it.'

'You're kidding?' He stared at me. 'He must be mad. If my wife wanted to start her own business, I'd get the flags out. Not that that's very likely,' he added bitterly. 'She's far happier spending money than earning it.'

'Anyway,' I said, keen to steer the topic away from our respective spouses, 'I never really planned to start a company, it wasn't my burning ambition. To begin with I just saw it as a way to make my daughter proud.'

'I'm sure you couldn't fail to do that,' he said softly.

I glanced at Gil. He was staring at me like I was the most fascinating thing on the planet and I knew I shouldn't encourage it but just lately Dan had been looking through me like I was invisible and it felt so lovely to be listened to.

'I've always made pies, ever since you showed me how to crimp pastry.'

'So . . .' His lips twitched. 'You make Cornish pasties?'

'No, no,' I clarified quickly, 'they are pies, big round pies.'

He laughed, a delicious gurgle of a laugh, and I laughed too. This was such fun, just being here chatting and laughing. I couldn't remember the last time I'd felt so relaxed.

I knew I should say something, edge away, start talking about something like what a terrible problem we'd had with maggots recently or how awful it was when one of our ewes died because she got her head stuck in the lamb feeder but I couldn't. All I could do was stare at his mouth. I hadn't noticed him move but there he was, right in front of me, so close that I could feel the heat from his face, smell his scent, outdoorsy and fresh, like Dan but where he smelled more often than not of lanolin, Gil smelled of the sea.

'Hetty.' He was staring at my lips.

'Hmm?' It was like I'd been hypnotized; I was completely under his spell. I could feel my body pulling me towards him.

'Would all finalists in the Britain's Best Bites competition please take their seats in the main theatre kitchen,' rang out the voice sharply across the tannoy.

I stepped away from him, but Gil reached a hand to cup my face.

'We should get back,' I said weakly.

'Wait.' Gil's eyes bored fiercely into mine. 'You and me, we were so good together.'

He was right; we had been. But that was a long time ago. I had a life, a daughter, a husband, for goodness' sake.

'We hardly started,' I said, shaking my head.

'Perhaps we should pick up where we—*Jesus*.'

He sprang away from me as the metal fire escape door was slammed back against its hinges and Joe appeared in the doorway.

'So here you are.' Joe had a thunderous expression and he was out of breath.

'Hi,' I spluttered. 'We were just coming—'

'It's . . . it's your daughter.' He thrust my phone at me. I looked at him again; it wasn't anger on his face, it was fear.

Time seemed to stand still. The sounds of the busy hall, the beeping of the reversing lorry . . . it all faded away.

Joe and Gil listened grimly as I pressed the phone to my ear. 'Poppy?'

'Oh Mum,' she sobbed. 'Please come home.'

'Darling, what's the matter?' Blood began to pump through my veins so loudly I could hardly hear her. 'What's that noise in the background?'

'It's the air ambulance. There's been an accident. Please hurry back.'

'Who's injured?' I yelled, forcing a finger into my ear. 'Who?'

'Dad and Bart. But Bart's worse, I . . . I think he's going to die.'

Chapter 22

The train was approaching the station. I was nearly home. As the engine slowed, my heart rate gathered speed with anxiety.

'Come on, come on,' I muttered impatiently.

It had been the longest afternoon of my life; I don't think I relaxed my muscles once during the entire journey. I had my arm through the train window, hand on the handle, waiting for the doors to unlock. I could see Naomi and Poppy on the platform, desperately trying to spot me.

I'd not even hung around to say my goodbyes in London. We'd already checked out of the hotel, so all I had to do was collect my overnight case from the luggage office at Olympia, jump in a cab and catch the first train back to Cumbria. Joe had texted me several times to tell me he was thinking of us and to ask would I please keep him abreast of the news. I hadn't replied. I couldn't face him yet, I felt so guilty about everything. I had tried to call Anna, but her phone was permanently on voicemail, but I had spoken to Naomi and she'd told me what she knew, which wasn't much: Cameron had been driving the trailer when it overturned and hit Bart and Dan. Bart had been airlifted to Cumbrian Royal Infirmary where there was a trauma team who could treat him. Because Dan's injuries were less serious, air paramedics had left him to travel to hospital by ambulance so they could focus on saving Bart's life. Viv had gone with him and

Poppy had had to be left behind, traumatized, and once again it had been Naomi to the rescue; she'd dashed over to the farm as soon as she could to collect her.

Finally, the doors unlocked and I flew out of the carriage and raced along the platform, my heart pounding with relief at just being back on my home turf.

'Mum, you're home!' Poppy wailed, throwing herself at me. 'It was all my fault.'

'Oh, baby girl. I'm sure that's not true. I'm so sorry I wasn't here when you needed me.'

I felt a surge of love for my red-faced, tear-stained daughter. So different from the giggling, happy one sharing pizza with her mates last night. I wrapped my arms around her tightly, pressing my cheek to the top of her head. Her body was trembling and for a couple of seconds I just rocked her from side to side, sending up a million thank-yous that she hadn't been injured too.

'It was an accident, Pops,' said Naomi levelly, ruffling her niece's hair. 'Goes with the territory in farming, I'm afraid. Glad you're back, though, Hetty. Nothing beats a cuddle with Mum.'

A pang of guilt shot through me for not being here sooner and I gave Poppy another squeeze.

'I repeat: an accident,' said Naomi, catching my expression. 'So *you* can stop beating yourself up too.'

She took my bag from me and with a hand on my back guided us towards the car park. It was pouring with rain and despite being June it was cold and grey and I shivered in my short-sleeved dress.

'Gran wouldn't let me go to the hospital with her and Dad,' said Poppy, still clinging to me, tears streaming down her face. 'But Cameron looked after me, made me hot chocolate for shock. He said he'd stay at the farm until one of us gets back.'

'And who's comforting Cameron? No doubt he'll be in shock too?' I asked.

217

'Tim's on his way to help,' said Naomi. 'So he won't be in sole charge for long.'

In other circumstances we'd have all laughed at that; Tim was as comfortable on a farm as a snowman in a heatwave. But I was grateful for any support today.

'Thank you,' I managed to say, despite the lump in my throat. 'Is there any more news?'

'Not since we last spoke, but Dan should be out of X-ray by now.'

'Oh God.' I felt sick. My lovely Dan, injured and in pain while I was standing on a fire escape making cow eyes at my ex-lover. I was a truly terrible person. I didn't deserve him. My mouth was so dry I could barely speak. 'And Bart?'

She shook her head and shot me an anxious look over Poppy's head. 'We can't get any information. Mum keeps asking the hospital staff but other than saying that Anna had arrived and that he was in the best possible place, they wouldn't tell her anything as we're not family.'

Anna and Bart had no other family. My insides clenched. Poor, poor Anna; she'd be a mess. At least the Greengrass clan had each other to fall back on for support at times like these; she had no one.

We reached Naomi's van with its Sunnybank Farm logo on the side of it. Poppy peeled herself off me and clambered into the middle seat at the front. Naomi opened the rear doors, stowed my bag inside and glanced over her shoulder to check Poppy was out of earshot.

'There is news, but I haven't told Poppy,' she whispered.

'Go on?' I stepped closer.

'Bart hasn't regained consciousness yet, as far as we know.'

'Bloody hell.' My stomach sank.

'He's going into theatre for surgery on his leg as soon as they can fit him in. They're waiting for the results from the scan to find out what's causing his unconsciousness, and in the meantime he's been sedated.'

I felt sick. 'Poor boy.'

She nodded gravely. 'But he got to the hospital within the golden hour; that will maximize his chances of recovery.'

A sob escaped and I pressed a hand to my mouth. I'd only been away from home for little more than a day. How could so much go wrong in such a short time?

Naomi rubbed my arm. 'You look like you're on your last legs, Hetty. Do you want to go home first?'

'No, please take me to the hospital,' I said firmly. 'I need to be there; I need to do something.'

Naomi dropped us off at the entrance and then headed back to the farm. Poppy and I took the lift up to the second floor and followed numerous corridors through the hospital to find the ward Dan had been assigned to.

'There's Gran,' cried Poppy, spotting Viv halfway down the busy ward. She was refilling a water jug from a tap. We rushed over.

'Where's Dad?' Poppy demanded.

Viv pointed him out and she dashed straight across. I made to follow her but Viv caught my arm.

'I blame myself,' she said in a wobbly voice. Tears shone in her eyes. 'This could all have been prevented. If only I hadn't let the dogs out.'

She didn't look her glamourous self today. Her bobbed hair, normally so sleek and perfectly curled under, was sticking out in all directions; there were stains down the front of her jumper, which may have been blood, and she looked old and frail. My heart went out to her. I took the jug and hugged her.

'If we're going to apportion blame, then I'm the guilty one,' I said. 'If I hadn't been away, you wouldn't have been at the farm. So we'll have no more of that talk.'

She rubbed a weary hand through her hair. 'Thank goodness all Poppy's friends had already been collected and were spared the ordeal.' She shuddered. 'It's a sight I'll not forget in a hurry.'

219

I put my arm round her shoulders and together we crossed the ward to where Poppy had draped herself over Dan in bed. He was propped up, naked to the waist with wires protruding from sensors on his chest. On his right side his hand and wrist were bandaged and his arm was in a sling, his other hand had a large dressing on it with a clip on his finger. His face was clammy and grey and contorted in pain.

'The wanderer returns.' Dan managed a weak smile and then winced as he tried to lift himself up. 'I've missed you.'

My face burned with shame.

'I leave you alone for five minutes,' I joked pathetically, sliding my arms around his neck. I breathed him in and closed my eyes, trying to swallow my tears.

Poppy moved to the end of the bed and sat cross-legged by his feet and Viv rearranged his pillows.

'Fractured his collarbone,' she said briskly. 'And a few nasty cuts to his hand. He'll live.'

'I'm glad you're here,' said Dan, kissing my hair. 'I might get a better class of sympathy.'

Viv chuckled and pressed a loving hand to her son's good shoulder.

'I know Bart's still really ill,' said Poppy in a small voice, 'but I'm so glad to have you two back in the same room.'

I smoothed a hand over her cheek. 'I won't go anywhere ever again, I promise.'

Dan gritted his teeth. 'I'll never forgive myself if, if anything . . . happens to that lad.'

I exchanged glances with Viv; I didn't know how much Dan had been told. Viv picked up her handbag and held out her hand to Poppy.

'Come on, let's go and find a vending machine, I bet your mum's parched.'

I shot her a grateful smile and eased myself gently on to the bed as I watched them leave.

'If you don't want to talk about it I understand,' I murmured, smoothing his hair from his forehead. 'But Cameron is usually really good at manoeuvring the trailer. What happened?'

'Where to start?' He frowned. 'It was one of those nightmare scenarios when everything went wrong at once.

'Cameron was driving the Land Rover and I got out to guide him while he reversed the trailer into position. Bart was waiting at the back to help me uncouple it from the jockey wheel and Poppy was trying to get the tractor out of the shed. The dogs shot across the yard and frightened Poppy, she hit the shed door with such a crash that Cameron's foot slipped off the clutch. The Land Rover shot back and the trailer tipped over. I managed to roll out of the way and it just clipped my shoulder. Bart copped the worst of it. It could have killed him. It still might. God, Hetty, it was awful.'

'You mustn't blame yourself,' I said, seeing Dan so close to tears.

He hung his head. 'The buck stops here. With me. Regardless of who's to blame. And I feel sick to my stomach.'

Just then a nurse appeared at the foot of the bed and unhooked a clipboard. Dan swiped at his eyes quickly.

'You must be Hetty,' she said with a smile and I nodded.

'Now, Dan, let's have a look at your obs,' she said, moving to the monitors and jotting down numbers on her chart.

'I'm fine,' said Dan.

'You are indeed. These can come off now.' She took the clip from his finger. 'Looks like you've avoided concussion, but just to be on the safe side, I want you to stay put for the rest of the day.'

'Ouch.' Dan pulled a face as she peeled his chest hairs away with the pads.

'Need any more pain relief?' she asked.

'I do now,' he grumbled.

'That was nothing,' she chuckled as Dan rubbed his sore chest. 'They have no idea, do they?'

221

I looked down and fiddled with the edge of the sheet. 'None at all.'

I knew she was referring to hair removal, but it felt as if she was talking about my indiscretions in London. Technically, I'd done nothing wrong, but would it have stopped at nothing if Joe hadn't disturbed us? Thank goodness I never got to find out.

'So how did you get on in London? Did you get your kiss?' she asked.

'Pardon?' I blinked at her, feeling heat rise to my cheeks.

'Harrison Finch?' She winked at me. 'I've been hearing all about a baking competition from your mother-in-law. Apparently, you've got the hots for him and if you won you'd probably get a kiss off him.'

'Oh,' I said with an awkward laugh. 'That.'

She prodded Dan. 'Listen to her, making light of it. Hasn't she done well?'

He groaned and rubbed a hand over his face. 'Sorry, love, with all this happening I never asked how it went in London.'

'No celebrity kisses,' I said, praying that my expression didn't give me away. 'I left before the results were announced.'

Which was true, but in fact I did know the result because Pam the Jam had called me and left a message on my voicemail.

The spring lamb pie from Hetty's Farmhouse Bakery had won the silver award, losing out on gold to Pemberton's Pasties. Joe had accepted it on my behalf. I'd won the runner's up prize of two thousand pounds and the honour of being allowed to put silver Britain's Best Bites stickers on my packaging. In theory, I now had everything I needed to make Hetty's Farmhouse Bakery a success. It was a fantastic outcome, or at least it would have been. Now it felt like a hollow victory. None of it mattered any more and the last thing Dan needed to hear was news of my success after the day he and Bart had had.

'Right, that's you done, Mr Greengrass. You can take these now.' The nurse handed him a glass of water and a small plastic pot with some tablets in it. 'You'll be in overnight, but unless you show any other signs of trauma, the doctor should discharge you tomorrow.'

She hung the clipboard back in its spot at the end of the bed and, with another friendly smile, left us for the next patient. Dan muttered that he didn't have any pyjamas and I offered to go and have a look in the patients' shop downstairs in the foyer but he shook his head.

'I want to know about Joe, did you see much of him?'

'Um, a little.' I bit my lip, remembering when I met Joe at Appleby Farm and how I promised Dan that from now on I wouldn't keep secrets from him.

'Oh?' He cocked his head to one side. 'Tell me more.'

He knocked the tablets back, and took a gulp of water to wash them down with.

'He told me that he came to see you after I left for Cornwall and that you had a row. I never knew that.'

He dabbed his chin and folded his arms across his chest. 'No, I didn't tell you because . . . Well, I guess I already felt bad enough about us splitting up, I went to him hoping for a sympathetic ear . . . Anyway, then Dad died and it put things into perspective. I loved you and wanted you back and I decided to do something about it.'

I nodded, taking this in. But after Mike's funeral when we realized Joe had moved away without telling us, why hadn't Dan mentioned it then? Had Joe told him that he had feelings for me?

Dan reached for my hand and squeezed it. 'What else did he say?'

I looked into his brown eyes and my heart leapt for him. Should I share my suspicions? It was so long ago, did it really matter now?

'Hetty, I can read you like a book, what is it?'

'A bit awkward really,' I said. 'I get the impression that he

223

may have been in love with me in sixth-form. A bad case of unrequited love, and that was why he lost touch with us.'

Dan choked, spraying me with water. 'What? Did he say that?'

I shook my head, taking his water from him and passing him a tissue. 'He just said he'd been in love, he didn't say who with.'

His eyes narrowed. 'He didn't try anything on in London, did he?'

I blushed. 'No, no, of course not.' *Joe* hadn't. Gil might have been about to, though . . .

'Well, it's all making sense now.' He nodded, staring into the distance.

'That's what I thought,' I said, biting my lip. 'I feel terrible, don't you?'

He blinked at me. 'I mean, about you winning the Cumbria's Finest competition. It was a fix.'

'He wasn't on the judging panel,' I gasped, appalled, 'so it wasn't a fix. I won on my own merit.'

'Can you be sure?' He picked at the bandage on his right hand.

I stared at him, fighting back a sharp retort and focused on deep breaths. Dan had been through hell today, and Bart was still going through hell. This wasn't a day for arguing, it was a day for kindness and love.

'As sure as I can be.' I leaned forward and kissed his cheek then stroked a finger along his stubbly jaw. 'Anyway, how Joe feels about me doesn't change the way I feel about you. I love you, Dan, and when you get out of here, how about we go away for a night, have a proper date, just you and me?'

He lifted his eyes to mine and his face softened into a sad smile. 'I'd like that. And I'm sorry for saying it was a fix. Perhaps I have got concussion, after all. I don't know what I've done to deserve you,' he said huskily, 'but it must have been good.'

I kissed his cheek again and seconds later Viv and Poppy returned carrying a tray of plastic cups.

'Look, if it's okay with you, I'd like to go and find out how Bart's doing,' I said. 'Your mum and Poppy will keep you entertained.'

'Sure.' He closed his eyes briefly and groaned. 'This is such a bloody nightmare. Give them my love and tell Anna I'll be along tomorrow just as soon as I'm allowed to move around.'

'She'll like that,' I said and pressing another kiss to his cheek, I left my family in search of my poor godson and my best friend.

It took me a while to find them. Bart was currently being treated on an adult intensive care ward due to lack of space in the children's unit. I pressed the buzzer to be let in and waited. There was a porthole window in the door and I looked through it to see if anyone was coming. My stomach churned; on the right-hand side in the closest bay to the door I could just make out the small figure of Anna, sitting on a chair next to a bed. All I could see of Bart was a mound under the covers. There seemed to be some sort of frame under the sheets at the bottom of the bed. Anna was leaning forward, her forehead resting on the bed. She looked like she was praying, which she may well have been doing . . .

A nurse opened the door and smiled enquiringly. I gulped in some air and pointed to Bart's bed and managed to stutter his name. She nodded and after I'd used the hand sanitizer, I tiptoed towards them.

There were six beds in this part of the ward, a nurse positioned at the end of each one. It was deathly quiet in here, only the faint sounds of the equipment beeping and whirring and ventilators sucking and hissing broke the silence. I stopped a couple of paces from Bart's bed to gather myself; my lungs were tight with the effort of not crying. My godson, who I'd last seen full of life and bouncing into the sickbay at school to visit Poppy, was lying motionless on his back with his head turned towards his mum. But his eyes were unseeing. His hair had been shaved and there was a huge dressing on the back of his skull. His face was covered with an oxygen mask, he had cannulas in both hands and two IV drips stood between the bed and a bank of flashing monitors. My legs trembled as I approached.

The nurse sitting at the end of Bart's bed looked up with a smile.

'Anna,' she said softly, shaking my friend's arm. 'Visitor.'

'Hmm?' Anna peeled herself up from the bed. Her face crumpled as she turned and saw me. 'Hetty. My boy, my beautiful boy.'

I dropped to my knees in front of her and held her close and cried with her while she sobbed soundlessly into my neck. All the time, she kept Bart's hand in hers.

'I'm here. It's okay, it's okay,' I soothed.

'Yeah.' Her eyes were red and her nose was running. 'He'll probably wake up any second and tell me he's been listening to me the whole time, won't he?'

'I hope so,' I said, smoothing her damp curls from her forehead. My heart went out to her, I couldn't imagine being in a worse situation than this.

The nurse handed us both tissues.

'Thanks, Kelly,' I said, reading her name badge.

'This is my best friend, Hetty,' Anna mumbled, swiping at her face. She looked exhausted.

Kelly smiled at me. She was about my age, with her blonde hair tied neatly back in a ponytail. I didn't know how she did it: look so calm and serene whilst sitting watching a fourteen-year-old boy fight for his life. But I was glad she did; I drew strength from her and bent over Bart. I kissed his cheek and then pulled up a chair.

'Anna, Bart is a fighter, he'll pull through this, won't he?' I looked at Kelly for answers.

'We're doing everything we can to give him the best

chance of making a full recovery.' The nurse stood and moved to take readings from the monitors at the head of the bed. She checked the cannulas and made notes. 'His obs are good but we'll know more when we get the CT scan results.'

Anna gazed at her son.

'I don't know what I'd do. I just . . .' She did a hiccupping sob. 'I'd do anything to swap places with him.'

'I know.' If anything like this happened to Poppy, I didn't know how I could bear it. My chest was tight and I forced myself to take deep breaths.

She leaned her face close to his. 'Bart darling, can you wake up? It's Mum, come on, open your eyes. Joke's over.' She attempted a half-hearted laugh but her cheeks were wet with tears.

Kelly placed a hand gently on her shoulder. 'We're keeping him asleep for now, Anna, remember? He's sedated for his own good.'

Anna nodded blankly at her. 'Course he is, I just . . . I, I, everything is so blurred.'

Kelly and I exchanged concerned looks.

'Why don't you two ladies go for some tea?' she suggested. 'Bart and I will be fine.'

Anna shook her head. 'He might wake up. I want to be here when he wakes up. He has to know I'm here, I'm all he's got.'

I shot Kelly a grateful smile for trying. 'Perhaps I'll manage to persuade her when the doctor's been.'

Kelly looked across as the door to the ward opened. 'Speak of the devil, or should I say *God*, here he is now.'

A clean-shaven man with dark skin, strong brows and thick glossy hair strode over.

'Bart's mum?' He looked from me to Anna.

She sat up to attention and swallowed hard. 'Yes? I'm Anna Croft.'

'Dr Parr.' He held out his hand and Anna grabbed it and held it with both of hers.

'What's happening? What's wrong with him? Is his skull fractured? And please don't fob me off, I'm a nurse.'

'Okay.' The doctor nodded. He handed his notes to Kelly and squatted down in front of Anna, balancing his elbows on his thighs.

'Right, Anna. He hasn't sustained a fracture, but there is some swelling on the brain at the back of the head where he suffered the injury.'

She whimpered. 'Oh God.'

'However,' he continued, holding her gaze, 'apart from the contusion, the scan hasn't shown anything that would indicate lasting damage.'

'Why is it swollen?' I asked, adding, 'I'm not a nurse.'

He scrunched his brows together and then turned to Kelly. 'Pass me the notes please, Nurse.'

She handed him the clipboard. He flipped over a piece of paper, drew a cloud-like shape on it and held it up to show us.

'A contusion, like Bart sustained, causes localized swelling. But the brain is very good at compensating for itself. It's made up of four areas, see?'

We both nodded and he separated the shape into four. 'But if one experiences trauma, as in Bart's case, and swells,' he adjusted his diagram to show one larger area, 'the other parts can reduce in size temporarily to compensate.'

'So he's going to be okay?' Anna's eyes bored into him. 'Is that what you're saying?'

I held my breath and wrapped an arm around Anna's shoulders, willing Dr Parr to say what Anna needed to hear.

He gave her a sympathetic smile. 'I'm saying we're confident that there are no secondary injuries and that there is no evident medical reason that Bart will remain unconscious.'

Anna started to cry softly and nodded her head. 'Thank you, Doctor.'

'When do you think he might wake up?' I asked, passing Anna another tissue from Kelly's box.

Dr Parr stood up and scanned through the notes on the clipboard.

'Right now, it's all about neuro protection,' he said, 'giving Bart's brain the optimum conditions to rest and avoid stress. We'll keep him sedated to give him recovery time. Then tomorrow we'll withdraw the sedatives and monitor him closely.'

I looked at Bart, at the fuzzy hair on his chin, his long blond lashes and high cheekbones, just like his mum's, and felt a swell of love for my sweet, kind-hearted godson. He had such a bright future ahead of him and I willed him with all my heart to get better as quickly as possible.

'In the meantime,' the doctor said, looking at me, 'he is booked in for surgery on his ankle. I suggest you try to persuade Anna to rest while she can. I'm afraid the waiting is going to be excruciating for her.'

'No way. I'll be here the whole time,' said Anna, not lifting her eyes from her son. 'I'm not leaving this hospital until I can take Bart home with me.'

'Thought you might say that.' Dr Parr smiled. He patted Anna's shoulder gently. 'In that case, I'll leave you in Kelly's expert hands and I'll see you tomorrow.'

The doctor left us then and Anna and I leaned closer and hugged each other.

'I'd better go too,' I said finally. 'I should get back to the farm and sort out—'

My voice broke off. I'd been about to say the trailer. Goodness only knew what state the yard would be in after it had tipped up. And I'd still have farm chores to do. But I closed my mouth; the last thing Anna needed to hear was about the details of the accident. I was half surprised she hadn't mentioned it. But as I looked at her, her eyes trained on her son, I realized that none of that mattered right now. She didn't have headspace for anything else; she didn't care how the accident happened or who was to blame, she just wanted her boy back.

'Of course.' Anna smiled at me sadly. 'Your family need you. It's times like these I wish Bart and I had a proper family around us.'

I fought hard to hold back the tears as I stood up. 'There's me, Anna. You'll always have me.'

'Promise?'

'Promise.'

'No matter what?'

I wiped my eyes, kissing her one last time.

'No matter what.'

Chapter 23

The next morning was Sunday. I set off early for the hospital in my Renault. The petrol gauge was almost on empty, but none of the petrol stations were open yet. I had enough to get myself to the hospital, but I'd have to stop on the way back. The roads were quiet and I got to the hospital in no time despite it being so far from home. I picked up a take-away coffee for Dan from the café on the ground floor and headed to his ward.

I found Dan out of bed and pacing the floor in borrowed pyjama bottoms. He looked like a caged tiger, but sexily so with his tanned, naked torso and arm still pinned up in a sling, and despite his evident frustration at still being here, I felt a flicker of desire for him. We kissed and then he took the coffee from me gratefully, telling me that he'd hardly slept a wink because of the noises that continued all through the night.

'I don't suppose any of us slept much,' I said, setting two bags down on Dan's bed. 'I lay there worrying about Bart and Anna and you, of course. Viv stayed over. I think she got up and put the kettle on. Then Poppy crept in beside me for a cuddle at dawn this morning.'

One of the bags I'd brought contained a clean set of clothes for him, the other was full of Anna's things. I'd been around to her house last night. It was a good job I did, she must have left in such haste that she'd forgotten to lock the door to her cottage. I'd tidied her abandoned kitchen and then gone upstairs and packed toiletries, make-up and several outfits, all the while telling myself that she really wouldn't need so many clothes because Bart would soon be home, and I'd tell her the same when I saw her.

'Anyway, how are you? How's the shoulder?' I asked.

He pressed a finger to his muscle. 'Sore. But the drugs help. I'll be fine once I'm home.'

He pulled the curtains closed around his bed and tried to unzip the bag I'd brought. I jumped up to help him. I put my hands on his waist and slowly pushed his pyjama bottoms down an inch, letting my fingernails graze his hips.

'You'll get me into trouble,' he murmured with a grin.

'So?' I wrapped my arms around his neck and kissed him and he responded, sighing with pleasure.

'The sooner we get home the better,' he said, cupping my face with his one free hand and pressing stubbly kisses to my neck.

'Promises, promises.'

The curtain was whisked back and a male nurse poked his head in and smirked at us.

Dan and I laughed guiltily and stepped away from each other.

'Want a hand getting a shirt on over that arm?' the nurse asked. His badge announced him as Chris.

'Please,' said Dan, yanking his pyjama bottoms back up. 'All my wife is managing to do is lead me astray.'

'Sorry,' I said with a chuckle, 'we've had two nights apart. Which is rare for us. I've missed him.'

'Don't apologize for a happy marriage, it's music to my ears,' said Chris. 'You'd be amazed how many couples row in here, even though one of them is in hospital.'

Dan and I exchanged smiles. The nurse untied the sling and slipped a shirtsleeve slowly over Dan's injured arm and shoulder and I waited in the visitor's chair out of the way. I felt very fortunate; despite our quibbles recently, we did have a happy marriage. Thank goodness Joe had interrupted Gil and me when he had. London already seemed like a distant memory and if it hadn't been for the Facebook friend request from Gil last night, it could almost have been a dream.

'How's everything at home?' Dan asked, his words shaking me from my thoughts.

'Loads better than I'd expected,' I said, taking a sip from his coffee.

And while Chris removed Dan's pyjamas and helped him into jogging bottoms and trainers, I brought him up to speed with the farm.

Our friends and family had rallied round and come to our rescue yesterday and when I'd got home from the hospital the strength of the community had reduced me to tears again. Tim had gone over to Sunnybank Farm after Naomi had collected Poppy and found poor Cameron trying to finish the job by himself. Between them they'd locked everything up and then Tim had driven him home. Cameron had been shaky and worried about the damage he might be blamed for but Tim assured him that he had nothing to be concerned about and we'd all been proud of the way he'd conducted himself. When Naomi got back from dropping us at the hospital, she went out on the quad bike with the dogs to check the sheep, and then Dan's friend Ian had turned up on his big tractor. He'd brought a couple of other men from the village with him and between them they'd righted the livestock trailer and parked it out of harm's way. The metal sides were twisted, but it wasn't a write-off. Ian's wife Jayne had put some chicken noodle soup in the bottom oven for us and left a fresh crusty loaf. And when I'd got back with Viv and Poppy, the yard looked as if nothing had happened. Even the chickens had been put away for the night.

'We're lucky to have such good friends,' said Dan.

'And family,' I put in. Unlike poor Anna.

Chris retied Dan's sling and tucked the ends in neatly.

'The doctor is doing her rounds; she'll be here within the next hour. Until then, I'll leave you two to it.'

'Can't I just go now?' Dan asked.

'No, you can't.' He waggled his eyebrows. 'Now do you want the curtains left closed?'

'You can open them,' I said, passing Dan what was left of his coffee. 'I need to go and see my friend and her son in intensive care.'

Dan gulped it down. 'Wait for me, I'll come with you.'

Chris shook his head. 'Sorry, you can't leave the ward until you're discharged.'

Dan rolled his eyes. 'Not even to go to another ward?'

'No. The last thing this hospital needs is a lump like you keeling over. You took quite a battering yesterday.'

'Probably better if you stay, Dan,' I suggested tactfully. 'At least you won't miss the doctor.'

'This is ridiculous, I'm not an invalid,' he muttered. 'He's my godson too.'

That was true; I sometimes forgot that as Anna and I were so close but there had been no other suitable male in her life and it had made sense that we were both Bart's godparents. We were his guardians too, if anything should happen to Anna before he came of age. We were as near to family as they had.

Chris hesitated. 'Technically you *are* an invalid. And you're in my care until the doc says otherwise. But . . .' He pulled the curtains back and looked over at the nurses' station. 'Yes, thought so. We've got a wheelchair on the ward. If your wife doesn't mind pushing you, you can go.'

I stood and picked up the bag of Anna's things. 'Sure. As long as you don't criticize my driving.'

'Thanks for doing this,' said Dan as I pushed him out of the lift and on to the ground floor.

'No problem. It's good practice for when we're old and you're decrepit.'

'Ha ha.' He raked a hand through his hair. 'Can't wait to get home.'

234

'For a shower?' I said hopefully, wrinkling my nose at his greasy hair.

'Watch out.' He gripped the arm of the wheelchair as I misjudged a corner.

'Whoops, sorry,' I grunted, desperately trying to get the wheels to go in a straight line.

'Yeah, I was holding out for a bed bath from that nice nurse from yesterday, but no such luck.'

'I'll run you a bath,' I promised. 'And I'll even throw in a dollop of my bath lotion.'

He reached up and touched my hand.

'Thanks. And then I'll have to get stuck into the insurance claim,' he said with a sigh. 'I hate paperwork.'

I frowned, knowing how much work that would entail. 'For the trailer? Do we have to?'

'Yes. And for Bart and Cameron. Bart especially.'

My stomach churned; I hadn't thought about that. 'Do you really think they'll claim for personal injury against us?'

Dan turned to look up at me and I stopped pushing. 'I'll insist on it. That's why we have insurance: for exactly this type of eventuality. Anything Anna needs. Or Bart. Anything at all. They'll have it.'

I carefully threaded my arms round his neck and pressed my cheek to his. 'You are a kind man. It's one of the many reasons why I love you.'

'Anyone would do the same.'

My heart swelled for this man. He was one of a kind and I adored him for it.

'Two people to a bed only, I'm afraid,' said the nurse when we buzzed to enter intensive care. The heat from the ward hit us like a furnace as she opened the door.

'But I'm in a wheelchair,' said Dan, doing his best invalid face. 'My wife needs to push me.'

'I can wheel you to where you need to go,' she offered firmly. 'Your wife can wait outside for a few minutes, can't you?'

But I wasn't really listening. I was looking over to Bart's bed. Kelly, the nurse I'd met yesterday, was at the foot of the bed again, keeping a watchful eye over Bart. She looked up and smiled and then inclined her head to where Anna lay slumped, head down, both her hands clasping Bart's. A ripple of sadness went through me. While I'd been in my own bed at home, Anna had been here with only the nurses for company.

'Oh, look at her,' I said, my voice catching in my throat. 'She must have been here all night.'

The nurse nodded. 'She has, poor love. We did our best to persuade her to take a break when Bartholomew was in surgery, but she wouldn't leave him; she sat in the waiting area of the recovery room and then followed him back here. No one else has come to relieve her. We don't ask, but I'm assuming the father isn't around?'

I pressed my fingers under my eyes, willing the tears back. 'She has no other family; we're all she's got.'

'We are Bart's godparents,' said Dan. 'And he was injured on my farm so I feel a responsibility.'

'And Anna and I are like sisters,' I added, watching as the nurse appeared to consider our plight.

Finally, she gave a simple nod.

'We do make concessions under difficult circumstances,' she said, standing aside to let me push Dan in. 'Just for five minutes and I must insist on complete calm or you'll have to take it in turns at the bedside. I have my other patients to consider.'

'We appreciate it,' said Dan. 'We'll keep it down, promise.'

Bart was lying in the same position as yesterday with his head angled to relieve pressure on the wound at the back of his skull. He'd been dressed in a hospital gown, which had been pulled down at the front to reveal his chest, which was dotted with sensors. The cage was gone and one leg was in plaster to the knee.

Kelly raised her eyes from her notes as we approached

and pressed a finger to her lips. 'Anna's sleeping,' she whispered. 'Finally.'

'Morning,' I said softly. 'This is my husband, Dan.'

She nodded. 'Anna told me all about you. How are you feeling today?'

'Fine. More importantly how's the lad?' Dan transferred himself to the visitor's chair and I perched on the arm.

The nurse tucked her hair neatly behind her ears and leaned forward to whisper. 'He's on strong pain relief but surgery to pin the ankle went well. The nurse on the night shift said he had a reasonably comfortable night. We've withdrawn sedation now so the next couple of hours are important. I'll be keeping a very close eye on him, and when he wakes I'll be looking for appropriate responses.'

'Shit.' Dan rubbed a hand through his hair. 'I'll never forgive myself if, if he—'

I interrupted Dan quickly. 'When you say "appropriate", what do you mean?'

Kelly's blue eyes softened. 'Can he poke his tongue out or squeeze my hand, can his eyes follow an object, can he answer simple questions. That sort of thing.'

'And if he can?'

She hesitated. 'Then I'll be happy.'

'We all will.' I nodded, understanding, and blew out a calming breath. I'd done some reading up on brain injuries last night. What none of us knew at the moment was whether Bart would have lasting brain damage or not. Anna stirred in her chair and I nudged Dan, reminding him not to make a sound. Her dress was crumpled from sitting in it all night, her curls were tangled and even though she was asleep, her face was etched with tension.

'Hetty said you were here yesterday evening, Kelly?' Dan whispered. 'And again early this morning, how long is your shift?'

'Twelve and a half hours,' she answered. 'That's how we do things in intensive care. Continuity is key in these cases.'

'*These cases?*' Anna's eyes pinged open and she blinked herself awake. She leaned across Bart and kissed his head tenderly. 'Morning, darling. Are you awake? Mum's here. I love you.'

She scanned his face, smoothing his fringe back, and then looked down at his injured leg as if noticing his plaster cast for the first time.

'Hi there!' I circled the bed so I was on her side and bent to hug her but she pushed me off.

'These cases?' she repeated, glaring at poor Kelly. 'This is my son. My *child*. Not just a case. A person.'

'Of course,' said Kelly calmly. 'And Bart is my top priority right now. His pulse and blood pressure are doing fine, let's keep it that way.'

Anna nodded but began breathing in a rushed, panicky way.

'You okay?' I asked, risking a light touch to her arm. 'Would you like some water?'

She nodded again but didn't look at me; her eyes were trained on Dan. I fetched her a cup of water from the machine, giving Dan a worried look as I passed.

'It all happened in a flash,' he was saying quietly when I got back. 'The trailer overturned and I tried my best to protect Bart, but his leg got caught and he fell backwards. I'd do anything to swap places with him, anything.'

I handed Anna the water and she mumbled her thanks. She was sitting bolt upright now and there was a wild look in her eye. 'You tried to protect him.' She had raised her volume and I was worried she'd attract attention.

'Keep your voice down,' I whispered. 'The ward sister said that if there was any undue noise—'

'*Undue?*' She reared her head back at me.

Kelly cleared her throat. She stood with her clipboard and made her way past Anna and me to Bart's monitors.

'You know what I mean.' I bit my lip and squatted down by her side, steadying myself by holding on to the arm of her chair. 'I've brought you some clean clothes, if you want to go and freshen up?'

She swallowed and closed her eyes briefly. Her eye-lashes glistened with tears. 'Thanks, but not yet, not till he wakes up.'

'Anna, love, I don't know what I can say other than sorry.' Dan's mouth was contorted with sorrow and I knew how much physical pain he was in himself. This was so unfair, all of it.

Anna gulped her water down in one and handed me the empty cup. Then she took a deep breath and addressed Dan. 'I can't do this any more.'

He inched his chair closer to the bed with his one free hand, wincing with the effort, and leaned as close as he could. 'Anna, you can, love. Stay strong. You're being so brave. Hetty said the scan didn't show anything serious on Bart's brain and now he's stopped being sedated it'll just be a matter of time. Hang on in there.'

She shook her head slowly, staring at him. 'That's not what I meant.'

Dan's brow furrowed.

'The farm's insurance policy will pay out, Anna,' I soothed. 'You probably don't want to think about any of that yet, but Dan and I don't want you to worry about—'

'It's not that. I need to tell you about something. Something that happened a long time ago. I can't keep quiet any longer, it's killing me.' Her voice had now gone eerily quiet.

My spine prickled. What was going on here? Something in her tone was really odd.

'Anna,' Dan warned, his voice low.

Anna turned her wild-eyed stare to me. 'Last night,' she said in a hoarse whisper, 'you said even if I didn't have a proper family, I'd always have you, no matter what. Did you mean it?'

'Of course.' I grasped her hand. 'What is it? You're scar-ing me.'

'Even if it's bad?'

I nodded and out of the corner of my eye I saw Dan lean forward and drop his head to his hands.

Anna held my gaze, emotions flitting too quickly across her face for me to catch them. My heart was hammering so violently I half expected Bart's monitors to start registering it.

'Anna,' Dan urged, 'think this through, love, think it through.'

'Oh, I have,' she said with a harsh laugh. 'All night. I thought about it while Bart was in surgery. While I followed him as he was brought back up to the ward, alone, wishing I had someone to put their arms around me and tell me everything was going to be okay. And I thought about how I'd feel if—' She gulped at the air, half sobbing, half choking.

'Oh Anna,' I said shakily. I didn't know what to do, whether to comfort her or leave her be. I'd known her for years, but now she looked like a stranger. I didn't know what was coming but my legs were trembling with fear.

Kelly crouched down beside her. 'Hey, Bart's neurology is looking good, his op was a success. Let's not worry about things we don't know about.'

'This is about things I *do* know.' Anna blinked at her and turned her gaze back to Dan. 'Bart begged to come and work with you on the farm. I was always worried that he'd hurt himself. I'm a nurse: I know the statistics, I know the risk. But deep in my heart I thought that maybe it was meant to be. You're the only father figure he's known.'

Dan swallowed. 'I was proud that he asked for a job; it's hard work, not many kids would be interested. I wish I'd turned him down now.'

'Then this stupid accident happened.' Her volume was increasing again and the two nurses at the end of the nearest beds looked over, concerned. 'And that was *not* meant to be.'

'Anna, you need to lower your voice,' Kelly warned.

But Anna shook her head. Her breathing was so rapid now I could see her chest heaving.

'If there was one person, Dan, one person on this earth I should have been able to trust him with it should have been you.'

Dan wiped sweat away from his forehead. 'I know. Don't you think I know that? This will stay with me for the rest of my life.'

'Sometimes accidents happen on farms. It's awful, but it's a fact of life,' I said urgently, pushing myself between her and the bed, forcing her to look at me. 'I can't imagine what you're going through but—'

'No,' she gasped. 'No you can't.'

She looked at me, her eyes huge, ringed with dark circles. She looked hollowed out, haunted, and tears sprang to my own eyes.

I glanced at Kelly, who sat tight-lipped and pale, looking anxiously over at the nurses' station.

'You promised you'd stick by me whatever, but I'm scared you didn't mean it.' Tears flowed down Anna's face now and her sobs were getting louder. Surely they wouldn't throw us out for crying too loudly, would they? I looked at Dan for reassurance but he wouldn't meet my eye.

'Anna, please, just say; whatever's the matter, please tell me. You're frightening the life out of me.'

'Hetty,' she managed to say through her tears, 'there's something you should know.'

'Please, Anna.' Dan pressed his hands to his face.

Anna's body was shaking like a leaf, but I couldn't comfort her. I was frozen to the spot, wedged between her chair and the bed, watching her lips, my own face already wet with tears.

'You don't deserve this,' said Anna. 'Neither of you do. But I lied to you.'

My breath escaped in a rush. 'That's okay, whatever you said—'

'Dan,' she looked past me to my husband, 'you are Bart's father.'

For a second no one moved, no one spoke, as her words settled around us. I twisted to look at Dan, expecting to see bemusement or confusion or denial.

But his face had turned white with shock. 'Are you sure?'

No denial.

Anna nodded.

I sank down to the floor as my heart shattered into a million splinters. I felt myself disintegrate. Noises echoed in my head from a distance but nothing felt real. None of this was real. My heart rate was speeding and my head was throbbing and hot like it was about to explode. Black spots blurred my vision.

Anna and Dan. Anna and Dan and Bart. Bart's father was my husband. Poppy had a brother. Dan had a son. A son. And Anna was my best friend.

The world went black.

Footsteps. Running. People had their hands under my arms. Someone held a cup to my lips and water ran down my chin.

'Anna and Dan,' I breathed.

Someone pushed my head between my knees.

Kelly's voice cut through the fog like a bell. 'One of you should leave.'

'Me,' I spluttered, lifting my head. 'I'll go.'

There were two nurses beside me, one hefted me up and then both of them returned to their own bays.

Out of the corner of my eye I could see Anna sobbing, head bowed. Dan was on his feet staring down at Bart. 'But you said the father was someone in Australia. I thought—'

'Of course I said that,' she spluttered. 'What else could I do? You were with Hetty.'

'So you were already pregnant when you left for your gap year,' I murmured.

'Okay,' said Kelly sternly, 'enough. You've got some talking to do by the sound of it. But this is not the time or the place. Nurse Black?' she called over to the nurses' station for assistance.

'Bart!' Anna lurched forward, leaning over the bed. 'He opened his eyes. Kelly, did you see? My baby boy.'

Bart's eyes flickered. He blinked and flinched at the light. The person in his line of sight was Dan.

'Sorry,' he rasped through dry, cracked lips. 'I got in the way.'

'Don't be sorry, son,' Dan whispered, tears leaking from his eyes. He touched the back of his finger to Bart's cheek. 'Don't be.'

'Bart,' said Anna, 'you're going to be okay, darling.'

Silently I picked up my bag and tiptoed to the door. I don't think anyone even noticed I'd gone.

Chapter 24

I drove home in a state of shock. I probably shouldn't have been driving at all but I had to get away from Dan and Anna.

In time I'd want facts. Hell, I'd want to know every last detail about why my boyfriend had cheated on me with my best friend. How could he have done that to me, and with her of all people? And when? Where had I been? How could Anna live with herself seeing me almost daily for the last fourteen years and keeping that sort of secret? And Dan. He had a son. All these years he'd had a son and Anna had denied him and Bart from having a relationship. Our past had been one big lie; goodness only knew what this was going to mean for our future.

Eventually I'd want to know all these things. But for now I needed space to take in this new situation. And in the meantime, I'd focus on the most important thing: Bart had regained consciousness. If his first sentence was any sort of indicator, it seemed as if he might be okay. My world may have collapsed around me but at least I could keep coming back to that. Because whatever else might be happening, none of this mess was his fault.

As I turned up the track to Sunnybank Farm, Ian was coming the other way. We slowed our vehicles as we came alongside each other, he in his battered old Land Rover and me in my Renault Clio.

'You here again?' I said, attempting a joke. 'Is there nothing to do on your own farm?'

Ian smiled at me and then did a double take. My eyes were probably swollen and bloodshot from all the crying.

'There's plenty,' he said with a frown. 'But Jayne says I need new trousers and wants me to go shopping with her. I'd rather chase escaped sheep all day than go shopping.'

I made a noise roughly like laughter. 'Show me a farmer who does like buying clothes. Anyway, I'm very grateful to you and so is Dan.'

Ian ran through the jobs he'd done for us: he'd borrowed our quad bike and checked for problems with the flock. He'd hauled a ewe and lamb out of the beck. Mended the latch on a gate that was swinging open, refilled the lamb feeder in the ewes-with-twins field and even watered my veggie patch.

'You did all that for us?' His kindness caused my voice to wobble.

'We know what it's like,' said Ian. 'Farming doesn't let up just because the farmer's ill. Same when Dan's dad died. Carsdale folk rally round. You concentrate on looking after each other. You'll let me know if there's anything else we can do, won't you?'

I thanked him again and he waved it away, asking how Bart and Dan were. I took a moment or two to find the right words.

'Bart has just come round, thank heavens,' I said. 'And Dan's coping with his injuries, but he's in shock.' Understatement of the year.

'Aye.' Ian nodded gravely. 'A chap at Coniston fell under a combine yesterday. Lost both his legs.'

I shook my head. 'Who'd want to be a farmer, eh?'

'It's in our blood,' he said, tipping his cap to me as he prepared to move off. 'We can't do anything about it. Father to son, down it goes. Or to daughter, in your Poppy's case. Never seen such a chip off the old block.' He chuckled. 'By the way, I was thinking about your shearing. I know Dan

245

and Cameron were doing it themselves this year, but Dan won't be up to it now with a knackered shoulder. There's a small team of clipping contractors who'd be able to do the job in exchange for parking their caravans in your yard for the duration of the season. If Dan's happy, they can fit your flock in first.'

'I'll get him to ring you,' I said. 'Thanks again.'

He smiled grimly. 'Right, I'd better go, or the missus will be clipping *me*.'

I waved him off and continued up the track to the house, thinking about what Ian had said about farming being in the blood and wondering about Bart.

Bloodlines. The secret to a successful sheep farm. We had to plan carefully to protect bloodlines, ensuring our tups didn't breed with their sisters. I pulled my car to a halt in the yard and Poppy ran out.

'How's Bart? Where's Dad, I thought he was coming home?'

'Long story.' I sighed.

I opened my arms and she ran into them for a hug.

Poppy and Bart . . . No wonder Anna had reacted so strongly when he'd asked her on a date. How were we going to break the news to my daughter that Bart was her brother? I shivered involuntarily and Poppy dragged me inside.

'Come and tell me everything. Gran's already got the kettle on.'

Half an hour later, I was alone. Viv had left for her own house and was dropping Poppy at her friend Matilda's on the way. Naomi had phoned to ask if everything was okay because she'd had a call to collect Dan from hospital and she thought I'd be doing that. I fobbed her off with an excuse. Dan could tell her the truth if he liked. That his wife was too angry and upset to be in his presence, because he'd slept with her best friend and fathered a child.

No biggie.

246

I wandered through the house for a while, unpacking my bag from London, putting a load of washing on and rooting through the freezer for something for dinner. Every so often I'd grab my phone to send Anna a text before remembering that the reason I needed to talk to someone was because of Anna, and I'd put it down again.

Outside the sky had cleared and when I opened the kitchen door to sit on the step and drink my tea, the air was warm and the view was postcard perfect: blue skies with powder-puff clouds above green hills dotted with sheep as far as the eye could see. Sunnybank Farm. Home since the day Dan had driven to Cornwall to collect me. I churned the memories of that summer over and over in my head. Everything had changed on the day we collected our A-level results. Even before Dan finished with me, he'd been distant; and looking back, Anna had avoided me too.

Had Anna and Dan gone behind my back while we'd still been together or had it happened afterwards, whilst I was in Padstow with Gil?

I took my phone out of my pocket and turned it over and over in my hand. I needed to talk to someone about this. I needed to say the words out loud; it would help me to process my thoughts. I could always ring Mum. Even though it was still only dawn in America, I knew she wouldn't mind me waking her. I'd spoken to her last night to fill her in on the accident. She'd made me promise to keep her posted with news. I scrolled to her number and my finger hovered over it but I couldn't call; the news of Dan's affair with Anna wasn't something I was ready to share with her yet. I needed to hear Dan's side of the story first. But I yearned to talk to someone, someone who'd understand.

As if in answer, the phone vibrated with a text message and I let out a long breath. Of course, this was who I needed to speak to, the one person who'd remember that summer as well as I did – Joe Appleton. I opened the message and my chest tightened as I read it.

> Hetty I'm worried sick about you. If I don't hear from you in an hour, I'm coming to the farm.

I texted him straight back.

> Please come now.

My second text was to my sister-in-law.

> Sorry to be cryptic, but please can you keep Dan away from the farm for a couple of hours? There's something I need to do.

While I waited for Joe to arrive, I did what I always did when I needed to take my mind off things: I made a pie. First the filling: a summer pie of feta cheese, fresh spinach from my garden, sundried tomatoes, chickpeas and toasted pine nuts. I mixed and tasted and adjusted the seasoning, setting it in the fridge once I was satisfied with it. After plunging my hands into cold water and drying them, I rubbed butter and vegetable shortening into flour, lifting and sifting until my trusty ceramic mixing bowl contained a mound of golden breadcrumbs. In went the egg yolk and ice-cold water. I mixed lightly, taking care not to overwork the dough, and turned it out on to my pastry mat on the kitchen table.

As my hands worked, my mind stilled. There was something timeless and grounding about making a pie. It nourished my soul and though I had to stop from time to time to brush tears from my cheeks, it felt like my own form of therapy.

The dogs began to bark, heralding the arrival of a car, just as I'd rolled out my circle of pastry for the base. I quickly wiped my hands on my apron and ran to open the door.

Joe's pristine, expensive car purred to a halt, a sharp contrast next to Dan's muddy Land Rover. Joe got out, reached into the back seat and produced a huge bouquet of flowers.

My heart thumped and for a split second I worried that inviting him over was only going to complicate matters. But then he saw me watching him and a smile lit up his face. His lovely, friendly, familiar face that had barely changed since he was eighteen had been missing from our lives for far too long, and before I knew it I was running towards him and throwing my arms around him.

'Whoa,' he laughed cautiously as I squeezed the breath from his lungs and pressed my face to the soft cotton of his shirt.

'I need a friend,' I managed to say. 'And a hug.'

'You got it.'

Even though I was probably crushing what looked to be really expensive flowers in the process, I leaned into him and revelled in the comfort of his arms and the subtle smell of his aftershave. After a couple of minutes of standing in our farmyard with the dogs woofing their excitement at our knees and my body trembling with sorrow and shock, I began to feel slightly less shaky and vulnerable. I pulled back and gave him a wonky smile.

'Thanks for that.'

He smiled. 'Pleasure.'

'Sorry about the mascara and dribble,' I said, noticing the wet patch on his shirt.

He shrugged and then kissed me on the cheek and presented me with the flowers. 'I know you've had a horrendous twenty-four hours, but before you make me a very strong coffee and bring me up to date, on behalf of Cumbria's Finest, congratulations on your silver award in the Britain's Best Bites competition. We – I – am very proud of you.'

Words choked in my throat and prevented me from replying. I lifted the bouquet to my nose and inhaled the perfume of peonies and roses, stocks and phlox, and had to work very hard not to cry again. I was a winner. But I felt like I'd lost everything.

If Joe noticed that I hadn't replied, he didn't remark on it.

He looked around him at the farm, which had been his playground for years; he'd hung out with Dan long before I'd ever met them. 'This place,' he murmured, shaking his head incredulously, 'has not changed one bit.'

'But it has,' I said, swallowing. 'It has.'

In the kitchen I made Joe his very strong coffee. We didn't have anything fancy so I put two big spoonfuls of instant coffee into a small mug and told him that would have to do. I made myself a cup of tea, shoved the flowers temporarily in the sink and Joe sat at the table while I finished my pie.

'So,' he said, wincing slightly at my coffee, 'tell me about the accident.'

And as I spooned my summer-pie filling on to my pastry disc I explained how several little mistakes had added up to the moment when our livestock trailer tipped, creating a chain of events so devastating that I thought we'd probably feel the ripples from them for the rest of our days.

'Dan is okay. Being discharged today with a fractured collarbone, bruises and stitches in his hand – but it could have been much worse.'

I set down my spoon and braced myself against the edge of the table, feeling my breath hitch in my chest.

'And Bart?' Joe frowned.

I took a deep breath.

'Dan's son, you mean?'

Joe choked on his coffee. 'What?'

'Yes. Dan and Anna have a son. Fourteen years old.'

An odd look flashed across Joe's face. It reminded me of the face Poppy pulled when I explained how to do a maths question and she insisted on working it through in her own head before finally accepting that I was right.

'She had Dan's baby,' Joe murmured.

My cheeks began to burn as he nodded slowly: he wasn't surprised. I felt a stab of pain. Everyone knew. Everyone except stupid Hetty.

'Bart sustained a blow to the head and was knocked unconscious,' I said softly. 'He's also had surgery on a smashed ankle. But he's awake again. Anna thought she was going to lose him and decided Dan should know who his real father is. And me,' I added as an afterthought. Which is what I felt like. An afterthought.

'Dan and Anna have a son,' Joe repeated. His mouth had gone dry and his voice came out as a gruff croak. 'I'm glad . . .' He paused and rubbed a weary hand over his chin. 'I'm glad he's okay.'

I arranged my features into a tight smile. 'So all change for the Greengrass family.'

I flipped the pastry lid over my rolling pin and laid it over the dome of the filling. Joe smiled softly and shook his head.

'What's funny?' I said tetchily.

'Watching you make a pie. Remember how I used to bring you and Anna pies and pastries from Appleton's Bakery? I thought that was going to be my life for ever. And instead, it's you who turned out to be the baker.'

'Only for the family.' I shook my head. 'Hetty's Farm-house Bakery isn't happening. I decided that before going to London, I just didn't have the heart to tell you. You were so focused on getting all your Cumbrian producers to London. But running my own business doesn't fit in with my life on the farm. Oh God.'

My face crumpled and I dropped into a chair. What life on the farm? Now that Dan and Anna's secret was out of the bag, could I even stay at Sunnybank Farm?

'I'm sorry, Hetty.'

Joe circled the table and wrapped his arms round me.

'I feel so betrayed,' I sobbed. 'You knew. You knew, didn't you?'

He lowered himself into the chair next to me.

'I . . .' He rubbed a hand through his beard and sighed. 'I knew some of it. I didn't know about Bart but I saw them together. And it broke my heart.'

'Tell me.' I gulped and managed not to jam my fingers in my ears. I needed to hear this.

He squeezed my arm. 'Okay. Remember when Dan, Anna and I went on that D of E expedition?'

'Of course.' I blinked at him, feeling my heart race. I already hated this story: Dan and I were still together then.

'The trip was a disaster.' He picked up an offcut of pastry and squeezed it in his hands. 'Everything went wrong. The weather was diabolical, I lost count of the number of times we got lost and then on the second day when the rain was coming down so fast on the Welsh hills that we could scarcely see our feet, Anna's partner Tasha slid on some loose slate and hurt her ankle.'

I nodded, remembering her being carried out of the mini-bus with her crutches. I urged Joe to continue.

'We thought she'd just twisted it and we tried to carry her down but we were weak from hiking uphill with those heavy rucksacks. Then she passed out and so we used the emergency phone and called for help and Tasha was taken off to hospital. When we eventually made it back to camp everyone was exhausted and worried about her. We asked if we could abandon the trip and go home but the assessor wouldn't let us. Said this was just another challenge and all part of the experience. One we could have done without, to be honest.'

He gave me a wry smile and flattened the lump of pastry into a long strip.

'Because Tasha had gone, Anna had no one to help her put their tent up. So I went to help her out. She was shaky and cold from exhaustion and still upset about Tasha's accident. She said she was dreading sleeping on her own that night. I put my arms round her and told her that I would always be there for her if she needed me.'

My heart ached for him; he'd always been there for both of us, me and Anna. I'd missed out on so many years of his friendship and hoped now he'd be back in my life for good.

'We had a campfire later on; the usual, all huddled on

damp grass, burning sticks and wishing someone had brought marshmallows. We had a few contraband beers to which the teachers turned a blind eye and the mood lifted. Then someone started drumming on those little camping saucepans and someone else started beat boxing, then Andy started singing that NSYNC song that Anna used to like.'

'"Girlfriend"?' I gave a harsh laugh. 'How apt. I wonder if the fact that I was Dan's girlfriend occurred to her at all while she was playing tonsil hockey with him.'

'Can you remember the lyrics?'

'I remember the gist of it.'

'It's about unrequited love.' He fixed his gaze on me and I felt my pulse race. 'About a girl who doesn't notice the boy who's in love with her.'

Poor lovely Joe. He'd twisted the strip of pastry into a heart and now he placed it on to the baking sheet next to my unfinished pie. How insensitive of me not to notice his feelings at the time.

I covered his hand with mine. 'Joe, I'm sorry if I ever . . . if you felt—'

He shook his head. 'Let me finish. The singing went on for a while and later I looked round the circle and couldn't see Anna. I was worried about her so I got up and went over to her tent.'

He looked at me intently, his dark eyes boring into mine, and even though by now I'd guessed what was coming next, it still hurt to hear the words. My stomach clenched in readiness . . .

'And there they were. Together. The two of them were inside her sleeping bag.'

I clamped a hand over my mouth and hot angry tears ran down my cheeks.

He cleared his throat and carried on. 'I went into our tent and pretended to be asleep when Dan came in.'

'And was that the only time?' I said in a whisper. Everything hurt: my head, my heart, my lungs, even my skin felt raw.

'As far as I know.' Joe nodded grimly. 'Yet *still* he managed to get her pregnant. If it's any consolation, he felt awful about it and decided he couldn't carry on going out with you after what he'd done. That's why he finished with you when we got back home. You know the rest. After you left for Cornwall, Anna made a snap decision to take a gap year and Dan was taken up with the farm. I realized that I'd been wasting my time hoping that the girl I loved would ever feel the same way about me as I felt about her.'

He stared down at the table glumly. I turned my chair to face him and took both his hands in mine.

'Why?' I demanded gently. 'Why didn't you tell me the truth? If you were in love with me like you say, then why keep me in the dark?'

'In love with *you*?' He looked at me surprised. 'Hetty, you were a mate, I loved you as a friend, but you were – you *are* – Dan's girl, I'd never have—'

I interrupted him with a gasp as I realized my mistake. 'Oh gosh.' I sprang up and away from him, feeling like the world's biggest idiot.

'It was Anna, not me. Of course it was. You were in love with Anna.'

Joe pressed a hand to his forehead and groaned. 'Yes. I'm sorry if I gave a different impression.'

'Dan *and* you. Both of you chose her. Not me. Oh no, Hetty was just the silly girl who didn't notice what was going on under her own nose.'

'That's not true.' He reached a hand to my shoulder but I shrugged him off.

'Go,' I said in a muffled voice through my tears. 'Please go.'

'Hetty, you are wonderful. I've always cared for you. I thought at the time Dan didn't deserve you and I told him as much when he came to see me to ask for my advice. I couldn't understand why he'd cheat on you.'

I stared at him. 'So Dan knew you'd seen him with Anna?'

Joe nodded. 'He was mortified. In fact, I think he cried.

254

But I don't think Anna knew, unless Dan told her. You know, there were so many times when I almost told Dan how I felt about Anna, but something held me back. She was so beautiful I thought I didn't stand a chance. After I saw them together I was so upset. Not just for myself but for you too. That's why I severed all ties with the three of you. It felt the right time to make a fresh start. I assumed that at some point in the last fifteen years, the truth would have come out.'

I hung my head and let the tears flow. 'Dan and Anna have kept it a secret all this time. How do we carry on from here?'

Joe stepped forward and gently pulled me into his arms. 'Look at the life you've built for yourselves. Don't throw that away over something that happened when you were kids.'

I waved my arm around the kitchen. 'But this has all been a lie. Maybe he only came to Cornwall for me because Anna turned him down. His dad had passed away and he needed someone to help run the farm. Maybe if she'd said yes, this would be *her* kitchen, *her* life with Bart, and because she's so perfect, she'd have probably gone on to have more children like I wanted. Maybe,' I finished with a sniff, 'all this time I've been second best.'

'And when he did come to Cornwall?' Joe raised an eyebrow. 'Were you still single? There seemed to be history between you and Gil, judging by the way you greeted each other.'

'Gil and I were . . . I was just . . .' My face burned like a furnace. 'He celebrated my eighteenth birthday with me. At the time he felt like the only friend I had. We got very close very quickly.'

Joe waited. 'And Saturday? You seemed to be getting on pretty well when I found you then too.'

I stepped away from him and lifted my chin defiantly. 'You don't get to judge me, Joe. You just don't.'

He sighed and scratched a hand distractedly through his beard. 'You're right. And I'm not judging, I . . . Hetty, I've spent a long time searching for someone to fill the gap in my heart that Anna left. Promise me you won't be too hasty to do the same with Dan.'

I acknowledged his words with a nod. Right now I was angry and sad and hurt. I felt cheated and lied to, and I didn't know who to trust.

Wordlessly, I began to crimp the pastry edges of my pie, binding the top with the base and sealing in the filling, pinching and turning, pinching and turning, just as Gil had shown me to do fifteen years ago. Joe watched for a moment and then stood up. He took an envelope from his pocket and set it on the table.

'You are a fabulous woman, Hetty. You don't know it yet, but you'll be okay. Here. Your prize money. And Gil asked me to pass on his number; I've written it on the envelope.'

I didn't look up until he'd gone.

Chapter 25

So now I knew everything. Joe had been in love with Anna and Dan had fallen for her charms too. I got it; she was pretty, funny, adorable. But now, fifteen years later, where did that leave us all? It was a mess and not just for the adults, for the kids too.

As soon as my summer pie was out of the oven I set it on the cooling rack and picked up my keys. Dan would be back soon and I didn't know what to say to him. Or how to *be* around him other than very angry. Outside, the steep hills beckoned. What I really needed was a good stomp up towards the fells with Rusty panting along beside me; today I missed him more than ever.

I pulled the door closed behind me, picked up a tennis ball from the yard, released Fern and Jake from their kennels and set off across the meadow.

The clouds had begun to thicken over Brant Hill, my destination, but I didn't mind. If anything, a gloomier sky mirrored my mood. The dogs set off joyously, looking for jobs to do. That was the difference between Dan's working dogs and Rusty, who'd never done a useful day's work in his life. Rusty had always been simply happy to be by my side, stopping when I stopped, sniffing at anything I showed an interest in, like a wild flower or a bird's egg fallen from a nest, whereas Jake and Fern were permanently primed and alert, waiting for instructions to gather sheep.

Having said that, I thought fondly, it was unfair to say Rusty hadn't been useful. He'd loved me unconditionally right from the first day he'd arrived on the farm. He'd allowed me to cry into his fur for weeks after my miscarriage seven years ago and the constant patter of his four paws trotting behind me everywhere I went became the soundtrack to my days.

I crossed the stile through the drystone wall at the edge of the meadow and struck a path up towards Brant Hill. The ewes largely ignored us as we passed but the lambs scampered away, nervous at the sight of the dogs. Fern was already ahead, sniffing at a tuft of wool caught in the thorns of the brambles and Jake stood on the wall before leaping off and flattening himself to the ground in front of me, eager to play. I threw the tennis ball as far as I could. He darted off to get it and for the next few minutes the two of them took it in turns to fetch it.

Fifteen minutes later I'd reached the summit of Brant Hill. The wind was stronger up here on the exposed hilltop and I found a rock to sit on, next to a patch of heather that was covered with a lacy spider's web. I leaned against the drystone wall behind me and looked down in the direction I'd come.

Below me the fields were dotted with our Swaledales and their remaining lambs. The farmhouse, sturdy and white, nestled into the side of the valley and across the other side of the river, I could see Ian and Jayne's farm, not white like ours but built from traditional stone: a long, low house with stables and a cowshed for their small herd of cows.

This landscape was as familiar to me as my own body. It had been my home, my life, since I was a teenager. Now I felt as if my claim on it was as delicate as the gossamer threads of web on the heather beside me. The clouds shifted, revealing a brief glimpse of the sun and its unexpected appearance made me squint. I closed my eyes and rested my head back against the wall. Suddenly the dogs barked and I sprang to my feet, blinking.

Coming towards me, arms pumping, was a short, round figure. The dogs, recognizing him, bounded off to greet him and I raised an arm to wave.

'Tim!'

'I read somewhere once that the best views come after the toughest climb,' he puffed, wiping an arm across his forehead. 'In other words, all the hard work is worth it in the end.'

'I'll take your word for it.' I smiled wanly. If that wasn't a metaphor for my current situation, I didn't know what was. Although at the moment my view still wasn't that great. 'How did you find me?'

'Naomi and I were driving Dan home and we spotted you with the dogs on the hill. You don't mind if I join you?' he wheezed, setting his rucksack down and opening his arms for a hug. 'Because I'll bugger off if this is a private party.'

'Pity party, more like,' I said, half laughing as I submitted to his hug. 'And no, I don't mind at all.'

Which was true. In fact, watching him take out a blanket, flask, mugs and assorted plastic tubs, humming tunelessly to himself, I thought Tim's laid-back attitude to life was exactly what I needed right now.

'Before you ask, I know everything,' he said with a kind smile, lowering his portly body to the blanket. 'Well, not everything. For example, I don't think I'll ever remember which towels I'm allowed to use from the linen cupboard, but you get my drift. Right, tea and a sandwich?'

He peeled the lid off one of the tubs and waggled it at me. My stomach growled and I realized I hadn't eaten anything since the bowl of Jane's soup last night.

'Thank you.' I bit into the sandwich, recognizing it as the rye bread Naomi sold in the farm shop. It was filled with tender beef and there was watercress and horseradish in there too. 'This is good.'

The two of us chewed in silence for a moment and I thought how bizarre it was that even in such crappy times as these, good food and easy company, on a rug on a Cumbrian hillside, could bring me such comfort.

'So Dan was at your house for a while?' I asked.

Tim brushed crumbs from his moustache and poured us both a mug of tea. 'Yes. He'd been in a hurry to get back but Naomi persuaded him to give you some space. I helped him have a bath and then get into some clean clothes.'

My head throbbed with the intense sadness of the day; only a few short hours ago, we couldn't wait to be home and alone together. How quickly things could change.

He chuckled. 'I know I shouldn't laugh but Otis insisted on supplying him with one of the shirts from his new collection. Dan looks like a cross between a pirate and Adam Ant. Very frilly.'

I managed a sort of smile at that. 'How is he?' I asked.

Tim threw crusts to the dogs, who'd settled at the edge of the blanket waiting for exactly that.

'Physically okay. Mentally . . .' He hesitated. 'He's worried to death about you. Hence me being sent forth to check on you.'

'And Anna and Bart? What does he think about his *other* family?' I asked, unable to keep quite all of the bitterness from my voice.

Tim eyed me with sympathy. 'He's very confused. It's been a huge shock, coming straight after the accident. He feels burdened with responsibility and guilt.'

I shuddered. 'It's like the summer Mike died all over again.'

'In what way?'

I paused to sip my tea and looked at Fern, wishing she'd come closer like Rusty would have done so I could ruffle her fur. But her gaze was fixed on the plastic tub of cake Tim was opening. 'Both of us changed our university plans and stayed in Carsdale to run the farm. Dan had to grow up overnight. He made the decision to follow in his dad's footsteps in the end, but a part of him has always resented the fact that he didn't get to train as a vet and an even bigger part feels guilty about it.'

Tim bit into a slice of buttered fruit loaf and held the tub out to me, I shook my head.

'It was a bad year for all of us,' he said. 'Did anyone ever tell you that Naomi and I nearly moved to Texas that summer with the boys?'

I looked at him in surprise. 'Never. I can't imagine her living anywhere but here.'

He wiped butter from his chin and swallowed his last mouthful. 'Yep. Earlier that year, I was headhunted by an oil company in Dallas. Same job as I was doing here but it had the full executive package: a ranch, swimming pool, plenty of room for horses, a great school for the twins. They were initially offering a five-year contract. I thought it was perfect; we could have a US adventure and then return to the UK in time for the boys to go to secondary school. But Naomi had already had the idea for opening the farm shop and asked for Mike's permission and he was thinking it through. I knew she would be torn, so before I told her about the offer, I went to see Mike and Viv behind her back.' Tim shot me a guilty look. 'She idolized her dad and I knew that if I got him on-side it would be a lot easier to persuade Naomi to come with me. Mike agreed that it was the opportunity of a lifetime and they were excited for us, so he went to see Naomi and said no to her farm shop plans. She was furious with him, accused him of treating her unfairly because she was a woman.'

'Poor Naomi.'

'I know.' Tim took a deep breath and shook his head. 'And I'll never forgive myself for creating that ill feeling.'

I frowned. 'But I thought planning permission for the farm shop was already in place when Mike died?'

'That was the worst part about it for me; he thought her business idea was great really,' he said. 'Mike applied for planning consent on her behalf, thinking that when we returned from the States, the project would be there for her to pick up. He also amended his will so that it made it clear that she would own the buildings and surrounding land.'

'Gosh.' I blinked at him. 'I had no idea.' Dan and I had been so wrapped up in each other that spring and had been studying hard for our A levels. Naomi and Tim were married with kids; our lives were completely different.

'I told Naomi about the job offer and because she was so mad with Mike, she agreed we should leave England. I resigned from my job, giving them three months' notice, and we made plans to leave in the summer. Then when Mike died everything changed again; there was no way Naomi was going to fly off to America leaving her little brother to cope with Viv and all the funeral arrangements. So we delayed our flights by a couple of weeks. Luckily, we hadn't found tenants for the cottage by then so we still had a home.'

My stomach twisted with guilt. During those weeks I'd been so determined to put our relationship behind me and mend my bruised heart that I'd tried to put Dan out of my head. I'd been having a carefree time, sowing my wild oats with Gil while Dan had been going through hell. I shifted my position, folding my legs underneath me and reached for the flask. There was enough left for half a cup each and I shared it out between us.

'Tell me about Dan.'

Tim spooned sugar into his tea. 'He went downhill as soon as you'd disappeared off the face of the earth. Viv phoned your parents, who told her where you were. Neither Viv nor Naomi could understand why he'd finished the relationship when he was so obviously still in love with you. Everyone told him to get in the car and go and find you but he refused, saying that you deserved better.'

'He said that?'

Dan had looked dreadful when he eventually did come to Padstow but I'd put it down to his dad's sudden death. No one had ever told me how much Dan had been suffering when I left. And because he'd been the one to finish with me, I'd never given his feelings a second thought.

Tim nodded. 'He only left the farm once and that was to go and talk to Joe. We'd been relieved that he was finally turning a corner and going out to see his friends again. But when he came back he was in an even worse state.'

I bit my lip; now I knew why. I gave myself a shake; this was Tim's story, I didn't want to get sidetracked. 'What happened about the job in Texas?'

'As soon as Naomi read Mike's will and realized he'd loved her idea for the farm shop she was overwhelmed. I knew she wouldn't be able to tear herself away from Sunnybank Farm then, so I told her the US job had fallen through. She started work straight away and has never looked back.'

I looked at him. His lovely kind face still rosy from his brisk climb, his thin dark hair plastered to his head. 'You sacrificed your job for her. That was incredibly kind.'

He shrugged. 'Going to Mike behind her back was a huge mistake. Huge. Naomi never really forgave her dad while he was alive and I've had to live with that on my conscience ever since.'

My heart went out to him. He had been such a good husband; I hated to think of him still feeling guilty. 'Have you ever thought about confessing?'

'I did. Last time Naomi came to stay with me in Inverness for our anniversary.'

'And?'

'I won't lie; she was mad that I'd gone behind her back. And she was upset that she'd given her dad such a hard time before he died. But after she'd calmed down, she said we'd had such a good life together, she wasn't going to throw that away. She forgave me and although it was one of the hardest things I've done for a long time, I'm glad it's out in the open. We had a really good talk and we've decided to make a few changes to our lives in the next few years. I'm going to scale back on my job and spend more time at home.'

I touched his arm. 'I'm glad. You were young, Tim, and it all worked out in the end. You can't feel guilty for ever for one mistake.'

He looked at me then, knowingly, and I realized where this whole conversation had been leading.

'You and Dan were even younger than us when you got together. You've grown up together. You were his only serious relationship.'

'And he was mine,' I said indignantly. 'And I would never have been unfaithful to him.'

'It was wrong, he knows that, but he was only eighteen and it was only once. He assured me and Naomi that.' Tim looked at me intently. 'I hope in time you can forgive him, like Naomi has done me.'

I blushed then, remembering my eighteenth birthday with Gil on the beach. That was only once too. Except, of course, I'd seen him on Saturday in London and look what had nearly happened . . .

'It might have been once. But look at the consequences,' I replied.

Tim sighed softly. 'I know, Hetty, the consequences are huge, but it doesn't make the crime any worse, does it?'

I stared at my hands, at the gold ring on my finger. The logic was right; but I was pretty sure my hurt and anger were justified. It felt as if I was looking at my past through a windscreen. Anna's revelation had been the stone that chipped that screen and shattered it into a million fragments. My life as I'd known it was a blur.

Tim began to gather up the picnic things and pack his rucksack. 'I can feel rain in the air. Come on, Dan's waiting for you. Do you think you can face him?'

I nodded and stood up, my pulse racing as I looked down the hill to the valley and home. Poppy would be back soon; Dan and I needed to get our story straight before then. Although I had no idea what that story was going to be.

264

Chapter 26

Naomi was waiting in the kitchen when Tim and I got back. There was no sign of Dan.

She pointed at the ceiling, reading my mind. 'He's gone up for a rest, but said to wake him when you got back.' She ushered me in and automatically put the kettle on. 'He'd like to talk to you as soon as he can.'

My stomach was in knots. I nodded and looked away, catching sight of my reflection in the mirror. What a state I was in. It had begun to rain on the way downhill and the wind had picked up too. My hair looked like old straw bedding from the sheep pens: sodden and matted. My nose was running and my cheeks felt like they would never lift upwards in a smile again. And on top of that I was so, so tired. I flopped in one of the armchairs and closed my eyes.

'Gareth Brookbanks just called.' Naomi paused from clanking mugs and rattling spoons. 'From Country Comestibles. Says he called and left a message on Friday?'

The joy that developing my idea for Hetty's Farmhouse Bakery had brought me had evaporated. Right now, the thought of me as a go-getting entrepreneur was laughable. I wasn't sure I could keep my family together, let alone run a business. I kept my eyes shut, but I knew she was looking at me, waiting for an answer.

'He wants pies for his shops,' I replied.

Tim whistled. 'That's a coup, getting stocked there.'

'Hetty's Farmhouse Bakery is an award-winning company, Tim. Locally and nationally. Of course he'd want her pies. Well done, love.' She nudged me with her foot until I opened my eyes and held out a mug to me.

'We've got eight hundred sheep to clip, a farmer with a fractured collarbone, lambs still to sell and a new branch of the family to absorb into the fold,' I said tetchily. 'Making pies for Country Comestibles is as far down my list of priorities as it could possibly be.'

'Well, this one's going down a treat,' Tim mumbled through a mouthful of the summer pie I'd made earlier.

Naomi raised her eyebrows and brushed crumbs from his chin. 'Oh, didn't you eat the picnic after all?'

'Um.' Tim looked at me for help and despite everything a gurgle of laughter escaped from my throat.

'I ate most of it,' I said, covering for him.

She narrowed her eyes. 'Hmm. If you say so. Look, I need to get back to the farm shop; Tess has got the afternoon off to work on her friend's garden and Edwin's on his own. We often get a rush in bad weather like this.'

I made to stand up but she placed a firm hand on my shoulder. 'No need. But just . . . Anything we can do, Hetty, anything at all. We're family. Please call and we'll be straight over.'

I nodded my thanks, my words stuck in my throat. Tim added his offer of assistance to his wife's and they walked to the door.

'Naomi?' I cleared my throat to help the words out. 'Did you see Anna at the hospital?'

'Yes, love.' My sister-in-law's gaze didn't falter. 'I collected Dan from Bart's ward and took him back up to be discharged by his own doctor. Bart was groggy but he recognized me. He asked me to persuade Anna to go home for a rest but she refused. She said she'd go as soon as she'd seen the consultant. The nurse said that if Bart continued to improve he'd be transferred out of intensive care this afternoon.'

'When he left, did Dan . . .' I paused to sip my tea, my throat was so dry it hurt to swallow. 'Did Dan kiss her?'

'Oh Hetty.' She smiled sadly at me. 'There's no need to worry about that. Dan clasped Bart's hand and told him to take care, but he didn't touch Anna.'

'Thanks.' That was something at least. I blew out a shaky breath and squeezed my eyes tight to ward off tears.

The kitchen door closed and after a minute or two the rumble of Naomi's van disappeared into the distance. The house fell silent. With a racing heart, I went upstairs and tiptoed into our bedroom.

Dan was fast asleep. He lay on top of our bed, naked except for his boxer shorts, one arm in a sling pinned across his chest, the other resting on top of the duvet. His broad shoulders and muscular chest were red with vicious bruises and my fingers ached to stroke them. His stubble didn't normally get this long and as I crept closer I could see flecks of silver at his temples. The curve of his lashes, his full lips, his strong jaw . . . I was still angry with him but I loved him too. My emotions rushed up at me and I had to clamp a hand over my mouth to stop myself from crying out.

'What a mess,' I murmured under my breath. 'Where do we go from here?'

He flinched in his sleep, his brow tightening and then relaxing, and I slipped out of the room, half relieved, half disappointed that I hadn't had to talk to him yet.

Outside, the dogs, now back in their kennels, started to bark and I crossed to the landing window to see what the disturbance was. I felt the blood drain from my face: Anna's car was coming up the track towards the house. I stepped quickly out of sight. Surely she couldn't think I'd want to see her today?

I stayed where I was, heart pounding, hoping that she wouldn't just walk straight in as she normally did. As far as

I was concerned *normal* rules had been suspended; no more open house at Sunnybank Farm. But there was no knock, no breezy 'cooee?', and after only a minute or so I heard her engine start up again. I watched her drive off and a chill ran down my spine; my best friend had left and the only emotion I felt was relief. Thank goodness; she must have had a change of heart at the last minute.

I leapt into action then to take my mind off matters and for the next half an hour I shut myself in the kitchen to avoid waking Dan and put the radio on while I tackled the pile of ironing. I only stopped when my phone rang. It was Poppy.

'Hi, Mum, how's Dad?' She sounded all breathless.

'He's in bed asleep. How are you?'

'Having a nightmare!'

'What's up?' I gripped the phone. What more could go wrong today?

'Matilda and I went to the park and when we came back her mum and dad had gone out so we're locked out and it's raining.'

I exhaled. 'Is that all? Why can't you phone them?'

'We did. They didn't pick up. Matilda thinks they've gone to some church thing in Holmthwaite. Can you come and get us? We're soaked.'

The two of them giggled and the relief at knowing nothing awful had happened made me smile.

'No problem, Mum's taxi is on its way.' I unplugged the iron and scooped up my bag.

I opened the kitchen door and paused, wondering whether to wake Dan and tell him, but decided against it. It was as I opened the door that I spotted an envelope with 'Hetty' scrawled on the front in Anna's writing had been pushed under it. She'd obviously driven over earlier to deliver it.

Not now, Anna, I thought, shoving it into my bag. It was still raining and I dashed to the car, dumped my bag on the back seat where I couldn't reach it and set off for Matilda's house. The petrol light came on straight away and I swore under my breath, wishing for the umpteenth time that I'd got a diesel engine so I could have used the farm's pump. I'd intended to fill up on the way back from the hospital, but I could barely remember the journey back, there's no way I'd have had the presence of mind to stop off at a garage. I glanced at the clock: four o'clock. My heart sank. The local petrol station only opened until noon on a Sunday. Still, I'd be fine, I'd never run out of fuel before and I'd driven on empty loads of times. Matilda lived on the road between the farm and Holmthwaite, it wasn't too far. I'd be fine . . .

I turned on the radio to stop myself from speculating on the contents of Anna's letter and turned out of Carsdale, heading uphill on the winding road to Holmthwaite. At the top, I suddenly felt the judder of the engine through the steering wheel. I snapped the radio off and listened as the car coughed and whirred and then cut out.

Shit. I lowered my head to the wheel and groaned.

I was facing downhill. Ahead of me was a small passing point, and using the clutch and brake, I steered the car as it slowly rolled down the hill. I pulled into the passing point, put my hazard lights on and retrieved my phone from behind the seat.

A text message had come through from Poppy.

Forget it Mum, we're fine now. We found a note from
Matilda's dad and a key under the mat xx

At least that was something, I thought to myself, peering out of the rain-smeared windscreen. The rain had eased off and was now just a slight drizzle; by Lake District standards it was nothing to worry about. But I was about a mile and a half from home and I didn't fancy abandoning the car on this hill. I had no choice but to phone Naomi to come to my rescue again.

She answered immediately and assured me it was no bother; the cavalry would be on its way shortly. I turned the radio back on quietly and unclipped my seat belt while I waited, watching the pattern of raindrops on the windscreen. I scrolled through my messages to kill time and then dropped my phone back in my bag on the passenger seat. The corner of the letter from Anna was sticking out. I stared at it and then, with shaky hands, I pulled it towards me. I didn't know if I wanted to read what she had to say, but inevitably, curiosity got the better of me and I tore the envelope open.

Chapter 27

Dear Hetty,

I know sending a letter is cowardly when I could have called in person, but as you now know I've been behaving like a coward for more years than I care to remember. Also, I really need you to learn some things, and I know you well enough to believe you'll read this to the end whereas if I knocked on your door I'd fully expect you to turn me away.

There are no words to describe how I feel about myself but 'disgust', 'shame' and 'grief' go some way towards it. In doing what I have done I have ruined the best relationship I have ever had in my life.

Hetty, I love you. So much more than as a friend. You're my best sister, role model and cheerleader all rolled into one. Since we were kids, you have picked me up, dusted me down and set me on the right path again. I have no right to ask for you to return that love.

I know Dan is out of hospital so by now he will have probably told you his version of events and I need to tell you mine.

Whatever I say, however I describe what happened on that horrendous Duke of Edinburgh expedition to Wales, you probably can't think any less of me than you do now. So on that basis I'm going to tell you straight and leave you to decide.

I've never been loved or cosseted by anyone. At best my gran tolerated me, at worst I was a burden she never asked for. Even though your parents had emigrated, they loved you. Dan loved you. Everyone at college loved Hetty Wigglesworth. And, for one night, I wanted to know what that felt like. To be as loved as you.

It had never crossed my mind to steal Dan from you. I had never wanted him as a boyfriend. And this is no excuse, I know that, but I was eighteen and after first getting lost on the mountain and then Tasha ending up in hospital, I was down and exhausted and homesick and, if I'm honest, a little bit drunk.

Please don't blame Dan for this. It was all my doing. We were sitting around the campfire and someone was trying to cheer us all up by singing. I was too miserable to join in and started to cry. I caught Dan's eye and he mouthed at me, asking if I was all right. I gestured towards my tent and he followed me. I didn't stop to think about how wrong it was, or what the consequences might be. It was one time, Hetty, please believe me. It never happened again; we both regretted it the next day and didn't speak for the rest of the trip. Dan was torn apart with guilt and couldn't live with what he'd done. So much so that he felt compelled to finish with you to punish himself. I didn't see him again until after my gap year, I promise.

The consequences from that night couldn't have been more life-changing. My horror eight weeks later when I realized I might be pregnant is indescribable. By then you were living at Sunnybank Farm with Dan. The happy couple. Meanwhile, I was in Thailand carrying his baby with no one to confide in and no one to blame but myself. Maybe if you and Dan hadn't got back together, I could have told him, but there was no way I was going to ruin your relationship a second time around. I was so lucky that the maternity hospital I was volunteering at took me under their wing and cared for me.

Spending my year abroad without friends and family around me was tough, but deciding what I was going to do at the end of my gap year was even tougher. Your letters kept coming, a true friend as ever. The thought that I'd lose you if our secret came out used to make me sob with fear. I couldn't see that I had a choice; I had to keep the father's identity to myself. I made just one concession to Dan in Bart's name, which no one else would guess. Bartholomew means 'son of a farmer'. I knew I'd have to return to the UK because I had no way to support myself in Thailand, but being the coward I am, I couldn't bear the thought of going somewhere new where I wouldn't know anyone and I knew that you'd welcome me home. So I took the easy option and came back to Cumbria.

I am so sorry that we've been living a lie right under yours and Dan's noses all these years. And Bart's and Poppy's, come to that. I felt that Bart would become a better person for having you both in his life. And I truly hope that you understand why I asked you to be his godparents.

As Bart has grown up, the deceit surrounding who his father is has been eating me up. It has been a privilege to have your friendship. I knew that I owed it to Bart and to Dan to reveal their true bond but I have been dreading the day that the story would come out for fear of losing you. Over the years, I've rehearsed countless scenarios in which I tell you all the facts. I never once imagined it would be across a bed in an intensive care unit while my precious boy was fighting for his life. I'm so, so sorry for blurting it out like that.

Now the truth is out there, I have no choice but to tell Bart quite soon that Dan is his father. After nearly losing him, I feel like I've been given a chance to be honest with him. I felt you should know so that you and Dan can decide what, if anything, you tell Poppy.

Hetty, I have so many regrets, so many, but the biggest is that I know how much this will have hurt you. It might give you some comfort to know that Bart and I will be moving out of the area as soon as we can. At least we'll be out of sight if not out of mind.

I have no expectations in sending you this letter other than that I hope you will be able to forgive Dan, even if you can't forgive me. He and I both made a mistake, but his ended a long time ago and my deception has gone on for years. You will always be the best friend I've ever had.

Love always,

Anna x

Oh Anna.

I crumpled the pages to my chest and cried for the pain my friend had gone through both then and now and for the loss of the simplicity of the friendship we had shared since we were teenagers. Could we get back from this? Could Dan and I recover from this? My head throbbed with the pressure of dealing with too much emotion. I closed my eyes and blotted out the world.

A gentle knock on the window startled me and I clutched at the letter as a face appeared beside me.

'Hetty?' It was Dan peering through the glass, frowning. 'Are you okay? You were miles away.'

No, I wanted to yell. I was anything *but* okay. I nodded and pushed the door open and got out.

'I'm fine.'

The rain had completely stopped but the air was warm and I felt claustrophobic in the humidity. We stared at each other for a long moment; he looked as tongue-tied as I felt. He had a petrol can in his hand and lowered it to the floor, scratching his jaw self-consciously.

'There's no instruction manual for this situation, is there?'

I shook my head and looked left and right but there were no other cars. 'How did you end up being the one to come?'

'Naomi rang to tell me what had happened. I wish you'd rung me.'

'You were asleep.' I ran a hand through my hair, not meeting his eye. 'Besides, you can't drive at the moment.'

'Tim brought a can of petrol over. He offered me a lift but I wanted some fresh air. Clear my mind. Why didn't you wake me before, at home? I asked Naomi to tell you to.' He touched my chin, forcing me to look at him.

My mouth had gone dry. Hardly surprising; I'd cried so much today I must have been completely dehydrated.

'I . . .' I lifted my shoulders. 'I didn't know what to say.'

'And you've been crying. What's the letter?' His eyes flitted to the pages I'd left scattered on my seat.

'From Anna. She says she's sorry and that she's going to tell Bart everything. So I guess we'll have to tell Poppy.'

'Shit.' Dan rubbed his fingertips over his stubble. 'I never knew about Bart. You do believe me, don't you?'

'I do believe you.'

And I did. Although he had kept his affair with Anna a secret, I didn't think he'd have been able to stand back and not be a father to Bart had he known. At heart, Dan was a decent man, I had to remember that.

He touched a finger to my cheek and my body trembled.

'Today must have been awful for you. It's been a shock for me. I mean, having a son . . . That's, well, I'm blown away.'

I stared at the ground, anger growing like a ball of heat in my chest. 'Yeah. My best friend gave you the only thing I couldn't.'

'That's not true,' he said softly. 'I've never been bothered about having a son.'

I looked at him, remembering his tears after the miscarriage.

'Okay,' he held his hand out to calm me, 'it would have been nice to have more kids but—'

'Well, now you have.' I folded my arms and looked down the hill towards Holmthwaite. 'Because you cheated on me. I know finding out about Bart was a shock to you, but let's not forget that Bart came along because you cheated on me. And you lied about Joe. All these years you pretended not to know why he cut himself off from us. And you knew!'

In the distance I saw a car making its way towards us and it crossed my mind to jump into its path and beg for a lift. I just wanted to get away, put an end to this hideous conversation. But I had to get through this. *We* had to get through this. One way or another.

'I know, I know and I'm so sorry.' Dan pulled me towards him awkwardly with his good arm but I sidestepped him. 'I'd made a mistake and lost you once through my own stupidity and I just couldn't risk losing you again.'

'Two nights. You were only away from me for *two nights*. And you jumped into bed with my best friend. How could you, Dan?' There was a tight band across my chest and my breath was coming in sharp bursts. 'You and Joe. Both in love with her.'

'Joe was in love with Anna?' He frowned.

'Yes!' I yelled. 'Do you know how that makes me feel? Do you? Second best, that's what.'

'Never say that.' He smoothed a hair back from my cheek. 'Never say second best. And I wasn't in love, I was just . . .'

276

He bowed his head. 'I don't want to say it; it makes me seem such a shit.'

'Say it.' I slipped my wedding ring off and rolled it around in my palms. He blew out a breath and raised his eyes up to the sky.

'Okay. I was young, I'd had a few beers. It started off as a cuddle and then . . .' His voice faded. 'I'm not going into details. I was never in love with her, never. Nor her with me. She was a mate. Your mate. I know, I know that makes it worse. We were sickened by our behaviour the next day. The stupid thing was that when she came back to Carsdale with a baby, I was relieved. I thought, great, she's obviously moved on and put it behind her. I never thought for a moment he was my son.'

I scanned his face. I didn't know what I hoped to find: guilt, regret, shame . . . I saw all those things but coming off him in waves was a bone-deep fatigue. I picked up the fuel can, poured in the petrol and then opened the passenger door. 'Get in before you collapse on me.'

He tucked himself into the front of the car and exhaled with tiredness. I got in too, turned to him and took a deep calming breath.

'This is going to take a while to sink in for me. So here's what I suggest. We park you and me and Anna for now and focus on the kids,' I said firmly. 'Whatever we're feeling doesn't matter. Bart and Poppy are going to be confused, possibly angry, and almost certainly needing a lot of support from their parents. We can't do that if we're at each other's throats.'

Dan looked at me with admiration in his eyes. 'God, I love you, Hetty.'

I clamped my lips together and started the engine, glad to be able to focus on the familiar actions of driving the car. I loved him too. But it would be a while before the words would be able to fight their way out of my bruised and angry heart.

Chapter 28

Viv's feet clumped down the narrow staircase in her little cottage and into the kitchen where I was sitting at the table. 'Right, love, I'm off to the farm.'

It was ten days since the accident, the shearing contractors were in situ and I had moved in with Viv for a while.

'Have fun.' I quickly lowered the lid of my laptop to hide what I'd been looking at. If she knew I'd been researching long-haul flights, she might tell Dan and I didn't want him to suspect a thing.

'Humpf, hardly.' She checked her hair in her compact mirror and puckered up to put on some lipstick. My mother-in-law had apparently been flirting outrageously with a Kiwi called George.

'You look very nice,' I said slyly, 'for sheep clipping.'

'In this old thing?' she said, waving a hand at her pretty pink and blue T-shirt tucked into jeans. Unfortunately, she didn't manage to hide the flush to her cheeks and we both laughed.

When I'd first moved to the farm, she'd always been kitted out in big baggy T-shirts, freebies from the feed suppliers or veterinary companies. Things that now accounted for at least twenty-five per cent of my own wardrobe. They'd be going in the bin as soon as I went home. Operation Be True To Me was well underway and ugly promo T-shirts did not form part of it.

My phone screen lit up with an incoming text from Gil and I quickly turned it over so she couldn't see who the sender was. I didn't want to have to explain that either. I'd got in touch with him that evening after Joe had passed on his number. I owed him an explanation; the last time I'd seen him in London, Poppy had announced that Bart might not pull through and I'd been beside myself with fear. I'd sent him a message to let him know that both Dan and Bart were through the worst and to congratulate him on his gold medal.

He'd replied straight away, thanking me for letting him know and saying how relieved he was to hear my news. He also added that his behaviour on the fire escape had been inappropriate and he apologized, hoping that it wouldn't stop us from being friends. Privately, I thought that us being friends wasn't a great idea, but I'd messaged him back and said of course not.

Since then things had moved on a pace in my life and I'd actually sent him several more messages asking for advice. Gil was turning out to be a very useful contact indeed.

'Viv?' I got up from the kitchen table and gave her a hug. She was stiff at first but I increased my grip, laughing until she relaxed.

'What's this in aid of?' She patted the back of my head awkwardly before wriggling free.

'To say thank you, for helping Dan and me out, for letting me stay here for a few days and for not judging me for it.'

While I stayed with Viv to give Dan and me some breathing space, Poppy was staying with Matilda. Dan and I had had a long explanation worked out ready to give her about the fact that I needed peace and quiet to get my business plans together for the bank while Dan had the shearing contractors staying in caravans in the yard. And that with his injured shoulder, it would be difficult to look after her. But as soon as we'd got to the 'you're going to Matilda's for a week' part, she'd yelled, 'cool!' and leapt onto her phone to Snapchat Matilda about it, so we kept the details to ourselves.

'Glad to help.' She tutted softly and shook her head. 'Such a messy business.'

I held my breath, hoping she wasn't going to take this opportunity for a full-blown discussion about her new grandson.

'It'll settle down in time,' I said, picking up her handbag and holding it out to her.

Her wise eyes searched mine. 'I couldn't wish for a better daughter-in-law, you know. I'm so glad it worked out for you and Dan that summer.'

'Me too,' I said huskily.

'Oh, good.' Her face brightened and she scooped her bag over her shoulder. 'Now, I really should be off.' She picked up the cake tin from the side. 'Mustn't forget my courgette cake. George didn't believe you could make a cake from green vegetables. So I'm proving him wrong. Want anything bringing back from the farmhouse?'

I thought for a moment. None of the things I was missing could be brought back with her. I missed stepping on to the silvery grass heavy with morning dew and watching the baby rabbits disappear into their burrows when I came too close, I missed the song of the curlews as they soared across the valley, I missed the smell of the fields and the feel of lanolin on my hands. I missed the sight of Poppy coming up the lane after school, bursting with stories about her day. But most of all I missed the presence of Dan beside me, his hand in mine at night, his cheery smile, his kind, thoughtful ways . . . It felt like a piece of my puzzle was missing and I couldn't rest until I'd fitted us back together. But that was something that would take time. I'd suggested this break from each other and he'd accepted it.

'No thank you,' I said eventually.

'Any message for him?' She waited, hand on the door knob.

'Tell him . . .' But before I could answer there was a knock on the other side of the door. Viv opened it and Oscar, my nephew, was there towering over her with a shoebox tucked under his arm, dressed in baggy khaki shorts, a long-sleeved blue-striped T-shirt and worn-out plimsolls, one of which had a big toe poking through.

'Hello, love,' Viv beamed, always pleased to see her family. 'I'm on my way out, I'm afraid.'

He flicked his fringe out of his eyes.

'Hi, Gran, I know; I've come to see Auntie Hetty. Uncle Dan says hurry up if you're coming because they've given out rain for later. The chippies have just arrived.'

'Clipping contractors, I think you mean,' I put in, giving him a wave.

He blushed. 'Oh, yeah. Them. So hurry up, Gran.'

'All right, slave driver.' She rolled her eyes with mock irritation. 'Better get my skates on.'

She set off and Oscar came in and put the shoebox on the table.

'What can I do for you?' I asked.

'Nothing, I'm working for Uncle Dan.' He leaned up against the kitchen worktop, fiddling with the sleeves of his T-shirt. 'He has employed me to drive for him while his shoulder's knackered. He sent me to give you that box.'

'Oh.' I was intrigued and fingered the lid, not knowing whether I could wait until Oscar had gone before ripping into it. Now I looked closely at it, I recognized the label on the side; it was the box Poppy's last pair of trainers had come in.

'Is there any cake?' he asked, scanning the surfaces hopefully.

'At Gran's?' I grinned. 'Need you ask?'

I pointed him in the direction of the cupboard and filled Viv's posh coffee machine up with water.

'So how's things, enjoying your long uni holiday?'

I rarely saw Oscar on his own, he usually came as a pair

281

with his brother, but Otis was currently abroad, having managed to secure an internship at Gucci in Milan. Oscar was a lovely boy, quieter and more thoughtful than his flamboyant twin, and usually managed to bamboozle me with science whenever I asked about his studies.

He didn't look up but carried on pulling the currants out of his grandmother's fruit loaf and lining them up around the rim of his plate.

'Actually, I've dropped out of uni.' He shrugged. 'So not great.'

My heart went out to him. 'Had enough of the properties of soil, eh? Go on, dish the dirt.'

He rewarded my feeble pun with a chuckle. 'They were all such nerds. And I just realized that I was doing a degree in something that in the end would lead me to a job that I didn't want to do. So I quit. Mum and Dad have been brilliant.'

'Of course they have,' I said, setting a latte in front of him. 'Because they just want you to be happy.'

He nodded and stared at his plate. 'I'm working for a while to save money for travelling next spring.'

'Good plan.' My eyes fixed on the shoebox and I pulled it towards me.

'So, I was thinking, you're going to need a delivery driver for your pies. I could do that. I love driving.'

I smiled apologetically. 'I won't be able to afford to pay anyone, I'm afraid. Hetty's Farmhouse Bakery is going to be run on an absolute shoestring to begin with. I'm planning on making deliveries myself.'

My business was back on track. I was keeping it simple to begin with: six flavours, minimum order of fifty pounds, delivery within a fifteen-mile radius. I was going to bake in the afternoon and evening and deliver early morning, then get back to the farm to help with the flock. Hopefully the business would grow, maybe in time I'd need to look at professional kitchens, but for now Hetty's Farmhouse Bakery would be just that: delicious pies baked in my own home.

'I've estimated the numbers,' he said, undeterred.

I suppressed a smile; he was Naomi's son all right. He pulled a piece of paper and a pencil from his pocket and showed me what he'd written. It had lines of formula and figures on it.

'I only want minimum wage, which is that.' He circled a number. 'I've estimated the profit on one pie.' He grinned sheepishly. 'Mum helped there. And I've planned out a proposed route too, based around the Country Comestible stores.'

I raised my eyebrows. 'That's very enterprising of you.'

Gareth Brookbanks had been amazing. I'd phoned him back after he'd left a third message about his initial pie order. I told him that I wouldn't be able to supply him for the foreseeable future and that Hetty's Farmhouse Bakery had had unforeseen catastrophic setbacks and that I might never be able to get my business off the ground after all. He'd asked if there was anything he could help with and before I knew it I'd poured the whole story out: about how Dan hadn't really wanted me to set up a business, about winning silver at Britain's Best Bites (although it turned out he already knew that), even about finding out that my godson also happened to be my stepson. Although he'd been expecting to do a deal about pies, he'd turned out to be a brilliant listener who, he'd reminded me, had had his own share of personal problems, and after I'd come to a tearful halt he'd given me a piece of advice: *What happens next is up to you.*

Such simple words but they had been my guide ever since. And from that moment on, everything had clicked into place. So much of what had happened recently had been out of my control. But my future was up to me. Enter Operation Be True To Me . . .

Oscar was now pointing out my break-even point by pie flavour and demonstrating through a complicated flowchart how my skills would be better spent making more pies (apple and dark chocolate being the most profitable) while his skills of efficient route-planning and safe driving would be best employed by delivering them.

'And Uncle Dan has said I can fill up my car with diesel from the pump at the farm,' he finished triumphantly. 'So the cost will come out of the farm business rather than your bakery.'

'So you've talked it through with Dan?'

'He's all for it.' Oscar chewed his lip. 'You don't mind, do you?'

I scanned the numbers before answering. Oscar had worked everything out for me; something I'd not yet found the time to do. And it was such a relief to hear that Dan really had had a change of heart about Hetty's Farmhouse Bakery and he hadn't just been paying lip-service to it when I'd told him of my plans before leaving the farm.

'Not at all. Oscar, this is impressive,' I marvelled. 'You've really got a head for figures.'

He scratched his head. 'Yeah, I'm thinking maybe accountancy for next year; don't tell Otis, he'll take the piss.'

I stuck my hand out. 'Welcome to the family firm.'

He punched the air before remembering to shake my hand. 'Yes! Thanks a lot, Auntie Hetty.

'Oh. I almost forgot what I came for; Uncle Dan needs an answer.' He shoved the shoebox to me and then excused himself to go to the bathroom.

I lifted the lid. Inside was a note from Dan:

I thought you might be missing home so here's a few reminders.

   Dan x

I was missing home, I thought.

Under the note was a posy of sweet peas tied with baler twine. I smiled at the twine, which had a million and one uses on a farm, although not normally for securing such delicate stems. I lifted them to my nose and inhaled their powdery scent. These would be the ones I'd grown amongst my runner beans; I bet the vegetable patch looked gorgeous. Next I lifted out a small framed photograph of Rusty. I'd taken this picture last summer at the top of the valley when he'd still had the energy for long walks. My throat tightened at the memory of him and I set the frame on the table. At the bottom of the box was a champagne-coloured silk nightdress edged with ivory lace. As I picked it up a second note fell from it and I smoothed it out to read it.

I found this in your underwear drawer. I think you bought it for a weekend away which never happened for some reason. I thought it was a shame that you never got to wear it, so, if it's all right with you, I've taken the liberty of booking us in to Prescott Hall on Friday night. I've made a dinner reservation for eight o'clock. Will you meet me there? Please send Oscar back with your reply.

A date night. With my husband. Love bloomed in my chest and tears sprang to my eyes as the downstairs loo flushed and Oscar loped back into the kitchen.

'Yes,' I beamed at him. 'Please tell Dan the answer is yes.'

Chapter 29

Prescott Hall was only a twenty-minute drive away from Sunnybank Farm but it might have been on a different planet. It was an eighteenth-century manor house built as a stately home for a family who'd made their money in tea plantations in Ceylon. But now it was a genteel hotel with a fine-dining restaurant catering to the deep pockets of Cumbria's elite and, for one night only, a farmer and his wife from Carsdale.

As I crunched across the gravel drive, my little trolley case bumping behind me, I paused and looked up at the graceful façade.

A date night with my husband. A shiver of nerves shimmered down my spine and I took a calming breath before going in.

I made it through the revolving doors, despite being slightly nervous that I'd get my case stuck. I didn't need a whole case, not for one night, but the alternative had been to shove my toothbrush, clean knickers and silky nightie in a Sainsbury's carrier bag and I decided turning up with that looped over my wrist might get me some funny looks.

I stepped into the foyer and paused to get my bearings. The place oozed effortless luxury. Tucked in next to the sweeping staircase, an elegant woman in an evening gown was entertaining the hotel guests on a grand piano with a refined version of 'Fly Me to the Moon'. Centuries-old wood panelling lined the walls and a huge crystal chandelier above the foyer beamed rainbows of refracted evening sunlight on to every surface. Smiling staff, carrying silver trays at shoulder height, glided along as if they were on wheels and even the other guests seemed confident and relaxed.

I was glad I'd put on my best dress.

Dan was on his own, leaning on the reception desk, and I headed over. My legs were so shaky that I wasn't entirely sure they'd carry me across the marble floor. He was in his best trousers and a shirt I hadn't seen before and his arm was out of its sling. Even his shoes had been polished. My husband was a handsome devil, I thought, with a small whoosh of excitement.

'Wow.' His eyes lit up as I reached him. He pressed a kiss to my cheek. 'I've missed you.'

I gave him a twirl, spinning round precariously in my high heels. 'You approve?'

'Definitely. You look . . .' His eyes shone and he shook his head in wonder. 'Gorgeous. I'm a lucky man. If, that is, if, you're still, you know . . .' He cleared his throat and raked a hand through his hair.

I couldn't help smiling. It felt good to be out together, dressed up. I couldn't remember the last time we'd had a date like this, just the two of us, dressed up and out somewhere fancy.

'Right, Dan, here's the thing.' I blew my cheeks out to psych myself up. I'd prepared a little speech and I was determined to get it off my chest before we went any further. 'I need to say something while we're alone.'

'Okay, Hetty, but—' Dan started but I shook my head.

'No, let me finish, I need to say this. It's been brewing all week. Sleeping with my best friend was possibly the worst thing you could have done.'

Dan looked at the floor, swearing softly under his breath.

'But you were young, you never repeated it, and it was a long time ago. And let's face it, neither of us ever got the chance to sow our wild oats, did we?'

'Excuse me.' A girl's head popped up from behind the counter. Her face was as red as a cherry and she couldn't meet my eye. She cleared her throat. 'Here you go, Sir.'

She pushed a plastic packet containing a toothbrush across the desk to him. 'I knew we had one somewhere.'

'Thank you,' he mumbled in a gruff voice. He flicked a sideways glance at me. 'Forgot my toothbrush.'

'Right.' My voice came out as a whisper.

The girl looked uncertainly from Dan to me. 'Did you still want to check in?'

We both nodded and I felt a bubble of laughter rise to the surface. Dan looked at me and his lips twitched.

'Oh yes,' said Dan, deadpan. 'There are plenty more wild oats where they came from.'

The girl, who according to her name badge was called Imelda, smiled cautiously while we filled in the registration form. 'And if you'd like to peruse the menus while having a drink at our bar, someone will take your luggage to your room. Just pop it over there.'

We smiled our thanks and I wheeled my case to the end of the desk where she'd indicated.

'And your luggage, Sir?' Imelda asked.

She blinked at him as he pushed the toothbrush back towards her.

'I like to travel light,' he said with a boyish grin.

I caught Imelda's eye and shook my head in despair as she slid our room key towards me.

She moved away to deal with some other guests and Dan and I giggled to ourselves. I tucked the key in my bag and we walked away from the desk.

'Well, I think we managed to check in without embarrassing ourselves in the slightest,' I said wryly.

He smiled. 'Yep, do you think she could tell we don't come to this sort of place very often?'

'I'd put money on it. "I like to travel light",' I mimicked

and rolled my eyes. 'Anyway, as I was saying before we were so politely interrupted—'

'Hold that thought. Let's find somewhere more private first.' Dan guided us to a small velvet couch in a quiet corner.

We sat knee to knee, bodies twisted so that we could look at each other, and I studied my husband's face. Every curve and line was so familiar and yet now I thought I spied a few extra grey hairs at his temple, a deeper line etched between his brows. My heart ached for us both that we were going through such a tough time.

'If I'm honest, I will probably never get over you cheating on me with Anna, and with Bart there as a permanent reminder, I'm hardly ever going to forget.'

Dan reached for my hands and hung his head. 'I guess not.'

'But,' I continued. I paused, taking in his hopeful expression. A million butterflies took flight in my stomach. Whatever I said now, I had to be able to stand by it; I couldn't change my mind next week, or next month or next year. It wouldn't be fair. On any of us.

I took a deep breath. 'I say we draw a line in the sand. We move on and deal with the consequences. Together. What happens now is up to us. Bart and Anna are such a big part of our lives, but I want you to know that this isn't something I shall drag out of the closet to use against you any time we have a row.'

'Thank you,' he murmured, blowing out the breath he'd been holding. 'That's so good to hear.'

He held up his hands to show me. 'I'm trembling.'

I turned them over, tracing the scars from the accident with my thumb, and pressed one of them to my chest. 'Me too.'

'So you forgive me?' He moved closer until his shiny shoes touched the toes of my one and only pair of heels, his eyes roaming my face.

I nodded. 'I can't promise that I won't get a twinge of jealousy about it now and again, and I'm still not sure how we're going to deal with Anna and Bart. But we're only human. We've both invested in this marriage, we've both made sacrifices. I'm not going to throw away this wonderful life over one night fifteen years ago.'

Dan's eyes looked a bit misty. 'You're such a better person than I am; I think I'd find it hard to move on if you'd been with someone else.'

I bit my lip and thought about Gil. *No more secrets.* 'I did have a brief fling in Cornwall, actually.'

'You got together with someone else straight after me?' Dan looked gobsmacked.

I tilted my chin up defiantly. I'd done nothing wrong; he had finished with me after all. 'Yes, Gil Pemberton of Pemberton's Pasties.'

Dan blinked. 'He was that guy in the pasty shop. I thought he was a bit curt with me when I came to ask you to come home. It makes sense now.'

'That's not surprising. I was an emotional wreck when I'd arrived in Padstow,' I retorted. 'He'd had to listen to me pour my heart out about you for weeks. Then you waltzed in and I followed you back to Cumbria as meek as a lamb.'

Dan was still staring at me incredulously. 'Did you ever hear from him again?'

'I saw him in London the other week, funnily enough,' I said, glancing towards the revolving doors where a man with a child buggy was having a few problems with his wheels. I focused my gaze on them, partly because of the ruckus he was making and partly to avoid eye contact with Dan. 'He was competing in the same pie category as me; he was the gold winner.'

'That must have been weird for you.'

'Just a bit.' I cleared my throat. 'Actually, it was good to see him; he's married now with kids. We've been in touch a few times over the last week; he's been helping me with my business plans.'

Dan was bristling with pent-up emotions, which under

the circumstances he didn't dare express. 'Oh, now I'm not sure how happy I am about this.'

'And he was the one who made me realize,' I continued, ignoring him, 'that some good has come from all this.'

He narrowed his eyes. 'Go on.'

'I told him about your and Anna's one-night stand. I said that no matter how much we all wanted it to be, it could never be brushed under the carpet and forgotten about because Bart had been born as a consequence. And Gil reminded me how distraught I had been when I'd heard Bart had been injured.'

I shifted in my seat, hoping that Dan wouldn't put two and two together and realize I'd been with Gil when Poppy had rung.

'Well, of course,' Dan murmured, frowning, 'he's our godson.'

'Exactly. I *love* Bart,' I continued, looking into Dan's eyes. 'I'm glad he's in our lives, so I have to embrace all that that entails, which includes his conception. Okay, maybe I won't embrace *that* part, but I have to accept it.'

'He's a great kid,' Dan said simply and then clamped his lips together as if scared to say too much.

I waited patiently.

'I'm finding this difficult,' he added.

I nodded encouragingly. 'It *is* difficult.'

'I love him too. Very much.' The flicker of cautious happiness in his eyes made me want to fling my arms around him: he loved his son, but I could see he was worried about the impact these new feelings might have on me.

'Bart is going to find this quite a shock,' I said. 'But one day he's going to realize how lucky he is to have you for a dad. And he's going to love you right back.'

'And you, Hetty?' The look he gave me made my stomach flip just like it did that first time he asked me out in the sixth-form common room in front of everyone. 'Do you still love me?'

I didn't even have to think about it. I wrapped my arms around his neck and kissed him like my life depended on it. 'Yes. Yes I do.'

Somewhere close by I heard someone cough discreetly and I broke off our kiss and tugged at the hem of my dress.

'Whoops,' I whispered, 'we'll get thrown out before we even make it out of reception at this rate.'

'On that note,' said Dan with a grin, 'I think this calls for a drink.'

He held his hand out to pull me up, but I grabbed his arm.

'Wait,' I said. 'There's something else. Another announcement.'

He winced. 'Oh dear.'

I took a nervous breath and launched into my surprise. 'You and I missed out on our years of freedom, we decided to forego university to stay on the farm, together. And I think a part of me will always be a bit sad about that. But I've been thinking. I've got my new pie business to spice up my life and it's time you had an adventure too.'

Dan's brow furrowed. 'Finding out I've got a fourteen-year-old son and getting hit by a livestock trailer is quite enough adventure for me for one year, thank you.'

'I said I love you and I meant it,' I said firmly, 'but I think some time apart would do us good.'

'You want us to separate?' His face fell.

I shook my head. 'No, no, not a separation, just a chance to find out who we are, without each other.'

He scratched his head. 'Where are you going with this?'

I took a deep breath. 'I'm not going anywhere, Dan, you are.'

From my bag, I fished out the information pack I'd downloaded from the internet and handed it to him.

'Borneo?' He stared at me. 'What is this? I can't just swan off to Asia for a holiday.'

'Oh yes you can,' I argued. 'And it's not a holiday. It's a two-month volunteering trip to assist with the orphan orangutans. You'll love it. Poppy's very jealous.'

'Two months . . . ?' He shook his head in disbelief. 'What about the farm? And the cost?'

'Just listen.' I touched a finger to his lips and smiled. My insides fizzed with excitement now that the news was out. I told him how I'd spent all week making arrangements. Naomi and Oscar were going to help and Cameron had agreed to do an extra day a week while Dan was away. I'd been to see the business advisor at the bank and had set up a new business account for Hetty's Farmhouse Bakery. Having a cheque for two thousand pounds seemed to smooth over most of his queries. Although I did stress that fifty per cent of that money would be paid as a donation to a charity in exchange for Dan's place on the project.

'Farm labour is all sorted. And I can't think of a better way to spend the prize money from Britain's Best Bites.'

His eyes widened. 'But I thought you needed that money to convert the kitchen?'

'Who told you that? Oh, Naomi,' I added, answering my own question. 'There'll be enough left over for the work needed, don't you worry about that.'

Sort of. There'd be enough to do most of it, anyway; I'd just have to earn the rest over time. It would be fine.

He ran his eyes over the documents I'd given him. 'This does sound amazing.' He looked at me, his eyes shining. '*You're* amazing.'

'I know. Can we have that drink now?'

'Definitely,' he said in a shaky voice.

Hand in hand, we crossed the marble foyer again in search of the bar but as we got to the middle my phone buzzed with a text message. I fished it out of my handbag and stopped to read the screen. The pianist had changed her tune and was now playing 'Somethin' Stupid'.

'It's from Anna.'

Dan shot me a sideways look. 'Are you two on speaking terms?'

'Yes. Well, *texting*.' I registered his surprise and shrugged.

293

'I had to check she was okay. I was worried about her mental health without anyone else around to support her.'

He slipped his arm around my shoulders and kissed my cheek. 'You're a kind soul.'

'Poppy and I have been in to see Bart.' I pulled a guilty face. 'Although admittedly I timed it so that I wouldn't see Anna. She's not there quite so much now that he's on the mend.'

'And? How is he?'

'Loving the attention. There was a group of adoring fans around his bed when we got there; Poppy was most put out.' I smiled. 'Physically he's doing well too, and very proud of his stitches. Coming home tomorrow, I believe.'

'Has Anna told him yet?' His Adam's apple bobbed. 'About me?'

I shook my head. 'That's what she's texting about. She was going to tell him as soon as he came out of hospital but I suggested that we tell the kids together – all of us, on Sunday, at ours, for lunch.'

Dan inhaled sharply. 'In front of Poppy? Is that wise?'

'It won't be easy, but it will be fair. No more secrets and everyone hears the same story. As a family. Is that okay with you?'

I watched his face to see his reaction. This affected my daughter too and I wanted it to be handled properly to protect her. Besides, I got the impression that Anna felt so guilty that she was quite happy to be guided by me. I'd invited her and Bart to lunch on Sunday in my kitchen, where many of the important moments in the Greengrass family history had taken place. This may well be the most important ever.

'As a family,' Dan repeated, going pale. 'What does Anna say?'

'She's agreed.'

'Does that mean you're coming home to Sunnybank Farm?'

294

I nodded. 'Normal service will be resumed as of Sunday morning.'

Dan folded me into his arms, wincing slightly at the pain in his collarbone. 'Thank heavens.'

Over by the piano, a man in a dinner suit began to croon along to 'Something Stupid'. Dan laced his fingers through mine and then we were dancing, cheek to cheek, laughing and ignoring the odd looks from everyone else.

'Like I love you,' he sang softly into my ear, joining in with the chorus.

'Ditto,' I murmured back.

And then his mouth was on mine and suddenly my insides were on fire.

'I'm not really that hungry,' he said gruffly, his stubble grazing my lip tantalizingly.

'Me neither.'

'Shall we?' He nodded to the big fancy staircase.

My eyes twinkled at him. 'Race you.'

And much to the amusement of the other guests, the farmer and his wife charged up the stairs to their room.

In the early hours of the next morning, I woke up, carefully slid from Dan's arms and padded across the thick carpet to the bathroom. I smiled at the abandoned room service trays which had contained our midnight snacks and the upturned bottle of prosecco in the ice bucket. As I got to the bathroom door, my little trolley case caught my eye. I'd left it unzipped from when I'd got my toiletries out and on top was my silk nightdress. Unworn. Again. Only this time I didn't mind one bit.

Chapter 30

On Sunday morning, I drove back to the farm. My heart was bursting with emotion: pure delight at being home and being with my family again and apprehension about facing Anna for the first time since the accident. And then there was the task we had ahead of us: breaking life-changing news to our children.

Poppy came flying out of the house to meet me. Her bright green eyes were full of sparkle and she danced around me as I climbed out of the car.

'Come here, gorgeous girl.' I held my arms out and she dutifully jigged close enough for me to hug her. I inhaled the loveliness of her, the fragrance of her dark copper curls, the fresh scent of her skin, and sent up a silent prayer that what the adults in her life were about to tell her wouldn't dampen her joy for long.

'This is so cool.' She pulled away, unable to contain herself in my embrace for more than two seconds. 'You are going to be blown away.'

'Don't tell me; you've tidied your room?' I teased, allowing her to drag me to the kitchen door.

'Mum!'

Dan was leaning on the doorframe and bent to press a kiss to my lips. 'Welcome home, Mrs Greengrass. I wish I could carry you over the threshold but my shoulder couldn't take the strain.'

'Dad!' Poppy said indignantly. 'Mum's perfect. Lovely and cuddly.'

'I think he's referring to his broken clavicle, darling,' I laughed.

'Exactly,' he agreed. 'Certain positions are still quite uncomfortable.'

He caught my eye and we shared a secret smile, remembering Friday night at Prescott Hall.

'Anyway,' he said, rubbing his hands together, 'are you ready for the big reveal?'

'Reveal?' I looked at them both; they were almost bursting with excitement.

Dan nodded. 'Poppy and I decided that an award-winning bakery should have a kitchen to match.'

'Surprise!' Poppy squealed as Dan pushed back the door. I stared at my kitchen, then blinked and rubbed my eyes. I couldn't believe what I was seeing.

I gasped. 'Oh Dan, I love it. I love it!'

'Phew.' He led me in to take a closer look. 'I hoped you would.'

The solid-wood worktops had been replaced with gleaming ivory granite. A new double stainless-steel sink and fancy chrome taps sparkled under the window. And the big corner cupboard at the end of the row which we'd never really used had gone and in its place was a professional-looking gas cooker.

'How did you . . . ? When did all this . . . ?' I gazed around in amazement.

'Mum's actually speechless,' Poppy giggled, holding up her phone to video me. 'Never seen *that* before.'

'Joe helped,' said Dan nonchalantly.

My eyes widened to the size of saucers. *'Joe's* been here?'

Dan nodded. 'I emailed him when I got out of hospital and asked if he'd ring me. We, er, we had a good chat. Sorted out a few things.'

'The mysterious Joe.' Poppy raised her eyebrows comically and folded her arms. 'Who I *still* haven't met.'

'You will, love,' said Dan, ruffling her hair. 'Joe and I have got to make up for lost time; he's going to be around a lot more in future.'

'I'm proud of you.' I gazed at my husband and swallowed a lump in my throat. 'That's the best news I've had all day.'

'Better than this?' Poppy skipped to a large grey American fridge-freezer at the far side of the kitchen.

'Gosh, I hadn't even spotted that.' I looked back at Dan in amazement.

'Watch!' She pressed a glass to a plastic chute and ice cubes rattled out.

'Very posh!' I agreed.

I floated around my kitchen, touching the work surfaces, trying the taps, pulling open the oven doors, and then returned to Dan.

I threaded my arms around his neck and fixed my eyes on him, my heart bursting with love. 'I'm overwhelmed. And I can't believe how much you've achieved in just a few days.'

'As soon as you said you were moving to Mum's for a bit, I got cracking. Joe came over and went through the report that that guy from the council sent you. And together we came up with this. Ian knew a chippy who could take that cupboard out, so—'

'What's a chippy?' Poppy asked.

'A joiner,' I told her. 'And that explains what Oscar said. He mentioned chippies and I thought he meant clippers.'

'He confessed to that slip-up.' Dan grinned. 'He was worried he'd given the game away.'

I laughed and skimmed the top of my hair with my hand. 'Nope. That clue went straight over my head.'

'The granite was a bargain because there's a fault in it, although no one but a genius would spot it. And Joe used his contacts in the catering trade to get good prices on the rest,' said Dan proudly.

'But still, it must have cost a fortune?' I looked worriedly at him, conscious that I'd just committed over a thousand pounds to fund his trip to Borneo.

'All taken care of.' He gave me a wonky smile. 'See out the window?'

I did as I was told but couldn't see anything amiss. 'What am I looking for?'

'What colour are the sheep?'

'White and br—' I stopped mid-sentence and searched the fields and hills. 'No brown ones. Where's the Soay flock? Have you moved them?'

'I've sold them.' Dan held up a hand as I began to protest. 'To a couple who've started a rare-breeds farm up in the Highlands. They were delighted to have so many lambs and fertile ewes to add to their flock and our tups will be able to breed with their own ewes later on this year.'

I seemed to be doing a lot of gasping. 'Sold? But—'

'There's more to life than sheep, Mum,' said Poppy, sounding at least twice her age.

Dan wrapped an arm around my waist. 'Poppy and I decided it together. Your pie business has inspired me to challenge myself. And who knows, maybe I'll get some new ideas on how to do that over the next few months.'

'I'm sure you will. I'm, well, I'm stunned!' I kissed Dan again and took a deep breath. 'Right, I'd better get cracking. Let's test the new kitchen out; Bart and Anna will be here for lunch soon.'

Poppy sighed dreamily. 'I hope it's pie. I've missed your pies. Matilda's mum and dad only eat salad.' She pulled a face of disgust.

'It is pie,' I laughed. 'Of course.'

Two hours later the Crofts were here and lunch was ready.

Bart was sitting with his leg propped up on a chair and was telling Poppy that everyone wanted to sign his plaster cast, even Ella James from the year above. A fact which made both of them lower their voices reverently. We adults were less at ease. Dan, after greeting Anna with the world's briefest kiss, was giving her a wide berth as if desperate to prove to me that she held no appeal for him in the least. Anna, who usually pitched in to help straight away, was hovering around not knowing what to do with herself, and when we spoke, our small talk was stiff and false. Finally, I directed her to the bottom oven of the Aga to get the plates out and she leapt at the chance to do something useful.

I untied my apron while Poppy ferried dishes of lightly steamed summer vegetables to the table. They'd been picked from my garden this morning: tender mangetout, baby courgettes and al dente French beans. Naomi's farm shop had supplied the tiny new potatoes which I'd roasted in sea salt, Lake District rapeseed oil and garlic, and my silver-medal-winning lamb pie which I'd reprised for today's menu took centre stage, golden and crisp and bulging with succulent chunks of salt marsh lamb from the local butcher.

'Looks delicious, Hetty,' said Anna softly, taking a seat by Bart.

'Thank you,' I said, choosing the chair at the opposite end of our long table.

Dan popped the lid of a beer for himself and eased the cork out of a bottle of wine. He poured some into a glass for Anna and me and I gulped at mine nervously.

Dan went to the fridge to add ice cubes to a glass of coke for Bart and when he sat down the three of us exchanged looks between us and I nodded.

'I'll start,' I said.

'Good, I'm starving,' said Bart with a grin. 'Hospital food has made me appreciate how good home-cooked food is. Even yours, Mum.'

Anna prodded him in the ribs. 'Cheeky.'

'Actually,' I cleared my throat, 'I meant I'll start the conversation we need to have.'

The kids both sank down in their chairs.

'If this is about me asking Poppy out on a date—' Bart began.

Dan choked on his beer. 'What?'

'Chill, Dad.' Poppy rolled her eyes. 'I'm thirteen.'

'It's not,' Anna put in. She tucked her blonde hair behind her ears and wriggled in her chair.

I took a deep breath. 'All I want to say is that whatever happens, you two, Bart and Poppy, mean the world to us. We love you and that will never change.'

Dan nodded. 'And any questions, at any time, we're here for you. All three of us.'

Bart and Poppy looked at each other, horrified.

'Well, this is weird,' said Bart.

'Freaky,' Poppy agreed solemnly.

'Bart, it's time to tell you about your father.' Anna's voice came out strangled and strange and Bart stared at her uncertainly.

'Bartholomew the extremely handsome Australian back-packer?' he said, attempting to lift the tension.

Anna swallowed and shook her head. 'That isn't his name. I named you for your father, not after him.'

Poppy looked at me and Dan anxiously. 'Should we leave?' she whispered.

Dan gave her a reassuring smile. 'No, love. You need to hear this too.'

'Okay,' she replied doubtfully. 'If you say so.'

Bart scratched the edge of his jaw and a bolt of recognition struck me. It was exactly the same gesture that Dan made when he was anxious. 'Mum, sorry, you've lost me.'

She held his gaze, her blue eyes fixed on his. 'I chose Bartholomew because it means "son of a farmer".'

His eyes widened. 'I'm the son of a *farmer*?'

'Not just any farmer.' Dan's voice cracked as he looked at Bart.

Bart stared back, his jaw falling as the penny dropped. 'Oh my God.'

'Dad?' Poppy gasped. 'Are you . . . ?' She looked at Anna and then at Dan. They both nodded.

'It's true, Popsicle,' I said softly, catching her eye.

'Poor Mum!' Her voice came out as a squeak. She skirted the table and pressed her body against mine in the tightest hug. My body trembled with love for my thoughtful girl.

'It's okay; it happened while your dad and I were on a break,' I said. 'All of us were free agents at the time.'

That was the tiny white lie that we'd all agreed on so that everyone could retain their dignity.

Bart's expression was still frozen in shock.

'Are you all right, darling?' Anna asked in a husky voice.

He lowered his chin to his chest, his eyes brimming with tears. 'Why didn't you tell me? Any of you?'

Dan got up from his seat.

'I didn't know myself until recently,' he said. He squatted down at Bart's chair and looked into his eyes. 'So finding out that you're my son has shocked me too, but I couldn't be happier. You're a great lad. Your mum's done a superb job with you.'

'Oh Dan, thank you for that,' Anna whispered hoarsely. He patted her shoulder.

'I don't get it?' Bart looked at her. 'Why keep it a secret?'

'Adults get things wrong sometimes.' She brushed tears from her cheek. 'But at the time I thought I was doing the right thing. I was only nineteen myself. I came back to England and moved back in with my grandmother. I couldn't tell her the truth because she'd have confronted Dan about it. And I didn't want Hetty or Dan to know because I couldn't risk losing the only people I loved.'

Bart nodded silently.

'And Poppy,' Dan looked at her. 'How do you feel about all this?'

Her brow furrowed as she took her place back at the table. 'So. Let me get this straight. The first boy to ask me out on a date was, in fact, my *brother*?'

302

'Shit!' Bart clapped his hands over his face.

Anna and I locked eyes. I held my breath; it had only been a matter of time before this would come up.

'Well, bro, that's me and you in therapy for the next thirty years,' Poppy muttered drily.

The half-siblings looked at each other and burst out laughing and after regarding each other cautiously for a moment, we three adults joined in too.

It seemed a good point to serve lunch, so with Anna's help we dished up. The kids asked question after question about our teenage years and what we'd all been like and the three of us were so relieved that it had gone so smoothly that we were only too happy to answer them. There'd be harder conversations later, I was sure, particularly between Anna and Bart, but the sense of weight having been lifted off my shoulders was immense. I was proud of both Poppy and Bart for the way they'd handled such a revelation.

'Has anyone else got any secrets they want to share?' Dan said, helping himself to potatoes.

'Yes,' I blurted out. 'I don't like eating Sunnybank lamb.'

'What?' said Dan and Poppy together, aghast.

'Why is that?' Anna frowned. 'I always wondered.'

'You knew?' Dan blinked at her.

She nodded. 'Hetty and I don't have any secrets.' She caught my raised eyebrow and heat rose to her cheeks. 'At least not any more,' she added.

I bit my lip. 'One day when Poppy was tiny, we sent a lamb to slaughter for a big family dinner and its mother cried for two days. She escaped from the field and stood in the yard where she'd last seen her baby, bleating. I kept thinking how I'd feel if I'd lost my child and I couldn't bear it,' I admitted. 'So I never cook Sunnybank lamb.'

'What do you do with it, then?' Dan asked, agog.

'She gives it to me,' said Anna. 'Bart and I have no problem eating it.'

'Sorry,' I muttered guiltily, 'but I'm glad I got that off my chest.'

Dan harrumphed. 'At least it's stayed in the family.'

Anna and I shared a smile.

'I've got a confession too.' Bart's ears had gone red. 'I don't think I'm cut out to be a farmer, Dan. I don't want to come back to work after my ankle has healed. I hope you don't mind?'

It was as I thought: the main attraction at Sunnybank Farm had been Poppy. Thank goodness that had been nipped in the bud before anything had happened that they would have regretted.

A tiny flash of disappointment crossed Dan's face and then he smiled. 'No problem. You gave it a go, that's the important thing. Any ideas what you might fancy doing?'

Bart nodded shyly. 'Sally says I can go and help out at the surgery. Cleaning up and stuff. I think I might like that.'

'A vet in the family?' Dan beamed at him and then at me. 'Amazing. Well done you.'

Anna pressed a kiss to her son's cheek. 'You'll make a wonderful vet.'

'Hello, still here.' Poppy put her hand up. 'For the record, Dad, I'm not *thinking* of becoming a farmer. I am one. Always will be. So there.'

'I'm very glad to hear it.' Dan grinned and raised his bottle. 'I'm proud of you, kids. Very proud. Cheers.'

'So how do you feel about being related to me, Bart?' Poppy asked through a mouthful of pie. 'Honoured, I'm guessing.'

'I'm okay with it,' he hesitated. 'Although there are some parts I don't want to think about too much.'

Anna frowned. 'What's that, darling?'

'I think he means the tupping part, Anna,' Poppy put in matter-of-factly.

'Tupping?' Anna looked at her.

Poppy looked at her kindly. 'The birds and the bees stuff. It's when we put the tups in with the ewes when they come into season—'

304

Dan coughed to try to hide a laugh and I kicked him under the table.

'Thank you,' I said swiftly, 'I think Bart said he didn't want to think about certain things.'

Poppy wrinkled her nose. 'Actually, me neither.'

'Dan, tell me about your trip to Borneo,' Anna said diplomatically, helping herself to more vegetables.

'I fly next week,' he said, looking only too pleased to change the subject. 'I'll be joining a group of volunteers at an orangutan sanctuary. We'll be helping with the rehabilitation of a group of animals that are almost ready to be introduced back into the wild.'

Bart and Poppy asked lots of questions and Anna and I took the opportunity to clear the table and have a moment to ourselves.

'Are we okay?' she whispered.

'Yeah.' I held my arms out and she came in for a hug. And I meant it. It was going to take me a while to get back to the level of trust we'd had before, but we were the same people deep down, I knew we'd get there.

'Poppy's a lucky girl to have you as a role model.'

I smiled. 'You're not so bad yourself.'

'Really?' She peered at me. 'Do you really mean that?'

'You're my dearest friend, Anna, one wet night in Wales can't erase the friendship you've given me.'

Together we carried dessert to the table: fresh strawberries and cream.

Dan was still impressing the kids with his planned adventure.

'But I'll be back in time for tupping,' he assured them.

Bart went pale.

'Don't worry, bro,' Poppy laughed.' This time he's talking about the flock.' She faltered for a second. 'I hope.'

'Something to tell the grandkids, I suppose,' Dan muttered red-faced.

'I'm not having kids,' said Bart and Poppy in unison. The

two of them giggled again and their pleasure at discovering their similarities was a joy to watch.

I smiled at my husband and he reached for my hand. And because it felt right to me, I reached for Anna's hand and squeezed it. She looked at me and swallowed and a tiny single tear trickled down her cheek.

'I love you, Hetty Spaghetti,' she whispered.

'I love you, Anna Bananna.'

Family, I mused, glancing around the table. A crazy mixed-up sort of family. But I loved them all the more for it.

A month later . . .

The mayor raised our big scissors (last used to free a lamb's head from some netting) to the ribbon and hacked away at it unsuccessfully. His wife tutted and took them out of his hands but she didn't have much luck either. I waved discreetly, trying to attract Poppy's attention to fetch some others but she and Bart were too busy filming on their phones to notice. The mayor took the scissors back and tried again.

Joe started laughing and Anna elbowed him in the ribs to shush. They were getting on remarkably well and I wasn't going to tempt fate, but I had high hopes that we'd be seeing Joe a lot more in Carsdale over the next few months. Joe and Dan had seen each other a couple of times before he'd left for Borneo and the two of them seemed to have picked up where they left off. I wondered now, looking at them, why Joe hadn't just plucked up the courage to tell Anna how he'd felt about her when we were kids, but perhaps it simply wasn't meant to be at the time. And Joe, I thought, watching the way he leaned towards her, would be perfect for Anna. She giggled at something he said and then went slightly pink when she caught me looking at her. Yes, definitely a bit of a spark there . . .

My mum fished a pair of nail scissors out of her clutch bag, or 'purse' as she liked to call it since she'd gone all American on me, and stepped in to intervene. The mayor snipped his way across the ribbon and finally he was through it.

It was lovely to have my mum here. Even if she did come

with plenty of opinions. She thought I was a saint to simply absorb Bart as my stepson as I'd tried to do. But to me it was the right thing to do and everyone benefited from it.

'I declare Hetty's Farmhouse Bakery well and truly open.' The mayor stood up straight and beamed, holding the tiny scissors aloft while the photographer from the local paper took a picture of me, him and his wife on our kitchen doorstep.

I thought my heart would burst with pride as everyone clapped. I cleared my throat.

'Thank you, everyone, for your support,' I said, hoping that no one else could hear the tremor in my voice. 'Hetty's Farmhouse Bakery represents the very best of Cumbrian life – hard work, wonderful ingredients and, most of all, love – and I'm thrilled that you could be here to share this special day with me. Thank you!'

I raised my glass and Joe shouted, 'To Hetty's Farmhouse Bakery!' and everyone chorused back with a loud, 'Cheers!'

All my favourite people were here, I thought, looking around as my guests filtered into my kitchen. All except one. I swallowed back the lump in my throat, reminding myself that it was my idea to hold the official opening while Dan was still away. And he was having a ball in Borneo, he'd already been there for a month and had settled into his temporary home at the sanctuary, although he did admit to missing us all badly.

Anna and Joe picked up trays of pie samples and milled around, handing them out to everyone. Viv and my mum, who hadn't stopped swapping gossip since Mum's plane had landed yesterday; Naomi and Tim, Oscar and Otis; Edwin – they were all here. Edwin had been promoted to shop manager to give Naomi more days off now that Tim had made a snap decision to take early retirement. Tess had come too, of course. She didn't mind a bit about Edwin's promotion, she'd set herself up as a gardening consultant and was looking to reduce her time at the farm shop and build her client list. We shared a common interest there, because her favourite client was my biggest customer: Gareth Brookbanks. I'd encouraged him to talk to Tess about his garden, which had got overgrown since his wife died, and she'd been happy to make a few suggestions. And now they seemed to have the perfect friendship: he cooked her dinner in return for a spot of weeding. I didn't know if it would lead anywhere but the last time I was in the farm shop, Tess did admit that she'd deleted her Tinder account, so fingers crossed . . .

'Congratulations, Hetty,' said Gareth. He raised his champagne glass. 'I look forward to our next delivery of pies at Country Comestibles.'

I chinked my glass of sparkling water against his. 'Thank you for coming and thanks for everything. If you hadn't given me that advice, I don't think any of this would have happened.'

'Someone said it to me a month after my wife died when I felt like I couldn't carry on. "What happens next is up to you." It made me realize that we can't control everything, but we do have a choice over our own actions. I've never looked back.'

'Daddy,' said a little voice, 'come and see the sheep!'

Gareth grinned at me with a mixture of apology and pride as his daughter tugged his arm.

'In a minute, Ella.' He blushed a little and leaned closer. 'By the way, thank you for sending Tess to me; Ella loves her and it's lovely to have someone to feed again.'

I watched them go and looked over to the wall where Freya and Lizzie from Appleby Farm were showing Freya's son Artie and baby Tilly the sheep. Next to them, Poppy and Bart sat on the wall, laughing at something on Bart's phone.

I felt a tap on my shoulder and turned. It was Poppy's teacher, Miss Compton.

'Well done on your Britain's Best Bites award, Mrs Green-grass,' she beamed.

'Call me Hetty, please.'

'I was just wondering . . .' She gave me a breathy smile. 'We're having an enterprise day at school next term and I wondered if you'd come in and give a talk about how you set your business up? It's always so inspirational to have successful parents come in and talk to the students.'

'Me?' I laughed, flattered. 'I'd love to.'

'Hello, Miss Compton,' said Poppy, joining us. 'Why are you here?'

I shot Poppy a warning look for being so blunt but if the teacher picked up on Poppy's tone she didn't mention it. 'My sister has a corner shop in Holmthwaite; she was invited today but couldn't come so as I'm a lady of leisure during the six weeks' holiday, your mum said I could attend in her place.'

'Fair enough,' Poppy said. Then she straightened. 'Do you think your sister would like organic eggs for her shop?'

Miss Compton laughed. 'Possibly. And I think she's going to be taking pies too. You must be very proud of your mum, Poppy.'

'Hell yeah,' said Poppy.

'Setting up her own business like that,' the teacher continued.

Poppy flopped her arm around my shoulders.

'I'm proud of my mum for way more than that.' She gave me a knowing look. 'Way more.'

I blinked back tears. 'Oh, Popsicle.'

'Excellent.' Miss Compton downed the rest of her fizz. 'I'll be in touch about that enterprise day.'

We said our goodbyes and Poppy blinked. 'Are you giving a talk on enterprise day?'

I nodded.

She whistled under her breath. 'You are such a cool mum.'

I smiled and felt my eyes brim. 'My work here is done.'

'You all right?'

I nodded. 'I'm fine. Just, you know, missing Dad.'

She took my hand. 'Come on, I've got something to show you.'

She dragged me over to where Bart was still sitting on the wall holding his phone in one hand and his iPad in the other. He handed me the iPad and Poppy swiped at the screen.

'There,' she said, wriggling beside me in excitement. 'Surprise!'

I peered at the screen, trying to make out what I was looking at. I cocked my head to one side. 'Is it . . . fur?'

'Yes!' Poppy jumped up and down on the spot. 'A red Border collie pup. Three days old. Jake's daughter. *Your* new dog.'

I gasped. 'Mine?'

Poppy nodded, giggling. 'She comes home in October.'

My heart leapt in my chest and I clamped a hand over my mouth. I looked at the picture on the screen again. 'Did Dad organize this?'

'Yep,' said Bart, grinning. 'He's not a *bad* bloke, I suppose.'

I looked up at him and realized he was filming me.

'Don't!' I laughed, 'I must look a mess.'

'You look beautiful, Mrs Greengrass,' said a faraway voice.

I froze.

Bart held out the phone. 'Someone else wants to talk to you.'

Dan's tanned face beamed out from the screen. He held a bottle of water up. 'Congratulations, my love, well done, I'm so proud of you. Sorry I can't be there.'

I looked at the man with whom I'd built this wonderful life and my heart wanted to burst with love for him.

'But you are,' I said softly. 'Because you're in here.'

I touched my hand to my heart. 'And you always will be.'

The Thank Yous

Firstly, a big thank you to Naomi Willcox who bid in the CLIC Sargent eBay auction to have a character named after her. All the money raised in the *Get In Character* campaign will help support children with cancer. Naomi, I hope you approve of Hetty's fabulous sister-in-law!

Over the last fifteen years I have met and have been inspired by many women who have had an idea for a food business and brought that idea to life through hard work, determination and passion for good food. They have started small, often from the kitchen table, fitting in the planning and producing and packaging and marketing amongst all their other everyday jobs. These women include Georgina Howard, Lucy Nicholson, Helen Colley, Mary Berry, Carey Shelton, Jean Johns, Marjorie Toms and Lynne Mallinson. Ladies, your stories have all, in some way, contributed to mine and I thank you very much.

The biggest thanks for this book must go to the wonderful Ian and Jayne Kirk, who own a sheep farm near to where I live, because I couldn't have written it without them. They have patiently explained every aspect of sheep farming from birthing right through to market day. I've been at the farm for shearing, lambing and even tupping. Mind you, I am still not entirely sure what a mule is . . .

Thanks, too, to Viv Sadler, who keeps rare-breed Soay

sheep and who kindly introduced me to possibly the prettiest lambs I've ever seen!

Thank you to Gina MacLachlan, who, as usual, was required to dispense medical advice. And a huge thank you to Kelly Rufus who came to my aid with her specialist knowledge of an intensive care ward and the treatment of specific injuries. I am in awe of you, Kelly. Sarah Williamson answered my Facebook cry for help to name a cat; thank you, Sarah, for coming up with the suggestion of Birdie.

As ever, thank you to Team Bramley at Transworld: my wonderful editor Francesca Best and assistant editor Molly Crawford for winkling out the best version of Hetty's story; my lovely publicist Hannah Bright; the fabulous marketing crew, Janine Giovanni, Julia Teece and Candy Ikwuwunna; and the ever-patient Sarah Whittaker who is responsible for my amazing covers. A heartfelt thanks to Hannah Ferguson at Hardman Swainson for your endless support and encouragement.

Finally, thank you to Tony, Isabel and Phoebe. Love you always.

Escape to the seaside with Cathy Bramley's wonderfully warm novel set on the Devon coast!

A MATCH
MADE IN DEVON

Sometimes you have to play a part to realize who you really are . . .

Nina has devoted her life to making it as an actress, although her agent thinks she's more best friend than leading lady. But with her onscreen character about to be killed off it might be time for a new role (on and off screen).

Luckily for Nina, life has a way of shoving you in the right direction. A falling-out with her agent and his new star client leaves Nina's life in tatters and her name in the papers. She is left with no choice but to flee the city, leaving nothing but an empty bottle of hair dye and her tiny bedroom behind.

Escaping to the West Country, Nina makes herself useful by helping her friend set up his holiday business in beautiful Brightside Cove. Soon Nina is learning there's more to life than London and more characters in a small village than on the stage. But she won't be able to avoid the drama for long – Nina's star is finally rising and it seems everyone wants a piece of her. So, when a beautiful man (and his adorable dog) catch her eye, it's not long before London and showbiz start to lose their appeal.

But can Nina really trade the bright lights of the Big Smoke for the calming tides of this Devon seaside village? Especially when, after years of chasing celebrity, it's finally pursuing her.

Will Nina choose the bright lights or has she met her match in Brightside Cove?

Originally published as a four-part ebook serial, the complete book will be published in summer 2018.

Read on for the first chapter . . .

Chapter 1

Maxine Pearce, the director, shoved her glasses to the top of her long charcoal-grey curls and clapped. 'Okay, folks, quiet please.'

In *Victory Road* Studio Two, on the outskirts of east London, everyone fell silent.

We were about to shoot my final ever scene in the show. This bit was so absolutely top secret that Maxine had insisted on the minimum number of crew on set. No one else knew what we were doing. It was all very exciting.

And I was part of it. The thought sent a rush of adrenalin swooping through me. Acting was my life. My dream. There was a sort of magic that happened to me when I took on a role. I ceased to be forgettable, plain old Nina Penhaligon with hamster cheeks, freckles and impossible-to-style hair, who on a good day would be classed as curvy, and on a bad day really needed to lay off the peanut-butter Oreos, and I became . . . anyone, anyone I wanted to be. And I loved every second of it.

Not much magic required today, however, because my character, Nurse Elsie Turner, was lying dead under a collapsed beam.

It would be heart-breaking for fans of the show; the first death of a character.

'Okay, Nina?' Maxine asked before giving final instructions to Mike behind the camera.

'Yep.' I tried to keep the tremor from my voice; never mind the viewers, my heart was breaking too. I was going to miss this lot.

Victory Road was a weekly drama set in the east end of London during the Blitz. Think *EastEnders* with gas masks and victory roll hair-dos. It had been my best part to date by far. I'd earned proper money and hadn't had to work for the temping agency for months. I detested office work, but needs must when you're a jobbing actress.

But after today it would be over; I squeezed back the tears, mindful of my make-up.

This morning we'd shot the cliffhanger ending to an episode in which I, Nurse Elsie, had been hurrying to take cover during an air raid when I'd heard a cry for help coming from a nearby house. I'd gone in to rescue the old lady who lived there just as a bomb exploded and the house collapsed around me. As the credits roll, the audience would be left on the edge of their seats. Will Elsie survive? Will she still be able to meet her boyfriend, Constable Ron Hardy, in the square where he's waiting with an engagement ring in his pocket? Will they be the first couple on the show to marry?

And only the people in this room knew the answers: no. I wasn't even allowed to tell my best friend on the show, Becky Burton, who also played a nurse. I understood the need for discretion but I felt bad about leaving without saying anything.

'And action,' murmured Maxine.

The atmosphere in the studio was crackling with tension. The ratings had dipped a bit recently and the management was hoping that a death would revive them. I was their sacrificial lamb. Apparently that was an honour because it meant my character was popular.

The sound effects began and we were transported to bomb-scarred London as the distant bells of fire engines and the wail of sirens filled the little studio.

Lamplight illuminated the wreckage of 33 Victory Road and two air-raid wardens, Ray and Godfrey, picked their way over the rubble looking for casualties.

'Over 'ere,' shouted Ray.

Ray, played by actor Lee Harwood, was the male lead. Drop-dead gorgeous. Shame I was playing a corpse and couldn't gaze up adoringly at him.

The beam of his lamp found my face. He dropped to his knees beside me and I managed not to blink under the glare. Godfrey leaned over us both as Ray checked for my pulse.

'Cor blimey,' Ray groaned, rocking back on his heels. 'It's Nurse Elsie. She's dead.'

Ninety minutes later it was all over. I'd packed up my bits and pieces and said farewell to the crew who'd filmed my last scene. Maxine, her stiletto heels tapping on the marble tiles, accompanied me through the revolving doors and out into the April sunshine. We squinted as our eyes adjusted to the brightness. It was the first of the month today; I wondered briefly whether the end of my contract had just been an April Fool.

'What an exit!' Maxine said as we stepped towards the bus stop.

Not an April Fool, then.

'So this is it,' I said, fighting the urge to grab her hands, fall at her feet and beg her to let Nurse Elsie live.

'You were marvellous today. Very professional.' She gave me a brisk smile. 'The reaction from the audience is going to be dynamite. It was a shame to kill you off but—'

'Maxine!' I warned as two teenage girls strutted towards us.

'Oh gosh, yes.' She tutted, folding her arms across her chest. 'Here I am enforcing an embargo on the storyline and then five minutes later blabbing it.'

'Ask her, ask her,' hissed the shorter of the two girls, pushing her friend towards me.

'Can we have your autograph?' The tall one shoved a scrap of paper and a pen at me.

'Of course,' I said, surprised to be recognized in public. I signed the back of what appeared to be a note excusing her from PE.

The two girls stared at the piece of paper.

'Oh.' The small one's face dropped. 'It's not her.'

'Told you.' The big one elbowed her sharply.

They screwed up my autograph, dropped it on the pavement and sashayed off.

Maxine and I exchanged wry smiles.

'At least they didn't hear what you said,' I said, scooping up the paper.

'Thank heavens. More than my job's worth if we had a story leak now.'

'Ditto,' I agreed. 'Not that I've got a job any more.'

Maxine smiled sympathetically. 'Sorry. But it's testament to your talent that you've lasted this long. The writers had originally only scripted you in for six episodes but you proved yourself worthy of more.'

I nodded, not sure how to respond other than to do the begging thing.

'When will you tell the rest of the cast that Nurse Elsie is . . . dead?' I said, lowering my voice on the last word.

'Not until the last possible moment. Can't risk the press getting hold of it. We'll let the rumour mill work its magic as long as we can: is she dead or alive? The love story between Elsie and Ron has captured the nation's hearts; the bookies are already offering odds on a wedding. This could really put *Victory Road* on the map. And you, too, Nina.'

'I hope so; it's such a good show.'

Maxine checked her watch. 'I'd best press on. You'll be at the party later?'

Jessie May, who played the flirty pub landlady, was having a birthday party in Soho.

'Of course,' I replied.

The press would be out in full force for this one; there was no way my agent Sebastian would let me pass up such an opportunity. He had recently told me that whilst I hadn't got star quality, there were plenty of parts out there for Miss Average (he was nothing if not brutally to the point), but that I had to show my face at showbiz parties, on the basis that someone might remember me and cast me in something. So that's what I did.

'Good.' She exhaled with relief. 'I was worried you might not feel like partying now that we've killed you off.'

'Actually, I . . .' I bit my lip, wondering whether to confide in her even though it hadn't been confirmed in writing yet.

'Go on.' She waited, one eyebrow cocked.

I couldn't resist; the opportunity to impress her was too great to miss.

'Strictly off the record, I've got a part in the new BBC period drama: *Mary Queen of Scots*.' I tried to look cool about it but my excitement was impossible to contain. 'So I'll be celebrating that.'

'Brilliant news!' Her angular face softened into a smile. 'Queen Mary?'

I blinked at her. 'The lead role? Gosh, no! My agent didn't put me forward for that.'

'He should have. Sebastian Nichols is your agent, isn't he?' Maxine furrowed her brow. 'Prince Charming himself.'

I nodded. Sebastian wasn't all that charming to me; ruthlessly ambitious, he only turned it on when he needed to.

'So who are you playing?'

'Eve, lady's maid to Queen Mary herself,' I said. In the distance I spotted an approaching bus and felt in my bag for my Oyster card. 'I'm just grateful to still be acting.'

Maxine took her phone out as the driver pulled up to the stop.

I jumped aboard and waved to her. 'Thanks for everything. It's been a joy working with you.'

'Likewise. But, Nina, hold on; something's niggling me.'

She rested the tip of her shoe on the platform of the bus, thus preventing the driver from pulling away. I shot him a nervous smile while Maxine tapped at her phone screen.

'Ah. Thought so. Cecily Carmichael.' She pulled a face. 'Not a name I'd forget in a hurry, more's the pity. I had a brief fling with her father – awful man.'

It struck me that that was the first personal piece of information she'd ever revealed to me; Maxine was notoriously private.

'Thought what?' I said, conscious of a chorus of tutting passengers behind me. 'What is it?'

'Nina, dear heart,' she held the phone out to me, 'that part is already spoken for.'

'What? Who?' I took the phone from her and stared at it. Somebody's Twitter profile filled the screen and it took me a second to take it in. 'No way!'

Maxine was right: another actress, Cecily Carmichael, had announced that *she* had got my part. The part I had set my heart on. The one that was going to keep me in acting and out of temping. Her Twitter feed was full of it. Disappointment trickled through me like iced water.

Soooo thrilled to announce I'm to play Eve in new @BBC drama #QueenMary #excited #perioddrama MORE news at 6pm!!

Cecily's timeline was full of congratulations. Even Benedict Cucumberpatch had wished her well, as had . . . Sebastian – *my Sebastian*? – had sent her his love.

'I don't understand.' I stared at Maxine in disbelief. 'And she says she has more news to come? This can't be right.'

She pursed her lips thoughtfully. 'Darling, they must be barmy to pass you over for her. She auditioned for us once; she had about as much facial expression as Big Ben.'

My heart was pounding so much I couldn't even absorb

the compliment. I needed this job; it was the only thing that had been keeping me going. It could be ages before something else came along.

'Is she getting on or not?' the bus driver grumbled.

'Not,' I replied. 'Sorry.'

Just then a young mum with a double buggy huffed up to the bus stop and Maxine and I helped her on to the bus.

'You need to be aiming higher than Eve the lady's maid,' said Maxine. 'And if your agent can't see that, he's a fool.'

'But it was better than nothing and if I don't act I'll never become famous and—'

She held a hand up to stop me. 'Fame is completely overrated and totally unnecessary for a serious actress. Which I know you are. I'll see you at the party and don't forget in the meantime . . . Nurse Elsie's story.' She mimed zipping her lips.

'Absolutely. Bye for now,' I called as the bus doors closed in my face.

The bus joined the stream of traffic and I waved through the window and tried to make sense of my thoughts. I had every respect for Maxine, but she was wrong about the fame thing.

My need to be famous wasn't driven by vanity, it was fuelled by fear. A fear of being forgotten.

Because when you've been forgotten by the one person you thought loved you most, the world becomes a much scarier place.

A Match Made in Devon is available now as a
four-part ebook serial:

Part 1: The First Guests
Part 2: The Hen Party
Part 3: The Frenemies
Part 4: The Leading Lady

Q&A with Cathy Bramley

What inspired you to write *Hetty's Farmhouse Bakery*?

I've met and worked with many women who run their own businesses, including lots of food companies. For a long time I've wanted to write a story which pays tribute to the hard work and sacrifice that goes into being a successful businesswoman. Running any sort of enterprise takes dedication and determination as well as passion, and quite often women entrepreneurs are still the ones running the home at the same time. So this book is my way of celebrating their success! This is also a story about being a role model for young people – in Hetty's case, her daughter Poppy. Not only does Hetty set a good example to her daughter by aiming high and giving her new venture a go, but when the family starts to fall apart, Hetty leads by example, showing Poppy that other things are important too, such as kindness, forgiveness and love. As a parent myself, this is the message I'd like to pass on to my own children.

Have you ever had your own business? If so, what was it?

I've had two businesses: a fitness company and a marketing and PR agency. The fitness company involved running group exercise classes and working as a personal trainer with individual clients. At one time I was teaching around fifteen classes per week; it was exhausting! I eventually stopped because I wanted to focus on the marketing agency. We worked predominantly in the food and homewares sector and had all sorts of lovely people as clients, from Mary Berry to Cartmel Sticky Toffee Pudding!

How do you get in the mood for writing? What always inspires you?

To get myself in the right frame of mind for writing, I take myself somewhere where I know I'll be undisturbed for a few hours. I make a huge pot of coffee, I light a scented candle and then I find some gentle background music on Spotify. I start by reading what I last wrote and then make a few notes for the next section. Then I pop my headphones in and off I go. Recently I've been listening to sounds of nature which somehow manages to block out the other manmade noises in my house! Music often inspires me. I was listening to a song by Scouting For Girls the other day and the girl they were singing about was exactly the character I had been thinking of for my new book.

You've captured life on a sheep farm so well! Did you do any special research to put yourself in Hetty's shoes?

I'm very lucky where I live in that I'm surrounded by farms and when I was researching *Appleby Farm* I went to meet several of the local farmers. This time I had to travel a bit further afield to visit a sheep farm. I met some orphan lambs, who were lovely, and went back to see the flock being sheared. Sheep are enormous close up – I was quite surprised. I was also very privileged to meet a lady who keeps a small flock of rare breed sheep in the field at the end of her garden. I was very taken with those and could quite happily have taken one home with me!

When you're not writing, what kind of books do you like to read?

I love books about strong or unusual female characters. I like to laugh and cry when I'm reading, and have a bad habit of wanting to read the funny bits out to my husband. I've never read a Marian Keyes book I didn't adore. I also love anything by Veronica Henry, Adriana Trigiani, Jill Mansell, Lucy Diamond and Milly Johnson.

My Golden Chicken Pie

I couldn't write an entire book about pies and not include a recipe, could I?!

I deliberated long and hard about what sort of recipe to include; Hetty's flavours are all so sophisticated and I didn't want to let the side down. But in the end I decided to plump for my favourite. Ladies and gentlemen, I give you the queen of pies, my Golden Chicken Pie . . .

Mmm, just the thought of breaking through the crispy golden layers of pastry to the unctuous filling below puts a smile on my face. There's something special about a home-made pie, don't you think? It's so comforting and mood-enhancing – a big, warm hug on a plate!

My first memory of eating pie at home is of my mum's shortcrust savoury minced beef pie. It was a family favourite and I learned to make shortcrust pastry at an early age. I loved rolling it out and then making pastry shapes with the leftovers. The secret to shortcrust, Mum used to say, was cold hands and a warm heart. Apple and blackberry pie was another regular on the Sunday lunch menu; home-grown apples, and blackberries picked from the golf course at the end of the garden, served straight from the oven with a dollop of cream.

But my favourite pie has always been – and I realize I'm about to slip in your culinary expectations – a good old chicken and mushroom pie from the chip shop. I was a vege-tarian for fourteen years from the age of twenty-three and the one thing I missed was not bacon, like so many other veggies, but takeaway pie and chips. When I finally went back to eat-ing meat to simplify family mealtimes after my eldest daughter started school, my first stop was the chip shop to reacquaint myself with my old favourite!

Over the years, I've made all sorts of versions of chicken

pie, with a variety of toppings from mashed potato to puff pastry. I've rung the changes with the fillings too, making it more (or less) calorific depending on my mood. This recipe for Golden Chicken Pie is as close to perfect as I think I'll ever get: it's got a lightness courtesy of the filo pastry, loads of flavour thanks to all the vegetables, and a lovely creamy sauce to bind it all together.

It's fairly straightforward to make so I do hope you'll give it a go. Serve it with some new potatoes and fresh green vegetables such as asparagus or sugar snap peas and maybe, if the occasion lends itself, a glass of chilled Pinot Grigio . . .

You will need . . .

Knob of butter
4 lean rashers of bacon, snipped into small pieces
1 onion, finely chopped
1 large leek, washed
200g button mushrooms
4 x 200g chicken breasts
250ml chicken stock
1 tsp mustard powder
1 tbsp cornflour
1 large handful of washed spinach leaves
Salt and black pepper to taste
2 tbsp low fat crème fraiche
4 sheets filo pastry
Olive oil or melted butter for brushing

Heat a large frying pan (you'll need one with a lid) over a medium heat, melt the butter and add the onion and bacon. Lightly fry, taking care not to let it go brown. Meanwhile, cut the leek into quarters lengthwise, chop into 1cm pieces and put them in the pan, stirring to coat them with butter. Quarter the mushrooms and tip into the pan. Cut the chicken into bite-sized pieces.

When the vegetables are soft – around ten minutes in total – add the chicken to the pan. Pour in the stock and bring up to a simmer. Stir, put the lid on and leave to cook for 5 minutes.

Mix the cornflour and mustard powder with two tablespoons of water in a cup. Pour into the pan, stirring until it comes to a gentle boil and begins to thicken. Cook uncovered for two more minutes and add the spinach. Once this has wilted, check the seasoning, adding more salt and black pepper to taste. Remove the pan from the heat and stir in the crème fraiche.

Grease the top part of a pie dish. I use a rectangular one, a bit bigger than an A4 sheet of paper. Decant the pie filling into the dish and have a clean-up while you wait for the filling to cool. Pre-heat the oven to 190°C (fan 170°C), gas mark 5.

Unroll the filo pastry and lay one sheet over the dish. Then take the remaining sheets and scrumple them up, each covering roughly one third of the pie. If there are any overhanging edges scrunch them up and then brush the top with olive oil or melted butter. Bake for 20–25 minutes until beautifully golden brown.

Cathy Bramley is the author of the best-selling romantic comedies *Ivy Lane*, *Appleby Farm*, *Wickham Hall*, *The Plumberry School of Comfort Food*, *The Lemon Tree Café* and *A Match Made in Devon* (all four-part serialized novels) as well as *Conditional Love* and *White Lies & Wishes*. She lives in a Nottinghamshire village with her family and a dog.

Her recent career as a full-time writer of light-hearted romantic fiction has come as somewhat of a lovely surprise after spending the last eighteen years running her own marketing agency.

Cathy loves to hear from her readers. You can get in touch via her website: www.CathyBramley.co.uk

 Facebook.com/CathyBramleyAuthor

 @CathyBramley

Want all the latest news?

Subscribe to my newsletter for monthly updates on my books, competitions, recipes, special offers and more!

Visit www.cathybramley.co.uk/newsletter to sign up.

Cathy Bramley

x x